THE KLENDORAN CHRONICLES

BOOK TWO

KEEPER OF THE DAMNED

KEITH JONES

authorHOUSE®

AuthorHouse™ LLC
1663 Liberty Drive
Bloomington, IN 47403
www.authorhouse.com
Phone: 1-800-839-8640

Published by AuthorHouse 01/06/2014

ISBN: 978-1-4918-4031-3 (sc)
ISBN: 978-1-4918-4030-6 (e)

Library of Congress Control Number: 2013922188

TABLE OF CONTENTS

PROLOGUE

RUBIS HORNSHANK stood on the deck of *Avenger*, after taking up his post as navigator for the main fleet of the foreign army. He wasn't a tall man, somewhere near five and a half feet; he was wide shouldered with short dark hair, a neatly trimmed beard, and piercing blue eyes. At forty three, having spent most of his years sailing the seas, his face was ruddy and wrinkled. As he stared out across the Sound of Sarl to the vast expanse of the Northern Ocean, he was reminded of their long, daunting journey ahead.

The ship rocked steadily, at anchor in the port of Verradune, nestled in the protective shelter of the harbour. *Avenger* would be the last to leave port; the other ships of their fleet fully crewed and supplied waited at anchor in the Sound. His home, a quiet and pleasant smallholding, lay to the north of Verradune, up the coast and close to the shoreline. He tried not to look too often in that direction, already missing his wife and two children, and he had only been aboard the ship for half a day.

In the long months since he had agreed to help the foreigners get home, he had regretted his decision many times. Now he had no other option than to see it through, knowing his younger brother, Theodin, would need him. Theodin had left four moons earlier, in one of the three swift, narrow hulled vessels of the advance party, fast little ships that would arrive at their destination over six moons before the wallowing sow he was presently standing on.

Someone shouting his name interrupted his musing. Rubis turned to look in the direction of the call, shielding his eyes from the sun with one hand as he turned.

"Rubis! Rubis!" Admiral Rolan Vellan hailed his navigator from the foredeck, indicating Rubis should join him with an impatient movement of his arm.

As Rubis climbed the short ladder to the foredeck he once again found himself regretting his decision. Admiral Vellan was a fool of the highest order. How such a man had ever risen to be commander of the main fleet was beyond the navigator's comprehension. Rubis had only formally met the man for the first time that morning as he boarded *Avenger*, and he had already seen more than enough of him.

They had been in separate meetings for months, large gatherings consisting of several hundred men, but never actually alone together. It was such a huge undertaking, with so many captains and commanders, that the navigator and admiral's paths had not crossed so closely. Rubis found this to be a good indicator of the man's attitude towards their mission: if he was going to trust navigation of any ship to a stranger, never mind an entire fleet, Rubis would want to meet the man and judge his character and capability. The fact the admiral had not sought a meeting showed over confidence and lack of foresight.

"Ah, Rubis; Rubis," said Vellan as he drummed a fist against the rail. "Isn't that a wonderful sight, miles upon miles of endless ocean?" Noticing his navigator's grim expression he changed the direction of the conversation. "Although I suspect you may not share my enthusiasm; you are, after all, leaving your home behind, whereas I am returning to the land of my forefathers, a land that no one living among our people has even seen. I wish this could have happened sooner, before the last of our Elders died. Finally the Ammelin people will return to our homeland and claim our birthright. It would have been so much better, a much sweeter victory, to have had the Elders lead us back to our ancestral home. But as your people say, 'Nothing is more peculiar than fate.'"

Once again, in Rubis' eyes, the admiral had proven himself a fool. Even after the several generations his people had lived alongside Rubis' own, he still didn't know the correct wording of one of the most common phrases in Sarl: 'Life is peculiar, but fate can be cruel.'

The navigator looked again towards his own home, nothing more than a white blur at the limits of his vision, to further imprint that sight in his mind, and said a silent prayer to the gods of wind and water that he would return safely, and soon. As he turned back to the admiral, the man actually seemed to be aware of some of the pain Rubis felt, but he kept silent, for which Rubis was grateful.

When at last he did speak the admiral seemed to have remembered some of the perils he had been warned of time and again, common perils to expect on a journey of this magnitude, dangers well known to those who had sailed the Northern Ocean. "Tell me, Rubis, what you expect of this voyage? I have heard from many others what they think we are likely to encounter, but please, tell me honestly what you personally think our chances are of reaching our destination."

Rubis was silent for long moments, estimating in quiet contemplation what he expected of the time of year and the length of such a voyage. When he spoke it was with sympathy for the losses to come, and genuine honesty of what he really expected.

"A quarter of your ships and a third of your men will doubtless be lost before the voyage reaches the safer waters of the Farren Ocean. The storms can be vicious and sink ships all too easily, carrying their crews with them. Any who escape the sinking ships will find there is no possible way they can be rescued and will perish just as surely as those trapped on board. We will also lose men from the remaining ships, both from disease and those swept overboard. If anything happens to the food or water stocks, getting replacements will be treacherous, if not impossible. But even with the grim estimate, you should reach your objective with enough men alive and healthy to accomplish your goals. If the gods are with us we could do much better, although we could also do much worse. Either way, by the time we know how well we are going to fare through the Northern Ocean, it will be too late to turn back. We will have no option other than to continue, and pray."

Admiral Vellan nodded morosely. "Honesty, that's what I like in a man. And that is what you have given me. Thank you, Rubis. I shall remember your words and fervently pray we make it through this safely; all of us."

Rubis found himself starting to grudgingly gain some respect for the man, but he doubted it would be long before Vellan once more proved himself to be a dolt.

Shortly after the sun had passed its zenith, *Avenger* left the harbour and sailed out into the Sound, taking its place at the head of the fleet. Anchors were hauled up, and the thirty eight ships of the main fleet unfurled their sails and turned their bows south, with more than one hundred and twenty soldiers aboard each vessel. The crews of the ships were mixed with about thirty percent of them being experienced Sarlen sailors, who had trained the Ammeliners as much as they could in the safer waters of the sound. Now it was time to put that training to the test, but if they encountered bad weather it would be the skills of the Sarlens that would bring the ships through—if the captains, who were all Ammelin, would heed their advice.

Rubis stood at the stern rail as *Avenger* steadily picked up speed, creeping out into the Northern Ocean, watching as the shore where his home stood became a dark smudge low on the horizon, then disappeared completely from sight. Admiral Vellan had taken the wheel for the maiden leg of their journey, a symbolic gesture that would likely not be repeated. Now he handed it over to his first mate, and fellow Ammeliner, Fermin Malik.

Rubis liked Fermin; he was much more realistic and not full of self-importance, the exact opposite to the admiral in many ways. The first mate was short but well built. He had shoulder length hair and a thick beard, whereas the admiral was tall and slim, the fair skin of his face clean shaven; something he might come to regret as the days passed and the sun, wind and salt air combined their efforts to peel his face like an orange.

Seven days of relative calm passed slowly for the crews, the late spring weather pleasantly mild. The grey sky and white-capped ocean were a true beauty to the eyes of Rubis. To most of the crew the sight was totally awe-inspiring and more than a little unnerving: so much water, with no land in sight. But while the weather held so did their nerves.

Then the first storm hit them.

It was the dead of night, cloud covered and moonless, on the eighth day of their journey. The wind had been steadily picking up speed all day, and at a warning from Rubis, Vellan had ordered most of the sails furled. The wind had increased to a ferocious roar, the first spots of rain hitting their cheeks as night fell, and soon the ocean before them became a towering mountain range of pitch-black water capped with white where the wind whipped at the crests.

The first mate held the wheel during the first hours of the storm, and the crew moved slowly through the rigging to stow most of the remaining sails. That first storm was short and furious, and as dawn crept in the storm abated and the clean up began. Two ships in the fleet, the *Crusader* and the *Retaliator*, had broken masts during the night. Several of the crew had also been swept overboard as they tried to cut loose the shattered rigging.

In the clear light of dawn—the first blue sky they had seen in days—spare masts were fitted to replace those that had been broken. This deeply concerned the admiral because each ship carried only one spare mast, and to lose two so early in their journey brought home to him the gravity of what Rubis had told him, and with more than another four months before they crossed over the equator into the calmer Farren ocean, Vellan wondered for the first time if this dream of returning to the land of his forefathers was purest folly.

As the fleet set on its way again, Admiral Vellan sought out Rubis. He found the navigator sitting by the wheel talking with Fermin.

"Rubis, could I have a word with you please?"

"Of course, Admiral," replied Rubis, casting a questioning look to Fermin. The first mate shrugged his shoulders, having no more idea what the admiral wanted than did Rubis himself.

As they moved aft, Vellan voiced his concerns to his navigator. "Rubis, the storm we faced last night, was that what we can typically expect? Or should we expect better or worse to come?"

"I am no weather expert, Admiral. The gods will send us storms as they see fit."

"Please," Vellan interrupted, "I want us to be friends on this journey. Please, call me Rolan, at least when we are alone; it is my given name."

"Well, Rolan," said Rubis awkwardly. "Last night's short storm was simply that; short. Like I said I know little of predicting the weather other than what I can see on the horizon. But I can assure you that as we head deeper into the ocean the storms will continue to grow increasingly fierce. Last night's storm was short and relatively easy to steer through safely. It was only due to the inexperience of your crews that you suffered any losses or damage.

"I personally have been in storms that have lasted for over a week, and have heard accounts from those who sail these waters more frequently than I that they have endured storms over a month long in the deep ocean. If we encounter one of them we can only hope last night's squall will have taught your men some important lessons that will not be soon forgotten."

"So, do you think we should turn back now, or can these ships truly ride out a month long storm?"

"As slow and wallowing as these ships are," said Rubis with a wry smile, "they are well built and can ride out storms with the best. As we progress through our voyage the crews will gain more experience. Those unfortunate deaths were a timely reminder to the rest of the crews—and the captains—to watch *Avenger* and follow our lead. Then once all is stowed the majority of the crew can shelter below decks until the storms passes."

"Well said, Rubis. I fear our inexperience in these waters has cost us dearly this first time. I will be sure to make it clear to the other captains tomorrow. We will make this a hard lesson well learned." The admiral turned and paced away from his navigator without further comment.

Rubis watched the admiral go, wondering if he really understood just how vicious these ocean storms could get. Watching Rolan struggling for balance as he walked across the deck, Rubis sorely wished he had more experienced hands aboard.

The next few months passed slowly with, as Rubis predicted, the storms continuing to worsen. The lesson of the first night had been well learned indeed, and even with the severity of the storms they now faced, they had only lost one more mast, and that had been a very rough night, day and the following night of harsh, icy cold weather.

They'd had many days of flat calm, and it was day one hundred and four when the mother of all storms rolled in from the west to pound their fleet. They could see it building on the horizon, the storm so black that it seemed to suck the light from the rest of the sky and swallow it within the roiling banks of towering black cloud.

The crews prepared their ships for what was going to be a very long night.

CONSEQUENCES

In a cave on the Farren Isles, Tobias and Xavier were waiting in readiness for their usual morning meeting with their fellow Circle members. Both were senior mages of the Circle of Five who governed, ruled and owned the islands and everything on them, Other than the five mages everyone else living on the islands were slaves, and also property of the Circle. After the meeting Tobias and Xavier would leave the islands, transported by magical means, and visit Empress Shatala at her palace in Zutarinis. It was time to inform her of the price she would have to pay for their aid in the slaughter of thousands of citizens from Zutar's neighbouring countries of Tibor, Gravick and Algor.

The previous year the Circle of Five had conjured and animated a great beast known as a *Draknor*. This beast and its Companions, *Feyhalas* in the old tongue, had been controlled by Shatala's minions. The Brotherhood of Divine Guidance had been handed complete control over the *Draknor*, sending it rampaging through their neighbouring countries, slaughtering thousands and bringing untold misery and famine to countless others. Shatala had requested the creation of the beast because she wished to conquer and reclaim those lands, which had rebelled many centuries before, winning independence from the Zutaran Empire.

One of her key goals had been to completely eradicate the mountain people from the High Plains village of Lokas. Unfortunately, for the empress and for Zutar, these 'mindless barbarians', as she had termed them, had thwarted her plans and destroyed the *Draknor*.

Now the empress would have to bide her time and make new plans, for she had sorely needed the secluded area around Lokas to move large numbers of troops undetected into Gravick and gain a foothold in their territory to consolidate a defensible staging point ready for a full scale invasion. The only other route presently open to her would be to march her army straight across the tundra and cross the Tiboran border then march on to attack Gravick's Middling Plain, costing her the element of surprise and risking heavy losses.

All business with the empress was forgotten as the other three Circle members entered the cave and took their places around a table carved out of the bedrock, at the centre of which stood the Nefferanian Stone; a huge magenta gem which was the source of all magical power on Klendor—or so it appeared to everyone, including the unnaturally perceptive Circle of Five. To touch the stone, even for the experienced Circle members, was instant death, the wash of raw power vaporizing flesh and bone in the blink of an eye. After prolonged use—Tobias, the eldest among them, was more than three thousand years old—and working in close proximity to the stone, the eyes of each mage had taken on the same purple glow as the stone itself.

In truth the Nefferanian had once been a space faring creature that, after being disorientated by a solar flare, had crashed into the planet's primordial muck that would eventually form the bedrock of the cave in which the Circle now held their meetings. Thin tendrils, each thousands of miles in length, which in space were spread out to collect all the nutrients the creature needed from the infinite microscopic particles of space dust, had flowed down to encircle the world that would become known as Klendor, and were now what those perceptive enough to recognize their raw energy referred to as lines of power.

Now after so many years the only secret that remained to the Nefferanian was its origins, and after long years of misuse of its incredible power the creature had only one wish; it wanted to die.

Tobias sat at his usual place and looked at each individual in turn. On his left sat Xavier, a huge man with short cropped hair, a thickly bearded chin and a wicked sense of humour. He also had the sexual appetite of someone of the age he appeared, somewhere around thirty, instead of the three thousand one hundred and seventy years he really was. Xavier was only two years younger than Tobias, and also felt some of the yearning Tobias constantly struggled with; to cast off his mortal shell and pass into the afterlife.

Next was Elaira, a slim thirty year old looking woman—who was really one thousand eight hundred thirty seven—with dark skin and vibrant red hair. Next came Meena, the youngest among them at only nine hundred and ninety nine—although she was the oldest in appearance, looking somewhere close to sixty. She had pure white hair and was very slim, almost skeletal in appearance. Lastly, sitting directly to Tobias' right, was Tamara, a beautiful if somewhat plump woman who appeared to be close to forty, though she was closest in age to Tobias, with only one year separating them.

The difference in their apparent ages was indicative of how old they were when each had mastered the Nefferanian's power. The three eldest amongst them were the offspring of a union between a Zutaren Empress and previous Circle mages, all of which had earned through their bargain the chance to father children with the empress.

Elaira had been the result of a union between the Circle and a tribal queen from the great desert of Etile. Meena had been a mistake. Her father had forgotten to take the herbs that all the mages took to keep them infertile and had foolishly gotten a slave girl pregnant. Meena was born eight months later. It was imperative that the mages took these herbs otherwise when their offspring were born half of their powers would pass over to their child, leaving them unable to again master the power of the Stone, making them once again susceptible to the ravages of time.

The fact that procreating meant a start to each mage's own slow death—by no longer being able to control the ageing process—was a mystery to the Circle. Although they thought they understood the fullness of its secrets, and had probed all the depths of the Stone's powers, the Nefferanian itself could still work against them in small ways. One of these ways was by limiting their number to five by splitting their powers and blocking the weakened parent from mastering its powers once again. To do this was a great strain on the Nefferanian, and now it was unsure if it would be able to accomplish this again as at least three of the mages were planning to procreate, in order to ascend into what they believed was the more powerful world of spirit. Most ardent in this course was Tobias, whereas Xavier and Tamara were content to delay a little longer.

The meeting opened with the usual daily business, attending to all that was involved in running a slave colony, and keeping those slaves in order. As they slogged on through the morning discussing production and exports Meena was becoming more and more restless, complaining about every small point, as usual. Finally, when Tobias grew weary of her incessant nit-picking, he asked, "What is the matter with you this morning Meena? You are being even more pedantic than usual."

"What do you mean by calling me pedantic," flared Meena, "I am nothing of the sort."

"He probably meant to say prehistoric," said Xavier with the barest hint of a smile.

"Prehistoric! Prehistoric! May I remind you I am the youngest among us, and only a third of your age," retorted Meena.

"Yes, my dearest Meena, that is true," replied Xavier in a flat tone. "But you are the one that looks like the walking skeleton here, you old bone bag."

As sick as Tobias was of Xavier's continual baiting of Meena, even he had to stifle a laugh to prevent an all out argument. Gathering himself from the edge of barely contained hysterics he managed to shout, "Enough! Enough of this pointless banter," in what he hoped was an authoritative voice. When all had calmed he asked, "Now, Meena. Will you please tell me what is troubling you?"

Meena gestured around the table. "How can you all sit here so calmly, discussing our normal routine business, when the very future of this Circle hangs in the balance?"

"Patience is a virtue, so they say," said Xavier. "I thought you of all of us would understand that best, being the vision of aged grace that you are."

Tobias glowered unconvincingly at his friend, but it was enough for Xavier to cease his baiting.

Turning back to Meena, Tobias said, "You are anxious to know what the reply will be from Empress Shatala when we lay before her the price she must pay for the use of the *Draknor?*"

"Of course I am anxious," said Meena. "Her answer could greatly affect our future. You all treat it as a trivial thing, giving this morning's meeting precedence."

"This meeting must take place Meena. The running of these islands does not cease because we have other business to attend to."

"I know that," said Meena. "But I thought that you, as the most eager to be done with this life, wouldn't be able to wait either. Her answer could mean the difference between your release into the world of spirit or being trapped indefinitely in that shell which you are so eager to discard."

"You seem to be forgetting something Meena," said Tobias, trying not to sound too much like a teacher stating the obvious to a particularly slow pupil. "It is only an hour after dawn here. The sun will only just be entering the sky over Zutarinis, and I doubt the Empress will be an early riser. Now, we still have time to conclude our business here and Xavier and I will still be there before Shatala finishes breakfast."

Meena grumbled something inaudible which Tobias took as her consent to carry on with the meeting, and quickly, before her simple error became all too embarrassing.

The meeting went smoothly after that, Meena being too fearful of looking stupid again to voice any more complaints. As they concluded their meeting Tobias said, "Xavier and I will leave immediately for Zutar and meet with Empress Shatala. When we return I will summon you all to the atrium and inform you of her reply."

Tobias walked away into the tunnel that would lead him back up to the surface. He didn't need to look to see if Xavier followed him— he could hear the large man's heavy breathing reverberating along the enclosed space—and Tobias deliberately slowed his pace so he and his friend would leave the tunnel side by side and walk together from the low building that sheltered the cave entrance from the elements and hid it from view.

The sun was still low in the sky, its orange light blindingly strong. As they worked their way through the warren of corridors and hallways that made up the central building of the Circle's palace, all was quiet and serene, slaves going efficiently about their duties. Serene, at least, until they turned a corner to find two slaves fighting.

"What is the meaning of this?" roared Tobias, his pace quickening to close the distance between himself and the slaves.

The two men instantly stepped away from each other, kneeling in subservience.

"Well?" said Xavier, coming up alongside Tobias. "You were asked a question. I demand an explanation or you will both suffer."

In answer one slave—slightly familiar looking to Xavier; then again all slaves looked the same to him—held out a hand on which was balanced a gold plaque. It was nothing new. Slaves were always trying to steal valuables in order to bribe ships captains to take them away from captivity. The slave holding the plaque spoke in a low voice. "I caught him trying to steal this."

"You did not!" protested the other. "You were the one trying to steal it. I was trying to stop *you* so we all wouldn't be under suspicion and have to suffer for your stupidity."

Tobias didn't know which slave to believe and in all honesty he didn't really care. Pointing to the slave holding the plaque he said, "Put that back on the wall, then go through that door," indicating towards an opening to his left, "and out into the courtyard. Walk fifteen paces, then turn and face the doorway. Understand?" The slave nodded and quickly set about his orders. To the other slave Tobias simply said, "Follow me."

As Tobias led the other slave away Xavier took up position by the door to make sure the first didn't try to run and hide. And not knowing what Tobias had in mind he didn't want to miss anything. His friend had a passionate hate for theives and undoubtedly had something impressive in mind.

Tobias led the slave up several flights of stairs, emerging at the top of a tall tower overlooking the courtyard, where he ordered the slave to stand on the low wall which surrounded the flat roof. Trembling with fear the slave complied, knowing refusal wasn't even an option. Tobias stopped close to the wall, spoke a few words the slave didn't understand and made a sweeping motion with his hand. After a few moments of silence Tobias ordered, "Walk forward."

"Please master," begged the slave. "It wasn't me who stole it, I swear"

"Walk forward," repeated Tobias in a voice that showed no emotion and brooked no argument.

The slave had no choice other than to comply, and as he took a hesitant step forward was amazed to discover the air solid beneath his feet. The slave looked back to Tobias, one foot on the wall and one seemingly in mid-air. The mage motioned for him to continue and the slave hesitantly took his other foot off the wall and began to edge forward in small shuffling steps, expecting his feet to encounter the end of this solid air at any moment. He was relieved when Tobias' voice commanded him to stop, even if his heart still pounded in his chest at the uncertainty of the situation.

Tobias leaned over the wall and looked down into the courtyard. Some thirty or so slaves had stopped working to watch this spectacle. He would have liked more to be present for what he planned but thirty would be enough that no other slave would doubt their word, which he knew would spread like wildfire. Tobias spoke another couple of words of power to amplify his voice, so even though he spoke in a normal tone his words boomed down to those gathered below like a voice from the gods.

"Slaves, hear me!" Tobias could feel the echoes of his amplified voice reverberating up through the stone under his feet. "We have been lenient with you so far, but obviously the rats are no longer an adequate deterrent. For your continuing theft and general disorder you have brought this lesson upon yourselves." He made a low sweeping motion with his arm, as if cutting the air with his hand. The slave suspended in mid air seemed to stumble, then plummeted head first, to the courtyard below. The second slave, frozen with horror, failed to move in time. Their heads met, shattering both skulls, spraying pieces of brain, bone and blood across the courtyard. The slaves witnessing this stood frozen in horror, some of them splattered in the disgusting mess.

Xavier, seeing this from where he stood in the doorway, nodded his head, satisfied this display would have the intended effect.

Without another word to the stunned slaves, Tobias descended from the tower, to where Xavier awaited him at the bottom.

"Good aim," said Xavier, obviously impressed by the gory display.

"Bad aim," said Tobias, with a shrug. "I was trying to drop the body at the second slave's feet. But it is of no matter. Hopefully this lesson will be discouragement enough."

"I should say." Xavier was still caught up in the moment of impact. "If that doesn't stop their thieving then nothing will."

"Shall we continue?" asked Tobias, reminding Xavier of their other duties this day.

Xavier motioned for his friend to lead on, "After you."

They worked their way through the palace, most of which consisted of a ramshackle spread of dilapidated buildings, to a small courtyard that contained a runic construct, carved into the bedrock. Stepping in through one of the three keyways—the only places it was safe to enter—Tobias spoke a string of ancient and powerful words, and both men disappeared in a flash of light and clap of thunder. As usual they did this with total disregard for the safety of anyone passing by, and one young slave, who didn't know better, was temporarily blinded and permanently deafened as a result. Not that the mages cared in the least.

Empress Shatala yawned and stretched, the thin silk sheets pulling tight across her naked body. She knew a servant had spoken to wake her. She didn't even acknowledge the old woman who had been her wet nurse and maid since the day she was born, ignoring the faithful servant as though she didn't exist.

Casting the sheets aside Shatala sat up on the bed, allowing herself a few moments before rising and striding to the steaming bath that had been prepared for her as she slept. Goose pimples covered her skin in the cool morning air, making her feel alive and invigorated. She slipped into the bath and laid back, the water covering her face and silver gold hair. As she sat up again two young women came forward and proceeded to wash every inch of her body while her old maid washed her hair.

With her bathing complete Shatala stood, stepped out of the bath and was towelled dry before a silk gown was placed over her shoulders to cover her nakedness.

Shatala walked slowly out onto a balcony that overlooked the palace grounds and took a seat as her breakfast was laid out before her, a selection of exotic fruits, warm breads, honey and preserves. While the empress ate the old maid brushed her hair, timing the strokes so as not to coincide with the tiny movements when Shatala leaned forward slightly to take a bite. Breakfast was always a slow and tranquil part of the day for Shatala, but not this morning. A disturbance from within her rooms heralded the arrival of Chancellor Vatarin, the empress's chief adviser.

"Why do you disturb me so early, Chancellor?" asked Shatala in icy tones as Vatarin stepped out onto the balcony and bowed low before her. She was angry that he would dare interrupt her breakfast yet knew it must be extremely urgent for him to do so.

"It is with news of profound importance, I assure you Em—"

Shatala cut him off, screaming, "Get on with it!"

Vatarin took a moment to compose himself before speaking, getting his words in order, knowing mindless babble would only raise her ire. "Mages Tobias and Xavier from the Farren Isles are here requesting an audience with you. I think you can already guess the nature of their business, Empress."

Shatala smiled nervously. She knew all too well why the mages were there; to inform her of the price incurred for their assistance. She had to wonder why they had waited so long. Five moons had passed since the death of the *Draknor*, five long months of nervous waiting. Abruptly she stood, walking back into her rooms and casting off her gown to stand there in all her naked glory, without a care that a man was present. "The blue dress today, I think," she said to no one in particular, her maids instantly scurrying into action lest they feel her displeasure.

Finally she turned back to her chancellor, silently standing still while the opaque dress was lowered over her head and belted at the waist, clinging provocatively to every curve. "Show them to my private audience chamber, Chancellor. I shall meet you there presently." With an impatient flick of one hand Shatala dismissed Vatarin. As the chancellor walked from the room, he reflected on how much the empress's dress sense had changed since the defeat of the *Draknor*. Before, when she was still sure of victory, Shatala's clothes were mainly see through, with only thin strips of silk hanging from a chain around her waist to give her some hint of modesty. Now, as if not wanting to draw attention to herself since the ruination of her plans, she dressed in what was for her a plain and concealing way, even if it would be considered outrageous anywhere else.

Vatarin worked his way along the glittering gold and white marble corridors and hallways that were the heart of the palace. Soon he came to a door, on the other side of which was a room where he knew the mages awaited an escort: one of them had hailed a passing servant who had alerted the chancellor immediately. This room was used for nothing other than a place for the mages to transport into and out from, to prevent the risk of anyone being injured or killed. Although this room was lushly furnished it was never entered or cleaned, except when the mages were already in the palace.

Vatarin knocked once to announce his presence and opened the door immediately, not waiting for permission to enter. The two mages looked at him as he stepped into the room, their twin purple gazes boring into him, weighing him to the last ounce. The chancellor felt cold fingers claw their way down his spine under that all-knowing stare. He coughed to mask his discomfort, and for an excuse to break eye contact.

"Mage Tobias and Mage Xavier, you honour us with your presence. If you will follow me gentlemen, I will take you to the Empress's audience chamber. She will meet us there shortly." With that he stepped back out of the room, holding the door for the *guests*. As the two mages left the room he closed the door, and without looking again at their strange eyes, he bade them follow him. As he made his way to the audience chamber, the mages walking silently a few paces behind, Vatarin felt inexplicably uncomfortable; but maybe it was just the thought of those gazes resting on his back.

It was a relatively short walk to the chamber, where, in attendance as ever, stood Night and Day—Empress Shatala's personal bodyguards—indicating that Shatala had arrived there ahead of the mages. As their names were almost unpronounceable, Shatala had taken to calling her guards Night and Day as a child, these names more than adequate to explain their differing colour. In size and shape they were almost identical, each one over seven feet tall and weighing around three hundred pounds—all solid muscle.

Vatarin knocked perfunctorily as he opened the door, indicating for the mages to precede him. Inside Shatala was lounging on a large pile of silk cushions, sipping a goblet of wine.

"Gentlemen," she greeted them, "what a pleasure to see you again."

"You do know why we are here?" asked Xavier, sceptical of her sincerity.

"Of course," she replied with an air of feigned casual interest. "You are here to state your terms for your aid in our little campaign last summer, a campaign, I must add, that did not go quite as planned. I hope you have carefully considered the failure of your creation before you state your demands."

"The price was for the loan of the *Draknor*, and in no way did we guarantee the outcome," replied Xavier. "Maybe you should look to lay blame at the feet of those responsible for guiding the beast for its failure."

Shatala's lips pressed together tightly, displaying her annoyance, before she said sharply, "The terms gentlemen?"

Tobias stepped forward to deliver the terms agreed within the circle. "First you must be married."

"Not to one of you gentlemen, I hope?" asked Shatala, a nervous smile curving her lips. "Nothing personal but at around three thousand years you are a little *too* old for me."

"No, Empress. That choice is yours alone."

"Well, this doesn't sound too bad. I had not planned to marry so soon but it could be arranged. Although I must admit I fail to see how the Circle gains from my marriage."

"That is only the first part of the terms," said Tobias. "Secondly you must bear a son. I am sure you have someone in your various orders in the palace that can *ensure* your first child is male."

Shatala shifted uncomfortably. She was starting to like the sound of this less and less; and she was sure the worst was yet to come.

"Your son," Tobias continued, "and yourself will then come to the Farren Isles to live with us for a while. Your son will stay until he is old enough to sire children for the female members of the Circle. You will be able to then return to Zutar, leaving your son in our care, after you have given birth to children for the male members of the Circle—that is Xavier and I. Your children by us will remain on the islands to be trained to one day take our places in the Circle. Those are our terms, Empress."

It took more than a few moments for all that Tobias had said to sink in properly. The full impact of his words hit Shatala like a charging bull. "What!" she shrieked, sitting upright. "You surely cannot be serious."

"Absolutely," replied Tobias. "If you were uncertain of the terms you should have questioned Xavier further before entering into the contract.

You seemed confident that you understood what would be expected of you when Xavier stated the terms of payment should be no more than the last time the Circle aided Zutar in such a venture."

"Are you honestly telling me that one of my predecessors, some ancient relative of mine, actually agreed to such terms?" asked Shatala. "What a fool she must have been."

"Be careful what you say, Empress," said Tobias, a raised eyebrow the only sign she may have overstepped the mark. "That 'fool' was my mother, as she was of Xavier and Tamara, all of us to three separate fathers. Meena's father was also conceived from that same agreement. They were our predecessors in the Circle. You should consider yourself fortunate; then there were four male members in the Circle. You will only be required to bear children for two."

"And give up my firstborn son?"

"As did my mother," said Tobias. "Her son was the father of the predecessor of Elaira. And as only an empress can rule Zutar to surrender a son to the Circle should not be so great a burden for you."

"And if I refuse?"

"That is your choice."

"What does that mean?" queried Shatala, seeking clarity. "You expect me to believe the Circle would just take my refusal, with no consequences?"

"Every action has a consequence," replied Tobias. "If you want to know what action the Circle will take against you in the event that you refuse, then the answer, quite simply, is none."

"None?" asked Shatala.

"None," confirmed Tobias. "Except to seriously consider any of your requests for aid in the future, and maybe refuse."

"Maybe refuse?"

"Nothing is set in stone, Empress. If the Circle can assist in the future, in a way that is beneficial to the Circle, then we would consider any request." Tobias was rather starting to enjoy this. His scrying of the time lines had made him certain Shatala would refuse, so he threw in, just to rile her, "Although we would have to insist upon payment in advance."

"And let me guess," said Shatala. "Payment in advance wouldn't be a first born son and two other children, would it?"

"That would need to be discussed at the time. Now, Empress, I must press you for a decision."

"Very well, Mage Tobias, if you must have an answer then I refuse to accept your terms. Not only are they unrealistic but they are also insulting."

"As you wish, Empress," said Tobias, not rising to the bait of 'insulting'. He simply smiled, turned and left, opening and closing the door for himself and Xavier.

"That was painless," said Shatala to Chancellor Vatarin as the door closed.

Vatarin had a feeling that the Circle of Five withdrawing their aid could prove *very* painful in future campaigns. Keeping his suspicions to himself he simply replied, "Quite, Empress."

In the atrium of the Circle's palace Tobias delivered the news that was greeted with mixed emotions. Tamara sighed heavily, Elaira was angry that the 'stupid child' had dared to refuse. Only Meena was happy with the outcome. "Well I cannot say I am sorry that the Circle will remain as it is for the foreseeable future. Although, I must admit, I was rather looking forward to hearing the last of Xavier's comments."

Xavier forced a smile, a merest curve of his lips, with a look that promised 'the old bone bag' would pay for that comment in the days to come.

2

DECISIONS

Lars had spent the whole of what had turned into a terribly long winter training to be *Fa'ku*. One day he would be the leader of the Lokan people, after his father, Alric, may Krogos keep that day far in the future. Lars had more on his mind than just his training, longing to return to Ragal, the city where the only girl he had ever cared for lived. He knew it would have been pointless approaching his father any earlier than now for two reasons. First it was winter, and even though spring was now thawing the ice and snow, it would still be a few weeks before it would be possible to start his journey back to Ragal. And secondly, his father had told him while they were guests in King Zief's city the previous summer that they would talk about it later. Lars had known then that he hadn't meant the next day, or even the next week.

So, during the winter, Lars had done his best to learn what his father had to teach him. Luckily for Lars he was a fast learner and seldom needed anything explaining more than once. But even though he got most things right at the first attempt, his father still continually hammered it home with endless repetiton until he was satisfied Lars had it perfect, every tiny detail permanently etched in his mind.

Now as Lars stood outside the crypt, waiting for his father to speak the *Karule*—a prayer to the gods and previous *Fa'ku*—he pondered how to approach the subject of his leaving Lokas Village to go and live far away. As his father left the crypt, resetting the rune spell traps behind him, Lars turned to walk down the High Plains at his side.

Alric had changed greatly in the past year. Not only had his manner changed since he had taken over as *Fa'ku*, but he had noticeably aged. The stress of fighting the *Draknor*—a beast of purest evil, thought to be only legend and myth a year ago—had added silver streaks to his dark, flowing hair. The most prominent of these was at his temples and in the centre of his beard, making him appear even more wise and mysterious than ascending to the position of *Fa'ku* alone accounted for.

After long moments of silence, Alric spoke to Lars, knowing he was mulling something over. "What troubles you son? As the winter has ebbed away you have become increasingly restless."

Lars took a deep breath and prepared himself for the berating that was sure to follow. "Father, I wish to return to Ragal. I know you said to talk about it later the last time I asked. I have waited, father. And I have been patient. I would now like you to seriously consider my request"

"I suspected that was what has been troubling you," was all Alric had to say at first. Then after a long pause he continued. "I know you are fully aware that you have a great responsibility to your people, so I will not labour the point. They will need you if anything happens to me, for leadership and spiritual guidance. Have you considered carefully your responsibility to you own people."

Lars had already worked out what he was going to say in response to this statement, as he had felt sure it would come into the conversation sooner or later.

"I know father. And I wish to serve my people to the best of my abilities when the time comes, may the gods keep that day far away. But I firmly believe by returning to Ragal, and gaining the increased knowledge I could learn there, I *would* be able to serve our people better. The extra experience I can get will only help to make me a wiser leader with a better understanding of the people beyond our lands. I may need that insight in the future. Lokas cannot remain apart from the other peoples of Gravick, Algor, and Tibor forever."

Alric stopped walking and looked at his son. "I can see you really have thought long and hard on this. And I am sure you have already worked out an answer to everything I would use to try and dissuade you. I agree with you my son; you probably would be better equipped to guide our people in this fast changing land of ours with all you could discover in Ragal. But I would bet anything you haven't worked out one important problem?"

"What is that?" asked Lars, frowning.

"How you are going to tell your mother you are leaving."

"I can go!" Lars gasped in disbelief.

"Yes, my son. In one moon's passing from now, when the winter has truly released its grasp, you can return to Ragal—and to Amelia." Alric only hoped she was pining for him as much as Lars was for her, otherwise he may arrive at Ragal to find she had chosen another.

As they walked past the charred remains of the *Draknor*, which had since hardened into several large piles of black cinder, Lars could think of only one thing to say, "Thank you father."

They continued in silence as they made their way down the High Plains to the village, Lars grinning inanely the whole time.

"Leaving!" shrieked Mira, Lars' mother. "What were you thinking? He can't leave, he's only just returned. You will have to tell him he has to stay. You *are Fa'ku* after all, command him if you must. I insist you do."

Alric raised his hands in a calming gesture towards his irate wife. "His heart is set on returning to Ragal."

"His heart is set is it," Mira interrupted. "Well my heart is set on seeing him stay at home, where he belongs. He should be with his family and his people. The world beyond the walls of our village is filled with danger."

"Hear me out, woman!" Alric was growing increasingly annoyed. Mira's lips were set in a thin line, her brow furrowed. But knowing her husband was at the limit of his patience she didn't cut in again as Alric continued. "Listen to me, Mira. He will be eighteen in a few weeks. Will you keep him here forever, out of harms way? He will be the leader of our people after me, he needs to experience life, otherwise what comparisons will he be able to use, unless he sees them with his own eyes, to guide and advise our Council of Elders. And Krogos knows they need guiding; half of them behave like children, or worse.

"More importantly, if we forbid him to leave, he could go of his own accord, running away one night to face even greater dangers. Or would you suggest we tie him up like a stalok? Or perhaps marry him off to the first maiden who passes our door? Either way he would be equally unhappy, forced into a life he does not desire."

Mira stood shaking silently for long moments. She knew her husband was right, *he* always was. But she was still seething that he had given in so easily, especially without talking to her first.

When she spoke she had to pause many times, until the right words would come to her. "I know what you say is true. But you are a man; you will never understand what a mother feels for her children. I know you love our children, but men differ from women with their concerns for their offspring. You always seem to think that 'experiencing life' is what will make them strong, whereas I only see it as putting them in unnecessary danger. I . . ." Her words faltered. After a long pause she spoke through a racking sob. "It's just that I will miss him. I won't . . ." Her voice cracked again as she broke down in uncontrollable tears.

Alric comforted her, hugging his wife close until the crying subsided.

Later that day, Alric made his way through the village to talk with Hakon, a fellow warrior and very good friend. Hakon was now well into setting up the forge he had promised himself he would build. They sat outside the new building, enjoying the warmth of the weak spring sun. Hakon had learnt the basics of working steel from a blacksmith in Ragal, and was determined to practice that trade in Lokas, ending the village's reliance on the flint they had to travel deep into the mountains to collect.

"Did you hear about the explosion yesterday?" Hakon asked Alric, rubbing a nasty looking purple bruise on his left arm. He and Alric had been good friends for many years and Hakon found it hard to remember to call Alric by his new title. Even when he did remember they both found it uncomfortable.

"No one told me yesterday, but I repeatedly heard all about it from the Elders this morning." He added with a laugh, "They seem to think your antics will be the death of us all. They're screaming hell and damnation, protesting that I should stop you before you kill yourself if not us all. What actually happened?"

"Nothing quite as bad as it was made out." Hakon explained, "I was stoking up the fire in my new forge, just to try it out. I still have to get some steel before I can do anything else. As I worked the bellows one of the stones I used for the hearth exploded with the heat." Hakon rubbed at the angry looking bruise again, before continuing. "Needless to say I have since replaced all of those stones with the same kind as the ones that remained undamaged by the heat. Unfortunately two of our most wizened and annoying elders witnessed the mishap and were nearly struck by flying shards and created a great fuss about it."

Alric smiled and shook his head at Hakon's explanation, but the warrior-blacksmith guessed there was something else troubling his friend. "What is bothering you?" he asked. "You seem distracted."

"Is it that obvious?" asked Alric, before explaining. "Lars is going back to Ragal. It is not a good time to be travelling in these lands. After the recent troubles people on the Middling Plains have been murdered for their possessions alone. And it will not look good if I send warriors to escort him; they may be attacked just for simply being in the wrong place."

Hakon mused silently to himself for a moment, before stating, "I'll escort him."

"You?" asked Alric. "Why would you want to go all the way to Ragal?"

"I could use the extra training Sarn promised me if I returned." He referred to the blacksmith he had learned the basics of his new trade from in Ragal. "I still have a long way to go just to get the forge up and running. The two of us travelling together should attract little attention, and can easily hide if trouble does come our way."

Alric was lost for words. "Thank you," was all he could manage.

"Think nothing of it, *Fa'ku*," said Hakon, finally remembering to use the honorific. "When do we leave?"

"Shouldn't you discuss this with Tara first?" asked Alric. "It may be better to talk with your wife before you commit yourself."

"I already have," Hakon assured. "We have spoken of it before. She understands the need for me to return and complete my training if this is going to be my new life. I must admit though, it's not as exciting as been a warrior, but it does have its rewarding moments."

"Well," Alric began, "all I can say is thank you again. I will really appreciate you going with him. Mira will also be relieved to know you are going with Lars. He will be leaving with the next new moon. We can talk more about the details later."

"I'll go and tell Tara," said Hakon. "At least I will have a cycle of the moon's phases to make it up to her." Hakon left Alric sitting where he was and went to find his wife.

One month later, just as the first moon was showing its last slice of light, Lars was organizing the few items he would take with him on the long journey to Ragal. He had a new bow, three spears and had even been allowed to choose a sword—which were normally only given to warriors on completion of their training. He had selected a sword with a long slender blade, a leather grip and a basket guard.

His mother and father were sitting outside their hut, fretting over the danger fraught journey their son would be embarking on the next day. Really there was little to worry about: it would have to be a group of extremely down on their luck bandits who would attack anyone for a few weapons. Besides, both Hakon and Lars were well trained in camouflage and concealment, and if needs be they could remain undetected all the way to Ragal even though that would greatly prolong the journey. And if the worst happened and they were attacked they were both more than capable of defending themselves.

With his few possessions set to one side Lars went out into the cool evening air to spend his last night with his parents. Kora, his younger sister, was bouncing up and down in the doorway, excited at the prospect of having more room.

"Lars, when you leave can I have your books?" asked Kora. "I mean, you can't take them all with you, can you?"

Alric sighed heavily as his daughter spoke. Lars knew he was none too pleased to have another bookworm in the family. Literature was scarce in their village and Lars alone had accumulated nearly as much as the rest of the villagers combined.

"No, I *can't* take them with me," Lars confirmed. "But I am not going away forever. I will be returning, one day. You can look after them for me in the meantime, if you promise to be careful with them." Kora's face beamed with delight. "But remember, you can't keep them. I'll want them back when I return."

Lars walked past his sister and went to sit on the ground in front of his mother and father. "Don't worry father, it's probably only a phase she's going through."

"No it's not!" shouted Kora from the doorway, before rushing inside to inspect her newly acquired books—even if they were only on loan.

"As I was saying father," Lars began again, "It's probably just another phase. Remember last year, after we defeated the *Draknor*, she wanted to know why she couldn't be a warrior when she was old enough, and was determined—no matter what anyone said—to be the first female warrior. That passed within weeks. And only last week she was going on about coming with me to Ragal, at least she was until I told her we were walking all the way. She's just excited at having something different. I seriously doubt she will read even one book before she finds something else that interests her."

"It seems I have been training you too well," said Alric, smiling. "I don't know if I should be more worried about Kora's flighty attitude, or whether I should be worried for my position as *Fa'ku* when you return. You speak with wisdom beyond your years."

"Can't you stay a little longer?" asked Mira suddenly, tears forming in the corners of her eyes. "There is still a frost in the air. Winter is not yet over." She bounced Bane up and down on her knee as she spoke, a little too vigorously, bringing a protesting squeal from the baby.

Lars smiled kindly at his mother. "Winter may not be completely over yet in Lokas, but in two days time I shall be on the Middling Plains. Winter *will* be over there already."

"What about the other dangers?" asked Mira, her voice breaking on a sob of despair. "There are bears and wolves in the forest, and what of these bandits we have heard so much about." Mira looked at her son pleadingly, a single, glistening tear tracing its way down her left cheek.

Alric cuddled his wife soothingly. "Come now dearest. We have been over this countless times."

Both Alric and Lars expected her sorrow to turn to anger, as it so often did. After a few tense moments she just melted into her husband's arms, whispering, "I know."

Theodin Hornshank docked the three swift ships he was navigating into the harbour of Grandor Town, the first large port they came to along the coast of Gravick. They ordered supplies and procured up to date maps of Gravick. The coastline had changed greatly from the ancient maps they had been supplied with. They had anticipated some changes but the differnces went way beyond their expectation. The captains and commanders held meetings once they'd had time to peruse the new maps and the soldiers discussed their options and modified their plans accordingly.

The ships had stayed in the harbour for only two days, making a show of taking on the supplies, before heading back out to sea. They now sat at anchor far out in the Southern Ocean, waiting to meet the main fleet and apprise them of the situation.

Over the two days the ships had been docked the soldiers, disguised as sailors, left the ships in ones and twos, making their way south, many miles from the town, to an easily located rendezvous point.

Theodin had disembarked with the soldiers and stayed with them. He had really always fancied himself more as a warrior than a sailor and this was his chance to finally experience the action and adventure he was sure such a life would lead him into. All would be bathed in glory when the Ammelin army arrived and destroyed Ragal.

They travelled mainly under the cover of night, using the daylight to simply observe the comings and goings of patrols and traders from safe vantage points.

After a few weeks spent on reconnaissance of Ragal and its surrounding lands he would finally get to use the sword he had sharpened religiously every day of their long voyage.

Feeling a little apprehensive about possibly having to kill another man, now that the moment was upon him, Thoedin used the confidence of the experienced soldiers around him to steady his own nerves. They would start small, picking at easy targets that could appear the work of bandits, not willing to draw too much attention to their presence until the main army was closer to their destination.

3

PERILOUS TIMES

Lars woke before the sun crested the horizon, excitement keeping him from sleeping soundly. He walked outside, with his fur blanket wrapped tightly around his body, to see his last sunrise above the mountains for some time. For a fleeting moment he wished he was staying, even though he knew he had so much to gain from spending time in Ragal, and longed to see Amelia again.

With the sun clear of the horizon he went back inside his hut to see his mother preparing breakfast. "You had better go and get some clothes on," she told him. "You are going to be aching all over as it is with sleeping rough. You certainly don't need a chill to go with it."

Lars left his mother to go and get dressed, taking his time and tidying where he slept. He thought she seemed more like her usual self this morning, but he didn't see the tears that dropped from her cheeks as he walked away. And even if he had, she would have blamed it on smoke from the fire anyway.

Dropping his pack and the few other items he was taking near the door Lars sat down next to the fire to eat his breakfast. Mira fussed about him, making sure everything was perfect for her son. There really was no need for the extra attention; it always was perfect. Alric and Kora joined him and they ate together, his father and Kora finsihing quickly and going to wait outside for him. Lars finished eating and stood to hug his mother and say his goodbyes. He had grown a lot in the last year and was now almost a head taller than his mother, and nearly as tall as his father. He hugged her tightly, promising to be careful. This was as

23

far as his mother would go to see him off. As always Mira wouldn't go to the gates just so the whole village could see her cry.

"Are you ready, son?" asked Alric, poking his head through the doorway. "Hakon's on his way. I can just see him saying his goodbyes to Tara."

"I'm ready." Lars kissed his mother on her forehead, and after one final hug left their hut. Kora was standing next to their father, brimming with excitement. She would go with them both to the gates to say her farewells. They joined Hakon as he drew near and walked to the north gate together.

"It's a fine day for travelling," said Hakon. "We have warm sunshine, with a bit of a chill carried on a light breeze. Perfect."

"Aye, it is that," agreed Alric. "So much more suitable than when we went to Ragal last year. By the time you get to the Middling Plains you'll lose the cooler air during the day, but the nights will still be pleasant enough."

They chatted as they walked through the village towards the gate. Hakon asked Alric to keep an eye out for Tara, and check on her from time to time to make sure everything was okay. Alric agreed without hesitation and told his friend he would also ask Mira if she could befriend her so Tara would always have someone to talk to if she got lonely. The two women already knew each other, but since Tara had come to the village Mira had been too busy with her newborn son, Bane, to make any new friends.

At the gate Alric turned to Lars. "Be sure to thank King Zief personally for me. Let him know how greatly we appreciate him sending Commander Benellan and his soldiers to help us fight the *Draknor.*"

"I will, father."

"Take care, my son," said Alric, offering his arm to shake in a warrior's grasp. "May Krogos smile down on your journey and see you safely back to us."

As they released Lars intoned, "He guides His faithful in all we do."

Alric and Kora then bid them farewell and watched as they set off down the High Plain towards the forest. After they left Alric walked up to the crypt to cast the runes for the day's reading, and Kora stood at the gate, watching as the two shapes of her brother and Hakon made their way down the plains. She found herself wondering if she would ever see them again, her mind racing with the possible dangers her brother might have to face. Shaking off the worrying train of thought she returned to her hut.

Hakon and Lars knew each other well enough, but found they had little in common to talk about as they travelled. Hakon had been a warrior until the previous year, and was now trying to learn to be a blacksmith, both of which Lars knew little about. He was good with a sword, having practiced against the other boys of their village, but had never shown any real interest in becoming a warrior, and he had little interest in learning the ways of forging steel.

Lars had always been too interested in reading to care about such things, enthused by all he could learn from scrolls and books. And reading was something he hoped to be doing a lot of during his stay in Ragal. But knowing all too well that he could only gain so much from reading alone he wanted to experience a lot more, and thought Ragal would offer a wider variety than Lokas ever could.

With no common interests the conversations each tried to start soon petered off as the other showed little knowledge of the subject in question. Both found themselves comfortable with the silence as they continued on through the day, enjoying the warmth of the sun and the wind rustling through the tall grass. Hakon did take the time to teach Lars whatever he could as they travelled, pointing out wildlife and tracks and asking Lars to name them. He wanted Lars to be as capable as possible of looking after himself in case the worst happened and they were separated one way or another, leaving Lars to fend for himself.

They reached the forest when the light was already starting to fade. The short, early spring days, would drastically reduce the distance they could travel in relative safety each day, leaving them with long nights of standing watch.

This first night Lars had first watch, meaning he would be awake until after midnight before waking Hakon to take over. They soon killed a couple of Tomol Hens and set them roasting. The light was fading fast, the air filled with tooting birdcalls and the baying of wolves. The flickering light the fire provided made them edgy, for it ruined their night sight, preventing them from seeing any stalking predators. And the crackling fire would disguise any twigs breaking under a predator's foot.

They ate some of the dark meat from the birds, saving the majority of it for the following day. The smell of fresh cooked meat, and the glare of the fire, attracted every biting insect in the vicinity. Hakon added some damp grass and twigs hoping the smoke would help drive away some of the blood sucking bugs.

The fire died down, and Lars allowed it to burn out as Hakon settled down. His night sight returned after a short while, the dim starlight breaking through the trees making every shape appear scary and dangerous. The trees seemed to form clinging hands reaching for him if he looked directly at them. He knew it was just an optical illusion and the trick was to look slightly to the side of any object he wanted to observe, using his peripheral vision to watch. Even knowing this he still found it unsettling. His only comfort was that he was not alone. He found Hakon's soft snoring strangely comforting.

The next morning, feeling little rested, they set off into the depths of the forest. Soon the undergrowth disappeared altogether, making spotting any predators easier. The forest remained much the same until they reached a part where the *Draknor* had trampled its way through the trees last autumn. Here ferns and other plants had rapidly filled the sunlit stretch. Great trees had been toppled to the forest floor, and knee high saplings were already fighting their way through the brush, stretching towards the light to eventually fill the gap in the canopy high above.

As Lars leapt from a fallen trunk, a bear reared up in front of him, disturbed from its basking in the warmth of the sun. Lars threw himself back against the trunk, leaving himself no way of escape. The furious bear swept a huge clawed paw towards him. At that same moment Lars felt a tugging at the back of his pack, and was hauled to safety by Hakon.

Lars reached for his sword, wondering why he hadn't when the bear had moved towards him. Hakon stayed his hand, indicating for Lars to follow, and slowly they moved back along the trunk, away from the irate beast. As they increased the distance the bear sank to its four legs, and ceased roaring, settling back among the ferns, eyeing them warily until they passed out of sight.

After they had travelled to a safe distance Lars asked Hakon, "Why did you stop me from killing it?"

Hakon looked at Lars in a strange way before his features softened and he explained. "Firstly, you have never tried to kill an angry bear, have you? You may kill it but the chances are it would rip your heart out with its dying breath. Secondly there was no need to harm the beast: it wasn't attacking you for food, you just disturbed its sleep."

"So it wasn't going to kill me then?"

"Oh, it would have killed you," Hakon assured him. "Of that you can be certain. All I am saying is that it wasn't purposefully hunting you. You just disturbed it."

Lars looked down at his hands. "I can't stop my hands from shaking."

"I don't doubt it."

"And in truth I never even thought of drawing my sword to defend myself until after you had dragged me to safety."

Hakon nodded. "That doesn't surprise me either. Being attacked by a bear is terrifying for anyone. Even me; and I have been stabbed with a sword, pierced by arrows, and tortured. Fear is a strange thing. It is hard to suppress the natural instinct to freeze the same way a startled rabbit does. But with the more experience you gain, the easier you will find it to override that instinct, which is the reason why all our warriors must train for years. And even then you can never predict how well you will react in battle. None of us can. Everyone handles it in their own way.

"Anyway, let us not dwell on things that have already happened. We have a long way to go before we are clear of the forest. We need to press on if we are to be at the edge of the Middling Plain by nightfall." With that Hakon started to move off, back into the darkness of the forest. After a few moments and several backward glances Lars followed.

They reached the outer edge of the forest earlier than expected— both had been going a little faster than before, eager to be clear of the forest and its concealed predators—allowing them plenty of time to hunt for their evening meal. Lars ate his meal quickly and prepared himself for his watch. They would keep the same pattern all the way to Ragal, making it easier for them to get into a routine

The next morning Hakon woke Lars early and after a few bites of food they set off onto the vast openness of the Middling Plains. Within two hours they had their first sight of what they presumed to be four mounted bandits. Hakon had at first believed the stories to be greatly exaggerated; now he was beginning to have doubts. As the bandits headed for them they went to ground, crawling away from where they had stood, using the cover of the long grass to hide them. Hakon wanted to avoid a confrontation if possible, so when they had crawled to a safe distance they sat still, watching as the bandits searched the area where they had last been.

The ragged look of these four men confirmed to Hakon they were indeed bandits, and one of them had a keen eye. He heeled his horse along the thin line of broken grass. It was difficult to see with a light breeze ruffling the waist high grass, hiding the signs of their passage.

As the bandits moved slowly towards them, Hakon, knowing their discovery was imminent, stood up with his hand covering his sword hilt. Lars also stood, trying to adopt a similar pose.

The bandits drew close and formed an arc in front of them. The one who had picked up their trail eyed them curiously. Turning to the man to his right he said, "Doesn't look like they have much, does it? I suppose, if nothing else, we might be able to sell their clothes and weapons."

The man he had spoken to looked directly at Hakon. "Where are you from?"

Hakon didn't see any reason not to answer. "We are from Lokas village."

"Thought so," he said before looking back at his companion. "Probably more trouble than they are worth. Mountain men always are. Might as well let them go."

The man he had spoken to—probably the leader of the small band—nodded, and tugged on his reins to move the mare away. The others followed in file. Hakon waited until they were over a hundred paces away before relaxing his stance. Looking to Lars he motioned with his head that they should continue and set out once more across the plains. As they moved on they stayed clear of Thoran, not wanting to prolong their journey by visiting the city. They would be welcome, and King Tomar would want them to stay a night or two. But neither of them wanted such a delay.

The next three days passed slowly, with nothing to hinder them. They saw more riders—no doubt more bandits—but were left alone. On the fifth day on the Middling Plains they stumbled upon a group of three bandits, who were hiding among the tall grass, waiting for them to come near.

They had no horses now although two of them were from the same gang that had approached them on the first day. The other man, lean and ugly with few remaining teeth, was completely unknown to them. He also appeared to be the leader now, motioning for the others to take up positions to either side.

"What you got for us, pretty boy," said the ugly man, looking at Hakon's scarred face.

Hakon looked at him with undisguised contempt. "For you, I have nothing but an abundance of disgust and a very sharp sword."

"Come now. No need for insults. You can make this easy for yourself and you can walk away." Then he looked at Lars adding, "We'll just take your girlfriend."

There was a hiss of grating metal as Hakon's sword flashed from his scabbard, slicing through the throat of the lead bandit. He looked at the other bandits, his piercing gaze resting for a few moments on each. "Well, are you going to fight and die? Or are you going to run like the cowards you are with piss running down your legs?"

The two remaining bandits glanced nervously at each other and hesitantly drew their swords. Lars gulped down his rising fear and also unsheathed his blade, ready to meet an attack. Metal clashed as the smaller of the two raced in and aimed a blow to Hakon's neck. That left Lars with the big man. He had probably been a farmer before the *Draknor* had ravaged their lands the year before, leaving him homeless and starving.

Lars had never fought with a real sword, only using the wooden practice swords, and was nervous at the prospect of hurting another man. Luckily, as he slowly approached, it appeared the farmer was no true swordsman either. Their blades met in a half-hearted attempt at a thrust from the farmer, Lars easily parrying the move. The farmer swung again, aiming high for Lars' head. Lars ducked and thrust his sword blindly forward, feeling resistance as the blade entered the bandit's flesh.

Opening his eyes as the body slumped against him Lars discovered that his sword had entered the man's ribcage, piercing his heart. Blood was running along the blade, dripping from the guard to the ground. Lars stood and pushed the farmer away, watching the body slide from his sword. He looked up in time to see Hakon send a crushing blow to the side of his opponent's head. The last bandit's skull shattered, spraying Lars in a gooey mix of blood and brain.

Lars dropped his sword and sank to the ground, shaking as adrenalin was replaced with shock. Hakon walked over to comfort him, knowing it was the first time Lars had killed a man, but never had chance. "Riders," he said, pointing to three horsemen galloping towards them.

Lars swallowed back the acidic bile he could feel burning his throat and pushed himself to his feet, bending to take hold of his sticky sword once more. Before he straightened up the bile came roaring back and he spewed the contents of his stomach into the pool of blood at his feet. Spitting several times to clear the nasty taste he shook himself and prepared to meet the next threat.

The three riders reined in before them, the first man dismounting immediately. Lars and Hakon both felt a moment of relief as they recognized the rider as Commander Turral from Thoran. After the *Draknor* had attacked Lokas, Hakon, with a fellow warrior named Hale, had followed the beast and had chosen to split up and warn their neighbouring towns, even though they were old enemies. When Hale had gone to Thoran—or Drakor as it was known then—to warn them about the *Draknor*, Turral had then been a gate commander. He had met both Lars and Hakon later that year and had fought alongside the Lokan people after the *Draknor* had attacked Thoran and the survivors had been forced to seek shelter in the mountains. Since the *Draknor's* attack, and the subsequent losses, Turral had been promoted to Commander of the King's Guard. It spoke of just how undermanned the city was that the commander of the king's personal guard would lead a patrol himself.

Commander Turral recognized them instantly. "Having some bandit trouble?" he asked Hakon.

Hakon glanced at the three corpses. "Trouble like that we can handle."

"So I see," said Turral. "It's all I've been doing for weeks now. Amazing, isn't it, how a disaster always brings out the worst in some people."

"Perhaps there was no good in them to start with," Hakon suggested.

"Not so," said Turral. "I knew two of these men before the troubles of last year. Both were good enough men with children and families. Like so many they lost everything to the *Draknor* and its companions."

"Even their dignity, their sense of honour?" asked Hakon sharply. "They do no honour to their dead families by attacking those they believe to be weaker than they are."

"True, true," Turral mused. "Anyway young man," he said, turning his attention to Lars, "it looks like you could use a wash. Straight south of here, around twenty minutes walking time, there is a deep stream where you can soak that mess from your clothes and skin. It shouldn't take you too far out of your way. Wherever it is you are going?"

"We are going back to Ragal," said Hakon.

"Well I hope it is under better circumstances this time and not another dire threat to our lands?" asked Turral.

"Not this time," Hakon assured him. "We are both going to visit friends we met there last year."

"It is not a good time for travelling."

"No," agreed Hakon. "But it is a journey we both needed to make."

"Well, good luck. I hope the rest of your journey goes more smoothly. But I need to get back to my patrols. I bid you good day." The commander mounted his horse, leading his soldiers away, heading in the direction of Thoran.

Hakon placed a hand on Lars' shoulder. "Let's get you cleaned up lad. There is nothing worse to get off your clothes than dried brain."

Lars visibly paled at the reminder, rigidly keeping his gaze straight ahead so as not to catch sight of any lumps. By the time they reached the stream the gooey mess was already starting to dry and took a considerable amount of effort to clean off.

They rested by the stream for a little under one hour, enjoying the heat of the sun and allowing time for Lars' clothes to dry a little. When they set off again steam rose in thin wisps from Lars' shoulders, the heat of the blazing sun quickly evaporating the remaining moisture now they were moving again.

After that encounter they had no more trouble. Neither slept well over the following nights; each felt the constant need to be extra vigilant, lest they be caught unawares.

Seven days later they had Ragal in plain sight. The Inner City stood high and proud, perched on the rocky headland, overlooking the ocean. The Outer City spread out in front and to the sides of the inner wall, with the two empty bastions projecting from each land-facing corner of the outer wall. Both were relieved to have the city, and the safety those walls offered, in sight.

Throughout the day the city grew larger before them as they closed the distance. They had hoped to reach the gates that evening but were still a couple of hours away when they lost the daylight, forcing them to spend another night in the open.

4

A WARM RECEPTION

Hakon and Lars entered the city of Ragal early the next morning. The streets were packed with storekeepers, market vendors and the citizens of Ragal themselves. Lars went with Hakon to Sarn Plat's forge, where the blacksmith was already busy hammering away, the thickly muscled arms, shoulders and back rippling as he worked the metal, his bald head shining with sweat in the dim light.

The blacksmith looked up as they entered. At first he stared at them questioningly, then a look of recognition passed over his face, and he grinned widely, displaying his few remaining teeth. "Hello again," he paused briefly until he could match a name to the face, "Hakon. Never really thought I would see you again. But by Alman it does me good to see you alive and well."

"I'm not that easy to get rid of," said Hakon, smiling warmly. "And I am pleased to find you also alive and well."

"What brings you here this time? Not another one of them *Draknor's* around is there?" asked the smith, echoing Commander Turral's own worries.

"No, nothing like that," Hakon quickly assured him. "I came back for some more training, if you are still willing to help me?"

"I would like nothing better. It has been some time since I last had an apprentice and all this time alone is making me think of giving up the trade entirely. How long have you got this time?"

"I was planning on staying until the end of summer. Maybe a little longer if the weather holds good."

"Splendid!" said Sarn. "This time I will have long enough to show you something worth knowing. You never know, after showing some natural talent for working metal last summer, you might even be half decent by the time you return home." Sarn looked briefly at Lars before asking, "What about the lad? Is he planning on becoming an apprentice too?"

"No," explained Hakon, "he will be staying in the keep as a guest of the king."

"And you?" asked Sarn. "Where are you staying?"

Hakon shrugged. "I'm not really sure yet. They will probably let me stay in the keep again."

"No need to bother them, lad," said Sarn, offering, "You can stay with me. Gert won't mind—you remember my wife don't you?" Hakon nodded confirmation. "She won't mind if you stay with us, at our home this time; in fact she would probably skin me alive if I didn't at least make the offer. I think she took quite a fancy to you last year."

"Well, thank you," said Hakon. "I would be grateful to both you and your wife if you could find space for me. But first I need to go to the keep with Lars. Make sure they haven't changed their minds about letting him stay."

Sarn nodded. "When you are finished with our good king, come back here and I'll take you to my home, get you settled in. It's been quiet lately and I would enjoy an early finish. Tomorrow will be soon enough to get you working."

Hakon and Lars left the forge and made the short journey to the keep. They hoped someone who they recognized would be on duty at the gates, and would deliver a message to King Zief or at the very least his aide, Tam.

At the gates they were relieved to find Tam standing between two guards. His thin, white straggly hair floated on the breeze, as he took names from the common folk who wished to petition King Zief to settle disputes and deliver justice. Tam's jaw dropped open when he saw Lars walking towards him. He managed a bow before saying, "Prince Lars, welcome back to Ragal. This is the second time you've done this to me in as many years, Your Highness. You find me dishevelled and ill prepared to greet someone of your high standing."

Lars frowned, wondering what Tam was meaning, then remembered that only the common folk came to the keep in the morning, with the afternoon being reserved for the noble's of Ragal and other high born. He smiled as he said, "Sorry Tam. I forgot. Please see to your people first and don't worry about me. I can wait."

Tam hastily rushed the commoners through. When he was done he led Lars and Hakon through the Inner City to the keep. "Will you also be staying with us this time?" he asked Hakon.

"No, I'll be staying with the blacksmith, Sarn Plat, and his wife."

"Ah, yes," said Tam remembering, "You spent your time here working with the old smith last year?" Hakon nodded.

Tam led them past the two guards on duty outside the keep, who wore red and blue chequered tabards, and on through the raised portcullis gate and double doors into the keep's grand entrance. Lars was awed once again as he looked at the two staircases that ran up either side of the hallway. He looked again at the elaborately carved balustrade where each baluster was carved in the form of a woman with her arms raised, as were the top newel posts where they reached to the ceiling high above. The base newels were carved with the women's arms along their sides. It was a really remarkable display of craftsmanship, clearly representing the carver's skill.

Tam offered them a seat on the red and blue upholstered, gold tassel fringed seats that were placed under the balcony to which the two staircases led. They waited there for what seemed only a short time before Tam reappeared, wearing the light blue and red livery. Tam's uniform was not like those the guards wore; all of his clothing was light blue except for his jerkin, which had two large squares of red and two of blue in the front panel. He had also tied his straggly hair back into a tight queue.

"The king will see you immediately, Highness," said Tam with a low bow to Lars. The previous year when Alric and Hale had accompanied Hakon and Lars, they had been required to kneel before King Zief in the throne room and announce the nature of their business in Ragal. This time Tam led them straight through the throne room to the anteroom beyond, where the King of Ragal was already waiting for them and sitting in front of a crackling fire. The king still had his black hair and beard closely cropped, but now grey flecked the hair of his head.

As King Zief stood to greet his guests, Hakon, Lars and Tam all bowed low. Zief bade them to rise and take a seat, indicating two chairs placed on the opposite side of the fire. When they were sitting comfortably and Tam had poured them all some mulled wine, Zief began. "I am pleased to see you decided to return to us, Lars, but not as pleased as I am sure a certain young lady will be. And what about you, Hakon, are you to stay with us as well?"

Hakon explained that he would be staying with Sarn and his wife, and that he was only back in Ragal to learn more about being a blacksmith.

When Hakon had finished, Zief said, "Well that's enough chitchat, pleasant though it is. Please tell me about how you destroyed the *Draknor*? I have heard Commander Benellan's report but would like to hear more."

"First," said Lars, "I must thank you. My father and all my people were extremely grateful to you for sending your soldiers to help us in the battle."

"It was the least I could do for our newest friends," said Zief, dismissing it with a gesture of one hand. "And all of Gravick was in danger. Ragal will never stand idly by and watch others suffer and do nothing. Now, tell me about the *Draknor*?" he finished eagerly.

Lars explained about what he had witnessed, Hakon adding comments from his own perspective of the battle. Then Lars told Zief the details of the Wind of Souls, how it had seared the life from the *Draknor* and its companions. He told of the severe losses, including the previous *Fa'Ku*, Lars' grandfather, and that if Zief's soldiers and the Thoranians hadn't made their way to the mountains and helped bolster their defence lines, the day, and all of Gravick, would have surely been lost.

King Zief seemed inconsiderate of their bitter losses as he said, "Well things will happen as the gods see fit. We all have to die someday."

"Yes," said Hakon hotly, "but most of us prefer to die in battle against other men, not some creation of evil. Or at the very least to die old and grey surrounded by those we hold dear."

Zief held up his hands. "Peace, Hakon. I am genuinely sorry for your losses, but I feel you misunderstand me. I am a fatalist. I believe everyone has a preordained destiny, and we will die when we are supposed to, one way or another. No man can escape fate. I would rather believe that when we die our spirits are going on to something better than wars and conquest, disease and death. Therefore although the moment itself is sad, it should also be celebrated as the spirits of your friends and family have been released to find a better place. And, on top of that, we have no worries that there is nothing but blackness and an end to our existence for us when we die: your Wind of Souls proves there is a life after death."

Hakon relaxed and nodded. "I am sorry if I spoke out of turn, Majesty."

"Nonsense," said Zief. "You spoke as anyone who has lost loved ones would. But I suggest in future you remember what I have just told you. We, all of us in this room, *know* death is not the end."

"Thank you for your understanding, Majesty."

Zief then turned his attention once more to Lars. "Right young man, I promised you last year that if you returned you could learn whatever you wished to know. So what are your interests?"

"My main interest is reading and studying old scrolls," said Lars. "I also would like to learn about horses, how to ride and care for them. And also," he added with a sidelong glance to Hakon, "I need to learn more of swordsmanship. I can handle a blade well enough in practice but in battle I lack confidence. We were confronted by bandits on our way here, and I only killed my opponent by luck and his own ineptness with a sword."

"Well, I'm sure those few things will be no problem. During your stay I am sure you will see many more things that interest you. If you discover anything else you wish to learn you only need to ask. First though, if you wish to learn from books, the best place to do that is in the library. If you desire it you could assist Felman. The gods know he could use all the help he can get. If you wish you could spend a few hours each morning in the library, then go on to your other lessons."

"I would like that very much," said Lars.

"Splendid!" exclaimed Zief. "Now that is agreed I will have to conclude this meeting. I must preside over the petitions of the common folk, wearisome though they often are. We shall talk again over the next few days and you can let me know how you are settling in. I will try and meet with you at least once a week during your stay so you can keep me apprised of how you are progressing with your lessons and if anything else has roused your interests.

"Tam will show you to your room, and let you get settled in," said Zief, adding with a smile, "And I'm sure a certain young lady will have heard that you have returned by now."

Hakon and Lars stood and bowed, Zief acknowledging them with a small nod of his head.

"Prince Lars," said Tam, after the king had dismissed them, "I will show you to your room, then I must attend my morning duties." He indicated with a motion of one arm for them to move towards the door.

"Thank you, Tam," said Lars, walking towards him as he opened the door. "Once I have seen where my room is I will go and visit Felman, to let him know I will be working with him."

"Very well, Your Highness," said Tam, closing the door behind them. "You are of course free to move around the keep as you will, but first you will have to check your sword into the armoury. We can do that on the way to your room, if you will please follow me."

Tam led Lars back through the Throne Room. It was already filling up with the common folk, petitioners for the king's justice and ruling. They passed the throne, slightly raised on its blue carpeted dais, and headed to a small door in the far left side wall. The door opened onto the foot of a spiral staircase that led up to the first and second floors. The portion of the second floor that could be accessed from these stairs was entirely taken up by the Royal apartments and the staircase guarded at all entrances. Other rooms were also utilized on the remainder of the second floor but were only accessible by using another staircase at the other end of the keep. Tam nodded to the guard and led Lars and Hakon up the stairs to the first floor, walking past another guard and out into the corridor.

Lars remembered the corridor they now entered as the one they had walked through on their first visit to Ragal the previous year. It was more richly furnished than where he had stayed before. The wall sconces had gold clips on the cages, and the doors were finely carved and richly appointed.

At the third door on the right, situated around the centre of the wall on that side of the corridor, Tam stopped and indicated with his hand. "This will be your room, Highness. But first we must go to the armoury, which on this floor is the last door on your left."

The armoury door was already open, leading into a narrow room. A middle aged, very lean man with silver hair was sitting behind a desk, dressed as a common soldier. He rose when Tam entered, eyeing Lars and Hakon with a cold stare. "Bollo," Tam named the man behind the desk, "this is Prince Lars from Lokas village. He shall be staying with us for some time." Tam turned his attention back to Lars. "Your Highness, this is Bollo. He is Sword-master and Armourer here at Ragal. You will have to leave your sword and other weapons with him. If you need your sword for any lessons, Bollo will take it to the fencing yard for you. As Sword-master he will also be responsible for instructing you in swordsmanship, so you will be seeing quite a lot of each other.

"After you have settled into your room, come back here and see Bollo. He will give you locations and times to meet him for your lessons. If you will please hand over your sword, Your Highness."

Lars hesitantly handed over his sword to the armourer, who unsheathed it and eyed it critically before placing it on a rack. Without another word to the armourer Tam led Lars and Hakon to the room he had indicated earlier.

Turning the gold coloured handle, the door floated open on noiseless hinges. Lars suspected—as he did with the clips on the wall sconce cages—that the metal wasn't actually real gold, but another metal which gave the appearance of richness. Walking into the room as Tam held the door for him, the first thing Lars noticed was two large windows on the far wall, the tapestry curtains billowing slightly in the cool spring breeze.

The room was huge, as Lars soon discovered as he walked within. On the left wall was a large bed, big enough to sleep four, with tall candlesticks placed on the nightstands to either side. In the centre, the stone floor was covered with a thick, floral patterned rug. To the right, four luxuriously padded chairs were arranged, two to either side of the large stone fireplace. The walls were hung with more tapestries, and thick candles were enclosed in wall sconces, one on either side of the fire.

Lars turned to Tam and asked, "Who else sleeps here?"

Tam allowed a small smile as he replied, "Only you, Highness."

Lars whistled through his teeth as he looked around the room again. This one room was larger than the hut he shared with his whole family back in Lokas.

Tam coughed to get Lars' attention. "I must go now, Highness. If you require anything before I return, please ask Bollo." Tam bowed low and left the room.

Hakon closed the door quietly and walked over to sink down into one of the chairs. "I think I have changed my mind. I might just stay here with you instead."

Lars sank down into an opposite chair. "I wouldn't blame you. I can't believe all this is for one person. And if you do want to stay here, the bed is more than big enough for four, let alone two."

Hakon looked around the room from where he sat. "A nice place to entertain your lady friend, isn't it?"

"I hadn't really thought that far ahead yet," said Lars as he felt the heat rising to his face.

"Yes, of course you haven't," said Hakon sceptically. "But seriously, as tempting as this place is, I will stay with Sarn. I have already agreed and wouldn't want to offend him by accepting a better offer. And his home is closer to what we are used to. I don't think this rich lifestyle would agree with me for very long." He smiled as he mocked, "Such rooms are only for the likes of you, *Prince* Lars."

"Don't you start," said Lars, good naturedly. "It's bad enough with Tam insisting on ending every word with 'Your Highness.' Although I noticed twice today he left out 'your' only using Highness instead; which is slightly better. I wish they would just call me by my name."

"Different people, different customs," Hakon reminded him. "You will grow used to it in time."

"I suppose I will have to," agreed Lars.

"Well," said Hakon as he eased his way up from the chair, "I need to go and see Sarn now. And you need to go and see Bollo. Seems a strange fellow, don't you think? But he moves with a deadly grace; I think he will be a good one to learn from." Changing the subject Hakon told Lars, "I don't know if I will be freely allowed access to the Inner City to come and see you regularly. If you ever need me for anything, or you just want someone familiar to talk to, you know where to find me."

Lars walked with Hakon to the top of the staircase in the main hallway, saying farewell as Hakon descended the stairs and left the keep. As Hakon passed through the doors and out of sight, Lars went back to the armoury to see Bollo.

Bollo stood as Lars entered. "Your training with me will be at first light everyday, before breakfast. Meet me each morning in the fencing yard, and be on time. Your sessions will end each day when the sun rises fully above the horizon. Do you have any questions, Highness?"

Lars wasn't sure whether Bollo disliked him for some reason, or if he spoke like that to everyone: direct and to the point, with little formality. It wasn't that he displayed a lack of respect, more a no nonsense attitude.

Lars shook his head, "No questions. I will see you tomorrow at first light." Lars left the armoury, the cool gaze of Bollo following him, and he headed down to the library.

Felman Spanril, the ancient, supposedly deaf librarian with very little pure white hair, was sitting behind his desk, snoozing as usual. Lars shook him gently to get his attention.

Several not so gentle shakes later and the librarian slowly opened one grey, bloodshot eye. "Do I know you?" he asked, picking up a peculiar shaped horn in a gnarled hand, holding it to his ear ready for an answer.

"I was here last year," said Lars, speaking loudly into the horn, even though he knew it wasn't really necessary. Felman could hear perfectly well but feigned deafness so he could avoid unwanted disturbances. Lars saw no harm in playing along with the old man's games.

The librarian still seemed confused for a while, then a look of recognition passed over his face, and he scowled fiercely. "You are one of those who brought that beast here last year. What was it called again?"

"The *Draknor*," Lars reminded him. "And we didn't bring it here. It came here by itself. We only came here to see if we could find a way to destroy it."

Felman appeared unconvinced. "Well, what do you want now?"

"I have returned to Ragal for the summer, to learn things I cannot learn in Lokas. I am going to be helping you every morning from now on." Lars scanned the books piled high on the floor and every other available surface, almost everywhere except on the shelves where they were supposed to be. "I'm going to help you get this place into some kind of order."

"Why would I need any help?" asked Felman. "I could, at a moment's notice, lay my hands on any book in this library."

"Yes, I'm sure *you* could. Unfortunately you are the only one who can do so. No one else can find anything in this place. I am just going to help you shelve all the books, organizing them into some semblance of order, and to arrange some sort of reference section to help people find any particular book or scroll quickly."

"I don't see the need," grumbled Felman, "My system has worked perfectly well for years. And no one ever uses this place anyway."

Aye, thought Lars, *that doesn't surprise me. Anyone who came in here would have to try and get some sense out of you before they could find what they are looking for.*

"I will see you in the morning," said Lars. "I have other things to take care of now." His foremost concern was staying in his room in case Amelia came looking for him. And Tam would be returning later, expecting to find him there.

He walked up the main staircase to get back to his room, past the penetrating stare of Bollo as he passed the armoury. Opening the door to his room, he stepped inside, admiring the fine furnishings before closing the door.

"And just where have you been?" said a familiar, sweet voice.

Lars spun round, expecting to see Amelia somehow standing there. His eyes had not deceived him on his first gaze around the room: there was no one there. Then he noticed dark, curly locks protruding slightly from the top of one of the deep chairs that was facing away from him. Lars crept up silently to the chair where Amelia sat. Crouching behind it he waited for her to rise. After a short time she peered around the corner of the chair only to find the room to be apparently empty.

Amelia stood, not noticing Lars crouched behind the chair as she looked across the room to the door. Sighing heavily she cursed herself for not standing up as the door had opened. She presumed Lars had looked in then left again on some other business. Feeling cheated she slowly walked to the door, and was reaching out towards the handle when Lars spoke.

"Can I help you, My Lady?"

Amelia jumped with shock and turned to see Lars sitting in a chair facing her. "How did you—?" she started, but it didn't matter. Lars smiled as he stood again and they rushed forward into each other's arms.

After an awkward kiss Lars held Amelia a little away from himself, staring into her green eyes, drinking in her beauty and eyeing curiously the white gem suspended by the thin silver chain on her forehead. She had not only grown taller and matured, she was even more beautiful than Lars' memories. "Oh, I have missed you," he said. "I don't think I realized just how much until I heard your voice."

"Nor I, until now," she said, stuttering in tearful joy.

A knock at the door disturbed their reunion. Lars gave time for Amelia to wipe the tears from her cheeks before he called for the visitor to enter.

Tam opened the door, looking uncomfortable that he had disturbed them. "Forgive me, Highness. I came to give you a full tour of the Inner City, and show you some other things we could teach you that you may find interesting. I did not intend to disturb you. I can come back later if you prefer?"

"It's okay," said Amelia. "The Queen has released me from my duties for the remainder of the day. I will show our guest around the Inner City and introduce him to several people I know."

"With all due respect My Lady, the king has requested that I see to it personally." Tam racked his brains to think of a way out of this uncomfortable situation. "I suppose, if it would not be too much of an intrusion on your privacy, that I could follow you, at a discreet distance of course. That way I could be available to answer any questions, and advise on any points you may miss, My Lady."

Amelia let out an exasperated sigh. "Very well Tam. If the king has ordered it who am I to countermand him."

Amelia linked her arm in Lars' and led him out of the room. Tam followed closely until they were outside the keep where he fell back out of hearing range as promised. Amelia led Lars around the left side of the keep's outer wall, where a cobbled path began, coursing all the way around the Inner City.

The first thing Lars smelled as he walked around the keep was the mixed smell of fresh straw and manure: the stable hands were mucking out while the trainers exercised the horses. Lars stopped, looking at the magnificent beasts as they pranced and kicked their way around the small exercise field. Still, even to his untrained eye, it was obvious the horses were happy with the limited confines of the paddock after been cooped up in the cramped stables.

Amelia looked at Lars as he watched the horses. "Can you ride?" she asked. Lars' only response was a shake of his head. "Well," said Amelia, "that is something we shall have to rectify."

Lars turned his adoring gaze to Amelia and blinked at her beauty. "I would like that very much indeed."

Amelia waved Tam forward. "Prince Lars would like to learn how to ride. That should be no problem, I presume?"

"Not at all, My Lady," replied Tam. "Prince Lars has already expressed an interest in that area. I shall speak with Enric," he referred to the Stable-master, "when we have finished our tour."

"Good," said Amelia, turning her attention to Lars. "After a few weeks in the training circuits and trotting around the Inner City, we shall be able to ride together across the Low Plain—that's if we ever sort out the trouble with these cursed bandits."

"You have bandit trouble on the Low Plains too?" asked Lars.

"Too much of it," confirmed Amelia. "And it only seems to be getting worse."

"What is King Zief doing about it? He doesn't seem the type to tolerate anything upsetting the smooth running of his kingdom."

"The king has ordered frequent patrols and for all trade caravans to be accompanied by armed guards," said Tam.

"Let us not talk of such depressing things," said Amelia. "This is a joyous day and we shouldn't spoil it with talk of Ragal's worries."

Amelia tugged at Lars' arm and they resumed their walk, with Tam once more following at a respectful distance. All the open space in the Inner City was covered with fine lawns and well-tended flowerbeds. Trees lined the path to either side. Most had lost their spring flowers as the first tiny leaves poked their way from the buds.

The first dwellings they came to were in the southeast corner of the Inner City wall. A long enclosed veranda adorned the front of the main building and every window was arched at the top. The outbuildings were plain and square, mainly hidden by bushes, shrubs and trees.

"This is House Farben," Amelia informed Lars. "Remember I told you about the five houses last year?" Lars nodded even though he remembered little of what she had told him.

The buildings were large to Lars, if small by the standards of Ragal's elite five noble families. No one seemed to be there so Amelia led him on to the southwest corner of the Inner City, where House Stalto was situated. The buildings here were large and grand, every corner, ledge and rail decorated with some frill or fancy, built, Amelia informed him, to resemble the Tiboran style. The main house was surrounded by tiered, immaculately maintained gardens. This corner of the city seemed also to be very quiet, except for a maid who was making her way from the main house to the laundry building.

"Ellie," Amelia called, obviously familiar with the maid. Ellie walked over to them, shifting the weight of the heavy basket in her arms as she performed an awkward curtsy. As she rose Amelia asked, "Is everyone away somewhere today?"

"No, My Lady," said Ellie. "My masters are inside with Lord and Lady Farben. Do you wish to see them? I could announce that you are here, if you wish, My Lady?"

"No," replied Amelia. "That won't be necessary; we won't disturb them. Thank you Ellie, you may carry on with your duties."

Ellie curtsied again whilst trying to balance the heavy basket, before heading once more towards the laundry building. As she walked away Amelia tugged at Lars' arm. "Shall we continue?" Lars smiled warmly and indicated for her to lead on.

Halfway around their circuit they passed the main gate into the Inner City. Seeing Amelia all the guards straightened from their usual more casual pose, the Guard Commander smartly saluting as they walked by. The guards were just starting to relax again when Tam appeared from the shaded cover of the tree-lined path. They straightened again instinctively. Tam just smiled and walked on, allowing them stand at ease once more.

Amelia led Lars along until they came to the northwest corner, where House Tremar was located. Here all was buzzing with activity: stable hands were busy strapping saddles to horses while young lords armed themselves and strapped on breast plates and greaves before mounting their horses.

"What is all the excitement about, Parlen?" asked Amelia as a young lord rushed by. Lars instantly recognized the name but not the young man. He had met Parlen at the midsummer feast the year before. Then he had been short and skinny with a nose far too large for his thin face.

Since then he had grown and filled out, his facial features altering so his nose no longer looked out of place.

"Bandits," replied Parlen as he tried to push his shoulder length hair under a rounded helm. "They were sighted this morning, and as House Tremar is the Duty House for this moon we are leading out twenty of the King's Horse to track down and arrest them, if they will come peacefully," adding with excessive youthful bravado, "If not we shall kill them all where they stand and leave their corpses to the crows."

"Mind your tongue, young man," said Tam, stepping forward. "That is no way to talk in front of a lady." Lars didn't understand what the problem was: warriors in Lokas always talked with their women of battle and hunting, but Parlen seemed suitably admonished.

"Forgive my coarse words, Lady Amelia. I am sorry if I spoke out of turn and caused offence." It was only then that he seemed to realize Lars was even there. Regarding him Parlen asked, "I know you, don't I?"

Lars was about to answer but Amelia beat him to it. "Surely you remember Lars?" said Amelia. "He came here last year."

"Ah, yes," said Parlen, "the young warrior from Lokas Village."

"I am not a warrior," Lars corrected. "But yes, I am from Lokas."

"Do you want to ride out with us?" asked Parlen.

"He doesn't ride," said Amelia. "And he is a *prince* of Lokas."

Parlen looked both surprised and amused that someone of Lars age couldn't ride a horse. After a moment he bowed to them both saying, "Well, Prince Lars, Lady Amelia, I must go now. Farewell."

"Farewell," said Amelia, "and return to us safely."

They watched as Parlen mounted his horse and rode out towards the gate with the other lords of the household, followed by the King's Horse. Once the sound of hooves clattering on the cobbled path seemed distant, Amelia led Lars on around the path, towards her own home, House Corban, which was located in the northeast corner.

"What was all that about?" asked Lars. Amelia turned him a questioning glance so he clarified his meaning. "All that stuff about their being 'Duty House' for this moon."

"Ah," said Amelia, "that. Well it is simple enough to explain. I told you about the patrols to take care of the bandits. Each of the other four Houses—the king's House is not included in this—take turns, one moon at a time, to lead out a party of the king's soldiers in times of trouble, whether it be a civil disturbance or trouble in the outlying lands of the Low Plains. Normally nothing ever happens so it is of little inconvenience to the Houses. But lately, with all the trouble from roving bandits after the *Draknor* was here last year, making hundreds homeless, hardly a moon passes without some kind of trouble."

By the time Amelia had finished her explanation they were within sight of House Corban. These were by far the grandest buildings, even outshining the towering magnificence of the keep. All was shining brightly, the buildings glittering in the sunshine. Tall, white marble columns graced the entrance to the main house, with black polished granite steps leading up to the door.

"Come on," said Amelia, tugging at Lars' arm. "Let's go inside, and you can meet my mother. She is the queen's sister," she added proudly.

Lars hesitated to tread on the steps, in case he left a mark on the highly polished surface, but Amelia pulled him on regardless. Lars stopped again, asking, "What about your father?" nervous about the response.

Amelia pressed her eyes closed. A tear began to form in the corner of her left eye. Lars wiped it away with his thumb, asking, "Did I say something wrong?"

Opening her eyes, Amelia forced a weak smile and shook her head. "There was no way you could know. My father and my youngest brother died late last year. After the *Draknor* was in these lands disease was rife. A blood plague swept through the city. For reasons no one understands it seemed to affect the nobles more severely than the common folk. It probably has something to do with them working the land and around animals. They pick up all kinds of diseases and infections and seem to have become more resilient. We in the Inner City lead a more sheltered life. Although no one ever suspected it could lead to problems it appears we have bred a weakness into the Five Houses.

"Other Houses lost family as well, although ours was the worst hit. To add to our sorrow my oldest brother was killed by bandits during the winter." Amelia paused for a moment to compose herself before continuing, "Now it falls to two of my cousins to represent House Corban as Duty House when our turn comes around."

Lars wanted to say something, but could think of nothing appropriate that could in any way ease her sorrow. Amelia continued after a moment and saved him from the awkward silence. "Please, Lars, don't mention any of this to my mother. She will only break down and that would embarrass her. She has already had young suitors wishing to take her hand in marriage, hoping to win House Corban for themselves. It is not something she is even willing to think about at this time. Now, please, let us talk no more of this. This should be a happy day, and I would not spoil it with things I cannot change, however sad." With that said Amelia smiled again and dragged Lars up the few remaining steps.

Entering the palacial home Lars felt cold, all the stone that surrounded him slow to warm in the rising heat of the day. He soon forgot the slight discomfort as he stared around the magnificent interior. Every surface was highly polished, whether it was stone or wood, and everything he could see had been carved at the edges to form flowing curves. Lars was drawn away from his amazement by the sound of footsteps on the granite floor, soon followed by, "Amelia, darling."

Lars looked at the woman coming towards them: she was old but nothing like the women of his home. Her skin was still fairly smooth, only her pure white hair and a slight stoop to her walk giving some indication of her true age. She also wore a white gem on her forehead, suspended by the silver chain. Lars remembered from the previous year that all the women of the five houses wore the gem and silver chain. Only the queen was different as hers was suspended on a gold chain. As she drew closer the woman spoke again.

"Who is this handsome young man you have brought to grace our home." Lars blushed at the compliment as the old woman carried on. "Is this your young love . . . Lars isn't it?" Lars nodded. "We have heard a lot about you young man." Now it was Amelia's turn to blush.

Gathering herself from her embarrassment, Amelia introduced them. "Lars, this is my grandmother, Lady Senara."

Lars bowed low. "It is an honour to meet you, My Lady."

Senara smiled at him. "From what I hear young man you are a prince, so it is I who is honoured." After a moment Senara spoke to Amelia again. "Come now my dear, your mother will be pleased to see you. You spend so much time with our queen these days your own mother barely lays eyes on you from one day to the next."

Amelia's grandmother led them through a series of gleaming corridors to the rear of the house, where Amelia's mother sat in the atrium, perched on the raised edge of an ornamental pond, watching the fish bask in the sunlight. The three of them walking out of the house caught her eye and she turned to see her daughter and her mother with a strange young man on her arm. Noticing the manner in which he was dressed she soon guessed who it was.

Lars saw Amelia's mother—and there was no doubt she was Amelia's mother, the resemblance to the queen was striking—turn her face towards them, her expression going from one of deep thought to pure joy at seeing her daughter. She rose gracefully and walked forward to embrace Amelia, before turning her attention to Lars, curtseying as she spoke.

"I don't think Amelia needs to introduce you, Prince Lars. Even if I had not seen you last year we have heard so much about you, you would be easy to spot anywhere." Lars and Amelia both blushed this time.

When Lars would have bowed, Amelia's mother stopped him, taking his hand between both of her own and holding it gently. Lars looked at her face and even though the family ties to the queen were obvious, that was where the similarity ended: where the queen was all grace and stern stares, Amelia's mother was all smiles and motherly tenderness, her beauty increasing tenfold as her smile lit up her face. The white gem she wore was much larger than those of Amelia and her mother. *Does the size have something to do with their position in the House?* Lars wondered. It was something he would have to ask about another time. Lars was taken away from his comparisons when she spoke again.

"My name is Talia," she said, still holding onto his hand, "and I am sure you already know I am Amelia's mother." Turning her attention to Senara, Talia asked, "Mother, would you please ask Kate to bring some chilled wine, whilst I show our guest to the parlour?"

Talia took Lars on one arm and her daughter on the other, leading them back through the house to a room that was large to Lars, though small compared to the rest of the house. She showed Lars to a large couch, sitting down next to him, at an angle so she could look at Lars without straining her neck. Amelia sat on the other side of Lars just as Senara entered the room and settled herself in a high, hard looking chair facing the three of them.

After the maid had poured the wine and left the room, Talia took Lars' hand again and began to speak. "Prince Lars . . ."

Lars held up his free hand to forestall her. "Please, My Lady, call me Lars. In my own village I am not considered a prince and it is bad enough that everyone in the keep names me so. Please, if you would simply call me Lars, I would be extremely grateful."

"As you wish," said Talia. "If you will do likewise and simply call me Talia."

"Of course," agreed Lars.

"Now," said Talia. "Amelia has told us about you but there is so much more I would know; if you don't find our questioning too intrusive."

"Not at all," said Lars, hoping he wouldn't come to regret saying so.

Amelia's mother and grandmother quizzed Lars for some time about his home, and what he intended to do during his time in Ragal, including some not so subtle questioning about his intentions towards Amelia. Quite some time had passed when Lars and Amelia finally left House Corban to find Tam still waiting outside.

Both the older women of House Corban said their farewells to Lars and Amelia on the steps outside, being careful to use Lars' title of prince with Tam being present. Amelia was about to lead Lars on along the cobbled path when a commotion from the direction of House Tremar stopped them in their tracks.

Lars, Amelia, her mother and grandmother, all being shadowed by Tam, made their way to House Tremar. As they neared they could see the same lords and horses they had seen earlier and knew they must have returned from hunting down the bandits. Lars thought they were back too soon, then he noticed the body of one of the young lords tied across the saddle of his horse, recognized the helm and knew it to be Parlen.

Lars tried to stop the women continuing, sure they would not wish to see the body, but after Amelia insisted that he tell her why he wished her to go no further, she pushed past him and ran up to Parlen just as they were pulling the corpse of her childhood friend from the back of his horse.

Lars came up a couple of paces behind her, seeing the deep gash across his throat and the broken spear shaft protruding from his ribs. Lars suspected the spearhead to be barbed otherwise they would have pulled it straight out after he had died.

Lars also noticed a gem similar to that Amelia wore suspended on her forehead, dangling on a chain around Parlens neck. No doubt it had slipped out of his tunic with the jolting from the horse and his body being slumped over. Once again he wondered what these strange jewels were or what they symbolized, but now was not the time or the place to ask.

Amelia stood in horrified shock for long moments. Then, turning away, she saw Lars and threw herself into his arms, sobbing loudly.

From there on the scene grew more and more grieved as women left House Tremar, wailing for their fallen son and brother.

Amelia finally listened to Lars' pleadings to come away and he led her back to House Corban, where Talia and Senara led her inside and put her to bed in her own room. Lars thanked them and excused himself to return to the keep with Tam to inform the king.

"These bandits grow too bold!" roared King Zief. His wife, Queen Seran, stood at his side, her face displaying no emotion. She had been informed as to Amelia's state and had sent a message that Amelia would be excused from her service until a moon's time in mourning had passed.

The king paced up and down in an agitated mood. "Only one moon ago I would have sworn we had defeated these bandits." The king spoke more quietly now, but there was still a shaking edge of fury in his voice. "Now they come back, somehow stronger and more persistent than before, and have the gall to attack my troops and slay one of my young lords. They will pay dearly for this with their own blood." Zief's voice was rising again with unchecked anger, spittle flying from his mouth as he raged. "I swear it on all the gods of creation that they shall pay!"

Just then a servant from House Tremar entered, carrying a small package and a message for the king. "Majesty, my Lord Tremar bid me bring this to your attention immediately."

The servant slowly un-wrapped the bundle of cloth, took out a bloodied spearhead and placed it before the king. "This is the weapon that the bandits used to kill Lord Parlen. Note the unusual markings and craftsmanship. My Lord is certain it is not from our lands."

"Indeed," said the king, looking carefully at the spearhead, wondering just who these insurgents were to be armed with such fine weapons, clearly too high in quality to be the property of simple bandits.

If one of those scum had come by such a weapon they would have sold it, not used it for fighting.

The king tapped his foot on the floor a few times then shouted, "Get me Commander Benellan. I want the perpetrators of this outrage found and killed, immediately!"

Tate Benellan, Commander of the King's Guard, was a hard man with a quick temper, swift and deadly with his sword. Lars had met him on several occasions the previous year and knew him to be exceptional in his abilities as a soldier and commander. He was also tenacious and would track down these supposed bandits whether it took hours, days or weeks.

Lars sat in his room, alone as the skies outside darkened. His only company was the crackling of logs in the blazing fire and the darkness: he had decided not to light the candles, and instructed the maid who started the fire not to light them either. His thoughts were all for Amelia. She had lost so much this past year. First her father and her siblings, and now she had lost a lifelong friend.

As the night dragged on he found he couldn't sleep. Every time he closed his eyes he saw Parlen's limp body and dead, staring eyes as they dragged him from his horse.

Finally, in the early hours of the morning, exhaustion from his long journey dragged him into the realms of sleep, where he dreamed fitfully, waking often, sweating and his heart pounding.

THE FORGOTTEN ISLES

The ship rolled ponderously as wave after mountainous wave crashed into *Avenger*. Rubis was struggling to keep a steady course along with Fermin, the first mate. Even then, with two holding the wheel and struggling to make the course corrections, rogue waves kept trying to push the ship sidelong into the next towering mass of water that raced towards them. Even Rubis had never known weather so fierce. As they crested one mountainous wave, with a trough so deep it was impossible to see the bottom in the black of night, he suspected if it had been daylight he would surely be able to see the ocean floor exposed between the huge walls of water.

The night was still pitch black, only being illuminated occasionally to stark whiteness by the streaks of lightning racing across the sky. Thunder boomed continually, drowning out orders and directions shouted between the crew.

They had been battling against this same storm continually for over three days and nights. The crew was thoroughly exhausted, and Rubis feared that if the storm didn't offer some respite soon, a rogue wave would push them sidelong and the ship would capsize before their tired bodies could correct it.

The masts were draped with the minimum of sail, just enough to stop them stalling before they crested the towering waves, yet not so much that it would push them too swiftly into the troughs beyond. Even with so little canvas Rubis had seen another ship founder after a mast had snapped under the strain, the ship sliding backwards down into the trough before the wave washed over them and took the crew and passengers into a watery grave. He wondered silently to himself, and later spoke his concerns aloud to Admiral Vellan, just how many ships they had lost that same way, and on top of that, how many ships had been blown so far off course that they might never find their way back to the fleet? And if indeed they still had enough ships to name it a fleet at all?

They fought on through the long night, and by the time the first light of dawn crept up onto the horizon, the storm had died away, leaving them in an eerily quiet calm. After three days and nights of pure, unrelenting hell, the peacefulness of the dawn was almost too much to believe. The few crewmembers that were still on deck collapsed where they stood, wondering if this was real, or if their ship had finally lost the battle and their spirits had been raised up to the heavens to live forever on peaceful waters.

It wasn't until they heard Admiral Vellan shouting orders to furl the tattered pieces of fabric that had once been sails that they came back to reality. The anchor was dropped, and the signal sent out for all ships to close up to *Avenger*.

"Rubis, Fermin!" Admiral Vellan called his navigator and his first mate to him. They would inspect the ship together and assess the damage. Everyone was exhausted but so much needed to be done before the crew could rest. After a thorough inspection of the deck, and orders being left to repair the shattered rigging and torn canvas, they moved below decks.

The smell of vomit was overwhelming. The whole ship would need to be scrubbed and aired before the stench would be reduced to merely nauseating; Rolan Vellan doubted if they would ever be totally free of the smell again. Moving down into the hold they found crates and cases and barrels—all their food and water supplies—bobbing around in several feet of water. Some of the fresh water barrels still seemed sound, but the majority of their food stores had been contaminated and would need to be tossed over the side.

The admiral turned to face his first mate and navigator. "Well gentlemen, we need to discuss our options, which I must admit at first glance appear to be none. Let us return to the deck. I'm sure we will all think much more clearly with fresh air in our lungs."

On the way to the deck any stray sailors were rounded up and set to drawing seawater and cleaning below decks. Others were set to working the bilge pumps to drain the hold, and then to tip overboard all the contaminated crates, restacking and securing those that remained in tact.

On deck they could see over a third of their ships, some fairly close, some others mere specks of darkness on the horizon. Rolan Vellan said a silent prayer that a lot more were still out of sight and would return to join the fleet by the end of the day.

They climbed the short ladder to the foredeck, where they would be least disturbed, and sat on the deck to discuss what possible courses of action they could take. Rubis propped himself in the space were the rails met at the prow, and the admiral and first mate wedged themselves against the anchor capstans.

When they were all settled, Admiral Vellan started. "The way I see it we have two options. Firstly we can turn around and try to make it back to Sarl with what water we have left, and live on a diet of raw fish, or, secondly, we can head for land. If the winds are kind we could reach Zant in less than one moon."

Rubis snorted loudly. Vellan stared at him then said a little sharply, tiredness making him ill-tempered, "You disagree, navigator?"

Rubis looked to both men before explaining. "Have your people never heard tales of the Jellan?" Both men's faces remained blank. Rubis sighed heavily before explaining. "The Jellan terrorize the peoples of Zant, who know them also by another name which I forget. To foreigners they are merciless. If we landed anywhere in Zant, the Jellan would be on us within the day. They would seize and burn our ships, and we would all be taken as slaves or slaughtered as the mood took them."

"We have large numbers here," said Rolan. "We could fight them off."

"You don't fight the Jellan," Rubis assured him. "Their numbers are huge. Just think about the size of Zant. Think of the amount of Jellan warriors it would take to terrorize a land so vast. Like I said, you *don't* fight the Jellan. If you fight them they will slaughter every last person and hang our heads from the nearest cliffs as a warning to any other foreigners who may think of landing their ships on those shores."

"Well," said Rolan in a defeated tone, "What do you suggest we do then, Rubis?"

"I will have to wait until tonight, to use the stars to accurately plot our position. Once I know exactly where we are then hopefully I will be able to advise you better. Until then I would not even like to make a guess about what trouble we may encounter."

"So be it," agreed Rolan. "Enough of this speculation for now; we will continue with what we know for sure. With what we know roughly of where we are, what can we expect of the weather from now on? Will we see more storms like this, or do you think we are over the worst of it now?"

"You can never predict the weather," said Rubis, "but nonetheless we are very close now to the Farren Ocean. The conditions in the Farren Ocean are a great deal milder, but they still have storms.

"Also, by now our three advance party ships will be reaching their goal, if they are not already there. When we arrive, at what will be the middle of autumn in those lands, all should be prepared. You should be able to march on Ragal before winter starts. And, from what you have told me of how close their town stands to the shores of the Middling Plain, we may also be able to use our cannons and bombard them to take their attention away from a land assault."

"That is encouraging news, Rubis," said Rolan. "Our people have long dreamed of the day that is now close so at hand; a day when we Ammeliners will have our revenge."

Rubis had heard the tale many times of how villages in the lands they headed towards had used strange and powerful magic spells to attack each other. The tale, as the people of Ammelin told it, was that after years of fighting between themselves and the vicious savage barbarians who lived in the town of Ragal, the Ammelin army was close to defeating their worst enemies. The Ragalans were envious of the cultured, civilized people of Ammelin and could not bear to lose a war to them. Sensing the end was close, the rulers of Ragal used the strange spells to send the town of Ammelin to the other side of the world, where they have waited and plotted to take their revenge against their lifelong enemies. And now with their tall stories of barbarism, where the whole world could be in danger, they had enlisted some of the people of Sarl to aid them.

In truth the people of Ammelin were the first to use these spells, trying to settle the long running battle. In retaliation, even though it wasn't ordered by Hagan, who was the ruler of Ragal, and King Zief's grandfather, three of the people of Ragal had bought these spells from the Zutaren traders. They each carried a spell with them when they went to Ammelin. The first two spells accomplished little, but for the third spell—the possessor of which hadn't actually wasted time having such trivial things explained to him as to what it actually did—all three of them joined hands and spoke the words of power.

As the last words were spoken, the village of Ammelin was surrounded in a shimmering light; then the entire village simply vanished. The place where the village had stood for countless years was the same as any other part of the plain, as if the Ammelin, the village and its people, had never existed.

Now, because the individual who had bought the third spell hadn't waited for explanations, he didn't know the village had been transported to the other side of the world. The three of them made up a wild story that the people of Ammelin had destroyed themselves using a defence spell. Unbeknown to them some boys had followed to see the spells being cast and had already returned and explained the truth of what had happened to Hagan.

After Hagan had listened to the spell-casters spouting their lies he ordered them seized and they were cut apart where they stood, the pieces of their bodies burnt along with the spells each had carried. Hagan ordered their names never be uttered again, that they should be wiped from the memory of Ragal Town. But, unfortunately, the one who had bought the disastrous spell had made a copy that a relative found and translated it from the old tongue in which such spells were spoken. Luckily the translation rendered the spell harmless, but copies left Ragal all the same, along with the story of Ammelin.

When Hagan found out about the copies he personally sought out and killed the man who had translated the spell, even though it was already too late, the story too well known. Most who heard the tale were horrified that such power existed and could be wielded by untrained people. They tried to forget the tale again just as quickly.

Later that night, after Rubis had accurately plotted their position, he went to see Admiral Vellan, who was in his cabin with Fermin. By this time over two thirds of the fleet had regrouped, an encouraging sign.

Rubis knocked at the door and waited for the command to enter. As he entered the admiral motioned for him to take a seat before making his report.

"We are in a better position than we could have hoped for," Rubis reported, "and further south than I would have expected. We are also many leagues further west than our course should have taken us."

"And this is good?" The admiral sounded doubtful.

"Yes," Rubis assured him. "It is very fortunate indeed. We are only two or three days sail from the Forgotten Isles."

"What are the Forgotten Isles?" asked Rolan.

"The Forgotten Isles," Rubis repeated, "was once one huge island, hundreds of miles across, with towering mountains near the centre. After years of earthquakes and volcanic activity the land began to sink, until now—so it is reported, though I have never seen them—only the peaks of the five highest mountains remain above the water line."

"I'm sorry Rubis," said Rolan, rubbing his brow as he tried to make his tired brain understand what he was been told. "But I don't see how this is going to help us."

Rubis' brow creased in confusion: surely it wasn't that hard to see how this would be useful. But then again he knew all too well that everyone was exhausted so he took his time and explained. "The mountaintops are still tall and form a cove providing shelter from the storms that have harried us so far. And the peaks themselves still remain forested and support life, although only animals live there now. We can fell trees to replace broken masts and rigging, and we can hunt for meat and gather some fresh fruit. We can replenish our fresh water supplies from streams that run down the peaks. With what we can gather there, it should be enough to take us all the way to the Farren Isles."

Admiral Vellan's mouth stretched into a wide grin. "Well *that* is splendid news indeed. Thank you, Rubis. For now, I think we have done all we can this day. Fermin, stand the crew down. We will stay at anchor here until the sun crests the horizon tomorrow, by which time all our ships that are going to return should have. Then we will set sail for these Forgotten Isles."

The next morning, by the time they were ready to sail, over eighty percent of their ships were back with the fleet. Orders were relayed to the fleet and slowly they got underway. Any other stragglers coming in later would be able to see their limping procession for most of the day.

They reached the Forgotten Isles at dusk the following day, sooner than even Rubis had hoped. The fleet moved into the cove, with a pilot at the prow of each ship to make sure they didn't run aground on a submerged mountain-peak, anchoring within the shelter of the cove.

The next morning, after a meeting of all the ships' captains aboard *Avenger*, boats were sent out from each ship to begin to restock their holds. It would take some time but they were all so happy that they could refit and restock that the delay didn't dismay anyone too greatly. For those among the army who were not too fond of life onboard ship, the numbers of which had greatly increased in recent days, it was a welcome opportunity to step onto solid ground.

Theodin Hornshank sat with the Ammelin soldiers around a fire in the Ragal woods. He was thoroughly pleased with himself this night: earlier that day he had killed a young lord from Ragal, his second kill of this mission. The first had been a farmer, who had spotted their party and was going to warn King Zief of their presence. It had been no contest, the unarmed farmer holding up his arms to try and deflected the blows as Theodin hacked and slashed at him. The whole incident had made him feel sick to his stomach.

Theodin had no idea who the second man had been, and he didn't particularly care, the thrill of the fight making up for his previous sour experience. He was just pleased to have proven himself in battle against a trained noble of Ragal. From what the Ammelin soldiers had told him of these people they all deserved to die anyway, peasant and lord alike. He would never forget the dizzy elation that swept through him as he plunged his spear deep into the young man's chest, moments before he swung his sword to slice deep into the throat of his victim. Neither would he forget the look on the young man's face as blood and life spilled from his body.

The captain of the advance party, a man named Spurlan Tannen, was issuing their orders for the next stage of their campaign, his gruff voice dragging Theodin from his thoughts. "We have done well today. One of their lords and four of their soldiers are dead. That means there will be five less for us to fight when we attack Ragal. We have hit them hard enough for our first encounter. We will lie low for a few weeks then we will attack another patrol together. After that we will split into four groups and start harrying the trade routes to try and isolate Ragal from the other Low Plains settlements. If we can disrupt trade, and kill any others who are travelling these lands, we should be able to make the battle when the main fleet arrives that much shorter.

"Our destiny is here for the taking and it is our duty to prepare the way. Our people will return to claim their birthright and punish those responsible for our exile."

There was a general murmur of agreement from among the men. Many would have cheered but they were too deep inside enemy territory to risk attracting attention.

A moment later a strange whistling sound filled the air, stopping suddenly when an arrowhead appeared through the front of Spurlan Tannen's throat. The man fell to the ground, choking on his own blood, his eyes beginning to glaze over within seconds.

Before the captain was even dead, a man, dressed in the livery of King Zief's guard, walked into the fire's circle of light. It was Commander Tate Benellan, looking as casual as if he was walking into his home.

"You are surrounded," he shouted. "Stay where you are and you might just live long enough to be imprisoned. If you chose to fight I will kill every last one of you."

The uproar that he knew would erupt took a little longer than he had expected, showing him these were not very experienced bandits. But sure enough, after a long pause, every man among them reached for their swords, preparing to fight their way out.

Two rushed straight at Tate Benellan, which proved to be a big mistake, and the last they would ever make. The first lost an arm and suffered broken ribs and a punctured lung for his troubles, and the second lost his head in one swift clean stroke. As the King's Guard moved in from the other side from where Tate had entered the fighting was pushed towards the commander. Another man went down from a heavy, cleaving blow that shattered its way through collar bone and ribs, the immense force sending the blade ripping through his lung and heart.

The next man was up close to Benellan before the commander had his sword free. The bandit unexpectedly froze, shocked and slack jawed in disbelief after seeing what the commander had made of his three friends. The man finally started to raise his sword and Benellan acted swiftly, head butting the man with a crushing blow that knocked him out cold, before bending forward with one foot on his enemy's chest to retrieve his sword, just in time for his next victim.

The fight was very short and extremely messy, their enemy quickly overpowered and brutally hacked apart with no remorse or regret by Ragal's finest. Under the confusion eighteen of those who shared the fire had escaped into the night. Tate knew this after counting the number of bodies, having done the same before attacking. He hoped that was all and they weren't more somewhere in the dark of the forest. Five of the enemy still stood in the clearing, having thrown their weapons away and surrendering. The King's Guard took two as prisoners to question later and slaughtered the rest, leaving their bodies to rot where they lay and feed the wolves of the woods.

Commander Benelllan looked around the battle sight and examined his victims more closely. "These are no simple bandits: they all wear the same armour. Something very strange is going on here," he said. Kicking over a corpse he knelt to examine the design and craftsmanship. Standing again he said, "I want to know who they are and what they want," adding as he turned to the two prisoners with cruel smile creasing his face, "and you two are going to tell me all about it."

Taking their two prisoners they headed back towards Ragal. It was going to be a long night.

Theodin woke in the dim light of dawn. His head was pounding, but that was nothing compared to the roaring pain from what was left of his nose. Somehow, after being knocked out by the most ferocious man he had ever seen, he had not received the killing blow he had expected as he sank to the ground.

Looking up, struggling to focus, he could see bodies laid all around him. It had been a slaughter. Now Theodin truly believed the stories he had heard of the savage barbarism of these people, knew firsthand the horrors they were capable of.

He pushed himself shakily to his feet and scanned the area. Blood covered bodies lay dead all around him, too many for his aching head to count. Many of the slain, on top of their wounds, had been trampled in the fight—which probably explained the rest of his aches and pains. Other than himself he had no idea how many of the advance party remained alive, and for all he knew the rest could have been captured or crawled off to die in the undergrowth.

A snapping twig caught his attention and he whisked his head around. His vision blurred and pain roared through his skull as he passed out, collapsing to the ground in a heap.

He awoke again sometime later to the sound of people talking quietly. Raising his head slightly he could see he was no longer in the clearing where the battle had been fought. All was silent again now and he wondered if he had imagined the voices. Seeing the back of a man, and recognizing the Ammelin armour, he croaked, "Are you the only one left alive?"

As the soldier turned around to look at Theodin several others stood from where they sat, concealed among the ferns. One of them brought him a water skin and he drank heavily, his head clearing a little with the cool water rushing down his throat. Theodin was helped to his feet and found there was a total of eighteen Ammeliners hiding together. He joined them and they sat in silence. Shortly after, a rustling in the forest around them announced the arrival of eight more Ammelin soldiers. They had been out on a roving patrol and had not been around the fire the night before, their presence remaining unknown to those who had attacked them. After returning to the clearing and finding the ghastly remains of their friends, they had moved on to the prearranged rendezvous, hoping at least some had escaped the slaughter.

The patrol was quickly briefed about what had happened and joined the rest, no one willing to broach the subject of what to do now.

After a long period in which no one seemed prepared to speak Theodin broke the silence. "Are there only twenty seven of us left?" he asked the burly soldier he recognized as Fellir.

"Aye," said Fellir. "We returned and searched the clearing after we got you away. I personally checked all of the forty seven bodies. All had died within minutes of receiving their wounds. Three of them were bound, slaughtered by those animals after they had already surrendered. Only two are unaccounted for; they must have been taken prisoner."

"What are we going to do now?" asked Theodin.

"Exactly what we were sent to do," replied Fellir, assuming command and talking loud enough for all the Ammeliners to hear him. "Only now we will have to do it on a smaller scale. At first we are going to lay low for a few weeks before attacking the trade coming into the area. Then we will work our way back here and hit them when they least expect it."

Theodin groaned and lay back. The thought of facing those soldiers again was not one he cared to contemplate just now. His vision swam wildly and he closed his eyes to stop the nauseating swirl. He calmed his breathing and when he could concentrate again he thought about home, wishing he had never left, and thought of his brother Rubis, who was now heading towards him with the main fleet.

"Are you still awake?" asked Fellir, dragging Theodin away from his thoughts. When Theodin opened his eyes the new captain of their much reduced force held up a water skin. "You should drink some more before you sleep again. You will be getting dehydrated; it will make you feel worse and slow your healing."

Theodin did as he was told, draining half of the skin in small sips, then sunk into a haunted sleep that offered little rest.

LESSONS

A loud clattering of steel on stone woke Lars, his heart pounding as he quickly sat up to see what the racket was all about. Bollo was standing in the doorway with Lars' sword settling to a rest at his feet.

"I thought I made it clear, Prince Lars." His voice was full of scorn for Lars' new title. "When I said first light I didn't mean when your eyes opened and you first saw the light. I don't know about where you are from, but first light in Ragal means when it starts to break into the dark of night. Soon now the sun will be up. If you think I have nothing better to do than walk up and down stairs to wake you up, you are sadly mistaken. Now, get dressed and meet me in the fencing yard promptly."

Bollo picked up the sword on the toe of his boot, kicked it up and caught it in one smooth movement. He left left the room then, not waiting for his new student. Lars quickly dressed in the same clothes he had worn all the way to Ragal. They were the only clothes he had brought and he had to admit they were badly in need of a wash.

As Lars left his room he realized he didn't even know where the fencing yard was. With all the commotion over Parlen's death yesterday he had forgotten to ask. He made his way down to the main entrance to the keep where guards were always posted. They gave him directions into the maze of trees, bushes and flowerbeds that crowded the centre of the Inner City between the five houses.

Just when he was sure he was completely lost he walked between two tall hedges and straight into a large paved area, the sides of which were surrounded by the same tall hedges. Bollo was standing opposite the entrance with his back to it, stripped to the waist and warming up with slow movements of his sword.

Again Lars noticed the strange gem suspended on a chain around Bollo's neck, but he certainly wasn't going to ask the Sword-master what they were. Lars was unsure how to address Bollo, unsure which title to use as the man had more than one role in the keep.

Bollo's body went beyond lean, not necessarily skinny, but not an ounce of fat showed anywhere. Skin pulled taut across his hard sinewy muscles as he worked his way through his exercises.

"You took your time," said the Sword-master without turning. He spun around then to look at Lars. "Take off your shirt and join me in the warm up. Your sword is over there," he added, pointing to a low stone bench with his own blade.

Lars looked at the hedge: the white frost of early spring coated everything. He shivered as he removed his shirt, laying it on the bench and taking up his sword. He stood there motionless, not knowing how to perform the warming up exercises.

Bollo sighed heavily at Lars' lack of knowledge. Slowly he took Lars through each individual exercise, making him perform them all until he got each of them right. Even then Lars looked awkward and slow compared to the flowing movements of the Sword-master.

By the time they had finished going through the warm up exercises it was time for the lesson to draw to an end. Bollo took the sword from Lars, making him hand it over hilt first in the correct manner. He told Lars to follow him as he made his way back through the maze of hedges and through the keep to the armoury.

After their swords were given a coat of oil and their blades checked for nicks and cracks—even though they hadn't been used, Bollo was a stickler for routine—they were stored in their correct places on the racks. Bending and flipping open the lid on a chest, the armourer lifted out a wooden practice sword. Handing it to Lars he said, "Before you come to my lessons in the mornings you will warm up in your room. Then, so you don't cool down, you will run to the fencing square, completing a circuit of the perimeter path of the Inner City first. You will also bring the practice sword with you to the lessons: you will need it for some of the later exercises."

Lars looked at the wooden practice sword, finding it similar to those he had used at home, and nodded to the armourer. Just as he was about leave, Bollo spoke again.

"Now before you leave, you can explain to me why you think you can turn up late for my lessons?"

Lars looked baffled at first. When he spoke he sounded tired. "The truth is with Parlen being killed yesterday it totally slipped my mind."

Bollo nodded thoughtfully, but his voice was ice as he said, "No excuses are acceptable. Parlen's death should be a timely reminder to you of your own failings with a blade. You are excused, Your Highness." Lars knew the armourer was mocking him when he said 'Your Highness' or called him 'Prince Lars', and those occasions he used the honorific were rare enough, and always in the same belittling tone.

Lars had no idea why the man seemed to have taken an instant dislike to him. He couldn't imagine what offence he may have caused, or how.

Lars glared at Bollo as the armourer turned away. He had been the best among the boys of his village with a practice sword and wondered why the man would think him so inept with a sword when he hadn't even seen Lars use one. Then he remembered when he had faced the bandits alongside Hakon, how he had nearly frozen with terror. Deciding Bollo's words may have some truth in them—facing someone with a practice sword where you knew you could not seriously injure them, or be injured yourself, was a far cry from the reality of battle, where you had to think past the terror and keep your head, in more ways than one—he sighed heavily and returned to his room.

A tray was placed on the small table in his room. The food was cold now, but Lars ate it anyway. He stripped off and made his way to the washstand where a pitcher of water, that was now only slightly warmer than the chill air, stood next to a bar of perfumed soap.

After he had washed in the cool water the bed still looked so inviting, making it hard to resist the urge to lie down. He forced himself to drag his clothes on, his nose wrinkling with the smell, and made his way down to the library.

Felman Spanril, Ragal's librarian by title only, as he seemed to consider sorting the books into some kind of order, or even shelving them for that matter, as no part of his job description whatsoever, was absent.

Lars waited for a long while but the librarian still didn't arrive, so he started sorting the books into some semblance of order: one pile for historical reference, another for tactics and warfare, a very small pile for herb lore, and many others. Any he couldn't catergorize he placed in a separate pile to ask Felman about. Once he had formed some sizable piles he cleared the first set of shelves adding those to the proper piles on the floor, then refilled them with reference books in order by title, writing them all down on a long list he was making.

By midday the first set of shelves were actually looking like they had some kind of order, but he knew it would take weeks to sort out the whole library. Felman finally arrived just as Lars stood back to admire his work.

"W-W-What are you doing?" screeched Felman. "You are ruining the careful organization that has been my work for over twenty years."

Lars was perplexed: did the man really believe books strewn all over the floor or stacked on every available surface—other than the shelves— was actually some kind of order.

"I am trying—" Was all Lars managed to say before Felman cut him off.

"Oh, you are trying alright. And right now you are trying my patience to the limit."

Lars started again. "I am *trying* to put the books into some kind of order so that *everyone* will be able to find what they are looking for."

As Felman was about to open his mouth again Tam entered and saved Lars from the next tirade.

"Good to see you are getting along so well," said Tam from the doorway, with a hint of a smile, adding very undiplomatically, "This place looks better already." Felman scowled but held his tongue.

"Anyway, Prince Lars, I have arranged riding lessons for you. Enric, the Stable-master, will teach you himself. If you go to the stables this afternoon he will start with the first of your lessons. Oh, and I forgot to tell you yesterday but your meals will be brought to your room; your midday meal should be there any minute now. If you will excuse me, Your Highness," Tam made a formal bow, "I have other business to attend to." Tam added to Felman before he left the library, "Prince Lars will be able to help you again tomorrow."

As Tam left, with Lars following shortly after, Felman muttered to himself, "Help like that I can well do without." He knew he should have made some grand gesture of defiance to the changes the young whippersnapper was making: something like sweep the books off the shelves, or mix up the piles on the floor. The only problem was he was feeling very old lately and any attempt at displaying his wrath would, he suspected, look both childish and pathetic. Instead he sat behind his desk and soon found himself dreaming of better days.

Lars ate his meal slowly, again resisting the temptation to lie down on the bed, before dragging himself off to the stables. He felt exhausted, but knew if he could make his way through this first day the next would be a lot easier, if he could get a good night of peaceful sleep. When he arrived at the stables the sight of the horses, mixed with a bit of excitement for his next lesson, temporarily washed away his fatigue.

After asking for Enric, the young stable boy—who clearly didn't know Lars was supposed to be a prince—pointed to a tall, broad shouldered man with pale skin and shoulder length blond hair tied back in a loose pony tail.

Lars introduced himself to Enric, omitting his title of prince, but clearly the man knew who he was anyway as he bowed low, announcing, "I am Enric, Ragal's Stable-master, at your service, Highness."

Lars sighed heavily. He was hoping to at least be treated normally by one person. It turned out that Enric had everything prepared for him, as he led Lars to an enclosure where a tan coloured horse was saddled and waiting. It wasn't a large horse by any standards, but to Lars, having next to no knowledge the animals, it looked huge. The only time Lars had been on a horse before was when they had been to Ragal the previous year, when on their return journey Hakon had been able to walk some of the way to build up his strength after been tortured in Balt, and Lars took his turns on the horse they had been loaned by Asten of Thoran.

There was a mounting block already at the horse's side. Even with the steps Lars still felt as if he clambered his way up onto the animal's back, showing little grace.

"This is Teari, she is one of the most placid mares we have in our stables," said Enric as he stroked the horse's neck. Waiting for Lars to settle himself comfortably, Enric asked, "Have you ever ridden a horse before, Highness?"

"Only a few times," replied Lars. "And I wouldn't so much call it riding; I believe clinging tightly and trying not to fall off would be a more accurate description."

"That makes my task a lot simpler, Highness", said Enric. "There is nothing worse than teaching someone who *thinks* they know about horses. It takes months just to train the bad habits out of them."

"Well, I can safely say the only things I know about them is they are bigger than me, can run faster than me, and most of all they make my backside sore."

Enric laughed before saying, "Well it is my job to teach you to sit and handle the horse correctly. Hopefully you will learn the correct posture after several lessons. Then maybe it won't hurt so much."

Enric untied the reins and led the horse away from the rail and mounting block. "All I am going to do at first is let the rope out a bit at time while Teari walks around in circles. As the circle gets larger I will be able to watch you and give you instructions to correct your posture. Then once you are sitting properly at the walk I will take the mare to a trot and we'll adjust your posture to suit."

The time passed quickly for Lars—even if he was only going around in circles—and after a few hours the lesson ended and Enric took the mare back to the rail by the mounting block. Watching Lars nearly fall of the horse, Enric showed Lars the correct way to mount and dismount, with and without the mounting block, letting Lars practice a few times before ending the lesson. "I think that is enough for one day, Highness. You are a fast learner. I think tomorrow I will show you a few basic moves to controlling the horse, then you can try going round without the lead rope. I will see you tomorrow, around the same time, Highness?" It was more a question than statement.

Lars nodded. "I'm looking forward to it already. And thank you for today, Enric."

"It was my pleasure, Highness," said Enric, bowing once more.

Lars walked away feeling sore and stiff, yet still strangely invigorated. He had enjoyed the lesson thoroughly, and couldn't wait until the day he and Amelia would be able to go riding together.

Returning to the keep Lars opened the door to the huge room and stopped. He still couldn't believe the whole room was for him alone. Closing the door he made his way to the fire and slumped in one of the chairs, relaxing until a knock at the door took him away from his thoughts of the day's lessons.

Tam entered with a tall, slim woman behind him. The woman, a head taller than Tam, with long dark hair turning to grey, and keen hazel eyes, looked at Lars as if weighing him to the ounce.

"This is Jeni, Highness," said Tam. "Jeni is the keep's seamstress. She has come to measure you for clothes more appropriate to your station here."

"Stand please, Highness," said Jeni, her stern face barely altering as she addressed him. "Arms outstretched and legs apart."

The seamstress tugged and pulled at Lars' limbs, measuring them every which way, even his inside leg, not pausing a moment before shoving her tape into his crotch. When she had finished, and Lars was blushing, she bowed stiffly and swept out of the room, calling over her shoulder, "I will bring the garments to you when they are ready, Highness."

"I apologize for Jeni's abrupt manner," said Tam. "She is a busy woman and seldom thinks of the courtesies required, even with the king."

"Think nothing of it," Lars assured him. "But I do have a question that you may be able to help me with." Tam raised a quizzical eyebrow. "When we were here last year, everyone kept saying 'Your Highness', now they seem to have shortened it simply to 'Highness'. Why is that?"

"Well, Highness," Tam started hesitantly, "some strangers prefer the full honorific, and get rather tetchy if it isn't used. But you seem uncomfortable enough simply being named as a prince, let alone being called 'Your Highness.' So I have spoken to those who you will come into contact with regularly. I instructed them to use the shortened version of the honorific, as it is normally used in Ragal. But if you would prefer it I could instruct them to use the full version again?"

"With the gods as my witness, no," said Lars emphatically. "It is more than enough as it is. I would prefer it if you all just called me Lars," Tam was about to open his mouth to protest until Lars forestalled him, "but I understand it is the king's orders and they must be obeyed." Tam nodded his agreement.

"Anyway," Lars continued, "enough of this. Have you heard anything of how Amelia is fairing after Parlen's death?"

"I have heard nothing so far, Highness. I am sure she will come and see you herself soon. Nothing keeps the Lady Amelia down for long. She is so lively. And the funeral is set for tomorrow, so things will start to get back to normal soon after that."

Tam left then, excusing himself to return to his duties for the king. Lars slumped down in his chair again, his eyelids instantly starting to droop. He was disturbed again moments later when a knock at the door announced the arrival of his evening meal. He was hungry but found he was too tired to eat and only picked at the meal.

As he settled down in his bed that night, he thought of Amelia. He longed to see her again, but was reluctant to disturb her during her period of mourning. And not knowing the proper customs in Ragal he wasn't sure if he was wise to visit her to try and console her, or to stay away. It was with these thoughts he drifted off to sleep.

"*Hello Lars,*" said a very familiar voice. "*It is a pleasure to see you again.*"

Lars' eyes flashed open as he recognized Melissa's voice and he found himself looking at the interior of the Chamber of Souls, or as those who were confined there named it, the Chamber of the Damned. It was a huge transparent cylinder with a domed top, that to his knowledge contained—although imprisoned would be a more accurate word— nine hundred and seventy eight souls.

Lars had first met Melissa, and the spirit of a madman named Paolen, when he had been to Ragal with his father the previous year. Melissa had helped them to find the information they needed to destroy the *Draknor*, and she had told Lars about their long imprisonment within the domed cylinder he now stood in and other containers that had been used in the past. He could only find the dome in his dreams and even Melissa was confused at how easily he could come and go from the prison that held their souls captive.

Although the spirits trapped there could see him, Lars couldn't see them. But sometimes he thought he saw a dot of spectral light as their voices shifted when they moved around him.

Melissa had hoped after giving him the information he needed to free the souls in the crypt at Lokas that he would also be able to free the souls in this chamber. Lars had felt useless when he'd had to destroy her hopes, because in the waking world he didn't know where this domed cylinder actually was. After an awkward silence, and feeling the need to ease Melissa's despair, Lars had told her he hoped to return, and would try to find a way to free them. During his time back at home in the mountains, although it often entered his mind, he still hadn't thought of exactly how he was going to accomplish this.

After long moments Lars said, "I'm happy to . . . hear your voice again, Melissa."

"I had hoped you would return. How long are you with us for this time?" asked the melodious voice of the spirit.

"I don't know to be honest, Melissa. I suppose I can stay as long as I want."

"Why are you visiting Ragal this time?" asked Melissa. *"Obviously there is no danger in the land, or you wouldn't be able to stay for long, I'm sure."*

"No. No danger," said Lars. "Remember last year I told you the king had invited me to come and live here for a while?" Melissa remained silent so Lars continued, "Well, I have returned. I am learning to ride horses, and swordsmanship; and I am also helping Felman organize the library."

"Ah. Felman is a sweet old man, isn't he," said Melissa. Lars wanted to say he was a cantankerous old fool, but thought better of it and held his tongue. *"He sometimes finds his way here in his dreams. I don't think he has any idea where he is, and he never speaks with us like you do. Other than you he is the only person we have seen in a long time."*

"Liar," shouted the familiar voice of the mad spirit, Paolen. *"You know there is one who visits us, repeatedly, and others before him."*

"But we do not speak of him or his predecessors," said Melissa in a firm tone.

"You mean you don't speak of him," hissed Paolen. *"You don't speak of him because he comes here in the flesh, all full of life and freedom, mocking us in our death and captivity."* Paolen's voice changed to one of maddened desire as he said wistfully, *"Oh, precious life."* It was only then he seemed to notice Lars, his voice shifting, and hardening in a deranged sort of way, as he turned his attention to their visitor. *"Oh, no; it's you again. Come to send us to oblivion, have you?"* Paolen's voice shifted once more to

one of total and utter madness. *"Actually, I have never been to oblivion; but it doesn't sound nice; too much sun for my pale skin."*

Lars was taken aback by Paolen's total changes in personality. He wanted to remind Paolen that he had no skin, not now, but he didn't wish to enrage him further. He had always known the spirit was mad, but now he seemed to be totally losing his grip on reality. It seemed their captivity was pushing them to breaking point. Even Melissa's calm, sweet voice seemed strained at times.

Lars tried to reassure Paolen. "I will try and help you, and free you if I can, Poalen."

"Oh, I'm sure you will," ranted Paolen, his voice dripping with sarcasm. *"And why would you wish to help the dead? You living are all the same, full of meaningless promises. You have no idea, no idea at all what an eternity of imprisonment means to us. We should have killed you when you first came here."*

"Paolen!" shouted Melissa. *"Stop that, now! Lars already knows we can't harm the living. Now, will you please leave us and let me speak with Lars in peace."*

Lars again noticed the strained edge in Melissa's voice; something that hadn't been there a year ago. After a tense moment Paolen moved away, rambling constantly to himself.

"Are you okay, Melissa?" asked Lars in what he hoped was a caring and concerned voice. "Maybe I shouldn't ask. It is just things seem a little strained, like there is some more tension in your captivity. More than I noticed a year ago."

Melissa sighed, invisibly composing herself. *"There is no reason why you shouldn't know the truth I suppose. The spirits trapped here constantly struggle to hold on to what is left of their sanity—"*

"Oh, great," muttered Paolen from the background. *"Tell him some more of our secrets why don't you."*

Melissa continued as if she had never been interrupted. *"We hold on to our sanity by new spirits being introduced into the dome. They tell us what is happening in the outside world, helping us to keep track of the passage of time in the world of the living; your world. Without that we become disoriented, disconnected from the passage of time. But the sad part is it also means someone has to die. We had a time since you left when new souls were imprisoned here in what seemed a constant stream. We had barely* introduced ourselves to one new soul when the next arrived. But now it seems ever so long since the last soul was imprisoned here.

"It is a double edged sword for sure. Not only does someone have to die, but their soul has to be imprisoned also. As cruel as it may sound, when things are really bleak, I find myself wishing someone would pass from life into the realm of spirit, so their soul can join ours and relieve us of the encroaching madness. If this goes on much longer we could all end up like Paolen.

"Sometimes, when I find myself thinking those thoughts, I try to pity those who will one day join us, but it doesn't help, it just adds to the despair." Melissa paused for a long while before asking, "Do you find me a cruel and heartless soul, Lars?"

"Oh, no, not at all," Lars reassured her, "I would never think that of you. And I'm not surprised you harbour such thoughts after you have been trapped here for so many years." As far as Lars was aware, which was as accurate as Melissa could be when he had asked her the previous year, she had been trapped as a spirit for over six hundred years. "Hopefully my return to Ragal will ease some of your suffering."

When she spoke next Melissa's voice sounded a little lighter. "I believe your return will make our captivity more bearable. You can help us keep up with the time line in the waking world. It's not the same, these short visits, but it is a great help."

"I will have to go soon," Lars told Melissa. "I have a lesson with the armourer at first light, and I must not be late. Hopefully I will return tonight, even though as yet I am still not entirely sure how I find myself here. Or more to the point how I get back to my body."

"I can't help you with that either, I'm afraid," said Melissa. "I imagine if you close your eyes here, and picture the place where your body lies, when you open your eyes again you may well find yourself there."

Lars tried what Melissa had suggested. The first few times he opened his eyes to see the dome again. Then on the fourth attempt he opened his eyes to total darkness, blinking a couple of times to make sure his eyes were really open. He felt panic rising inside and forced his eyes shut once more, opening them again to find himself back in the dim light of his room.

A gull cried outside as it hovered on the wind and Lars rushed to the window, throwing open the shutters. Light was just beginning to edge into the night sky. He dressed quickly and rushed to the corner to take up the wooden practice sword. He worked his way through the exercises that Bollo had taught him, then rushed down to the keep entrance and out onto the cobbled path to complete a circuit of the Inner City path.

Everything was silent as Lars ran in a steady rhythm, with only the sounds of his breathing and feet pounding to keep him company. The pathway was damp and Lars had to watch his footing on the slippery cobbles, having to throw his arms out to steady himself more than once. The guards eyed him curiously as he passed the gate, snapping to attention as the strange young prince ran past them. Lars suppressed a groan before nodding acknowledgement when they saluted. He carried on around the path, past House Tremar, only slowing a little when he reached House Corban. Although there was little chance Amelia would be awake at this time of the morning, he gazed intently at the windows, hoping to catch a glimpse of her. Nothing moved within the dark house. Lars carried on back to the front of the keep then dashed into the hedge maze and weaved his way towards the fencing yard.

When Lars rushed into the square, with sweat running down his back, Bollo was just removing his shirt. Lars set the wooden sword on a bench and removed his shirt also, used it to wipe away the sweat and took up the practice sword once more. He joined Bollo in the warm up exercises as he worked his way through them without waiting for instruction to do so. This received an approving nod from the stern Sword-master.

With the warm up completed, Bollo also took up a wooden practice sword and stood facing Lars. "You seem to know something of handling a sword, which can sometimes be a disadvantage. I need you to forget what you already think you know. I will show you the correct way to handle a blade, and show you exercises that you can practice to keep your form right. If you follow my instruction, and once you leave here carry out those exercises daily, there will be few who will be able to best you.

"In saying that, you will have to bear in mind, that there will always be someone better than you. Someone who's faster, stronger, younger, and knows a few moves even I don't. Over confidence can be as deadly as your opponent's blade. Don't fall victim to it. But if you listen and learn you will at least be somewhat prepared for those unexpected and unknown moves, and you will likely be able to turn the enemy's blade aside easily enough. Do you have any questions?"

Lars shook his head. The sweat was cooling on his body and he just wanted to get on with the lesson.

That morning Bollo showed Lars three of the most basic moves, and some other exercises to help improve his fitness and stamina, making him practice them over and over again until he was satisfied the form was as near to perfect as he expected of these early lessons.

Lars walked away from his lesson with Bollo, again dripping with sweat, feeling the biting chill of the early morning air. As he trudged back to the keep he could hear the Sword-master walking just behind him. He suspected that if he turned Bollo would be grinning, pleased at exhausting his student. He refused to give the armourer the satisfaction, instead pulling himself up straighter and adding a spring to his step. His tired muscles protested with every pace, but he was determined to put on a good show.

After several moments he found himself thinking of the summer: if he had to start everyday at first light, in the summer months it would practically be the middle of the night. Then he truly would be exhausted. Feeling a little deflated he carried on.

Dragging his body up the steps, he turned towards the corridor to his room. For the first time since he had returned to Ragal he noticed the statue that stood at the centre of the wall at the rear of the balcony. Pausing, he eyed the figure curiously, spending just as much time looking at the door behind the statue. It was still barred and locked as he remembered it from the year before. He was about to approach the door when he heard Bollo's voice as the Sword-master entered the keep, presumably talking to one of the guards, and Lars carried on to his room where he let the wooden practice sword clatter to the floor and collapsed onto his bed.

He was awakened a short while later by the maid with his breakfast, followed shortly by the seamstress, Jeni, with his newly made clothes. He managed to swing himself off the bed while she placed them down, before showing him each set of clothes she had made, telling which garment went with which. Lars wasn't really in the mood for it but he tried to pay attention, and he couldn't help noticing the dark circles around the seamstresses' eyes. Then he realized just how quickly the clothes had been made.

"Have you sat up all night making these, Jeni?" he asked.

"Not all night. Still, it was a late finish for me and three of my ladies, Highness."

"Well, I really don't know what to say," said Lars. "Thank you doesn't quite seem to cover it. But nevertheless I thank you wholeheartedly. And please thank your ladies for me also. Tell me, please, why the hurry?"

Jeni smiled at his heartfelt thanks. "We already had a lot of work on. With spring upon us, and summer fast approaching, every noble in Ragal wants a new set of clothes, not to mention the orders we are already receiving for the summer feast. Your clothes were extra on top of that, so we either worked late into the night, or you wouldn't get them until late summer."

"Well," said Lars, "as I have already said, thank you doesn't seem enough. If there is anything I can ever do to repay you please ask."

Jeni seemed surprised at this. None of the other nobles in the Inner City seemed to give a second thought for the toils of the seamstress and her staff. "Not tearing them or wearing them out in an unduly short time will be all the thanks I need, Highness."

"Consider it done," said Lars. "I shall treat them with the uttermost care."

"While I'm here, you might as well tell me what you will need for the midsummer's feast?"

Lars looked at the clothes on his bed, quite easily the finest he had ever owned. Jeni seemed to sense he was considering which of those before him would be appropriate for such an occasion. "No use looking at those, Highness. Whilst you are a guest in the king's household he will expect you to be dressed in the finest garments available. Those on the bed are for everyday wear."

Lars had no idea what to request, so he simply said, "After seeing these fine clothes I am sure I could leave it to you to create something appropriate. I trust your judgement completely."

Jeni blushed at the unexpected praise. "Well I'm sure I can think of something. And I already have your measurements, Highness. I will leave you now for I am sure you have a full day ahead, as do I." With a respectful bow she glided out of the room, easily as graceful as any queen, her pride swelled by Lars' kind words.

As the door closed Lars dragged himself away from the very tempting bed, and forced himself to walk the short distance to the washstand.

After the refreshing water and a filling breakfast he felt almost revived, and didn't have to force his body to make each step as he practically sprang down the steps and on to the library.

Entering the library the only indication he had that Felman had arrived before him was the soft snoring coming from behind the piles of books on his desk. Lars quietly carried on with the work he had started the day before, and by the time he was due to leave he had actually created some room on the floor that would serve as a pathway to the desk, so that people wouldn't have to dodge and weave their way through the seemingly endless stacks of literature.

Just as Lars was about to leave Felman woke himself with a huge rattling snore. The librarian eyed Lars critically. "Oh, you're here again are you, disrupting my careful systems again no doubt." Then thinking it had been Lars who had woken him he added, "If you insist on ruining my life's work, the least you could do is be quiet about it. Can't an old man get any peace and quiet these days?"

Lars shook his head at the old fool's comments, wondering how the librarian could consider the mess he had created as anything other than disorder and chaos. As he turned towards the door he found Amelia was standing there, waiting quietly. Lars' face cracked in a wide grin. "I was wondering when I would see you again."

Amelia didn't return his smile as she solemnly said, "I came for my grandfather," she indicated towards Felman. "I am to escort him to Parlen's funeral." Lars looked stricken that she wasn't there to see him, and noticing his expression she added, trying to force a smile, "I will come and see you in a few days, Lars. I just need some time. All this death is hard for me to handle."

Felman, who was grumbling away to himself until that point, finally noticed Amelia was there. Poking his head over a stack of books his face transformed as he smiled with genuine warmth and said, "Hello, Amelia dearest. How is my lovely little granddaughter today?"

"I am here to take you to Parlen's funeral service, grandfather."

Comprehension dawned on Felman's face. "Oh, I am sorry. It had completely slipped my mind. I have such trouble remembering things these days, addled old fool that I am."

"You are not addled, grandfather," said Amelia, frowning.

"I am not so sure anymore. Some days-"

Amelia cut him off from saying anything more, telling him his explanation wasn't necessary. She walked to the desk and took his arm, helping him from his seat. With a brief, almost curt farewell to Lars, she led her grandfather from the library.

7

ENTRAPMENT

All the nobles of Ragal looked on as Parlen's body was carried through the maze of shrubs and hedges to the graveyard. Every nobleman and woman of Ragal lined the route, and as his body was placed on a bier they filed into the ceremonial area that stood before the enclosure of the graveyard itself. In Ragal the nobles called this area The Window Of The Gods, where they believed the Gods of all Creation could look down upon them, bearing witness to the service in honour of the dead, and bless their returning to the ground from which all life had sprung, while the soul would be lifted up to the spirit world.

The ceremony was a long and complicated affair. Firstly, a prayer to the gods was recited by the ruling Lord of the deceased's House. This duty was performed by Lord Harnen Tremar, Parlen's father. As he stood next to the body of his son Lord Tremar looked down on the pale face for long moments. His body already wrapped for burial, only Parlen's face showed, and the gem on the chain around his neck, which rested on his chest. Tears spilled down Harnen's cheeks as he spoke the blessing to the gods, a blessing he found hard to give after they had so cruelly taken a beloved son from him.

After Lord Tremar stood aside, it was then the turn of those present to give an account of what they knew of Parlen's life, speaking only of the good and honourable deeds he had done and what they thought were his best qualities, so that after his burial all would remember the young lord in the best light.

When it came to Amelia's turn to speak she stood on unsteady legs, her tears hidden by a black lace veil. It only seemed brief moments since she had stood here to give the same service to her father and siblings. Her heart was already heavy with loss, but she forced herself to go on. She moved forward to stand next to Parlen's body, trying not to look upon the pale, lifeless face, lest it block from her mind all the things she had thought of to say. Standing for a moment to compose herself as best she could she suddenly wished Lars could have been by her side, to hold her hand and lend her strength. She imagined he was there and felt slightly comforted. When she spoke her voice cracked at first and she took another moment to calm her emotions, coughing to clear her throat. Then she spoke again, her voice soft but clear, carrying easily to all the nobles assembled.

"I have known Parlen as long as my first memories allow. We were born within several months of each other and spent much of our young lives playing together and tormenting each other. As the years passed and we both grew older we were always the best of friends. We always talked together of the future and what we would do before we grew old. When we were younger we both had such plans. We would travel the known world, rule empires, bringing all the nations to peace with one another. As we matured our dreams became somewhat more realistic. We both desired to serve our king and queen the best we could, living long and happy lives in our service to Ragal.

"The day I was taken into our gracious queen's service, Parlen and I spoke for long hours. Now that one of my ambitions had been realized he wondered what the future held in store for him. He said he still wished to serve the king, and hoped that some day he would rise to be Commander of the King's Guard. He also told me he would . . ." Her voice cracked again as she thought about whether what she was about to say was appropriate, but Parlen had been so sound in his conviction that she thought she owed it to his memory to speak his words.

"He also told me he would gladly risk his life in service to the crown, and if the gods demanded the ultimate price for this service then so be it. Parlen said to me that if the gods had decreed he should die young then he wanted it to be in the glory of battle, not from some sickly wasting disease or a stupid accident.

"I suppose that is why he always tried to fill every moment of his life with adventure, embracing every opportunity, living his life to the full. I think he was determined that whenever the gods called him home he would have lived a full life no matter how short it may have been.

"But these will not be the things for which I will best remember Parlen. I will always think of my friend as one with a sympathetic ear and willing shoulder for me to rest my head on in bad times, his witty remarks and infectious laughter, finding something funny in all manner of strange things. And of course, his wide, caring smile. These are the things I will choose to remember Parlen by."

Amelia lifted her veil and steeled herself for something she had already decided she must do. Bending forward she kissed his cold forehead. Standing straight again she let her veil drop, whispering, "Goodbye Parlen. Sweet dreams." On wobbly legs she made her way back to her place, and fell sobbing into the arms of her mother.

Each noble approached the bier in turn, speaking only a few words, until finally it came around to the last speaker of the ceremony. King Zief stepped forward, speaking loudly and clearly.

"Those who took Parlen from us have paid with their lives; although that is no comfort to a grieving family. We also have two of their number in our cells." Everyone's head shot up at this remark; it was the first they had heard of the captured prisoners. The king continued, "I will be going to question them shortly, and I intend to get to the bottom of this outrage. But we are not here to talk about the prisoners; I am here now to speak about Parlen.

"I must admit, that like many of our other young nobles, I did not know as much of Parlen as I would wish. Still, I knew him well enough to be sure he was a young man of great promise. Commander Benellan and my own dear brother, Bollo, both held him high in their estimations, and are sure he would have one day risen to command my guards. Unfortunately, that will never be. Yet all Ragal can be proud, my lords and ladies. His death was a noble one, in a way he himself had prepared for. Nevertheless that is still scant consolation. Rest assured, one and all, I *will* get to the bottom of this mess and make those responsible suffer for these attacks."

The king then placed his hand across his chest in salute, and said, "Parlen, lord of Ragal, go now to your rest. May the gods bless your brave soul and keep you safe." With that he reached down and took the gem and chain from around Parlen's neck, placing it carefully in a pouch at his side.

Parlen's head was then wrapped in the same white linen as the rest of his body, before being carried from the bier and lowered into the ground. All stood in silence as the soil was pushed over the shrouded figure. When the grave was filled, the king dismissed the nobles, who were all returning to House Tremar for the wake. The king himself would only attend the wake for a short time, having business at the keep to attend to.

Less than an hour later Zief walked to the top of the stairs onto the keep's wide balcony. Crossing to the rear of the balcony, he pulled a key from his pocket and opened the lock on the wooden door situated behind the statue that had intrigued Lars. Few in Ragal knew what this room contained, though all who entered the keep, staff and nobles alike, were all too aware it was out of bounds. Not that they could enter anyway: there was only one key for this lock, which the king kept on his person at all times. He removed the lock and lifted the bar, placing them to one side.

Slipping inside, he placed another bar across the door to stop anyone entering while he was within. Once secure in the knowledge he wouldn't be disturbed, he turned at the top of the narrow stone staircase, and gazed at a thing that had awed him for years. The room was almost completely filled by a huge transparent domed cylinder, stretching all the way up to the stone roof of the keep, leaving only enough room around the inside of the stone walled room to walk around its circumference.

Zief had no idea how the dome had been made, but he knew a little about its transportation from old Ragal. When the village of Ragal stood on the Middling Plains, before the southern ocean had crept away from the Sea Plain completely, the Chamber of Souls was housed in a wooden keep in old Ragal Town, and it was much smaller. At that time the Low Plains were called the Sea Plains, because at each high tide the plain would flood. Each year the floods became shallower until they stopped encroaching up onto the plain at all, then it was renamed. Over the six hundred or so years that the rulers of Ragal, both new and old, had been imprisoning the souls of their predecessors and nobles, the nature of their confinement had changed numerous times. At first it was only a spell enshrouded wooden box, but as times changed so did the materials used until today they used a magnificent crystal dome that had been enlarged by the use of Farren Isles magic to fit the confines of the room that had been especially built to house it.

At first only the souls of their rulers were held in the Chamber, believing their close proximity would be beneficial to the new king, that he would one day be able to communicate with them and ask for advice. That changed when Zief's grandfather, Hagan, had declared his people would build a new and magnificent city on the Low Plains. The practice of soul entrapment was then extended to all those who were now considered nobles.

Each of these nobles was required to wear a peculiar, magically fashioned gem at all times. The men wore theirs on a chain around their necks, whereas the women wore theirs suspended above their forehead. The strange gem absorbed the soul of the wearer when their body died, taking in all that would otherwise have passed on to the spirit world. The nobles, men and women alike, believing the gem to be a symbol of their elitism, never questioned this, at least not openly, for which the king was grateful. The nobles easily accepted that it was just something granted by their ruler, something rare and precious, to be returned to the king before burial.

Zief descended the narrow stone staircase to the floor of the chamber. Walking the few paces from the bottom of the stairs to the dome, he pulled out the only moveable part of the dome: a small tray placed at the rim, made of the same transparent material, its location only visible by an ancient symbol painted above the handle.

Pulling the tray out, the king gently reached into the pouch at his side and withdrew Parlen's chain and gem, gently placing them into the tray and closing it again. Waiting a few seconds to ask the gods to forgive this entrapment of a free soul, Zief touched the ancient symbol. It was a strange device, curving out at either side, surrounding a smaller symbol at its centre. For a moment nothing happened. Then a faint light began to grow within the gem, gaining in brightness with each passing second, before being released in a streak of white light.

Parlen's soul fled the gem only to be greeted by the confines of the dome. After a short time the light began to fade, until it eventually winked out. Zief knew that was the last time he would see Parlen's soul, but he also knew it would be trapped for all eternity within the dome.

Opening the tray again he withdrew the chain and gem and placed them back in his pouch.

Zief looked at the dome for a long time, wondering if there was any point to what he had just done. With all the souls that had been imprisoned over the years if this dome was ever going to be of any use then it should already have been so. The king shook his head, deciding not to worry over it for the time being. He knew nothing of magic to understand the workings of such a thing. After a moment he decided one day he would have to contact the Farren Isles personally to ask about how it could be used to benefit his people.

Walking back to the top of the stairs he removed the bar and left the Chamber of souls, barring and locking the door on the outside once more. Just as he snapped the lock shut, a voice startled him.

"Hello, Your Majesty," said Lars, as he walked up the last few stairs and onto the balcony. Zief spun to face him, angered at being surprised. Seeing Lars take an involuntary step backwards his anger fled.

"Forgive me Lars," said Zief, taking a moment to steady his breathing. "You startled me. I didn't think anyone of importance remained in the keep. How can I help you?"

"I wasn't really in need of help, Majesty. Just at a bit of a loose end with everyone at Parlen's funeral. I was just looking around a bit." Lars paused a moment, then asked a question he had been wondering about even before the king came out of the door behind the statue. "What is in that room?"

King Zief had used the same excuse many times to visiting nobles and readily supplied it to Lars. "It is a storeroom. Nothing interesting, just a load of things we brought with us from Old Ragal. None of which is of great value; at least not to anyone else. Still, we keep these things locked away because they have great sentimental value to my family. Sometimes, when there is great sadness in our city, I feel comforted to be surrounded by familiar things."

The king waited for any further question from Lars. Seeing nothing forthcoming he said, "If you will excuse me Lars, I have other business to attend to." Lars bowed formally and the king began to walk away, stopping again after only a few paces. Turning to face Lars he said,

"Before I forget, I have something for you." He walked back towards Lars, drawing Parlen's chain and gem from his pouch. Many of them were similar in size, so it would be impossible for anyone to tell this one was once Parlen's. He let the gem drop and held onto the chain. It swung there for a few seconds before he handed it across to Lars. "This is for you. Wear it always while you are with us, even when you sleep. It will identify you as one of my household should anything befall you."

"Thank you, Majesty." Lars bowed again. "I am honoured." As he straightened up he placed the chain around his neck and slipped the gem into his tunic. Before he had finished the king was already walking away again, to his next piece of important business for the day, something he was actually looking forward to.

King Zief met Commander Tate Benellan at the top of the stairs leading down to the dungeons, the meeting being prearranged earlier that day. Commander Benellan and the two guards standing watch on the stairs saluted as the king approached, and with a motion of his hand Zief indicated the commander should go ahead of him down the stairway.

The darkness on the stairs was all consuming, made eerily so by the sound of trickling water as it seeped through the stones and ran to the ground.

At the bottom of the stairs, the Dungeon-master, a big, ugly, bald man named Tauros, stood shabbily to attention and saluted as the king and the commander entered his domain. Tauros enjoyed his job thoroughly, mainly because he was a small minded and cruel natured man who took pleasure in the opportunity to inflict pain on those committed to the dungeons, finding them weak and harmless. His actions were quick and he was unnaturally strong, making up for his slow brain. No prisoner who had ever tried to escape had made it past him, and all had regretted the attempt only as few moments later. He also enjoyed being able to shout at people a lot, or whisper quietly as to what was in store for his charges, watching them cowering in fear. He drank in their despair, lived for it.

It was not often that prisoners were held in the dungeon, so he rarely got to practice his art. But even when the dungeon was empty he stayed at his post, sleeping and eating his meals there, enjoying the dark dankness of the place. When he had gained the position and walked in the despairing darkness for the first time he had felt at home for the first time in his life.

"Take me to the prisoners," said the king. Tauros was about to ask which ones until his brain caught up and he realized there were only two, and both of them shared the same cell.

The Dungeon-master turned and selected a key from the huge ring that hung on a chain from a studded waist belt. Placing the key into the hole he turned it, moving it silently as the well oiled tumblers rolled, unlocking the heavy, iron clad door that led into the corridor beyond. Cell doors were set equidistantly along either side, twelve in total.

Picking up a new torch from the stand at the entrance, and lighting it from the one already blazing in its wall sconce, Tauros led them into the corridor, stopping at the first cell on the right. The door had a small square metal grille set into a thick wooden frame. Tauros held the torch up high, letting its flickering flame light up the cell. The king and Commander Benellan came to stand before the door. Taking the torch from Tauros, Commander Benellan instructed the Dungeon-master to wait outside.

Looking at the torch King Zief said, "What in the name of all the gods is he still using those things for. I'll have to see Tam about getting some candles down here."

Both men peered into the dimness of the cell. The two prisoners were cowering in the far corner, barely visible in the dim light. Benellan called them forwards, and both slowly edged towards the door, shading their eyes against the light.

The king started the questions immediately. "What are you doing in my lands? Why are you attacking my people? And don't think you can lie to me. I can see by your armour you are no simple bandits, and not from anywhere I know of either."

Both men spoke in the language of Sarl. It had been decided long ago that since all the Ammeliners spoke both the language of Gravick and the language of the land their village had been mysteriously transported to, that if captured they would feign ignorance of the language, whilst listening carefully to what was said in case the people of

Ragal spoke about anything useful to their cause, thinking them unable to understand.

Not one to be easily fooled, King Zief was having none of it, and Commander Benellan had heard them talking in the language of Gravick around the fire, before his soldiers had attacked them.

"I know you can understand what I say so don't play games with me." The two prisoners started again, pretending they didn't understand but Zief cut them off. "Stop that. You should know you were overheard talking our language, with only a slight accent I might add, by my commander here, before you were captured in the forest. So I suggest you cooperate. Otherwise, I may have Tauros return and, shall we say, persuade you to loosen your tongues."

Both prisoners remained silent. "Very well," said Zief. "If you want to play dumb, so be it." The king looked to the door where he could see the Dungeon-master at his desk. "Tauros!" he called. The Dungeon master lumbered forward, halting before the king and saluting. "Stretch them," Zief ordered.

The Dungeon-master's mouth curved in a vicious grin. Sifting through the huge bunch of keys, Tauros selected one and turned it in the noiseless lock. The prisoners instantly shuffled to the back of the cell where they cowered together in a corner. With a slight push the door glided open on silent hinges. Tauros stepped into the cell and grasped each man by their upper arms, his grip tortuously strong, dragging them behind him as he headed back into the corridor. They both fought to escape but neither could break the Dungeon-masters hold on them.

The king and Commander Benellan stood back as Tauros dragged the two struggling prisoners from the cell. Tauros headed into the blackness of the tunnel beyond the cells, without any need of further light. But soon enough the tunnel was lit up as Benellan held the torch aloft and followed the Dungeon-master ahead of his king.

After about thirty metres the tunnel came to an end in front of an open doorway. Tauros dragged the prisoners into the room beyond, letting them drop to the floor once he was far enough inside that they wouldn't be any hindrance to King Zief and Commander Benellan.

Tate Benellan lit the torches surrounding the torture chamber while Tauros set up the racks. After they were prepared the Dungeon-master lit a small brazier and stood a metal bowl with a long handle on top of the coals, adding a few chunks of pitch into the bowl from a bucket a short distance away from the brazier.

One of the prisoners, seeing only the king between himself and the door, made to try and escape. Zief had been ready for any such attempt, and kicked the man in the head before he was fully up from the crouch he had tried to move into, ready to spring past. The booted foot connected well and the prisoner instantly slumped to the floor, knocked senseless by the impact.

With all the torches blazing, the torture chamber could be seen properly now. Strange looking spiked torture beds and stretching racks filled the room. Chains hung down from various positions all across the ceiling, some with hooks, others with strange and deadly devices for torture. Storage racks were set in recesses around the walls, hidden in deep shadows, holding all manner of tools for inflicting pain, or, if required, a swift death.

Tauros hauled up the other prisoner, who even though he wasn't dazed, couldn't have forced his body to run, fear turning his legs to jelly. After stripping off the man's armour, Tauros slammed the prisoner down on the bed of one of the racks, securing his feet by thick, steel manacles. Pulling each arm out to the side he fastened another set of manacles, which were connected to a chain, around each wrist. Lastly he fitted a thick leather band around the prisoner's chest, hooking chains onto thick steel rings that were bound into it. He then secured the other prisoner in the same manner and proceeded to stretch the first man.

First Tauros turned a wheel that pulled tight the chains that were attached to the prisoner's wrists. The mechanism worked so it pulled on both chains evenly, forcing the arms away from the body, increasing the tension until he could hear the sockets making noises he knew to be close to popping.

Next the Dungeon-master turned a second wheel that pulled on the chains secured to the leather band around his chest. With the prisoner's feet securely held in the fixed manacles, his torso and legs were stretched until he felt his body would be torn in half. The prisoner tried to scream at the pain, but this seemed to only increase the pressure on already strained joints, forcing him to suck breath in a series of quick gulps.

Satisfied that the first prisoner was suffering a considerable amount of pain, Tauros turned his attention to the second, proceeding in the same manner.

With both prisoners stretched, and struggling to draw breath, King Zief walked between the two rack beds, looking them over with a critical eye. After a long time, Zief took the chin of the prisoner to the right side of him in his hand, gripping the jaw tightly and digging his fingers into the joint. Turning the pain-stricken face towards him he asked, "Once again I will ask, and I suggest you don't toy with me. What are you doing in my lands?"

The man started gibbering in Sarlen. King Zief released the chin and, in one swift movement, forced his elbow into the man's stomach, forcing out the breath that was so painful to draw. "I've already told you that I know you speak my language. Don't play me for the fool, or this will only be the start of the pain inflicted on your body. Our Dungeon-master has ways of causing you pain that will make this rack seem like a minor irritation. He can remove limbs and even some internal organs without you losing too much blood. He can keep you alive long after you will wish you were dead.

"Now, one last time I will ask you; what are you doing in my lands?"

Ziefs words were met only by a grim mask of defiance. But even so the man's eyes still showed his fear. King Zief shrugged slightly. "Maybe I should ask your friend. He seems to have recovered somewhat since his fall against my boot." Turning to the man on the left rack, who was already watching, the king said, "Would you care to answer my question?"

The prisoner's only response was to look away from the king and stare up at the ceiling. This man showed no fear at their ordeal, a willing martyr to their cause; a complete fool. If the man wished to die then Zief had absolutely no qualms obliging him, but only when he was ready and not at the prisoner's choosing.

The king reeled back and landed a heavy punch to the left side of the prisoner's face, followed quickly by another to the ribs. The man still showed little fear as he winced with the sharp pain as his ribs cracked. Drawing his sword, Zief ran the razor sharp blade across the man's chest, the weight of the blade cutting clean through cloth and flesh to the ribs. Blood oozed fiercely from the wound. Zief looked to Tauros, "Seal it."

Tauros took the bowl from the brazier, using a miniature ladle to check the consistency of the pitch. Standing before the rack the Dungeon-master poured a thick line of boiling pitch along the length of the cut with complete disregard for any cloth that was sealed into the wound. The prisoner's back arched in pain as the surrounding skin was scorched, burning with a smell reminiscent of roasting pork as he tried to stifle a scream.

The renewed pain his sudden movements caused the prisoner in his joints spread fire throughout his body. He had to fight to stop his body instinctively convulsing, otherwise his limbs would be torn from their sockets. The boiling pitch caused the skin around the wound to instantly blister and turn an angry looking red. Tauros, at an indication from the king, picked up a second bucket, pouring cooling, soothing water over the molten pitch. At this release from the searing heat the prisoner lapsed into unconsciousness.

The king, Commander Benellan and Dungeon-master Tauros moved away and sat to the side of the room on a long bench that ran along the wall nearest the door, waiting for the prisoner to regain consciousness. There was just no pleasure in causing pain when the one you were hurting wasn't awake to feel it.

After several long moments, Tauros, growing bored with waiting, walked up and poured the remainder of the bucket of water over the prisoner's head. The man came to, trying to clear his nose of water. Once the immediate danger of drowning was over, pain erupted throughout his body, nearly sending him back to the reassuring, dark comfort of unconsciousness. He groaned at the pain with eyes closed, but was soon brought back to full awareness as Tauros prodded at a huge blister that was half covered in pitch.

King Zief looked at the two stretched men before him. Both were looking back at him to see what horror he would visit on them next. "Now you have had a little time to contemplate the seriousness of your situation," said Zief, "would either of you care to tell me what you are doing here? And bear in mind, if you answer my questions truthfully, I will let you return to your cell. Remain silent and the pain you will receive will be only from your own lack of cooperation. This can all end now; you only have to tell me what I want to know."

The man to Zief's right looked terrified and stared straight at him. The prisoner on the rack to his left, even though he must have been in agony, slowly turned his head away to stare at the ceiling once again. Zief knew the defiant one wouldn't talk, and if he started to torture the frightened man he might find his courage and die without saying a word. Having been in this situation many times before, Zief knew the tricks and pitfalls.

Leaning towards the man on the left, he ran a finger along the blistered edge of the pitch. "Either of you can stop me at any time. You need only say the word." Zief released the tension on the hooks connected to the torso belt and removed it. He then ripped open the torn remains of the prisoner's shirt and moved over to a wall, where a rack for tools was mounted in a recess, enshrouded by shadow, returning with an instrument of torture, one of his personal favourites. It consisted of four thick steel hooks each connected by a chain to a large ring. He pushed two of the hooks deep into the defiant prisoner's thighs, turning them until they broke the surface of the skin again. The other two hooks were pushed through his chest muscles, breaking the skin on either side of each nipple. Zief reached up and placed the ring over a hook suspended on a chain from above the rack.

Moving to the other side of the rack, Zief started to pull slowly on another chain, which moved with a smooth click around a well-oiled pulley. It was something the king had demanded, of the torture chamber and the dungeons as a whole, intending that everything moved silently so not even the merest whimper would be blocked out by the creaking, groaning sound of protesting metal. Zief smiled to both the prisoners in turn, as he pulled on the chain, slowly running it link by link through his hands.

After long agonizing moments the chains connected to the hooks in the prisoner's flesh started to pull tight. As link after link was pulled slowly down, the hooks pulled at the flesh, lifting the prisoner up from the bed of the rack, until he was suspended by four elongated strips of skin, the prisoner sucking air through his teeth as his jaws clenched with the pain. Zief pushed the chain into a cleat to hold it still while he walked around the rack again to stand between the two prisoners.

The king eyed the prisoners casually, gracing each of them with a smile. "Now would either of you care to talk?" Once again only silence greeted him. "Very well, I gave you the only chance you will get. If you wish this to be hard on you, so be it. I have tried to be nice, to make this easy on you, but I have neither the time nor the patience to continue in the same manner. Now you leave me no choice."

Zief moved back to the other side of the rack and removed the chain from the cleat, pulling on the chain hard and fast. The prisoner's body arched in response, his joints, already strained, protesting at this new attack.

"Do you wish to talk yet?" snarled the king, all traces of the smile gone from his face. "No?" he questioned, giving them the briefest of moments to respond.

Zief pulled hard on the chain once more and heard a satisfying pop as shoulder dislocated from its socket. The prisoner screamed in agony, and Zief bellowed, "Still want to stay silent, do you? I warned you, you have already had all the niceties you are going to get from me. I have no patience with fools."

Zief let the prisoner's body fall back to the bed of the rack, not letting the man rest a moment before hauling sharply back up. Up and down the prisoner's body moved, in a series of sharp movements, slapping to the table each time he was released. The man howled in pain, and the second prisoner had his head held and eyelids forced open by Tauros to make sure he watched this display.

Suddenly one of the hooks tore free of the flesh, leaving a nipple waving around on a flap of skin. Even the blood that sprayed over him didn't make Zief stop, he just pulled all the harder. A second chain pulled loose, then a third. The man had passed out by this stage, his body limp and head lolling to the side. Still Zief kept on going, pulling all the harder. This was purely for the benefit of the prisoner who was being forced to watch.

The fourth and final hook pulled free with a spray of blood, pumping from a severed artery, a lump of flesh still hanging on the hook. Zief ordered Tauros to seal the wounds and Commander Benellan took the Dungeon-master's place at forcing the other prisoner to look on. The smell of searing flesh filled the chamber as the hot pitch was poured over the wounds. Personally Zief didn't think the man would survive the night, but hopefully he wouldn't need that long.

Zief turned his attention to the other prisoner. Unhooking the chains and hooks he had already used, he laid the ring on the second man's chest and started to push the first hook through the flesh of his thigh.

"No, no," whimpered the prisoner. "Please, no."

"Oh, so you do speak my language after all," said Zief. "I was beginning to think we had captured a pair of idiots who could only spout nonsense." Pulling the hook from the man's thigh he asked, "Are you ready to answer my questions now?" The prisoner nodded resignedly.

"Good. Now first of all, what is your name?"

"Petan," said the prisoner, croaking through his parched throat.

"And your friend?" asked Zief, indicating to the unconscious man on the other rack.

"His name is Charla."

"Now then, Petan, maybe you can tell me what you and your friends were doing in my lands? And maybe explain why you think you had the right to kill one of my young lords?"

Petan licked his lips nervously. What he was about to say would endanger their cause, but he didn't want to suffer the same fate as Charla. "We have come from a long way across vast oceans, to return to the land of our birth, and to seek revenge for the manner of our departure from our ancestral home."

"And who exactly are you?" asked Zief, more than a little confused at the response. "Where was this homeland you speak of?"

"Our homeland is Gravick," said Petan. "Our village was called Ammellin. I believe you will have heard of my people," he added bitterly.

King Zief stood frozen with shock. *Ammelin*, he thought with contempt. Surely there was no way it could be possible? After long silent moments he said, "I think you had better tell me all you know, since the day your village disappeared from these lands."

"Even though there is no one still alive from that time," Petan began, "the story of our village has been passed down through the generations, so it would never be forgotten. Ever since that day my people have worked towards our revenge.

"When the rune spell was cast everyone in the village was momentarily dazzled by the bright light. They all felt a fierce, cold wind buffeting all around while they were temporarily blinded. When the wind stopped there was a marked change in the temperature of the air. When my people could see again, they thought their eyes were playing tricks on them. Instead of seeing the grassy plain they expected, all they could see, for miles around, were marshes and swamps.

"Before everyone's sight had returned our village began to sink into the swamp. Everyone had to quickly gather only those possessions they could carry. My people moved away, distraught as they watched their homes sink into the sucking swamp. But that wasn't the worst of it. If anyone stood still for more than a few moments they also would start to sink. So my people began their long trek to safety, hoping to find some help, or at the very least discover where they were.

"That first night revealed a sky very different from that which we had left. My people began to despair. What had happened had deeply shocked them all. Having no idea where they were my people continued on in a totally unknown direction that could be leading them further into danger. That first night three people were lost to the swamp, slipping into gripping mud, too tired to fight for long, and knowing nothing of the nature of bogs my people knew not how to rescue them.

"Over the months that followed, many others succumbed to the swamp; some to the sucking bogs, some to strange insects stinging them with their poisons. Others died simply from starvation, and some from eating the fruits of the swamp which we now know to be poisonous.

"Four months later my people found the edge of the swamp. Over a third of those who were transported into the dread marsh were dead or lost. It took another month of travelling to reach civilization from there. It was then my people discovered that we were in a land called Sarl."

Petan sighed heavily before finishing. "The village of Ammelin as your people would have known it had been transported half way around the world, to the great swamps of the north."

Amazement from this unlikely story was written over Zief's face. Even Commander Benellan looked thoughtful. Tauros just looked confused.

"So, Petan, what are you and your people doing in my lands now, after so many years?" asked Zief.

"We found the people of Sarl knew a great deal about building ships, but with our numbers diminished by the swamps, we had too few soldiers to mount an immediate attack. So our people have bided their time, building the numbers of people and the ships we would need, during the four generations we have been in Sarl."

"And what do you want of us now?" asked Zief.

"Revenge; it's as simple as that. Revenge for what your people have done to mine. And to return to the land of our forefathers, to our birthright," said Petan.

"No," Zief mused to himself. "There has to be more to it than that."

"I know of nothing more," said Petan.

"And what are your plans now?" asked Zief. "Surely this small force is only an advance party? How many soldiers will your leaders bring against us? And when will they come."

Petan didn't get time to answer Zief's questions. Charla groaned as he regained consciousness. "Say no more, you fool."

"Be silent you," Zief bellowed, striking Charla across the face with the back of his hand. Turning his attention back to Petan he roared, spittle flying into the man's face, "Answer my questions." But the few words from Charla had been enough to renew Petan's courage. No matter which way Zief chose to torture them over the next hour, neither would speak another word.

Eventually the king gave up his questioning and ordered them released from the racks. Tauros was about to return the two prisoners to their cell, when Zief stopped him with a boot on Charla's head. "Kill them. Here."

Commander Benellan approached and spoke softly, for the king's ears only. "Are you sure you want to do this, Majesty? We may get more from them tomorrow."

"No, I think we have all we will get from these two. Kill them. I don't want any Ammeliners stinking up my cells, eating my food." Zief looked to Tauros, "Take care of it, Dungeon-master." Tauros grinned evilly as he grabbed the first, Petan, hauling him to the slaughter. There was no chance that Charla would try to escape in the meantime, his injuries too severe to be able to even drag his tortured body along the floor. The king and Commander Benellan left the torture chamber to the sound of screams, Tauros taking evil pleasure in ending the lives of his victims as slowly as possible.

Tate Benellan was slightly puzzled by Zief's decision, and the manner in which the king had commanded it. "Majesty, I'm not sure I understand. Why kill the prisoners?"

"Simply because they *are* Ammeliners, Commander, is reason enough for me."

"I still don't understand, My King," said the commander. "This makes no sense to me."

Zief stopped, and Commander Benellan halted too. After a short while the king resumed his walk while he explained. "I am sure, Commander, you will have only heard the common story of Ammelin and how my grandfather had the three who cast the rune spell named evil and killed." The commander nodded to indicate that he had indeed heard this version of the story. The king continued. "Well, let me tell you something in confidence. Let me tell you the truth of it. But it goes no further, understand?"

"Of course, My King," said Tate. "My loyalty to you is absolute. I will carry it to my grave."

King Zief nodded in approval of his commander's vow. "The war with Ammelin, if it could be truly called a war, was something that had grumbled on for years. The people of Ammelin always tried to seek revenge for an old battle, and when any opportunity arose they would attack our people.

"My grandfather, Hagan, was part of a large family, but over the years three of his brothers, one of his sisters, and his father were all killed by the Ammeliners. He grew up hating them with a passion. He wanted nothing more than to see their whole village decimated. For several years the Ammeliners had used rune spells against our town. The effect of these spells wasn't great enough to overwhelm us, but we still lost men, women and children. They didn't care who they killed.

"My grandfather had vowed he would avenge those deaths, and those my own family had suffered also. He was already hatching a grand plan that would end the war once and for all when news came of what the three had done with the rune spell. Hagan was infuriated that someone could have beaten him to his lifelong goal. He named the three as evil and had them slaughtered as a show to neighbouring villages that this sort of warfare would not be tolerated, that our village had no need of magical weapons.

"My grandfather died a happy man, thinking his lifelong enemies were dead before him. But this!" said Zief, pointing down the tunnel towards the torture chamber, his voice rising. "Those men, and the knowledge that more Ammeliners are roving in our lands, attacking our patrols and supplies, is what angers me. It pisses on my grandfather's memory.

"I swear to you commander, I will see an end to these attacks and the whole Ammelin race. When they come we will crush whatever army they bring, and any survivors will be thrown into these cells to be slaughtered at my leisure.

"Do you understand now why I hate them so?"

"Yes, Majesty, I do," said Benellan, pleased at the prospect of another good battle. "We will be ready for their army whenever they come. They will all pay with their lives for having the raw nerve to attack your great city."

8

SEELI

Lars was laying on his bed, thinking about all that had happened since he had returned to Ragal, the crackling and heat from the fire lulling him towards sleep. It had been a particularly long day of sword practice, library reorganizing and horse riding. A soft knock at the door interrupted his mental review of the day's lessons. It had been six days since Parlen's funeral, and in that time he had only seen Amelia once. Even then she had averted her eyes.

Now Lars wasn't really in the mood for visitors. He was starting to think he had made a grave mistake returning to Ragal, and he was beginning to suspect Bollo positively hated him. No matter how hard he tried the armourer always criticized every move he made. He seemed unaware of the notion of offering encouragement and praise when it was earned. The most Lars could expect if the move he performed was correct was a curt, almost contemptuous nod.

Sliding his legs off the side of the bed Lars dragged himself to a sitting position. "Come!" he shouted to whoever had disturbed him.

The door opened and a mass of brown curls appeared around the door. Amelia looked up and in that moment Lars forgot all his doubts. Just seeing the overwhelming look of sadness on that beautifully perfect face made Lars' heart ache for her.

He stood as Amelia entered the room, closing the door behind her. Lars approached to stand before her. She looked at him for a while then threw herself into his arms, whispering, "Hold me." Lars' arms slowly encircled her in a firm, reassuring hug.

After long moments Amelia pulled away to look Lars in the face. "I'm sorry," she began, but Lars stopped her, laying a finger on her lips, shushing her. He led her to a chair in front of the roaring fire and eased her down into the seat. She looked totally exhausted from her days of mourning, her face paler than usual, green eyes sunken and surrounded by dark rings. But she still looked like an angel to Lars.

Lars pulled another chair closer and sat down in front of her, taking hold of her hands. "How are you?" he asked with genuine concern.

Amelia was silent for long moments. She closed her eyes and took a deep, shuddering breath before answering. "I have never been good at handling death. I remember when my grandfather died I was devastated for months. I have seen how other people handle their losses and wonder how they can be so strong. Just the other day I saw Parlen's mother, we only spoke a couple of words before I broke down, crying. *She* had to comfort *me*. Surely I should have been the one offering her comfort? But she was as proud and strong as ever. I just don't understand it, Lars. I mean . . . I mean, I understand about death, and that eventually it comes to us all, but I don't know how others cope with such a loss."

"We all cope with death in our own way, Amelia," said Lars. "I suppose things were different for me. In my village, small though it is, death is almost commonplace. With the raids over the years, and the winter taking its yearly toll on the sick, young and elderly, and with the attacks from the *Draknor*, I have seen a lot of death and a lot of people I know lose their loved ones. My own grandfather was one of those to die last year, thankfully not before he saw the *Draknor* destroyed.

"I have seen the lowest villager stand strong as he set his loved ones on the funeral pyre and watched the flame consume them. And I have seen the strongest warrior fall to his knees sobbing in uncontrollable grief. The point is no two people handle death in the same way, and the way you handle your grief is a part of who you are and not something that can easily be changed or overcome. Niether should it be something that you should seek to change. The deep emotion you show at the loss of those close to you, Amelia, only shows others just how much you care. No one will rebuke you for it. Still, no matter how upset a person feels about death, we all have to understand life goes on for the rest of us."

Amelia looked up at him and managed a weak smile. "I need to talk of something else to take my mind away from Parlen. Tell me, how are your lessons going?"

"My riding lessons are going really well. Enric has had me riding around the Inner City today, and he says next week we will try the bustling streets of the Outer City. The library is reaching some form of order, although Felman is driving me mad. For every two books I put on a shelf, another one ends up on the floor."

"My grandfather likes his own ways," said Amelia. "He doesn't like change. You have not mentioned your lessons with Bollo, aren't they going well?"

Lars groaned. "I'm sure the man positively hates me. Everything I do, no matter how well, he either criticizes, or the most I get in approval is a grunt."

"He is a hard task master, our king's brother."

"King's brother," Lars spluttered. "No one told me that!"

"Oh. Well no one probably thought is was important to mention it. Bollo does not like any of this business of kings and princes. He is the only one who has managed to stop everyone saying 'Your Highness' after every sentence. I think he actually had to threaten to cut someone's head off first before anyone would go against the king's decree. And I heard even the king has recently agreed to honour his wishes."

"Well I wish everyone would stop calling me 'Prince' and 'Highness,'" said Lars sullenly. "I am nothing of the sort but no one listens to me. In the mountains I was only a boy. The only difference between me and the other boys was that one day I would be *Fa'ku*, and only if no one opposed my right of ascension. It made no difference to anyone else in the village that one day I would lead my people. They all treated me like what I was; another boy of no standing, not even thinking of becoming a warrior."

"Well then," said Amelia, "It seems you have found a kindred spirit in Bollo. You two should get along just fine." Lars groaned again and Amelia laughed for the first time since Parlen's death. It felt good to be able to laugh again, and she felt her sorrow lift a little.

Amelia left a short while later, promising to come and see him again soon, and Lars prepared for bed. He tossed and turned, not being able to find a comfy spot. And the chain and gem the king had given him was annoying no matter which way he faced. He had worn the gift from the king every night, not taking it off as the king had said, but this night he slipped it over his head and hung it on the bedpost.

Bollo had mocked him the first time he had seen Lars wearing the gem. "Oh, so we are a proper little king's boy now aren't we, Your Highness," he had said, lifting the chain with the point of his sword. Lars had ignored the comments; the king had asked him to wear it and he would.

Lars drifted off to sleep not long after. He was woken only moments later by a strange, desperate whimper and opened his eyes to find himself inside the Chamber of Souls.

"*Hello Lars,*" Melissa's sweet voice greeted him. She sounded almost her old self, no sign of the strain he had heard in her voice the last time they had spoken. "*It seems so long since we have seen you.*"

"It has been a while," agreed Lars. "Although I must say I have no idea why I haven't found my way here in my sleep recently. Maybe I am just more tired than normal. But I am pleased to hear you are sounding better, Melissa. Happier than the last time we spoke. You sound more like your usual self."

Paolen moved forward then, muttering nonsense as he came. Again Lars thought he saw a wisp of light as the invisible soul of the madman moved towards him. "*Who's that you're talking to Melissa?*" asked Paolen. "*Oh. It's him again. What do you want now?*"

Lars looked toward where Melissa's voice had come from before. "Good to see some things never change though," he said with a shrug, a smile and a shake of his head. Melissa laughed softly.

"*Well, boy, we're too busy today,*" said Paolen. "*If you are here to blast us to oblivion, you had better just get on with it and go.*"

"How many times do I have to tell you, Paolen, that I mean you no harm," said Lars. "I don't wish to blast you anywhere. And even if I did, I wouldn't know how to."

"*Why should I trust you? What have the living got to offer the dead?*"

"Release, for one," replied Lars. "I may not be able to offer much to other souls, but to those of you who are trapped in this Chamber of the Damned, I may one day be able to offer you the freedom that has been so long denied to you."

"*Release! Freedom! Pah!*" Paolen spat the words out as though they were a vile taste on his tongue. "*I knew we should have killed you when we had the chance. I still could. I could you know. Don't believe everything our sweet Melissa tells you, boy. I should have killed you. Oh yes, I should have kill-*"

"Be quiet, Paolen," Melissa cut in sharply. "*I'm sure you have something else to do other than pointlessly rant away at Lars.*"

"*Oh, but we are doomed, Melissa,*" he said with his voice once more crossing well past the boundaries of sanity into Paolen's usual world of endlessly tortured madness. "*His coming here heralds our doom.*"

"*I said that is enough, Paolen! Now leave us please so we can talk without your constant interruptions.*"

Lars could hear Paolen drifting away, a wisp of light marking his passage, muttering to himself. "*We are doomed, all of us, doomed. Why won't anyone listen to me? No one ever listens to me,*" he finished sulkily.

When he could no longer hear Paolen, Lars turned back to Melissa and found he could also see a thin wisp of smoky light where her spirit hovered. "I can see you," he said, the awestruck expression clear on his face. He looked around the dome and could now see hundreds of similar wisps. "I can see all of you." He laughed softly to himself.

"*What do you mean, Lars?*" Melissa asked, before asking for clarification of his statement as if she couldn't believe what she had heard, "*You can see us?*"

"Yes," Lars confirmed. "I can see all the spirits trapped in this dome. You appear to me as small wisps of white light that leave a trail like a falling star behind them when you move. A few even seem to have a shade of colour to them, only very faint and can only be seen at the right angle. And there is one over there," said Lars pointing to the far side of the dome, "that burns a bright red."

"*Those with the colour are the newer souls among us,*" explained Melissa. "*The bright red soul is the newest addition to our numbers. He has only been with us a short time.*"

"Why are you and most of the other souls a milky white colour?" asked Lars.

"*Every soul has its own colour,*" Melissa explained, "*but the soul of a person is not meant to be held captive. After a long period of time imprisoned here our colours begin to fade until we lose them completely. Those new to us*" *still burn brightly with the memories of life, as we all should until the gods decree it is our time to move on to the next plain of existence. This prison of ours drains us of the finest memories of the lives we once knew, until we find ourselves bordering on madness—or in some cases crossing over—as we try to grasp onto the fleeting memories that continually drain away from us."*

"I am truly sorry for what you have lost, and I still aim to free you from this dome one day."

"Thank you, Lars, though I fear it may already be too late for some of us. Still, anything you can do will be greatly appreciated."

Lars was silent for a few moments, certain that there was something he was missing in what Melissa had told him. Unsure what was niggling at the back of his mind he pushed it aside already having another question that he wanted to ask. "What did Paolen mean he is too busy today?"

"He is busy talking with our newest arrival," said Melissa. *"He is the bright red soul that you pointed out."*

"What is his name?" Lars asked.

"We don't know yet," Melissa informed him. *"When spirits first cross over there is a certain amount of confusion and disorientation. It takes time for them to accept they are dead, and even longer to accept they have been imprisoned for eternity. Normally when someone dies and they cross over into the spirit world they will find loved ones waiting for them, and find themselves in familiar surroundings they know from their lives. This is all intended to comfort and reassure them during the period of transition. When a soul is trapped before it can leave its body, as we all were, then thrust into this dome, normally surrounded by strangers, well, you can imagine the effects this can have on the sanity of a soul."*

"If you have been trapped here since you passed, how do you know what is supposed to happen when you die?" asked Lars.

"That is another thing of great sadness among us," said Melissa. *"A long, long time ago, before we were brought here, before your great grandparents were even born, a free spirit came to us, a spirit named Seeli. She had left the Spirit Plain to see how her daughter fared. She had died when giving birth to her daughter and was anxious as to how the rest of her family would treat the child. She wondered if they part blamed the innocent baby, as she had seen happen before when other mothers had died in childbed.*

"Seeli was greatly comforted by what she saw at her home. Her daughter had grown to an age of more than three years in the short time Seeli had been away from this world. Time runs differently on the Spirit Plain and in only a few moments there a month or a year may pass here. Her husband was playing with their daughter, laughing and playing horses, the young girl giggling hysterically as she was bounced around the room on her father's back. Seeli stayed on this plain for a time, watching as the rest of her children came home at the end of the day.

"The last person to enter the house that evening was a woman unknown to Seeli. The woman's stomach was round and heavy in the latter stages of pregnancy. The stranger was greeted warmly by Seeli's children, most of the youngest calling her 'mother'. Seeli was surprised at her own emotions; she felt no jealousy, only joy that her husband had found happiness again and that her children had someone to be a mother to them. The woman crossed over to the young girl—who had been named Seeli after her mother—cradling the child in her arms, 'How are you today little one?' she asked the young Seeli. The young girl looked directly at the spirit of her dead mother. 'We have had a strange visitor today, but daddy can't see her. She is still here, watching us.' The girl pointed directly to where the spirit of her mother hovered. No one else could see her spirit, only the innocence of a child allowed her mind to comprehend what was there for all to see.

"The young girl was asked to describe this stranger that only she could see. When she perfectly described her dead mother all in the room broke down in tears, even the strange woman who her husband had taken for a wife. Seeli stayed with them a little longer. Later she said goodbye to her little daughter and left the building. She soared into the sky, full of joy for her family and happy for herself because she knew her family would be well cared for.

"She soared high and swooped low in her joy, passing through buildings as if they were made of air. As she approached another building her senses tingled with danger, but she was moving too fast to stop herself. She slammed into the prison that was our home before this dome was constructed. The spells holding our spirits inside did nothing to prevent other spirits entering. Once her spirit was inside Seeli was trapped. At first she refused to accept her freedom had been taken away from her. She would talk with no other spirit here. A long time passed before she stopped fighting against the magic that holds her here still. She finally told us what had happened, and when *she found out we had not come to be here the same way as her, she told us all about the wonders of the Spirit Plain."*

"Where is she now?" asked Lars.

"*Oh, she is still here,*" replied Melissa gravely. "*Although now she is even tighter in the grip of insanity than Paolen, so far withdrawn into herself as to be lost in a well of despair. Her spirit colour even lost the white after a time. Now she is grey bordering on black, like her moods. She rarely talks and when she does she only ever rants nonsensical madness.*"

"Can I see her?"

"*Her colour is so dim even some of us have trouble seeing her at times. Her spirit is like a shadow.*"

"No, no," said Lars. "I meant can I talk with her?"

"*You can try, although you may not get any response.*" Melissa led Lars over to the side of the dome. Following the bright white colour of Melissa's spirit was easy now he was growing accustomed to it, but when she stopped Lars had to strain his eyes to see the grey haze where Seeli's spirit lay. Compared to the way the other spirits floated in mid air, he found it hard to believe that Seeli's spirit could slump so close to the ground, looking so dull and pitiful.

"Seeli? Seeli?" Lars spoke softly to the spirit at first, and was completely ignored. He had to kneel down, lean in close and raise his voice before the spirit would respond. "Seeli! Listen to me. I am going to free you all, one day soon."

A spark of light seemed to flicker in Seeli's spirit as she spoke. "*And pray, how exactly do you think you can free us. Paolen has told me all about you and your false promises.*" She spoke with such anger, bitterness and hatred that Lars shifted back a little.

"Don't listen to Paolen, Seeli. I *will* free you all. It is my highest priority to discover a way to release all the souls trapped in this crystal prison." Seeli didn't respond again, but the faint flicker of light stayed within her spirit. Lars turned to Melissa. "I must return to the waking world. It must surely be near dawn. But before I leave I have a question: you said that the child could see Seeli's spirit. What did you mean?"

"*Oh, Lars, you have so much to learn,*" said Melissa. "*Spirits surround you everywhere you go on the Living Plain, only as people grow do they close their minds to them. The living can still see us, but you have become so used to ignoring spirits that your mind no longer registers their presence. Most people*" *are frightened of spirits and try to deliberately blank us out at a very young age. Young children are different. They observe with the eyes of the innocent, not yet fully understanding what it is they are seeing. Most animals see spirits all around them for their whole lives. It is only humans who have feared and completely avoided spirits for so long that they have stopped seeing what is all around them."*

"I feel there is so much more you could tell me," said Lars.

"Oh there is."

"That shall have to wait for another night. I must leave now." Lars closed his eyes, and when he opened them again he was still in the dome. Closing his eyes he tried again, imagining himself laid on his bed in his room. When he opened his eyes again everything was dark, the mattress of his bed soft beneath his back. He stood and crossed to the windows, throwing open the shutters. Pale dawn light was just edging into the sky. Lars dressed quickly and went through his warm up exercises with his wooden practice sword. Minutes later he left his room to run his circuit around the inner wall and on into the maze of hedges to meet Bollo for his lesson.

He had a few moments to think on last night before Bollo showed up. He had promised Seeli he would free the souls. How could he have been so foolish? He had already promised Melissa he would free them if he could, but he had told Seeli she would be free soon, and he didn't even know where this Chamber of Souls was located yet, let alone how he was going to release them.

The scuff of Bollo's boots brought Lars away from his thoughts. The king's brother was he? Well, Lars now had a plan how to stop Bollo mocking him every time he used an honorific, and now was the time to try it.

"Are you ready, *Your Highness*," Bollo mocked.

"Yes, I am ready, *Prince Bollo*," Lars returned.

Bollo looked at Lars with a hard, piercing glare. "The last person who called me that was lucky to walk away with his head still on his shoulders."

"Truly?" said Lars, taunting the Sword-master.

"Yes," Bollo confirmed through tight lips. "You would do well to remember that."

"Well I suppose that's plain enough," said Lars. "But I like being called 'Your Highness' and 'Prince' about as much as you do. It grates on me every time someone calls me that. In the mountains I was a boy, no more. I wasn't even training to be a warrior, which gave me even less standing among the other children. Then I come here and all of a sudden I'm a prince, by the king's decree. I don't have the benefit of being the king's brother, so I have to suffer it. And as if that isn't bad enough, you choose to mock me with these unwanted titles every chance you get."

Bollo looked thoughtful for a while before saying, "Well, what would you have me call you?"

"Lars. Just call me Lars. It is my given name after all. I hate all these titles. They don't suit who I am, or where I am from."

"Very well, Lars. Shall we proceed with the lesson?"

That morning the lesson seemed to go a lot smoother. Lars still suspected Bollo hated him, but they seemed to have reached an understanding and Bollo became more the teacher Lars had expected. Lars also now suspected that Bollo had been trying to goad him, seeing how far he could push with his mockery, and how well Lars handled it when he snapped. To Lars' credit he hadn't overreacted, had instead turned the taunting back on him.

As they were walking away from the fencing yard that morning, Bollo stopped Lars. "From now on the lessons will start at the same time each morning. As we head into summer it would be impractical to keep starting at first light, otherwise we will be doing lessons in the middle of the night. Don't worry about knowing what time to get up, I will come and fetch you. We will run the circuit of the wall together, before we start our lessons."

Lars was amazed by Bollo's change in attitude. Even if he still spoke with the same curt tone, the king's brother seemed a completely different man. And what he said next shocked Lars even more. "You did well today, Lars. We might make a swordsman out of you yet." With that Bollo strode away into the keep, leaving Lars standing there, dumbstruck.

9

THE FIRST NIGHT

The next three days passed quietly for Lars. He continued with his lessons and the library actually was looking somewhere near tidy, even though there was still a long way to go. Lars hadn't seen Amelia again either and he was once more beginning to doubt if she was going to come to him. Also he'd had no further dreams of the dome, which was puzzling him.

As he was leaving the library that morning he was met by Tam. "The king requests your attendance."

Lars followed Tam to the anteroom at the rear of the throne room, wondering why he was been summoned. Tam had no idea why, so Lars searched his brain to think of anything he may have done to displease the king. As he stepped into the room all his worries were swept aside.

The king sat in his usual chair, with another chair placed on the other side of a small table. "Come, Lars. Please sit." Lars sat as Tam poured mulled spiced wine for them both.

After a sip the king looked to Lars. "I'm sorry it has been so long since you arrived before I have had a chance to speak with you. I had intended to see you within the first few days but with certain unfortunate circumstances I am sure you can appreciate I have been busy. So tell me, how are your lessons going?"

Lars explained about how far on he was with his lessons, and that this afternoon he would be riding the mare he had been training on through the Outer City streets. All the time he was talking Lars suspected the king was only half listening, distracted by some other matter.

When he had finished the king asked if he had thought of anything else he wished to learn. Lars had thought of nothing so far, and his days were quite full already. Once the library was organized he would have his mornings free to spend reading, or had intended to. Now he was sure that King Zief had something else in mind for him.

After a brief silence the king asked, while staring into his goblet, "Tell me Lars, do you know what the bastions are for at the front of the outer wall?"

"I know a little, Majesty," Lars replied. "Amelia told me about them last year."

"Did she tell you about the weapons that were planned to be mounted on them?"

"Amelia told me what she knew of them," said Lars, confused as to where this conversation was leading. "She said her grandfather was one of the designers?"

"Ah, now there was a truly gifted man. His death was a great loss to us all. He was completely the opposite of her other grandfather, our devoted librarian, Felman."

The king was quiet for a long time, silently musing to himself. Lars was beginning to think he had forgotten he was there, when the king raised his head to stare directly into Lars' eyes. "Now I have a problem, Lars. One I think you may be able to help me with. Since the death of Amelia's wiser grandfather I have had no one suitable to work on improving the long range defensive capabilities of my city." That wasn't strictly true, but a little flattery never hurt. Over the years Zief had appointed various seemingly gifted people to the task, working under a vow of secrecy. Most had died in their attempts, and the only two to survive were badly injured. One had lost both arms at the elbow, and the second had lost huge chunks of his face and his eyesight too. Now all that remained to him were the scrapings from the bottom of the barrel, and Lars.

"Now, Lars," King Zief continued, "you have come to stay with us, and you seem an exceptionally bright young man. With the attack of the *Draknor* last summer, and the continued threat from bandits, our lands are unstable. Such instability has caused wars in the past and I would see my people protected from any future conflict, and be able to repel any future attacks on my city. I would like you to look into the possibility of making the weapons we planned those bastions for a reality."

"Me?" Lars was so shocked all he could do was repeat himself, "Me?"

"Yes, Lars: you. I sense something special in you. I know you can do this. Of course you will be provided with all the notes Amelia's grandfather made, and those of the men who tried to follow his work. I will expect a progress report one moon from now. Now, go and enjoy your riding lesson."

Lars doubted he would ever be able to enjoy anything again. As far as he could see the king might as well have issued him his own death warrant, with just the date to be added to complete the document. As he rode through the Outer City streets that afternoon he found his mind drifting away from his imminent death as he relaxed into the simpler things life had to offer.

When he returned to his room that evening he found two things waiting for him. Both were equally unexpected. The first thing he noticed was Amelia standing in the centre of the room. The second thing he saw was what she was reading, slowly fingering through a report from a stack that was piled high on the floor before her. Books were stacked in waist high columns, at least ten columns with between ten and twenty heavy tomes in each. Amelia closed the book she held and placed it back on the pile she had taken it from. "You have all my grandfather's notes here. Why?"

Lars bade her to sit, and taking a chair opposite told her of the king's request, even though order sounded more fitting. It wasn't as if he was given an option or chance to refuse. "King Zief wishes me to see if I can improve on the designs. He is concerned about these attacks and wants to arm the bastions with these weapons."

"Why would the king wish to arm the bastions after so long?" Amelia mused. "Bandits are nothing new, and they would never dare attack the city anyway. The day they killed Parlen was the boldest they have ever been."

"I suspect that is why the king is concerned," said Lars. "I think he believes this is only the beginning of an escalation in their raids. Though in all honesty I doubt all the bandits in Gravick could form sufficient numbers to threaten Ragal. Maybe there is more to this than we yet know. If there is, the king did not choose to confide in me. I only know what I have told you."

"You will be careful, won't you, Lars," pleaded Amelia. "You remember what I told you about my grandfather, don't you?" Lars nodded, he had thought of little else since King Zief had told him what he was to do. "Good," Amelia continued, "I couldn't bear it if anything were to happen to you." Amelia smiled warmly at Lars, the first true smile Lars had seen from her since Parlen's death. "Let us not talk of such things anymore," she continued. "I came here to spend some time with you." Amelia grinned mischievously as she stood and walked the small distance to where Lars sat, easing herself down into his lap and wriggling around so her legs hung over the chair arm.

All that wriggling brought an unexpected reaction for both Lars and Amelia. Lars felt the blood rising, and not only in his face. Feeling him harden beneath her, Amelia giggled softly at first. Lars' mouth hung open in embarrassment. Amelia leaned forward and covered it with her own. After a moment to recover from the shock Lars responded eagerly, showing just how much he had missed her.

After several moments of inexperienced doubt Lars reached up to cup one of Amelia's small firm breasts in his hand, caressing it gently through the soft material of her dress, half expecting her to slap his hand away, and hoping she wouldn't. To his surprise she leaned into his hand, raising his excitement.

After several minutes of their inexperienced fumbling, Amelia suddenly leaned back, swung her legs around and stood. To Lars' dismay she turned away from him and crossed to the door. Just as Lars was about to rise to stop her leaving, Amelia barred the door and started walking slowly back towards him, swaying her hips teasingly. Amelia pulled Lars to his feet and led him towards the bed. As they drew closer Lars stopped her and whispered, "I've never done this before. I've heard men talking about it but have never . . ."

"Neither have I," Amelia whispered back, then giggled, "But I too have heard all the theory." Amelia turned around with her back to Lars. "Untie the laces for me." With another nervous giggle she turned around before she changed her mind.

Lars started slowly, nervous excitement getting the better of him. His fingers were shaking so much he had trouble at first. When the dress fell to the floor Amelia was left wearing only a white linen shift. Lars nervously lifted it over her head and let it fall to the floor beside the dress. He looked down the length of her milky white body, from the hair flowing down her back to the heels of her feet. Just then she turned and Lars' gaze slowly travelled upwards, along the length of her soft thighs, the curve of her hips and across her slender, flat stomach up to her breasts. "Your turn," Amelia said with a mischievous yet clearly nervous smile.

She removed his tunic and shirt first, tracing a finger across his young, firm chest. She knelt before him removing each boot slowly before reaching up to untie the cords of his trousers. She slowly pulled Lars' trousers down over his hips and was surprised when his manhood sprang out at her. Every time the women had talked about sex she had seen them wiggling their little fingers and mentioning maggots when they talked about their men. Amelia had expected Lars' to be no bigger and was suddenly unsure of what they were about to do.

Lars saw the doubt in her face. "We can stop now if you wish," he said, hoping the answer would be no, and she wished to carry on.

Amelia stood to face him. "No. It took me a lot of time to build up the courage to do this. If we stop now, I honestly don't know when, or if, I will be brave enough to try again. Lars kissed her softly on her cheek and eased her back onto the bed. They fumbled around each other for what felt the longest time to them both before they were ready. Amelia had to guide him in and at first she thought she would split. As Lars eased his way in she felt her maidenhead break, and let a sharp gasp escape her.

It was over quickly and messily, the prolonged excitement too much for Lars to be able to hold on for long. Lars rolled aside and Amelia cuddled into his side, resting her head on his chest, listening to his deep breathing and pounding heart.

Lars reached out and turned her head towards his, craning his neck awkwardly to kiss her. "Are you okay?"

Amelia smiled one of those smiles Lars loved so much. "I'm fine. Just a little sore; but I've heard that's normal the first time, and it only gets better from then on. Are you okay?"

"I don't think I could possibly be better. Now I understand what the warriors used to tell the boys who were training with them. They used to say that the feeling during the rush of battle made you feel truly alive, with heightened senses tuned to every small change, and the only thing that bettered it was the elation at the release of emotions between a man and woman who deeply loved each other, when they coupled and became one." Lars let his head fall back to the pillow. "Now I know what they meant. Although I am not quite sure how they could rate battle and the probability of death anywhere close to what we have just done."

They were both silent then and lay there, cradled in each other's arms, drifting off to sleep almost simultaneously.

Amelia woke in the dead of night to find she was alone in bed, the covers pulled up under her chin. She sat up to see Lars sitting naked in front of the fire, reading through her grandfather's notes. Seeing her sit up Lars looked up and smiled. Amelia slid out of bed, only remembering she was also completely naked when she saw his body reacting at the sight of her nakedness.

Lars looked down the length of Amelia's body. There was a thin smear of dried blood on the inside of her left thigh, but that didn't deter him at all. He pushed himself to his feet and crossed the short distance to where she stood, sweeping her back towards the bed.

Their lovemaking was longer and more intense the second time, with each of them being able to relax a little and feel each other's pleasure. At first Amelia felt sore, though the discomfort soon eased and she relaxed into the rhythm of their love.

They both dozed for a short time after, before drifting into a deep sleep. They were startled awake several hours later to someone hammering at the door. Lars knew who it was before he even got his first foot to the floor. He threw open the shutters to confirm his suspicions. Dawn was creeping into the black of night. Amelia was looking at him curiously as he crossed the room, towards the door.

"Who is it?" Amelia asked.

Lars replied with certainty. "It is Bollo, here to get me for my lesson. Pull the covers up and pretend you are sleeping."

Lars opened the door to see what he had expected; Bollo stood there waiting with their swords in his hands. "Why is it you bar your door?" the smile on his face suggesting he already suspected he knew the truth. "Who is she?" he asked, tilting his head up to indicate towards the bed, expecting it to be one of the maids.

Amelia poked her head above the blankets and Lars tried feebly to explain her presence away. "Amelia came to visit me last night. She fell asleep from exhaustion after her mourning. I put her into my bed and I slept before the fire."

Lars followed Bollo's gaze, from Amelia's naked shoulder where the blanket had slipped away, to her dress and Lars' own clothes laying crumpled together on the floor, and back to Lars trying to hide his nakedness behind the door. The armourer leaned closer to Lars. "I think the lady will require assistance with the laces of her dress. Be outside in ten minutes. Amelia should be able to slip away unnoticed before I am finished with you this morning. She can go after the changing of the guard; that way the new guard will have no suspicions that she has spent the whole night here."

Bollo left then and Lars barred the door once more. He helped Amelia into her dress and tried to make her hair look presentable with only his fingers for a comb. With Amelia dressed Lars quickly clothed himself, snatched up his practice sword, and was halfway to the door before he realized he hadn't said a word or exchanged a kiss since Bollo had caught them. He quickly paced back towards her, kissed her passionately and said, "I must go. I will see you again soon, yes." Amelia nodded and smiled, and Lars felt a relieved grin split his face. He kissed her again and left without another word.

Bollo was waiting outside, looking stern and disapprovingly at Lars. The armourer turned and without a word set off at a hard pace to run a circuit of the Inner City. He ran faster than usual and Lars struggled to keep up. By the time they completed the circuit and made their way to the fencing yard Lars was flagging badly. Without a word Bollo took up his sword and began working his way through the warm up exercises. Lars joined in and could feel his muscles resisting, his usual relaxed movements feeling forced and awkward, and this was only the warm up.

The lesson that morning was hard and fast, Bollo only speaking when giving instruction. Lars was thoroughly exhausted as the lesson drew to a close. He thought the lesson was over but Bollo told him to sit on one of the benches that were placed around the yard.

The armourer paced back and forth, staring coldly at Lars for a while before speaking. "How could you treat a woman's maidenhood so lightly? She was still a maiden, I presume?" Lars nodded and Bollo sighed heavily. "I could have quite easily struck your head from your shoulders for what you have done. She is a lady of Ragal, not a tavern wench. I don't know how things are done in the mountains, but here we respect our maidens and only bring dishonour on our families by acts such as yours.

"We were all young once," Bollo continued, "and every lord or lady in this city knows how desire can easily drive you towards dishonour. That is not an acceptable excuse and will not help you in the slightest if word of this gets out. I only hope for your sake and Amelia's that she returns home with her absence unnoticed.

"Enough of this!" said Bollo, berating himself. "The gods know I am not one to be lecturing you about such things. I had enough, shall we say, indiscretions tarnishing my youth. I learnt from those mistakes. Hopefully, if nothing else, this has taught you at least one valuable lesson. It is one all warriors and soldiers should understand, and no doubt the way you are feeling now should emphasize the point."

"I don't understand," said Lars.

"Before battle it is wise to refrain from love making," explained Bollo. "It saps your strength, and it is strength you will sorely miss once battle is joined. After the battle do as you will, but before save yourself for the fighting and you may live to use the brain between your legs another day."

Lars nodded. "I understand."

"I hope you understand more than that," said Bollo, turning towards the exit from the fencing yard.

"I do," confirmed Lars, standing and walking alongside the Sword-master back to the keep, hanging his head low in shame.

After Lars had left the room Amelia waited nervously. She wanted to slip away as soon as she heard the guards change, but from Lars' room it was difficult to hear anything other than gulls screaming outside the windows and maids scurrying like so many rats along the stone corridors of Ragal's keep. And there was always the danger that if she delayed too long a maid would enter the room with breakfast for when Lars returned.

On top of her problems getting out of the keep, she had other worries preying on her mind. As much as she loved Lars, Amelia had really wanted to wait until after she was married, and she was certain they would have been married regardless, one day. Unfortunately she had been persuaded to act early to guarantee a strong bloodline and now regretted her actions and her deceit. It made her feel guilty for the enjoyment of the experience.

In the back of her mind Amelia knew that it would have to be an outsider she married. If she married one of the lords of Ragal the chances were high that her children would be born deformed or weak and die young. Hundreds of years of interbreeding between the five main houses of Ragal—even before they lived separately from the common folk—was already beginning to show its effects on the noble children of the Inner City. New blood needed to be introduced into their lines. Who could be better than a prince from the mountains, from a strong, hardy people?

Amelia guessed the other noble houses would all have to take similar actions over the course of time, all the nobles knowing this day was coming for them all. Many would bide a while yet before taking such an action, finding it strange to their way of life. For House Corban, now so few in numbers and on the edge of slipping from this world entirely, time was no longer a luxury.

Amelia cracked the door to listen and stole out of the room after the scurrying footpads of a maid moved away into the distance. Checking both ways she made her way unseen across the balcony into the opposite corridor, having already decided to take a route via the library. If she were seen coming down the stairs in the main hallway everyone from the king down would hear of it by the end of the day.

At the end of the corridor she turned right along another passageway, making her way to the end and going down the stairway to the bottom, coming out in sight of the library. Making her way along the corridor Amelia heard the shuffling steps of a maid coming down the adjoining corridor ahead and to her left. With nowhere else to go she slipped into the library and hid behind the door.

Time seemed to crawl by as the footsteps grew louder. There had to be more than one maid she was sure, or maybe her nerves were playing tricks with her senses. Three maids passed the door in quick

119

succession, and just as Amelia was about to steal a peek a fourth came hurrying up behind them. This time Amelia waited until all was silent before slipping back out into the corridor. Up ahead she turned left into another corridor that would lead her back to the main hallway and out of the keep.

She listened carefully in the shadows at the end of the corridor before stepping out into the hallway. She still didn't know if the guards had changed yet but she couldn't lurk about in the corridor either. Committing herself she stepped into the hallway. All was still quiet so she quickly made her way to the exit from the keep, and there, standing by the portcullis winch wheels, were the same guards she had passed coming into the keep the night before.

She paused in mid-step but there was no turning back now. Completing her stride, the pause barely noticeable, Amelia walked straight past the guards who inclined their heads and murmured, "My Lady," as she swept past. She received the same show of respect from the two guards posted outside the keep. As she walked away she could hear their soft whisperings and knew they were talking about where she had spent the night. There was nothing to do now but try and keep her dignity and walk away in the slow graceful way befitting a lady, when all she really wished to do was lift her skirts and run for home.

Amelia stepped through the door into House Corban. Closing the door she leaned her head against the cool wood, wishing she hadn't been seen—and she was honestly trying her best not to be seen either—but that, too, had been part of the original plan, a plan she now wished she'd had no part in. As risky as it was, if she wasn't seen it would be near impossible to pressure Lars into marriage, as her elders had insisted. The worst part to Amelia was she felt certain that Lars would need no pressure, would willingly take her as his wife, and that this sly betrayal could only sow the seeds of mistrust into their perfect relationship.

"Amelia, sweetie, you are back." Amelia spun around at the sound of her mother's voice. Talia stood looking at her daughter with a slight look of relief. Senara, Amelia's grandmother, stood at Talia's side looking anxious. "Is it done?" asked Talia.

Amelia looked at her mother and grandmother, neither could meet her stare. "It is done! My betrayal of Lars' trust is complete!" she shouted, her voice echoing loudly in the hallway. Tears formed in her eyes and through blurry vision she forced her way between the two people she least wanted to see in the world at that particular moment and ran headlong down the corridor, up the curved marble staircase, and on to her bedroom. Amelia threw herself down on her bed, burying her head into the thick pillow. She was so ashamed of what she had done that she wished she was dead, effectively ending her House and her mother's scheming.

After she had cried herself quiet she heard footsteps in her room and felt the mattress sink as someone sat down on the edge of the bed.

Talia ran her fingers lightly through Amelia's hair. "I'm sorry Amelia, darling, to have asked so much of you. But it had to be done, for the future of our House."

"Go away," said Amelia, the words muffled through the pillow.

"I know it is hard," her mother continued, sweeping away a lock of her daughter's hair from a tear-streaked cheek. "Still, I cannot totally regret this sorry state of affairs. You know how desperate our situation is with your father and brothers taken from us. There is no one of our immediate family left to inherit, and if after a year of mourning I haven't accepted a suitor the king will name one for me. Even before the blood plague took your brother he was too young and sickly and may never have grown to inherit. Our house will pass to your cousins, vultures who we never see unless they can smell how rich they may become. They will care nothing for you, and then it would be up to them who you would marry. Whoever is chosen will care little if anything of your wishes and only for the power they could gain.

"This way we can assure the future of this House. Lars will be able to take the name and title of Lord Corban, and your children will be strong and healthy. If the blood plague should strike again your own children should be safe, saving you much heartache. It is the continued practice of breeding only within a select group that has created these problems. Now we need to breed those weaknesses back out, to secure the future of this House."

"Go away," Amelia repeated. "Leave me alone."

Talia granted her daughter's wish. As she reached the door she paused, looking at her daughter sprawled out on the bed. "This way is the best for all of us, darling. In your heart you know it is." Talia left her daughter alone then to weep and brood.

As her mother's steps retreated along the corridor Amelia turned on her side, bringing her knees up to her chest. *It may be best for you, mother,* thought Amelia bitterly. *It may even be best for me, that my children will be strong. But I doubt Lars will share your views. What if he refuses to marry me? What if he returns to the mountains, never wishing to look upon my treacherous face again? What then, mother dearest?* With her bitter thoughts tormenting her, Amelia lay there for a long time, with fresh tears of despair running down her cheeks every time she pictured Lars' reaction if he should find out what the women of House Corban had plotted between them.

Eventually exhaustion took her into a fitful, nightmare filled sleep that consumed the whole morning.

LARS VELAREN

L ars returned to his room after the morning's lesson with Bollo to find Amelia gone. He had expected as much, and the knowing grins he had received from the guards as he entered the keep let him know she had not left unnoticed. Now the room seemed empty and lifeless without her presence.

Even with Lars' sense of loss at not finding Amelia waiting for him, one thing still troubled him. If, as Bollo had told him, that a woman's maidenhood was given paramount respect, why would Amelia cast hers aside so easily? Lars knew he hadn't pressured her at all. The whole thing had being initiated by Amelia. It could have easily been stopped before they went too far. And if it was revealed, it could possibly cost Lars his head, and would definitely cost Amelia her honour. Why, he wondered, knowing all the pitfalls, would Amelia take such risks? She was certainly no lackwit who was easily led. Nor was she reckless even though she acted it occasionally. No matter how Lars thought on it he couldn't accept that Amelia hadn't understood the risks; so the question remained, why?

Lars was troubled and wished Amelia had stayed in the room. He had a few questions to ask, and he wasn't sure he was going to like the answers. Unable to do anything about the situation he pushed it aside, to be dealt with when the time was right. He washed and dressed ready for a morning in the library. Another tedious morning with Felman was the last thing he wanted just now and he had to force himself to walk the short distance to the library.

All through the morning the same thoughts kept troubling him no matter how much he tried to ignore them. He would find himself with a book halfway to the shelf as his mind returned to the present or discover that he had put books in the wrong order, making him curse and be ever more determined to keep the troubling thoughts from intruding. But the more time that passed the less he liked the whole situation and had a sinking feeling his conversation with Bollo wouldn't be the end of it.

It was early in the afternoon when Lady Talia Corban was summoned to the keep. King Zief received her in his anteroom, where they could talk more privately. The afternoon court had ended early when no petitioners from Ragal's noble houses, or any visiting nobles from other lands, had come seeking the king's ruling or guidance.

Tam held the door for Lady Talia as she gracefully entered, stopping to curtsy once she was clear of the doorway into the antechamber. King Zief stood and inclined his head slightly, before asking her to be seated. Once Talia was seated the king sat again, indicating for a waiting servant to fill the two glasses already placed next to the pitcher of chilled wine set on a small table between them.

King Zief waited silently as the servant poured. With a sharp gesture Zief dismissed the man. Tam closed the door, standing outside in the throne room to make sure they weren't disturbed. Tam already knew the nature of the problem for which Lady Talia had been summoned: he was the one who had brought it to the attention of the king, hoping it could be dealt with quietly before the gossipmongers blew it out of all proportion. He liked Lars well enough and hoped this could be brought to a satisfactory conclusion without any need for bloodshed.

Zief took a few sips of the wine, stalling for time as he still couldn't think of a polite and kind way to tell Lady Talia about Lars and Amelia. He placed the glass back on the table and looked up to see Talia staring at him expectantly. It made it so much harder with her being the queen's sister, and now he had his first doubts that maybe he should have let his wife, Queen Seran, deal with this situation. But it was too late for that now. He would just have to get on with it.

King Zief cleared his throat to give himself a few extra seconds before he started. "I have grave news for you, My Lady. A great dishonour has been done on your daughter and your House." The king paused, not sure of the most tactful way to go on. "Did you notice your daughter's absence from your home last night?" Talia shook her, a look of puzzlement clear on her face. "Well, how can I put this? I will speak plainly, My Lady, and if any offence is given, it is unintended. Your daughter, Amelia, spent the night in the room of a visiting prince." Talia's jaw dropped open and Zief confirmed what he was sure she must be thinking, "The *whole* night."

Talia purposefully eased her grip and let the wine glass slip through her fingers and drop to the floor, were it shattered into countless shards. Adopting the rehearsed look of outrage she had been practicing all morning, Talia stood and paced slowly to the one window in the room, looking out over the ocean, a pleased smile gracing her lips while she had her back to Zief.

Her stomach fluttered wildly, knowing she had to carry this through now it had begun. Talia turned, feigning anger and shock. "How could this happen," she tried to shout, her voice coming out in a pitiful whine. Clearing her throat she spoke with real anger, anger at what had brought her to this desperate situation, causing her to use Amelia in this deceit, after the loss of her husband and children to the blood plague. "I suppose this 'visiting prince' is this Lars she brought to House Corban to meet my mother and I? And she speaks so highly of him, this uncivilzed barbarian."

The king tried to assuage her anger. "Yes, it was Prince Lars, Lady. He is not from anywhere we would count as civilized, and whilst he is surely a smart young man, he does not know our customs." Actually Zief considered Lars and his people very civilized, only choosing his wording in an attempt to calm her rage. If she thought of Lars as a mindless barbarian, maybe she would have mercy on him.

"What do you intend to do about this, Majesty?" asked Talia, grinding her hands together.

"That decision lies with you, Lady Talia. As the ruling member of your House, until you name another lord, these weighty decisions rest firmly on your shoulders."

"I could ask for his head, could I not?" asked Talia.

That was the last thing Zief wanted, but how could he explain it to an irate mother. "That is your right, My Lady. But I would urge you to seriously consider the implications of such an action. If we executed a prince of Lokas, we could be pushed into a war we can ill afford at this time." Actually Lokas Village posed no threat to Ragal with its distance and small numbers. Still, Zief didn't need another enemy right now with an army of Ammelin due to show up outside his walls any day now. Most of that was known to only a select few, and he could hardly state these reasons to Lady Talia.

"Well if the situation is so grave, that only leaves me one choice," said Talia.

"My Lady?" questioned King Zief, wondering where this was leading.

"With my daughter's maidenhood lost, she will not be able to marry another lord of high standing now, as she deserves. This Prince Lars will have to marry her, taking responsibility for his shameful actions." Talia hoped she had not played her hand too early, knowing she should have ranted and raved a lot more. She just wanted this over with, wanted to run home and curl up until the butterflies in her stomach stopped kicking up a storm.

Now King Zief was clearly puzzled. "You have that right, My Lady. Although you must understand, unless you marry again before the wedding, with Lars of eligible age, the title of Lord Corban would pass onto his shoulders."

"I am sure between myself, my mother and my daughter, that we can keep one barbarian in line, Majesty."

"Very well, Lady Talia, as steward of House Corban the choice is yours. If that is what you wish, I will see it is carried out."

"Thank you, Majesty. I think my daughter and I need to have a long talk, if I may be excused?"

"By all means, My Lady, you are excused." The king paused a second. Something was amiss here, but he couldn't quite put his finger on it. After a moment he called, "Tam!" Tam opened the door and Lady Talia curtsied once more and swept out of the room. When she was gone, King Zief looked to Tam, "Find me Prince Lars and bring him here." Tam closed the door and went to do the king's bidding.

Talia paced slowly back to House Corban, trying to look stern and perhaps a little outraged all the way home. Only when the door closed behind her did she allow her mask to drop, letting out a long sigh. Relieved, her mouth spread out in a victorious smile. It had been easy, and although she thought it may have been a little too easy, Talia was sure all would proceed as she desired.

Lars was just walking his mare into the stables when Tam found him. "King Zief requests your presence immediately, Highness."

Lars knew something was amiss by Tam's formal tone. He didn't need to ask what. Handing the mare over to Enric he followed Tam silently to the anteroom, where he found the king looking remorseful for what he was about to do.

"Sit down Lars," said Zief resignedly. "Do I need to explain why I have called you here?" Lars shook his head. "Do you understand the gravity of the situation?"

"I think I do now, Majesty."

"Good. I don't expect you to know all of our laws and customs but a woman's maidenhood is something to be respected no matter where you live. I trust this is so in Lokas also?"

"Yes, Majesty, it is." After the night Lars had spent with Amelia he had thought nothing could ever make him regret it. Now found he was ashamed of his actions.

"Lady Talia, as ruler of House Corban, could have demanded your head over this. Instead she has demanded you marry her daughter to rescue some honour from this embarrassing situation. As king it is my right to offer you another solution. If you do not wish to marry Amelia you could quietly leave Ragal, never to return."

Zief felt he should be ranting or at the least giving Lars a stern lecture over his actions, but found he just didn't have the heart for it. After his meeting with Lady Talia he suspected this seemingly spontaneous coupling had been set up in advance, intending to trap Lars into marriage. And although he knew all too well the scheming Talia was capable of, he found it hard to believe Amelia would have agreed to be a part of this unless she truly had feelings for Lars. It presented him with an awkward situation.

With no proof he could do no more than convey Lady Corban's wishes. He felt sorry for Lars, watching the young man as he agonized over the situation, and wondered whether he should just order Lars away. He could have a lot happier life away from the devious Corban women. After a moment he decided it was for Lars to choose where his future lay, sat back and waited for a response.

Lars didn't know quite what to think. The idea of leaving Amelia was painful, beyond what he thought he could bear. And he had no wish to leave Ragal in disgrace either. To do so would shame his people and threaten their new friendship with Ragal. It was not something that could be easily explained to his father.

But he couldn't help thinking that he had somehow been betrayed by Amelia, who knew exactly how such an act would be perceived. If she had wished to keep their coupling secret she could have left his rooms soon after and no one would have suspected anything. Instead she had been the instigator and had then spent the night in his bed, surely knowing it would be impossible to keep it a secret. The only thing Lars was certain of was that, for all his suspicions, he simply loved her too much to leave her now.

"I will marry Amelia," he said quietly.

Zief held up a hand. "Before you finalize your decision I should explain to you all the implications. If you marry Amelia not only will you gain a wife, you will also gain the title of Lord Corban and become ruler of their House; not a small responsibility that should be lightly entered into. Your children will be the future heirs of that House, and your duties here in Ragal may mean you would never be able to return to your home in the mountains, except for short visits. It is a heavy responsibility to be a lord in my city. You would be giving up your family, your home and your future as *Fa'ku* in favour of Ragal. With that in mind you may want to take time before you make your decision. Perhaps you should sleep on it?"

Lars shook his head firmly. "No. My answer will be the same tomorrow as it is today." Even though he himself was not a warrior the people of his village lived by a common ethic. "In Lokas we live by a code of honour and that honour demands I marry Amelia. I would not willingly or knowingly bring shame on my people." Now though he could only think how his mother and father would receive this news, agonized over it, knowing his father's anger would be great though not as great as his mother's sorrow.

"Are you certain?" asked Zief.

Lars nodded and forced a smile, the resigned smile of the condemned. "Yes, Majesty, I am."

"As you wish," said Zief with a heavy sigh. "Now that is settled there is one more thing you need to consider. Although you will be Lord Corban in title, as one not born of that House, you will retain your own name. That presents us with a problem; your surname."

"I have no surname," said Lars, confused.

"That is precisely my point. Everyone in and around Ragal have birth names and family names. You will need a surname for the ceremony and in the future. Do you have any idea how we could come up with a surname for you?"

"Not really," said Lars honestly. "For any clarification in Lokas we quote lineage. I would be known as Lars, son of Alric, son of Wulfric."

"A bit of a mouthful, isn't it?" Zief paused for a while in thought, even though he had already given some time to this subject. "When Ragal and many other villages or towns started using surnames the lineage was altered to create a family name, so instead of Lars, son of Alric you would become Lars Alricsson. Not a bad name though I think we need something more fitting for a lord of Ragal. I have been trying to think of what you were named by the souls in your caverns when you dreamt in the crypt, but it eludes me."

"Velaren," Lars supplied.

Zief clicked his fingers and pointed in one smooth motion. "Velaren, that's it. How would you feel about being known as Lars Velaren? It's a name filled with meaning in the old tongue and is different enough that no one would mistake you as been born of Ragal."

Lars was unsure but nodded anyway. Surnames had little meaning to him, something used by other villages, so he had never even thought of needing one, or what it would be. "Lars Velaren," he said, trying it out. Zief watched him as if anticipating an answer. "I think that would be suitable, Majesty."

"Splendid!" said Zief. "I will inform Lady Talia of your acceptance of her terms. Now, I'm sure you have many important things to be getting on with, as do I. We will talk again soon."

That seemed to be the only dismissal Lars was going to receive. He stood, bowed and left the room. He walked slowly back to his own room, dragging himself up the stairs and down the corridor. He closed the door behind him and barred it, not wishing to be disturbed. Glancing at the heaped documents he decided he had little enthusiasm to read anything, so instead pulled off his shirt, tossing it onto one of the chairs, and laid down on the bed. The weight of the chain and stone pulled uncomfortably across his neck. He removed it and threw it on top of his shirt.

Later he heard a knock at the door and ignored it, presuming it to be one of the maids with his evening meal. This was confirmed moments later when he heard the bronze tray scraping on stone as it was placed on the floor outside his door. He was going to leave it there but decided the uneaten meal would only invite a string of enquiries. He wanted no more questions this day. Peeling himself off the bed he unbarred the door, placed the tray on a table and barred the door again.

Looking at the food for long moments he couldn't bring himself to eat anything. Returning to the bed he fell onto it face down and started to doze. Some time later, but he was unsure whether it was minutes or hours, he was roused by someone trying to lift the door latch.

"Lars. Lars?" He recognized Amelia's soft voice. After a moment reflecting on the day's events he found he didn't really want to see her either. What could he say to someone who he loved and hated all at once, someone who he was sure had betrayed that love and used it to trap him? He presumed she left then when he heard no more. He loved her still and had already decided he would forgive her, holding himself equally to blame for the situation he now found himself in. But now was not the time to offer his forgiveness. It was the unsubtle way the entrapment—and that was the only word he could think of to describe it—had been executed. He refused to believe it had been unplanned now, after the event. It was so obvious he was sure the king suspected it also.

He wondered what sort of situation had forced her into such desperate actions, suspecting he already knew the answer to that also, understanding just how badly House Corban could be affected. If that was the true reason behind her actions why didn't she explain the situation to him and he would have willingly married her. Like he really needed any incentive! Then at least their marriage could have started on a more equal footing, on his terms.

What did she think? Did she believe that she could mould him, making of him a puppet lord who said only what his wife wished him to say? And to think of maybe never walking the slopes of his beloved home again, except in the briefest visits. He hadn't missed the mountains when he had thought he could return freely. Now he longed to see those towering peaks again, changing colours from white to grey, red then purple as the sun travelled its daily course.

And could he ever trust Amelia again after such a betrayal? These thoughts were still plaguing Lars when he finally drifted into a deep sleep, opening his eyes to find himself in the tall cylindrical dome once more, hundreds of specks of light filling the interior, looking like nothing so much as stars in the sky. Then one of the stars moved, coming towards him.

"*Welcome Lars,*" said Melissa. "*As always it is a pleasure to have you visit us.*"

Lars at first wished he hadn't come to the dome this night, but soon found his sour mood lifting as he gazed on the souls and heard Melissa's musical voice. He still couldn't understand why some nights he found himself there and others he didn't. There seemed to be no pattern, no obvious reason that would influence his visits either way. He had discovered the previous year that alcohol seemed to block his, what could only be called, spirit walking. So far this year he had studiously avoided any strong drinks, wanting to return to the dome. Now he was beginning to wonder whether he was mistaken and it had merely been a coincidence. And with the visits still being infrequent there was no way he could test his theory.

"Hello Melissa," he replied finally.

"*Are you well, Lars?*" asked the spirit. "*You seem . . .*" Suddenly Melissa laughed. "*I was going to say you seem dispirited, but that is not a word to use in this situation. You seem, should we say, distracted.*"

Lars, smiling, waved the comment away. "It's nothing to concern you." His gaze travelled around as he spoke and fixed on the bright red of the newest spirit. "Have you discovered anymore about your new arrival?"

"*He is very withdrawn. We can't get a word out of him. His death must have been very traumatic, the binding a great shock. He still refuses to believe he is dead. Only time and patience can heals the wounds his soul has carried over. I fear it could take some time yet before he will accept his fate."*

"And Seeli?" asked Lars. "How is she coping after my last visit? I fear I may have done more harm than good giving her such promises."

"Not so," said Melissa. *"She is still a solitary soul but she has opened up a little and begun to again share her life experiences with other spirits imprisoned here. Remembering our lives and sharing our memories are all that is left to us now. Without that we would all be like Paolen, or worse."*

Lars could see the grey spirit moving slowly around the dome, stopping occasionally when nearing other spirits. He was pleased to see his words had helped in some small way, but still wished he could do more. The trouble was he still knew so little about his surroundings. He was kept busy enough that he had no time to explore the keep and he was fairly sure he had already seen everything of interest there. And the dome was so huge he couldn't imagine where such a thing could be hidden.

"I'm pleased Seeli has improved a little," said Lars. "Maybe I could help with the newcomer also?"

"I'm not sure that would be wise," replied Melissa. *"He is still confused and angry."*

"I would still like to try."

"Very well," said Melissa, the white speck of her spirit moving aside to let Lars cross to the red soul.

"Hello," he began as he drew close to the spirit, not wanting to shock or scare it. "I would like to talk with you if I may, maybe ask you some simple questions."

"You!" hissed the spirit. *"What are you doing here?"*

Lars took a step back, and not because of the clear anger in the voice. He was shocked to find he recognized the voice, and was finding it hard to come to terms with the fact that the spirit was now trapped in this dome. The last time he had heard that voice was outside House Tremar.

"Parlen?" he asked finally.

"Yes, it is I," said the spirit, regaining some of his usual composure upon hearing a familiar voice. *"Can you get me out of here? These floating lights keep telling me I am dead. Occasionally they take on human form and that is very unsettling. I feel so alive, never more so. What they say can't be true; can it?"*

"I don't know an easy was to say this, Parlen, so I will state it plainly. You *are* dead. The floating lights you see and hear are other spirits. They look the same to you as you do to me."

"How can this be?"

Lars couldn't think of any way to make this easier on Parlen so he simply spoke the truth the way he knew it. "You were killed by bandits when you rode out with the soldiers to intercept them. Your body was brought back to Ragal where you were buried." Lars paused for a while before he continued. "How your spirit came to be interred here I don't know." Although he had his suspicions, now, he kept them to himself.

"How long will I be trapped here?"

"I have no idea how long you will remain here. From what Melissa has told me-"

"Who is Melissa?" Parlen interrupted.

"She is a spirit like you, trapped in this place. I will introduce you. She has been here a long time." He thought it best not to say exactly how long lest the spirit of Parlen despair and descend into madness. "Melissa knows far more about this dome than I do."

"And what about you?" asked Parlen. *"You appear as you did in life and not just a speck of light like these other spirits. When did you die anyway?"*

This was something Lars had been dreading Parlen asking. "I am not dead, Parlen. I come here in my dreams. How I can come and go without being trapped is something Melissa could also explain far better than I. It has something to do with my body being firmly anchored in the world of the living. I don't entirely understand it myself. I'm not sure anyone does."

Lars thought for a moment before speaking again. He had decided he wouldn't make any more rash promises, but the more he was learning about this dome and its prisoners the more determined he became to release them all.

"Do not despair too greatly Parlen," Lars began again. "I intend to release all the spirits in this dome from their captivity. It may take some time, so you need to be patient. If you speak with the other spirits here, share stories, the time will pass that much quicker for you and you won't feel so alone. Now, I will introduce you to Melissa, who in turn will introduce all the other spirits here."

Lars looked around for Melissa. She was one white spirit among many and he couldn't pick her out, forcing him to call her name instead. "Melissa?" he said questioningly and immediately saw one of the spirits starting to move towards him.

As the spirit drew near Lars said, "Melissa, this is Parlen. He is a young lord of Ragal, a good and honourable man whom I have met and spoken with several times. Please welcome him and let him meet the other spirits." Lars wished he could stay longer to help Parlen adjust. He had lessons to get to and didn't want to be late. "I have to go now Parlen. It will be nearing dawn and Bollo will be coming to get me for my first lesson. I will return soon."

Lars closed his eyes and opened them again to the darkness of his room. He was finding this much easier each time he returned. He was going to get out of bed to look out of the window to gauge the time when a knock at the door announced Bollo was already there.

Lars leapt out of bed and dressed quickly, snatching up his practice sword as he made his way to the door.

"Good morning," Bollo greeted him. "I trust you slept well."

That wasn't how Lars would term it. He nodded all the same, not wanting to discuss the troubling things he had discovered; especially not with the king's brother. He pushed his thoughts aside and concentrated on this morning's lesson.

"We are going to step your training up a notch today, starting by running two laps around the Inner City," Bollo explained.

Not waiting for a response from Lars he turned on his heel and headed towards the stairs. They completed the run quickly and made their way to the practice yard. As they entered Bollo swung around unexpectedly, bringing his practice sword up at a level with Lars' neck. Lars didn't have time to bring his own practice sword up to meet it and instead had to crouch while the sword swept above his head then spring backwards before Bollo could bring it back towards him. He brought his own sword up then, ready for the next attack.

After a slight pause Bollo moved in again, attacking with a speed and viciousness that surprised Lars. Bringing his sword up and planting his feet to keep a good balance, Lars met the attack with several blocking moves then started trading blow for blow with Bollo. After several minutes of furious fighting Bollo stopped and stepped back a couple of paces.

The Sword-master nodded approvingly then bowed, before turning to enter the practice yard properly, saying over his shoulder. "I think that is enough of a warm up. Let's begin today's lesson."

Lars took a few deep breaths to compose himself with the sudden change in Bollo's manner then strode forward into the yard to begin his lesson. Bollo taught Lars several new moves that morning, all aimed at one final move that resulted in decapitating your opponent. Lars personally found this a bit worrying but was sure Bollo had a good reason for teaching him these moves.

"You did well today, Lars," said Bollo, as the lesson ended. "Do you have you any questions before we leave?"

"Only one," said Lars. "What is this obsession with cutting off heads? Almost everything you taught me today was aimed at decapitation."

"That is a simple one to answer," replied Bollo. "In a battle if you waste time cutting off limbs you are using valuable energy you will sorely miss later. If you go for a body assault aiming to crush ribs or run your blade through stomach, chest or are even lucky enough to pierce the heart, even though most of these injuries will prove fatal it is rarely immediate. Then, as they crash to the ground and you move past them to your next opponent, they are still alive and can stab you through the groin.

"A groin wound is a messy and painful way to go; not something I would wish on anyone. They could also stab you in the buttocks or hamstring you as you pass. Both of those wounds make it impossible to keep your balance properly and you would soon be cut down.

"The reason I like going for the neck is that it is always immediately fatal and eliminates all these possibilities. There are enough uncertainties in battle with everyone fighting so close together, making it so easy to be killed by a blade you didn't even see. If you can at least remove one of these dangers it greatly improves your chances of surviving the day."

"I can understand that," said Lars, and he truly did. The problem was that he had seen someone almost decapitated by one of the *Feyhalas*, and remembered the nauseating rush he had felt after killing the bandit. He didn't know how he would handle all that blood spraying into the air, and more than likely, all over him as the body toppled.

"You did well again today," Bollo stated again as they started walking back through the maze of hedges towards the keep, and Lars was taken aback by the unexpected praise. "Especially with the attack when we entered the fencing yard. But you only did well due to your youth and quick reflexes. You have to learn to expect an attack at any time and from any direction. Your youth and speed will not stay with you forever. If you learn what I can teach you, in time instinct will replace the advantages your age provides you with, and give you the edge your youthful agility gives you now.

"You could be a good swordsman Lars; really good. It will require a great deal of dedication from you. And you will need to abstain from alcohol to apply yourself properly. It is a foul thing for a soldier or warrior to drink. It clouds the mind for longer than the initial effects last; slows your wits and your reflexes. More good people have been killed when drunk or suffering from the after effects than I care to remember.

"Even our latest victim of the bandits, Parlen, was fond of strong liquor and drank daily. He was a good man and more than adequate with a blade. I can't help thinking he might still be alive today if he could have stayed away from alcohol. It seems to have become a curse of the rich. Poor people don't drink much or often because it is simply too expensive. But the nobles here can buy large quantities of the strongest drinks from all across the land, and do so regularly.

"They seem to think it is some kind of competition as to who can drink the most, as though it is something to be proud of. Personally I find their behaviour disgusting and intolerable when our own lands are not even secure. Our soldiers should be outside these walls day and night, removing the threat from the land and making the roads safe for innocent people to travel, not spending their nights in the taverns of our great city."

Bollo stopped for a moment looking up at the flags snapping in the breeze above the keep. They were nearing the edge of the maze now and would soon be in clear sight of the keep. Lars stopped also, looking at Bollo.

"I should not really speak so, Lars. I am sure our noble and wise king knows exactly what he is doing and has plans well in hand to remove these cursed vermin." With that Bollo strode away and disappeared into the keep, leaving Lars to follow on behind in his own time.

When Lars reached his room he found the door slightly ajar. Pushing it open he saw Amelia sitting in a chair next to the cold and empty fireplace. Catching the movement of the door she looked up to see Lars standing in the door way.

At the sight of her the bitterness of her betrayal he had been holding in check welled up in Lars and overflowed. Without looking at her he walked into the room, resting his practice sword against the wall by the door. Crossing to the bed he removed his jerkin and hung it over the end of the bed. He still preferred to wear the clothes he had worn on his way to Ragal for his lessons with Bollo, finding the clothes of his home gave him more freedom and didn't cling annoyingly to his skin when he sweated.

He walked across to the wash stand and poured some of the warm water from the pitcher into the bowl. After washing himself thoroughly he finally turned to Amelia. "How can I help you, My Lady?"

"I just wanted to see you," replied Amelia.

"I thought you had already gotten everything you wanted from me?"

"It wasn't my idea, Lars," said Amelia, confirming his suspicions. "I didn't want to hurt you. I love you too much for that."

"You have a peculiar way of showing it," said Lars angrily. "Do you always sleep with those you claim to love, intending the whole time to trap them into doing what you want?"

"I didn't want to trap you at all, Lars. It was my mother's idea. She is concerned about the future of our House and if I don't marry soon she would be forced into a wedding of the king's choosing. More than likely it would be a power hungry fool with no care for my mother or her wishes; a man with ambitions of his own, someone who would have no love for her or me. Then I would be married off to the first free man he could find and likely never see you again. This way seemed best for everyone. You and I could stay together and my family would stay together in House Corban, where we belong."

Amelia could see her words were having little effect on Lars, his anger too great to see her reasoning, but she pressed on regardless.

"Can't you see that it was done with only the best intentions," she continued. "I love you so much and didn't want to lose you. And I love my mother and wouldn't wish to see her forced into a loveless marriage.

She is still grieving over the recent losses to our family. My father was her whole world."

Lars looked straight at Amelia at last. "Then why didn't you simply explain all this to me, instead of trapping me the way you did?"

"I was just wondering that exact same thing," said a voice from the door that had remained slightly open since Lars had entered. Amelia and Lars both looked up to see King Zief standing in the doorway.

The king walked into the room, accompanied by Tam, who closed the door firmly behind them to stop anyone else overhearing what was said. The king sat down opposite Amelia and indicated with his hand for Lars to sit next to her. For a few moments the king stared between the two of them, seeing the anger of betrayal still clear on the face of Lars, and Amelia looking ashamed and uncertain after being caught admitting the deception.

"I suspected something amiss in all this," the king began. "I must say though that I had hoped it was just my overly suspicious nature reading more into the situation than was actually there. Discovering I was correct makes me feel that not only did you betray Lars, the man you claim to love, but me also, your king. And your mother lied to me so that Lars would be steered into this marriage."

The king looked directly at Amelia then. "And what was your mother thinking. Does she really believe I would marry her off to someone who cared nothing for her? By all the twelve gods she is my wife's sister! If only for that reason alone she should know I would never have treated her with so little regard.

"But pushing me into a corner like this has left me with little choice other than to act in the best interests of the realm. If Lars no longer wishes to marry you and become Lord Corban, your House will be dissolved and another elevated from the ranks of lesser nobles from one of the estates around Ragal."

"What would that mean to Amelia?" asked Lars, unsure of what the king meant.

"Normally," Zief began, "it would mean Amelia and her family would lose their home and be cast onto the streets of the Outer City, to scrape a living; though I must say that has never happened in my life time. Amelia's mother, related by marriage as she is, would be more fortunate. I would have to grant her a small estate and a modest allowance. And then I would have to choose a husband for her, who, with Lady Talia no longer being from the Five Houses, would have to come from a much smaller selection of available lords than would have otherwise been the case.

"So, Lars, you can see the future prosperity of House Corban is nothing for you to feel responsible for. This deceit has freed you from any obligation you may have felt towards them. If you choose not to marry Amelia you need not concern yourself with their welfare; her family will not become destitute. You would be free to carry on with your life and put this whole sordid mess behind you."

King Zief waited for a few moments to let Lars assimilate this information before asking, "Do you still wish to marry Amelia and become Lord Corban?"

Lars was silent for a long time, staring at the floor. Amelia looked at him expectantly, Lars in turn refusing to meet her gaze. Finally he looked back to the king, "I will need time to think about it, Majesty."

"Lars," pleaded Amelia.

Still refusing to look at her he shook his head and said, "Not now."

"Take as long as you need, Lars," said Zief. "If you wish to talk about this at any time find Tam and he will arrange a meeting. We shall leave you now." The king rose then to leave but had to say, "My Lady," to get Amelia to follow suit. As they left the room Lars heard the king say to Tam, "I would like to see Lady Talia. Bring her to me, now!"

Lars sat there for a long time, lost in his thoughts and feelings as he tried to resolve the issue within himself. He found it was too much to contemplate just now, and soon gave him a headache. He needed some distraction. Dressing quickly he headed down to the serenity of the library. It was looking so much more organized now than when he had first started. Almost all the books were shelved and categorized accordingly. He had numbered each shelf and recorded them all in a reference book, listing the title and it's location by alphabetical order. The library had once been as it looked now and Lars had found a similar book to the one he had written, which gave him the idea of how best to create some order in the library.

He was sure Felman could have told him as much if the cantankerous old librarian could stay awake for more than a few minutes at a time and didn't view all Lars' efforts with undisguised contempt. Lars knew that Felman could be quite reasonable at times; he had spent a lot of time in the library the previous year and when they were leaving Felman actually spoke to them in a civil manner.

Then they had suspected that he had simply been feigning sleep while surreptitiously watching what they were doing. This year though the old man seemed genuinely tired, sleeping most of the day through, and appeared truly disgruntled whenever he was disturbed. When the morning was over Lars looked at the library. He thought it would only take a few more days to finish the reordering and decided he would soon need another activity to fill his mornings.

At least he would if his decision about Amelia led to him remaining in Ragal.

When he got to his room though and saw the piles of documents for arming the bastions he knew he already had enough to occupy him. Maybe more than he could handle.

He picked up a document from the top of the nearest pile and started browsing through it. It was fascinating stuff and he backed up to a chair without stopping reading, easing himself slowly down as he turned the page. It seemed a complex system of weights and leverage, cranking and release mechanisms. It appeared to be a giant sling of sorts and Lars could see no apparent flaws in the design to explain why they failed.

He was no engineer, with only a rudimentary understanding of how things were built. It would take a lot more reading, mainly through the failure reports, to find the weak spots and try and correct them.

The other documents and manuscripts in the same pile as he had taken this one from were all on the same 'war engine' as they were termed. As much as he wanted to keep reading about the first one he took a document from another pile, deciding it would be best to understand a little of each before starting on any particular weapon in depth.

The next document concerned a giant bow that could propel a spear as tall as a man over a great distance. Looking through the design Lars could already see a potential flaw. The layers of wood that formed the bow were laminated, as was common, but the bows that were made in Lokas also had layers of soft calf skin from the stomachs of young staloks bonded between them which held the wood together better when it flexed, stopping it from splintering. Again it would take a lot more reading but at least he had a starting point for this one. He was about to pick up a scroll from the top of the last pile when a knock at the door announced a maid carrying his lunch.

He ate his meal slowly, thinking about Amelia, while skimming through one of the reports concerning a weapon called a cannon. All that he achieved through thinking about her deceit was a ruined appetite. Placing the tray to one side he rose and went to the stable. The rest of the day passed slowly, his mind continually betraying his wishes and leading him back to Amelia. That night he slept little and felt physically and mentally drained when Bollo arrived for his first lesson of the day.

The lesson with Ragal's Armourer and Sword-master was interesting, as they always were, and passed quickly but left him exhausted. To prevent sleep creeping up on him again he washed, ate and dressed quickly before heading down to the library.

As he entered the library all was quiet, too quiet, indicating Felman wasn't present. Lars decided this was an ideal time to record the rest of the books, which were still stacked on and around Felman's desk, shelving them as each was added to his reference book.

When Lars got close a faint yet unpleasant smell greeted him. As he came past the last of the books he could see Felman, slumped in his chair, pale and dead. Lars reached forward to check the pulse to confirm this. The skin was cold to the the touch; too cold. As expected no life burned in that old body any longer.

Lars stood frozen for a moment, unsure of what to do; then the shuffling of feet in the corridor outside the library quickly led him to a decision. He raced to the door and pulled it open to see two maids just passing the library, carrying blankets. As the door banged open the maids turned to see what the commotion was about. On seeing Lars they both curtsied awkwardly, struggling with their loads.

Lars didn't have time for such niceties. "I need one of you to leave what you are doing and go and find Tam for me now. Bring him straight here." The maids looked at each other, undecided who should go, so Lars made the choice for them. "You," he said pointing to the one on the right. "Leave your blankets here and find Tam." When the maid was slow in reacting Lars lost his patience and roared, "Now!"

The maid dropped her blankets, bobbed a nervous curtsy and disappeared down the corridor. Lars sighed and turned to the other maid. "Apologize to your friend for me when you see her next. I am sorry for my curtness but it really is rather urgent."

The maid curtsied again and muttered, "Yes, Highness," before sweeping off down the corridor and out of sight. Lars went back into the library and closed the door. He didn't want to just sit and wait for Tam so he started ordering the books as had been his intention this morning. He soon found the sight of Felman too unsettling him so he returned to the corridor and picked up one of the blankets. Gently he covered the body with the blanket and tried to continue with his work, although he found it difficult to concentrate.

It seemed a long time before Tam arrived. Lars jumped as the door opened on creaky hinges, his nerves getting the better of him. "What is the problem, Highness?" asked Tam from the doorway.

Lars waved him towards the desk and pulled the blanket away when Tam was close enough to see. "I found him dead this morning when I came to library," said Lars, looking at the corpse. "I didn't know what to do so I thought it best to get you."

"Quite right," agreed Tam. "I will need to inform the king and then House Corban. Can you wait here Highness, so no one disturbs the body until I can arrange for it to be moved to the chapel?"

"Of course I will."

"Thank you, Highness," said Tam. "I will try to return as quickly as possible." With that he hastily left the room and Lars was left alone again with the body. He covered it again with the blanket and returned to his work.

His mind kept drifting back to the former librarian. Even with his waspish comments Lars had liked Felman and could understand some of his frustration. Lars had suspected the surliness came as much from an inability to bring some order to the library himself and not just from his cantankerous nature.

It felt like an incredibly long time before Tam finally returned with four male servants bearing a stretcher. The stretcher was laid on the floor and the men gently lifted the body from the chair to the stretcher. Rigor mortis had set in so some joints had to be broken to straighten the body out, each crunch making Lars wince.

With the body straightened and covered once more the four servants picked up the stretcher and carried it from the library. Tam approached

Lars. "The rest of the day will be given over to mourning and tomorrow for the funeral. The rest of your lessons for the day will be cancelled, Highness. Your lessons will resume as normal in two days time."

Tam turned then to leave the room but Lars stopped him. "How is Lady Amelia?" he asked.

"Distraught," replied Tam, "As is to only be expected. She was very close to her grandfather and their family has suffered much loss already this past year. With that and the worry of what will become of her family I fear it has all become too much for her." Tam paused for a second. "I must leave now, Highness. There are many arrangements to be made. But you should know that the king has not yet spoken to Lady Talia as she was visiting her estates outside the city yesterday. This news has now forced him to abandon that meeting for the next few days at least."

Lars nodded and Tam left the library. Lars stood there for a long time, thinking about going to see Amelia then deciding against it. He cared about her deeply but was still unsure what to do and didn't want to add confusion to her pain.

Instead he continued with his work and when he left the library later that day it was fully ordered once more.

QUESTIONS AND ANSWERS

The next couple of days passed in a haze for Lars. The funeral for Felman took place with all its sombre formalities. Lars wasn't invited to attend, which didn't really surprise him. He slept little and when he did he was haunted by dreams of Amelia and what he was going to do about the whole situation. The only trouble he had was that he was still so angry about how he had been tricked. His mind was clouded by emotion, making it impossible to think clearly. Until he could settle this inner trumoil his judgement would remain suspect and he wanted to make the right decision, not take some rash action based on his feelings that he would later regret.

The worst of it was that if she had simply explained the predicament her family faced he would have married her in a heartbeat. He loved her and he couldn't get away from that fact. He didn't hate her by any measure but he hated the way her actions made him feel. If he could just find it in himself to forgive and forget then everything would be okay between them. It was the forgiving part he was having trouble with though. And now on top of all the other issues he had to try and decide how the death of her grandfather would influence his decision, or if it counted at all.

Instead of letting the problem consume him he threw himself into reading through the piles of paperwork still cluttering the floor in his room, trying to make sense of them and find some answers. Much of the information was simply repeated and he soon reduced the piles to three short stacks that could easily fit onto a desk and still leave him room to work. He was pretty sure he had the problem with the giant bows, which he had found were called ballistae, hopefully solved. He also had several ideas for the catapults, which were named trebuchet in the documents, involving padded leather to absorb some of the shock on one of the designs.

There were already two designs for trebuchet, one designed for large rocks and another for what could be considered nothing less than giant boulders. The smaller used a sprung design and the larger utilized a stack weights. Both would need several modifications to function as intended.

But the cannon design was still giving him a considerable amount of trouble. He knew very little of metal so could see nothing wrong, which had led him to where he was now heading. It was early afternoon and he was walking the streets of the Outer City to Sarn Plat's forge, needing to ask the advice of a blacksmith. As he turned into the yard before the forge he saw Hakon coming out of the smithy with a hammer and horse shoe, heading for the only horse tied in the yard at the time.

Hakon saw Lars and waved him over. "I'm surprised to see you here. Just give me a minute to nail this shoe in place and I'll be with you."

Lars was amazed at the deft way Hakon handled the hammer and nailed the shoe, the horse standing placidly, chomping at a bag of hay. Hakon finished up and fixed Lars with a quizzical stare. "You don't look too happy. Are you having problems at the keep?"

"Only one that anyone can help with," replied Lars.

Hakon was confused but shook it off. "And what would that be."

"I think we will need Sarn's help on this one, too" said Lars. "And I would rather explain this just the once."

"Very well," said Hakon, and led him into the forge to see Sarn.

"Welcome, Highness," Sarn greeted him.

"Please don't call me that," said Lars. "It's bad enough that everyone in the keep insists on it."

"Okay then, Lars, to what do we owe the pleasure of this visit?"

Lars explained about the task the king had set for him. First he explained about the problems with the ballistae and trebuchet, showing them the plans and the improvements he had decided upon.

Hakon and Sarn examined the plans and the suggested modifications. Sarn looked at the trebuchet, which had two distinct designs, and pointed to where Lars suggested putting the padding on the smaller of the two. "This won't work as you hope," he explained. "I have seen similar weapons before, in Tibor, and they rely on that impact to launch the rock from the cradle. If you pad it too thickly there you may well stop it from breaking but you will reduce the effective range of the weapon. I think the true problem with this one is that they have bored a hole through the wood for the pivot. I would suggest making a metal cradle to hold the arm from where it pivots with the pivot on the underside and banded around the outside to keep the arm whole."

Sarn took a shaved piece of charcoal from the pouch in the leather apron he always wore in the forge, and sketched in what he suggested, extending the cradle to the base of the arm where it struck to launch the rock, and a little way above the pivot.

"This will support the base of the throwing arm," said Sarn, "while leaving the top of the arm flexible enough to stop it breaking. I would also strengthen the strike plate better, and that should be okay for the smaller version." Then he turned his attention to the larger design which used the weights to propel the rock, with a winch to pull the arm back.

"The problem with this one is the same as the first. They have bored through the throwing arm, where a cradle to hold the arm would make it stronger and more durable, it creates a weak point where the stress of the weights and the load meet." He then took up the plan for the ballistae and gave it a cursory examination. "You know a lot more about bows than I ever will," he said, handing to Hakon.

Hakon looked it over. "The hide is a good idea, but I would also make the layers of wood thinner with more of them and it should last well."

"Thank you," said Lars. "Your suggestions are great, and I'll certainly put them to use. Now, I have one other design for you to look at. It is the main reason I thought to come and see you." He laid the document for the cannon on the table and watched as both men bent to look at it.

Hakon looked up after only a few moments, shaking his head. Sarn though continued examining it for a long time, writing down several calculations on the side of parchment. Finally he looked up at Lars. "I am no expert but I would say this thing isn't strong enough. It would blow apart and likely kill any who tried to use it."

"It already has," Lars informed them. "At least once that I know of, if a long time ago now. No one has tried to improve on the design since."

Sarn pointed with his piece of charcoal, naming the parts as they were recorded in the document. "I would say the metal needs to be a lot thicker around the explosion chamber. It could also use several bands for extra strength, one either side of the explosion chamber and one around the muzzle. These changes could all be incorporated into the cast. I have never seen anything like this before but it would certainly be a formidable weapon if you can get it right."

"I will have to show the king these changes," said Lars. "I think he will want to know who helped me with these."

"I would rather be kept out of this," said Sarn. "But the king isn't stupid and will probably be able to figure it out easily enough. I can only hope he won't ask for my assistance. But I care more about the safety of this city than my own work and will come if the king asks it of me."

"Thank you again, both of you, for your help. The king seems eager to have these weapons in place as soon as possible and your ideas will be greatly appreciated. He says they are to repel bandits, but I suspect another reason, a greater danger he knows about but isn't willing to have it become public knowledge just yet."

Lars said his farewells and left the forge then to return to the keep. Hakon accompanied him out into the yard. "I will be returning to Lokas soon. I presume you will be staying here for a while?"

"Yes," confirmed Lars. "I have a lot yet to learn here." He paused for a moment, undecided whether to tell Hakon of his other problems. He finally decided that he could really use another opinion. "I may also be getting married," he blurted.

Hakon simply looked at him and raised an eyebrow.

Lars continued to explain his problems with Amelia, how he felt about the situation, and what the consequences would be for which ever decision he reached.

"It could be worse," said Hakon, explaining further at Lars' startled expression. "Since I have been here I have discovered that the women of Ragal seem to try and marry into the most powerful or wealthy noble families. Most are in fact encouraged to do so by their parents. There are some exceptions but in general that is the way it is.

"Amelia may have tried to trap you into marriage but at least you know greed was never an issue in her decision. She has done this to save her family. I would say she picked you because she loves you and if she must marry before she is ready it would be best to do so with a person she already knows and cares for. You need to see this from her point of view. Family aside, she would be faced with losing you and being thrust into a marriage with someone she neither knows nor cares for; and who will likely have as little regard for her.

"She will then be stuck with someone who just wants to marry into the family for the power and wealth it will gain him." Hakon remained quiet for a long time, watching Lars, allowing his words to sink in. "Amelia obviously loves you and trusts you to treat her family with respect. I can't condone her actions or approve of the honourless way she acted, but there are always two sides to any story. It is up to you to decide how you will react to her deceit. Only you can make that decision." He finished and waited for a response.

Lars could find nothing wrong in what Hakon had said, and he realized he had been angry with Amelia for all the wrong reasons. He still felt though that she should have just explained it all to him. He realized then that she must have been unsure of his reaction and didn't want to risk him refusing; then she would have been left in the same predicament.

"I need to speak with her," whispered Lars.

"I think it would be best," agreed Hakon.

Lars nodded, holding up the plans he had brought with him. "Thank you again for your help. I hope I will see you again before you leave?"

"I'll make sure of it," replied Hakon.

Lars nodded again. "Good. Good." He walked away then, heading back to the Inner City, lost in thought. He wanted to go and see Amelia straight away but didn't know if it would be wise. Her family would still be mourning the death of Felman. His visit could be taken the wrong way.

Instead he returned to his room, laid down the documents, and threw himself onto the bed. He was too hot and sat up again to remove his shirt. The chain and stone that Zief had given him was also becoming irritating so he removed it and hung it over a post at the head of the bed.

Laying down again Lars took a long time to relax. Just as he was drifting into a sleep a knock at the door announced the arrival of his evening meal. He picked at the meal without interest and placed the tray outside the door when he was done so he wouldn't be disturbed again.

It was well into the evening now and was starting to cool down. He closed the window shutters and drew the tapestries. Returning to his bed he lay down in silence and darkness. Occasionally he could hear people in conversation as they passed by his door. Soon enough the keep settled down for the night and was finally quiet. Eventually he drifted off to sleep.

Opening his eyes again he was pleased to find himself back in the crystal dome. Again he wondered about his visits here and why they were so far between lately. He thought he already knew but would need to experiment over several more nights to verify his suspicions. He had intended to do so already but had put it off with all the commotion around the keep.

Lars could see Melissa's spirit drifting towards him and was surprised to find he could discern hers from all the others. In fact with each visit to the dome he found that although at first glance most appeared the same, if looked at closely each had a slight shade of colour, or pulsed, shimmered and moved in their own unique way.

Melissa's spirit also seemed to be growing in size, taking on some shape and form. With time Lars suspected she may appear to him as she had looked in life. Lars presumed it was his familiarity with her that was causing him to be able to see more of Melissa's spirit.

Lars also noticed another new spirit in the dome. This one was a darker shade of red than that of Parlen, not as eye catching or vibrant, yet still clearly very new to the spirit world.

Melissa reached him then. "Hello Lars. It is simply delightful to see you again," she said in the most normal and least strained tone of voice Lars had heard from her since his return to Ragal. Then finished, mock petulant, "Although I must say your visits are becoming too infrequent for my liking."

"I know," said Lars. "I feel the same way. Hopefully, soon, I will be able to come here more often. I think I have discovered the reason for my visits ceasing and will hopefully be able to correct that without any adverse effects." Changing the subject totally Lars glanced towards the new spirit. "I see you now have Felman among you."

"How did you know who it was?" asked Melissa.

"That was also amongst my suspicions, in the same conclusions I reached as to why I have not been coming here often." Lars paused before he explained, sure he would be stopped at any moment, expecting Melissa already knew what he was about to say. "I believe it is all because of the strange stones all the nobles of Ragal wear. I am now sure the function of these stones is to trap the soul of the wearer when the body dies. I am also fairly certain that wearing one is the reason why I have not been coming here in my sleep.

"With the soul temporarily trapped in the stone it enables the king to somehow release you into this dome. And as you well know once inside there is no escape."

"The king," gasped Melissa. "How do you know this?"

"I have had my suspicions for a little while. The king gave me the stone after Parlen's death. The next time I came here Parlen's soul was trapped in the dome. I believe the stone I wear was once Parlen's." Lars was also certain he now knew where the dome was, and was surprised he hadn't realized this before, even though the size of the dome was too large for any single floor of the keep. He didn't say as much to Melissa; he was unsure as to how he could get into the room, the only key he had ever seen being in the posession of King Zief. He simply refused to raise their hopes again until he had a clear plan of how he would free them.

Melissa sounded shocked and disgusted when she spoke again. "How could he do this? How could they all do this to us? This would mean the kings of Ragal have been imprisoning souls for over six hundred years, condemning those who thought themselves friends to an afterlife of torturous imprisonment. You must let everyone know about the stones. This cannot be allowed to continue."

A loud knock sounded and Lars felt himself wrenched from the dome and back into his body. Knowing Bollo would be waiting for him outside the door he leapt out of bed and dressed quickly. In a way he was glad he hadn't remained in the dome any longer. He couldn't possibly tell all the nobles about the stones as Melissa would surely have insisted. The nobles probably wouldn't believe him anyway, and the king would find out what Lars was accusing him of, leaving him in a precarious position.

He picked up his practice sword and opened the door, surprised to find Amelia standing there.

"What are you doing here so early," he asked, surprised.

"Early," said Amelia, confusion wrinkling her brow. "Are you well Lars? It is just before midnight."

"Oh," said Lars. "Sorry. I was sleeping and when I heard the knock at the door I presumed it was morning." He paused for a moment to gather his thoughts, feeling slightly uncomfortable at being caught unawares. "Please come in. I am happy to see you. And may I offer my sympathies for your recent loss."

"Thank you," said Amelia as she walked into the room. Once inside she turned to face Lars, waiting for him to close the door before speaking again. "And *are* you pleased to see me Lars, truly?"

"Oh yes," replied Lars fervently. "I have wanted to come and see you for the past few days. Only today I wanted to come and tell you what I have decided. But I didn't want to disturb your mourning, thinking my visit may be taken the wrong way."

"And what have you decided?" asked Amelia, looking nervous, not knowing where to put her hands as she fidgeted continually.

Lars didn't want to increase her anxiety so he answered quickly. "I have decided that although I greatly dislike the way you tried to trap me, you did it to protect your family's future, and I would very much like to marry you if you still want to."

Amelia seemed to melt with relief. Tears flowed freely down her cheeks. She closed the short distance between them and threw herself into his arms.

"I would like nothing more," she mumbled into his chest.

PLANS

"**I** need your assistance in a matter of some importance to me," said Empress Shatala, facing Evarlen and Taneera on her first visit to the Brotherhood since their immense failure with the *Draknor*.

"As always, we are yours to command, Empress," Evarlen assured. "If it is within our power it shall be yours."

"I want to press forward with the attack on the eastern lands," said Shatala, "bringing them back under my rule. The commanders of my army though seem to feel it best to delay, inventing reason upon reason as to why we should wait. What I need from your Order is to scour the lands for reasons why now is the best time to move."

"We shall search ceaselessly, questing with our souls, into the lands you have specified," said Evarlen. "We will look for signs of disorder and chaos that would be beneficial to any attack we could mount, seeking for any reasons to demonstrate that a delay would be costly to us."

"You have understood my needs perfectly," said Shatala. "I know I can count on you to deliver what I need."

Shatala left the room then, leaving the two men alone. "It begins again," said Taneera.

"So it does," agreed Evarlen.

Theodin Hornshank was sitting with his back to a tree, slowly scraping a sharpening stone along the length of his sword's blade, when Captain Fellir announced it was time to move out. Theodin was becoming disillusioned with the whole campaign and was seriously starting to doubt the wisdom of his leaders. His brother and the whole fleet should be joining them soon, and they had achieved little since the night attack by the Ragalan soldiers.

They had been harrying supply wagons and farms, but couldn't do anything on a larger scale due to insufficient numbers and the very real danger from the constant patrols from Ragal.

Theodin now believed they should lay low until the fleet arrived. Their attacks had only served to alert Ragal to the coming threat. The Ammelin army needed the element of surprise to attack the city. Otherwise their soldiers would break against its walls, be forced to fall back and mount a blockade. The army, after a long sea voyage, would be too weak and ill equipped to mount a siege. After voicing his concerns his opinions were quickly disregarded and had been ignored ever since.

When the main fleet arrived, they would find, the same as the advance party did, that Gravick had changed greatly from the maps they possessed. The fleet would have one advantage; they would make port at the Farren Isles and be able to purchase up to date maps then. This had been something the commanders had discussed long before the advance party sailed, knowing such things to be a very real possibility. That had not been an option for the advance party, not wanting to run the risk of alerting anyone to their presence.

Thoedin stood and joined the Ammelin soldiers, ready for the next in a seemingly never ending series of skirmish style raids. Their attacks were constantly taking their toll on the already too small band. They had lost three more since the night they were attacked by Commander Benellan, reducing their numbers to twenty six. They were now desperately undermanned, scarcely enough to have any real impact.

They had been moving from cover to cover each night. Now, though, it was becoming increasingly hard to find enough places close enough to the trade routes, anywhere with a secondary place of safety to retreat to, so they could attack and dissolve back into the forest before the patrols could find them.

All the men in the advance party had wanted to see the place where the village of Ammelin had once been; see what they were fighting for. It seemed now that with the great changes in the land, since the

Ammelin people had been attacked with foul magic by Ragal, it lay too far away from their objectives to visit. Many of those who had arrived would never return to the land they were fighting for, their bodies left to rot, unburied in a clearing far from any home they had ever known or dreamed of.

Theodin continually longed for the fleet to arrive. He would be glad to see his brother again, and pleased to get this war properly underway and hopefully soon over with. Then he could return home, to the family he so missed.

He was beginning to feel he had made a mistake and should never have left at all, and could only hope that day would soon come to pass.

Rubis Hornshank stood at the prow of *Avenger*, enjoying the cool spray from the ocean as the bow pounded into each wave. The ocean was calming somewhat after the most recent storm of this seemingly cursed voyage. There had been little damage and no one had been killed, but it had battered the fleet and spread them out once more.

Now they were well into the southern ocean and had the Farren Isles in sight, a dark smudge on the horizon that grew clearer and larger with each passing minute. They would make port there and re-supply with all they would need to finish the final leg of the voyage, so they would be able to march on Ragal immediately after disembarking. That way they could carry from the ships all they would need and not have to delay to forage from the land. This had two benefits; first they would find it hard to feed such a force, the time needed slowing them immensely. Second, if they were forced to raid farms the people of Ragal would be alerted to their presence and they would lose the greatest weapon they had; surprise.

Rubis wondered how his brother had fared these past months, living in a hostile land full of the Ammeliners oldest enemies. Or, after the voyage the fleet had suffered through, if the advance party ships had even made it to their destination. They could have sunk below the waves, never again to see the light of day.

Now they were in unfamiliar waters and sailing using only old maps, as had the advance party, the only benefit to the main fleet being their planned stop at the Farren Isles which the advance ships would have avoided if at all possible. Hopefully the advance ships had all made it through and would meet up with the main fleet as they sailed away from the Farren Isles.

"That is a marvellous sight," said Admiral Rolan Vellan, coming up behind Rubis.

"Aye, that it is," said Rubis, turning to face the admiral. "One I have often doubted we would ever see."

"I think every man on every ship of this fleet has shared those doubts at one time or another over this treacherous voyage," said Vellan, not voicing the concern the whole fleet shared over the fate of the advance party. "It would be hard not to. But we have come through the worst these oceans can throw at us and will soon reach our objective. This fleet may have suffered heavily but now we can once again concentrate on the reasons we started this whole mission."

"I only hope we can find somewhere remote to beach the ships while the army disembarks and unloads their supplies," said Rubis. "Once that is complete the ships can then head out to sea and split up as previously planned. At least for a few days, until it is time to complete our mission, may the gods grant us a swift victory! After that . . . well, we will all have to make our own future."

"And may that future be long and bright for us all," said Vellan, leaning on the rail and looking towards the islands they were rapidly approaching. "It is, as you say, for us to make."

"I only hope these Farren Islanders can be as discreet as they are reputed to be," said Rubis. "If word of our fleet passing through here reaches the wrong ears the whole southern continent will be on alert and we will have no hope of making land without facing some opposition and the armies of those countries being ready for us."

"I know," said Rolan Vellan. "All too well do I understand the risks; our mission could be over before we even know it."

Both men fell silent then. Soon they were close enough to see the main island's largest harbour: huge warehouses pressed close to the water followed by rows upon rows of small white houses spreading up the hillside beyond, to where they crowded up against the outer wall of what could only be described, for its size alone, as a palace. The pale stones and squat towers looked impossibly smooth from such a distance. Beyond the palace the island was covered in trees, stretching for miles towards the interior. Where the hills sloped towards the ocean the land was sectioned off into huge fields, cultivated and filled with more crops than the people of these islands could use in ten years.

An escort ship came out to meet them, the Harbour-master and a whole host of pilots on board. The escort drew up alongside *Avenger* and the Harbour-master came aboard to discuss their needs and barter a deal. He was a tall man, his dark, silver streaked hair tied back and his beard neatly trimmed.

"Gentlemen," he began, offering a small bow. "I am Maladin Carn, Harbourmaster of Port Fall. Welcome to the Farren Isles. How may we be of assistance to you?"

"I am Admiral Rolan Vellan and this is Rubis Hornshank, my navigator. "We need supplies for four weeks at sea and two weeks of dry rations for when we reach our destination. And we need maps of the eastern lands of the southern continent."

The remainder of the voyage should only take them a little under three weeks. After the problems they had experienced so far Admiral Vellan wasn't in any mood to trust the whims of the ocean and wanted to make sure they were well supplied to cope with any unforeseen delays.

"How many men and ships in your fleet?" asked Maladin.

"We have thirty two ships and forty eight hundred men."

Maladin was handed a slate slab framed in wood, and a stick of chalk by one to the pilots. He started writing on the slate, tallying up exactly how much they would need and how much it would cost. After several minutes he looked up. "How are you going to pay for this?"

Admiral Vellan produced a pouch from within his coat and dropped it onto the slate. Maladin eyed it curiously, as did Rubis, wondering what was inside. Maladin picked up the bag and eased open the drawstring. Upending the bag he tipped the contents out onto the slate. Precious gems sparkled in the sunlight in a myriad of bright colours. Maladin picked up several of them, one at a time, raising them up to catch the light of the sun, holding them close to his eye and judging their clarity and value.

Placing several of the smaller stones back in the bag he handed it back to the Admiral. "We will have you re-supplied and ready to sail before nightfall. My pilots will guide in the first ten ships immediately. The remainder will be brought in as space becomes available."

"Thank you, Harbourmaster," said Rolan. "Your assistance is greatly appreciated. As would be your discretion," he finished, holding up the bag containing the remaining stones.

"That will not be necessary," said Maladin, holding up a hand to refuse the stones. "All transactions on these islands, no matter how small or large, are conducted with the utmost secrecy. Indeed you are fortunate in the time of your arrival, for even our masters cannot control the coming and goings of other ships, and an emissary from Grandor departed just this very morning. So the passing of your fleet will be known only to us. You will need to travel swiftly though from here. Soon you will reach the waters where the fishing vessels drop net; then others will know of your presence."

As promised they were ready to sail again by nightfall. The maps they had been supplied with led to a lot of questions. Once out of sight of the Farren Isles the fleet dropped anchor and all the ships' captains and the commanders of the army met aboard *Avenger* to discuss the huge changes in the land from what the elders had told them, and how it would affect their plans and strategy.

After the meeting had been in progress for several hours a cry from the deck disturbed their deliberations. Vellan and several of the captains went up to the deck to see what the commotion was about.

Rubis was already there and greeted the Admiral with good news, long awaited by all in the fleet. "The ships of the advance party are approaching, Sir."

"That is encouraging news," said Rolan.

They all waited quietly while the ships came up alongside, one at a time, and the respective captains came aboard. All on deck greeted the new arrivals with a huge amount of uncontained joy and enthusiasm, more than a few amongst them seeing relatives for the first time in ever so long.

When the initial excitement calmed down the meeting resumed. With the three extra men, who could give insight from what they had seen with their own eyes, plans were made to take their revenge on Ragal and return the Ammelin people to the land of their birth.

Back on the Farren Isles, Tobias, Xavier and Elaira had watched the Ammelin fleet sail away.

"Now that *is* interesting," said Xavier, as the last ship dropped below the horizon. "I wonder just how interested the little empress would be in this information."

"Why would we trouble ourselves to offer any help to Shatala again?" asked Elaira. "She has already proven she is untrustworthy and unwilling to honour her debts."

"Nevertheless," said Tobias, "Chaos is ever our friend. The more these people fight amongst themselves the more they will need what we can offer. War slows down the advancement of their weaponry, especially when it is easier to get what they require from us. Their squabbling takes away the necessary time they need to utilize, to invent on their own, what we can so readily offer. If they were to advance too quickly they would need us less and less until eventually they would have no need of what we can give them at all; and that just won't do."

"So, do we tell Shatala?" asked Xavier.

There was a long pause until finally Tobias said, "Yes. We will tell her." Then added, looking at Elaira, "But I think maybe you should go this time. Her last meeting with Xavier and I will still be too fresh for her pride to overcome."

"And just why do you think it should be me who goes?"

"Because, my dear, Shatala also needs to be reminded of the debt she still owes us. That will undoubtedly require the tact and diplomacy only a woman can give. Meena is totally out of the question for a task of this sort and Tamara is already occupied with a delicate matter in Zant."

"Alright," said Elaira. "I'll do it. But I swear if she parades around in front of me half naked I'll deflate her breasts and put warts around her crotch. That will soon put an end to her stupid, immature games." Without turning to look at him she added, "And stop grinning like a lunatic Xavier, or I'll do the same to you."

"Thank you, Elaira," said Tobias. "Your assistance in this matter is greatly appreciated."

"I would like to say you are welcome," said Elaira, "but I'm not that good at lying. That girl irritates me immensely. I'm not sure I am the best person for this. I will try and keep my personal feelings under control and refrain from strangling her. I will be back shortly."

Elaira left then and headed to one of the transport circles. She heard Xavier burst out laughing as she walked away, had expected him to do so, and simply shook her head. It was amazing to her how a man of more than three thousand years could still act like an immature adolescent. Still, it was his childish wit that made him good to have as a member of the Circle, a counterpoint they needed against Meena's morose grumblings.

In Zutarinis Empress Shatala stalked through the palace, frustrated after another pointless meeting with the commanders of her army. Her personal guards, Night and Day, followed her as always, their huge and silent presence a deterrent to any would be assassins, or even any who simply wished to discuss policy. She wanted to launch an attack on Gravick as soon as possible. Feeling the need to salvage something from the fiasco of the previous summer, she wanted to use the devastation the *Draknor* had caused to help them infiltrate and conquer that infuriating country, then move north and south respectively into Tibor and Algor.

The commanders though seemed to be conspiring against her, continually thinking of reasons to delay or completely abandon her plans. Shatala wanted to have them all beheaded, and would have if Vatarin hadn't advised her that if she did so the army could rebel and seize the palace and forcefully remove her from power, as had happened three hundred years earlier. That had calmed her ire then and helped to keep it in check since.

That particular empress had been allowed to live out her days, with the army in control, until her daughter was old enough to take the throne, when she was moved to an estate in the country and never seen again. Shatala didn't want to live like that. Zutar was her empire. No one was going to take it from her, forcibly or otherwise.

Vatarin's words had struck home that she was not above reproach, her position not as secure as she had believed. The true power was with the army. Without them she could not progress with her plans. She had to keep them on side and have their respect.

Her fuming contemplation was disturbed by Vatarin rushing towards her; not running exactly but as close to it as she had ever seen from him. Shatala stopped, taking a few deep breaths to calm herself as her chancellor approached, intrigued by what could have gotten him so flustered.

Vatarin slid to a halt in front of her, offering a bow. "Farren Isles . . . Woman . . . Mage," he gasped between breaths.

Shatala took a step back, a frown of distaste marring her brow, as she looked at the sweating face of her chancellor. "Calm yourself and tell me what is so important for you to dare present yourself before me like this."

Vatarin could see anger rising in his empress and feared he was about to lose his head if he couldn't explain himself and quickly. "Forgive me, Empress, for appearing before you in such a disgraceful manner. A female mage has come from the Farren Isles with a message of some importance. I fear they seek retribution for our arrangement with them and sought you out immediately. I have shown her to the throne room to await you convenience."

Shatala turned away and walked a few paces, thinking, before looking back at Vatarin. "How do I look?" she asked.

Vatarin was stunned by her vanity but answered accordingly, "Gloriously regal, as always, Empress." He looked at her and decided she was dressed somewhat modestly; at least compared to her usual attire. She wore a pale blue dress that although it had opaque panels, and clung to her skin in a dangerously alluring way, essentially covered her well enough for people to actually have to use their imagination. "Your beauty, as always, outshines all others."

"Good," said Shatala, adding with a motion of her hand, "Lead on, Chancellor."

Shatala walked through the palace, its splendour shining all around in hues of white and gold. Her mood was momentarily lifted by Vatarin's words but soon started to sink again at the thought of meeting with the Farren Islands mage and Shatala felt some foreboding at what the arrival of a Circle mage could mean.

Maintaining a graceful air as she glided through the palace was not easy. Arriving at the throne room Shatala allowed Vatarin to open the door and announce her presence. Elaira was sitting to one side, looking bored as she lounged on a pile of cushions. Shatala herself didn't walk up to the throne but instead towards a low couch opposite Elaira, finding herself somewhat irritated that the mage didn't rise and prostrate herself. Unsure of where this meeting was heading Shatala didn't rise to the obvious insult.

Sitting down she asked, "How can I help you?" Shatala paused, looking at the woman before her, tilting her head to the side with a questioning frown. "I'm sorry but I don't know your name. I don't believe we have met before?"

"We have met, but not for several years," the mage corrected. "Empress, I am Elaira. And *I* am here to help *you*."

Shatala's frown deepened, suspicious of the Circle's intentions. "And just how do you intend to do that?"

"Are you still planning to bring the eastern lands of this continent into the protective embrace of your empire?"

"That would be desirable," agreed Shatala.

"I possess certain information that may be of some use to you."

"Go on," said Shatala, intrigued.

"War is fast approaching Gravick," Elaira explained, "from an enemy the people of Ragal thought they had defeated decades ago. A large army has travelled by sea all the way from the northernmost continent of our world, intent on crushing Ragal and bringing their people back to Gravick. This war could last for some time if they are forced to lay a siege. But whether it is long or short, suffering, disease and chaos will rule that land in the near future, causing further disruption that will turn their eyes away from Zutar and aid you greatly."

"And what do you require from me for delivering this information?" asked Shatala.

"The Circle wants nothing at all."

"Really?" asked Shatala sceptically.

"It is in the best interests of the Circle for you to know this." Elaira paused for a few moments before continuing with the second reason for her visit. "Although while I am here it would be remiss of me not to mention the debt you owe us for the aid you received last year."

"I was wondering when that would come to the fore."

"Unfortunately," said Elaira, "you made a bargain with the Circle. We require payment."

"The stated terms are repulsive to me," said Shatala with obvious distaste. "And I thought I had made it clear to your fellow Circle members that I could never meet your demands. I believed that to be the end of it."

"If you were unclear on the terms you should have clarified them before agreeing. And the Circle will never forget a debt but treat each situation as we see fit. We can not be held responsible for your ignorance in this matter."

"Ignorance!" fumed Shatala. "I was told the price would be the same as the last time you helped my country in this manner."

"And did you seek to discover what that price may have been?" asked Elaira.

"We kept no records that disclosed that information."

"Well, again, you should have sought to clarify that very issue with Tobias and Xavier," Elaira reiterated.

"I could never have children to those men, to have them sweating and grunting over me. Then after carrying each child and giving birth, to watch it taken away, never to see them again," explained Shatala, pleading to the mothering instinct she hoped Elaira possessed. "Even though they would be children I wouldn't really want it would be a hard thing for me to do. And then, after all that, my first born son from another relationship, possibly even from a marriage, would also have to be given away; that I could not bear."

"It may seem hard to you," said Elaira, having not been swayed at all by Shatala's words. "Yet you should consider yourself fortunate."

"Fortunate!" shrieked Shatala. "How do you think me fortunate?"

"When your predecessor made this same bargain," explained Elaira, "there were four men in the Circle for whom she had to bear children. And she did so willingly, honouring the bargain, as we fully expected you to do."

Shatala sat in silence for a few moments before responding. "Very well, I will agree to your terms, with one condition."

"Go on," said Elaira.

"Tobias is to be the first," explained Shatala. "I'm not sure I could face the fat man just yet."

"Now that I can understand," said Elaira, grinning broadly. "I will inform Tobias. I will leave you now, Empress. I hope the information I provided will be of some use to you."

"Oh, it certainly will be," confirmed Shatala, knowing that with this knowledge the commanders of her army could no longer resist her plans. She would have them mobilize immediately, travelling to the northern Zutaren coast, waiting there until spring before marching through the mountains and out onto the High Plains of Gravick, decimating the population there and using Lokas as a staging area for the full scale invasion she had long dreamed of.

First though she had two more pressing concerns, and as Elaira stood and bowed, Shatala also rose and accompanied the mage and Vatarin to the room from which the mage would transport herself back to the Farren Isles. The empress didn't want to wait for Vatarin to do so and return to her before the first matter that occupied her thoughts could be voiced and the necessary steps taken.

When Elaira entered the room set aside for the mages and closed the door behind her Shatala looked at her chancellor and said, "I am going to speak with the Brotherhood."

"Now?" asked Vatarin.

"Now," confirmed Shatala.

They walked through the palace side by side in silence, Night and Day only a few steps behind, until they reached the door to the Brotherhood's wing. Shatala motioned for Vatarin to open the door, "Please announce my presence."

Vatarin pulled at the door but it was locked. He soon resorted to pounding, shouting, "Open this door! Your Empress commands it!"

If any within moved to comply they weren't quick enough for Shatala's limited patience. Looking to Night and Day she commanded, "Break it down!"

There was no room in the corridor for both men to swing, so Night stepped forward, pulling the huge sword from the scabbard strapped to his back and looked to Shatala, waiting until the Empress withdrew, before attacking the door and reducing the area around the lock to splinters in short order. Night sheathed his sword and raised his leg; with one huge kick the door flew open, booming as it struck the wall behind, the noise echoing along the corridor. Night walked into the room beyond, holding the door open for Shatala to enter. Day stepped through first, unsheathing his sword and holding it ready to counter any threat.

Shatala stepped into the room just as the door on the opposite side of the room crashed open and Evarlen shouted, "What is the meaning of this outrage!" before his eyes rested on Shatala. "Forgive me Empress," he said, approaching and bowing low, Taneera, as always, present at his side. Fuming within, Evarlen struggled to contain his anger, but was sure it showed in his voice as he asked, "How can I be of assistance, Empress?"

"First you can explain to me why this door was locked?" said Shatala. "No one delays my entry to any part of this palace."

"Our Brotherhood has regular meetings to discuss ways to advance our arts for the benefit of all," explained Evarlen. "It is imperative that these meetings remain undisturbed lest valuable ideas be lost forever as creative trains of thought are disrupted."

"Well, I would suggest that in the future you place a servant at this door, to answer any requests."

"We have always commanded all of our servants to leave this wing before commencing the meeting, needing absolute certainty of uninterrupted debate," replied Evarlen, but seeing Shatala's ire rising once more he quickly continued, "Though having seen the error in this, in the future a servant will be posted at this door," he said, eyeing the wreckage that had formerly been what he referred to, "for instances such as this. Again, Empress, please forgive us. No insult was intended."

"Very well," said Shatala. "Your apology is accepted. Now, I have another question for you. You have been monitoring the lands of Gravick, Tibor and Algor, have you not?"

"Certainly, Empress, it is as you commanded. We have kept a constant watch on those lands. We still search for something of use to you and what you wish to accomplish."

"Then why have you not seen an army approaching by ship from the north, intent on destroying Ragal and its people?"

Evarlen frowned in thought before asking, "This army is not yet within sight of land, I presume?"

"That is so," agreed Shatala.

"Then that is why we have not yet detected them," Evarlen began. "Questing with the soul over water is very difficult, dangerous and chaotic. Even the best among us cannot do so easily. And sight of land must be maintained at all times lest the soul become disorientated and never be able to find its way back to the body."

"Nevertheless, the fact remains that you have failed me again."

"Empress," Evarlen began in protest but was cut off by a curt movement of one hand by Shatala.

"You *have* failed me," said Shatala, deciding on a whim, "And I have already decided what your punishment should be. You will accompany the army on the invasion of the eastern lands, using your arts to speed up the war, quell any resistance, until those lands are subjugated and once again under my control."

"You wish for *me* to go, Empress?" asked Evarlen, stunned.

"You misunderstand me," explained Shatala, a malicious smile curving her lips. "I want you all to go. You, your second, third and fourth. I want your whole damned Brotherhood gone from my palace! General Taridene will lead the army; I will inform him that you will be accompanying them and that you will have no powers of command whatsoever. You are to defer entirely to him, in all matters. You should liase with the general in the interim until the army marches, so he can tell you what he will require from your Brotherhood so all of your order will know if you need to pack any special objects or . . . potions," she finished with a slight shrug, not being able to think of a better term.

"As you command, Empress," said Taneera, speaking for the first time, seeing Evarlen was incapable of any reply that would allow him to keep his head on his shoulders.

Shatala eyed the man with a look of distaste but quickly dismissed him from her mind. "I will leave you now. You have my orders and many preparations to make."

Feeling very pleased with herself Shatala turned and swept from the room, closely followed by Vatarin and her bodyguards. Once away from the depressing darkness of the Brotherhood's wing and back into the sparkling grandeur of the palace proper, Shatala turned to Vatarin. "I need you to find three men from whom I can choose the most suitable for me. They must be young, healthy and noble. Most importantly they should be free from any obligation or prior commitment.

"In short, Chancellor, I want you to find me a husband, preferably one without a mind of his own. I don't want an ambitious man who will challenge me or dare question my decisions. I just want someone with good looks, excellent health, and of sound mind. I want to be married and pregnant within the course of the next moon."

"What of your commitment to the Circle, Empress?" asked Vatarin.

"If I am pregnant already, then the Circle will just have to wait its turn," replied Shatala with a sly smile.

"Unless you have a son," Vatarin reminded.

"For the past twenty four generations the first born children from my line have been female," explained Shatala. "And if, by some strange occurrence, I am different, they will still have to wait until my son is old enough before they can get what they want."

"As you wish, Empress," said Vatarin. "I already know of several suitable candidates."

"Get them to come to the palace this evening and I shall meet with them. For the present I need the commanders of our forces to meet me again in the war room. Now they will have no excuse to delay. The army will have to start preparations immediately. I want them to march the day after my wedding."

"When will that be?" asked Vatarin.

"Ten days should be sufficient for all that needs to be accomplished."

"Ten days," said Vatarin, thinking. "Then there is not a minute to spare, Empress. I will locate the commanders and have them report to the war room. Then I will find your selection of future husbands and have them attend the palace this evening. Will they be coming to the throne room?"

"The throne room will suffice," agreed Shatala. "I don't want to give them any opportunity to relax. It shouldn't take too long."

DISCOVERY

The previous few days had passed in a blur for Lars. The Inner City was abuzz with the news of a wedding. The keep's seamstresses were positively run off their feet with orders as the nobles all wanted to look their very best.

Lars had more than enough already to keep himself occupied and was thoroughly enjoying the serene peacefulness of the library each morning. The whole place was well ordered now and he was enjoying simply picking a selection of books that took his fancy and reading through them, gathering knowledge he may find useful in the future.

It was the third morning after Amelia had visited him and he was perusing a scroll about divination. He had found a selection of scrolls all concerning reading signs to discern the future. One even dealt with rune reading, the preferred method among his people.

The door creaking open disturbed his reading. Lars looked up to see Tam entering.

"Good morning, Highness. Congratulations on your forthcoming marriage." He held out a silver chain, from the bottom of which hung a key. "The king wished you to have this," he said, passing the key and chain over to Lars. "It is for the drawers in that desk, which I feel certain, will need to be organized as much as the rest of the library did."

"Thank you," said Lars, remembering the only scroll he had ever seen taken from that desk; that scroll had been the one which showed them how the Wind of Souls could be used to kill the *Draknor*. He guessed though that the king had no idea what was locked in that desk and kept his face neutral to hide his sudden excitement.

"The king also wondered about how you were progressing with the task he has set you."

"Arming the battlements," said Lars, aghast. He had completely forgotten all about what he had discussed with Hakon and Sarn, and the improvements they had suggested. "I have some suggestions ready now for when the king wishes to see them."

"I think he would like to see them now, Highness."

"I will go and get them," said Lars. "Should I bring them to the throne room?"

"That would be best; the king is already there. I will let him know you will be there shortly, Highness."

Tam turned and left then, but Lars waited for a moment before rushing up to his room to get the papers. Tam seemed a little tense, which was unusual. Lars wondered why until he arrived in the throne room to find the king pacing up and down in an agitated manner.

Zief turned upon seeing Lars approach. "You have them?" he asked eagerly.

"Yes, Majesty," said Lars, wondering why arming the battlements was such an urgent matter for a few bandits that even if they all joined together could never mount a serious attack against Ragal. He knew there was more to it but doubted he would find out the truth until the king was ready.

Lars was quickly ushered into the antechamber. The king took the plans and laid them out on a table, going through each in turn, muttering "Yes, yes," and, "That could work." Finally he looked up at Lars and asked, "You had help with these?"

"Some," Lars admitted. "Although I have to say that they would rather not be involved any further in this project."

"Very well," said Zief. "I will respect their wishes if at all possible." He didn't need to ask who Lars had gone to for help. Lars had been followed when he left the Inner City, and had been seen visiting the blacksmith. "I have a team of men ready to start making these weapons. They may need to call on you if they have any trouble reading the plans."

"Of course, Majesty," said Lars. "I will be ready to assist them, should they need my help."

King Zief scooped up the papers and holding them up said, "Thank you for these, Lars. If you are not needed before then I will let you know when they are ready for testing."

That seemed the only dismissal Lars was going to recieve. Tam opened the door and Lars bowed and left the room. He wished to go to the library and find out what was locked in the desk. But it was nearing midday and he needed to go and change before his horse riding lesson. When he arrived in his room lunch was already waiting for him. He quickly ate the meal, taking bites in between changing clothes, and was heading out of the keep again only a few momenst later.

This particular riding lesson was very exciting for him, one he had been eagerly awaiting for some time. They would be venturing outside the city for the first time, out across the Low Plains. Lars was quite confident now and was quickly becoming a competent rider. If all went well today, and there was absolutely no reason to think it wouldn't, this would be his last lesson. Then he would have his afternoons free to pursue other interests.

The afternoon passed too quickly for Lars and before he knew it they were riding back towards the city. The ride across the open plain had been very calming for him after spending so long in the city, and he felt some of the tension leaving him that had been building since Amelia's deceit, even though his ire was no longer directed at her. Even the plans for their wedding had not managed to completely erase his anger and he would find it rising unexpectedly, leaving him with a short temper more often than not.

Enric was pleased with Lars' riding and commented as much, receiving a wide smile from Lars. At the stables in the Inner City Lars dismounted and handed the horse to a stablehand, patting Teari affectionately. He thanked Enric sincerely, pleased that he would now be able to ride out as and when the mood took him.

When he returned to the keep Amelia was waiting in the room for him. "My mother would like to see you," she said without preamble.

Lars had been dreading this moment. He knew it would have to come one day and had honestly expected it to be sooner after the wedding was announced. He had completely forgiven Amelia for her deception, but knowing it was her mother that had persuaded Amelia to do so was still a bone of contention within him. Lars wasn't sure how he would react when he stood face to face with Lady Talia.

"Very well," he said finally, indicating for Amelia to lead the way.

Amelia looked at him and shook her head. "I think you should perhaps wash and change your clothes first. You stink of horse."

Lars nodded and closed the door. Crossing to the wash stand he poured some cold water into the bowl and removed his shirt. The wash was brisk and brief. As he was drying himself he heard Amelia rise from the chair and walk up behind him. Laying her hands on his shoulders she said, "You seem tense."

Massaging his shoulders first she worked her way down his back then caressed his chest and stomach. Reaching the waistband of his pants she didn't even pause, but unbuttoned them and reached inside. "Maybe I can do something to relieve some of that."

Their lovemaking was passionate and over quickly. Lars had to admit he did feel a lot more relaxed, although he still had a nagging doubt that would change when he came face to face with Amelia's mother. When they reached the entrance to House Corban he felt more anxious and tense than ever.

Amelia led him inside and Lars found Lady Talia and Amelia's grandmother waiting there for him. "Prince Lars," said Talia, curtseying. "Welcome to our home."

"Lady Talia," said Lars with a tight nod and tighter smile.

Talia fidgeted nervously, clearly worried by Lars' manner. "Please follow me. We have prepared some refreshment." Lady Talia led the way towards the rear of the house, and the atrium situated there.

Amelia looped arms with Lars, stepping slowly to allow some distance to build between themselves and her family. "Please be nice to my mother," she pleaded. "It would mean so much to me if you could both get along."

Lars smiled and tried his best to relax. When he sat down in the atrium, and was offered a drink, he managed to remain courteous and his voice didn't sound strained even to himself. Arrangements were slowly agreed upon and a date was set for the wedding. It would take place in six weeks, long enough for all the necessary preparations.

The conversations were civil at first and then relaxed into an almost friendly exchange, and when Lars left House Corban that evening his manner was pleasant as he said his farewells to Amelia's family.

Amelia walked outside with Lars, onto the sweeping steps that fronted the home. "Thank you for being nice to my mother. I know it couldn't have been easy for you."

"It wasn't so bad," said Lars. "When I looked at her I could see that what she did was only to protect those she loves, the same as you. It would have been unfair not to forgive her for doing that for which I already forgave you."

"Well, thank you anyway," said Amelia. She leaned forward and kissed him. "I will come and see you again tomorrow evening." She giggled girlishly. "Maybe you will need a little tension relieving?"

"Oh, I am sure tomorrow will be much too hectic for me. Some relief from the day's trials will be most welcome." He kissed her again. "I should go now." With one final kiss they parted and Lars made his way back to the keep, turning to wave to Amelia every few steps until the curve of the path took him out of sight.

Back in his room he undressed for bed, making sure to remove the strange stone the king had given him. This would be the first night of his experiment to discover if the stone was what had prevented him from visiting Melissa for so long in his dreams.

Lars already felt relaxed and sleep came quickly. As expected he soon found himself in the dome, confirming his suspicions about the stone. He would need a few more nights to be certain but all the evidence was indicating that the peculiar stone was the reason for the gaps in his visits.

He stood for a while simply watching the spirits drifting around the dome, leaving small trails of misty light in their wake. He was still finding the more he visited the dome the better he could see the souls, finding it easier to identify each. Very occasionally they appeared to be more than the pinpoints of light and actually took on some shape.

Lars could see Melissa talking with Parlen and Felman, both the new souls easily discernable by their vivid colour. He looked around and could see Seeli close to him. He walked over to her grey spirit where it hovered at the edge of the dome, just above the ground.

Crouching down close to the spirit he spoke softly. "Seeli. Seeli. I know you can hear me. I don't want all the spirits to know what I am going to tell you. I have discovered some new and important information about this dome and also believe I know its location." He had already told Melissa most of this but he suspected Seeli needed to be told personally to lift her hopes, relieving the constant state of depression the spirit existed in.

"Don't lose hope," he continued. "I am still working on finding a way to release you all from this prison." Lars felt bad saying this as he had done little recently. He vowed to himself to begin again with renewed vigour. "I *will* find a way to free you all. You will once again be able to soar freely through the skies."

Seeli still didn't say anything but a faint pulse of light from her spirit showed she had heard and understood.

"*Hello Lars,*" said Melissa from behind him.

Lars stood and turned to face Melissa. Again her spirit seemed to be taking on more substance than just the speck of light, like an aura being cast, pulsing ever so faintly, ethereal in its appearance. "Hello Melissa, how are you? Are Parlen and Felman settling in well?"

"*Yes. Both of them have accepted they have crossed over into the world of spirit and are now trapped in this dome. I have told them not to lose hope, that you are doing all you can to release us lest they sink into despair. It has been hard enough for them to adjust, especially for Parlen, him being so young when he died.*"

"I know it was hard for him, the sharp wrench from his body. Then first being imprisoned in the stone, only to be released from one prison and find he was equally as trapped." Lars paused for a few moments, looking around at the other spirits and that of Parlen. "Hopefully his stay will be short and he will never need to suffer prolonged imprisonment as you, Paolen and Seeli have had to endure. How is Paolen? He has not come up to me raving for quite some time."

"*He is as well as can be expected. The arrival of two new souls has given him a distraction from his usual musings and he spends a long time talking with them. Some days he seems quite normal.*"

"Good," said Lars. "I was just telling Seeli I am still working to free you all and I am actually starting to make some progress. It will take some time but I am confident I can find a way. I will have to go soon. Time seems to run differently in this dome compared to the world of the living. For a full night there I only seem to get a short time here. Do you know why that is?"

"I don't know," Melissa admitted. "*Perhaps it is the nature of your visits here, distorting time in some way, or at least the way you perceive it? Or maybe you are asleep longer than you think before you come here, so that although the time may seem short, it is actually the same.*"

He remained there a bit longer, chatting with Melissa about daily life in the keep. Melissa liked to try and find out as much as she could about life in the new city of Ragal; it helped to slow the creeping despair that constantly lurked in the dome, ready to overwhelm the unwary. But all too soon he had to leave.

Lars closed his eyes and opened them again to find himself in his room. Throwing aside the covers he swung his legs over the side of the bed, got up and walked over to the window. Opening one of the shutters he found the sky to still be completely dark.

He returned to bed, pulled the stone and chain from the post and looped it around his neck. As much as he liked his visits to the dome he was finding the next day he felt a little more tired, slowing his wits. He needed some good, undisturbed sleep; the stone would make sure he didn't return to the dome again for the remainder of the night.

The next morning's lesson with Bollo was more intense than was usual even from the demanding Sword-master. It started before they had even entered the fencing yard. Halfway through the warm up run Bollo stopped suddenly and swung his practice sword at Lars, nodding approvingly when Lars ducked under the blow and rolled away, coming back to his feet at a safe distance and quickly adopting a defensive stance. There was no let up in the pace all through the lesson from then on.

As they were leaving the fencing yard Bollo commented, "You have mastered the basics now, and done so sooner than I would have normally expected." He stopped suddenly and looked directly at his student. "You're good Lars, really good. You have the natural ability to become an exceptional swordsman; perhaps even a Sword-master, like me. In the morning we will start on the more advanced lessons. Only time will tell how far you can progress."

"Thank you," was all Lars could manage, a little stunned by such praise from a man who rarely commented on anything other than to berate Lars for executing a move incorrectly. It was not the first time he had praised Lars' ability but was far from normal. Bollo walked away then, leaving Lars staring after him for several seconds before following him back to the keep.

Back in his room Lars ate, washed and dressed quickly. He was eager to get down to the library and use the key Tam had given him to open the locked cupboard in the desk. He knew the desk contained one important scroll and could only guess what else he might discover hidden within.

Lars opened the door to find Tam standing there with a hand raised, ready to knock at the door. "The king requires your attendance. He is meeting with the engineers this morning to discuss the new weapons."

"Very well," said Lars. "Lead on," He left the room and followed Tam along the corridor, his eagerness for the morning suddenly deflated.

King Zief walked through the streets of the Inner City, accompanied by a guard of six loyal and trusted soldiers, all of whom would remain silent about anything they saw or overheard this day. Zief stopped outside a yard with a sign above it saying 'Farrier and Blacksmith'. Set at the rear of the yard was the forge of Sarn Plat.

The king walked across the yard and entered the open door. Stepping inside the gloomy building the heat hit him like a hammer. Resolutely he walked forward, wondering how anyone could bear to work in such heat. Two men had their backs to him, one so broad shouldered to be unmistakable as the blacksmith. The other man Zief had met the previous year.

The king coughed loudly to get their attention. Both men turned slowly, neither of them displaying any shock at their unexpected visitor. "Your Majesty," said Sarn and both men bowed. "We are honoured by your visit. How can we assist you?" He said the last in a manner that suggested he knew exactly why the king was there and had been expecting this visit for some time.

"Lars has not shared with me the names of those who helped him with the plans for the new weapons," said Zief. "As king it is imperative that I know of everything going on in my city, so it was easy enough to figure out. My engineers are having trouble with the plans and all of them have their own ideas of how best to implement the suggested improvements. In short they need your help, direction and guidance; the whole of Ragal needs your help; *I* need your help. Can we depend on you?"

"I am ready to serve," replied Sarn, who then looked to Hakon. Hakon seemed thoughtful for a few moments, then nodded.

"Good," said Zief. "My engineers are waiting for us."

Sarn looked at Hakon. "Bank the fire and I'll stow the tools." They went about their business and left the king standing, waiting impatiently. When they were finished Zief looked agitated but remained silent.

Following the king and his guards back through the city Sarn and Hakon received strange looks from the people in the streets. Many of them whispered to each other, no doubt wondering if they had been arrested and what possible crimes they could have committed for the king to come for them personally.

Lars had followed Tam to a small group of buildings at the north side of the keep, set at the point where the grounds surrounding the keep met those of House Corban. Trees hid them from view from the pathway around the Inner City and even though Lars had spotted them from the roof of the keep he hadn't sought to discover what they were for. They were too small by far to hide the crystal dome and therefore of no interest to him.

Tam led him to the largest of the buildings, one that backed right onto the outer wall. It wasn't large but had tall doors and a high roof. Stepping within, the building felt and looked as if it had not been used for a long time. It had been cleaned and new workbenches had been built against the rear wall with racking above holding an array of tools.

A group of seven men waited next to the benches and Tam quickly ran through the introductions naming them, "Ban, Harold, Grant, Paol, Fren, Rohen and Yannet," none of which were particularly distinguishable from any others living in Ragal. They stood silently for what seemed a long time until the king arrived. Lars was surprised to see Sarn and Hakon walk in behind him.

The king addressed them all without preamble. "Gentlemen, I appreciate your attendance here today and also your discretion in this matter. I would like to stop these weapons becoming public knowledge until they are ready to be positioned on the bastions and tested." Zief looked at each man in turn, his expression making it clear he would not tolerate any word of the weapons leaving the group.

"I will now share with you all some information that is known only to a privileged few and must remain secret. I am entrusting every one of you with this information, trusting you will not pass it on." Zief paused for a few seconds, giving them chance to appreciate the seriousness of what he was about to tell them.

"An old enemy we thought long defeated has returned to our lands. I don't know how many of you have heard the story of Ammelin." Gauging their expressions at the mention of that name he could see they all had. "I can see there is no need to elaborate on that point. A lot of the attacks we thought to be perpetrated by bandits has proved to be not so. Our patrols have intercepted and captured some of these raiders.

"After questioning the prisoners we discovered them to be Ammeliners, who say their village wasn't destroyed but transported to the other side of our world. We believe them to be an advance party for a main force coming across the oceans to attack Ragal. I want these new weapons perfected and in place before they arrive. I have no doubt that we could defeat their army but these weapons will save countless lives of your fellow citizens. With these new weapons we could crush them before they even reach the city walls.

"Now, gentlemen," he addressed Lars, Sarn and Hakon, "I have assembled you here today because our team of engineers," he indicated the group of seven men with a sweep of his hand, "are unable to decide between them the best way to implement the modifications you have suggested to the original designs." The last part he said with obvious disdain for the inadequacy of the team of engineers.

"I would like you to discuss the problems among yourselves," Zief continued, "and agree on a way forward so we can begin building these weapons and have them ready for testing within two weeks."

The king had set them quite a task and Sarn wanted it done with so he could return to his own forge. Quickly taking charge of the situation he got the engineers to hang the plans up on the wall and discussed them with the group one at a time, adding notes to each plan, confirming the exact form and specifications for the modifications.

Lars found the engineers to be an obstinate lot, each with their own ideas, most of which Sarn summarily overruled. Lars could see why they had not progressed at all and guessed they would have argued a whole lot more had the king not being personally overseeing the discussion. As it was the day dragged on interminably until nightfall, when candles were lit as the final notes were added. Sarn sternly told the engineers, "Stick to the new plans. You all have to be united in a common goal, not pulling in opposite directions, working against each other as you have been. If the king has to go to the trouble of calling me here again I will not be pleased."

"Thank you gentlemen," said Zief, leading Lars, Sarn and Hakon aside. "Your help here today is greatly appreciated. You have done our city a great service." He led them towards the door as he talked, Tam opening one of the huge doors as they approached. "Thank you again and I bid you a good night."

They walked out into the cool night air, the darkness enfolding them as Tam closed the door again. They could hear the king raise his voice as he addressed the engineers. "These decisions are final and I don't want to hear any more news of you all arguing like a bunch of old women over these plans. Just build these war machines and build them well; then you may redeem yourselves somewhat in my eyes. I want to see some progress and soon. The blacksmith will not be the only one displeased if we have to go through this again. Goodnight gentlemen."

Lars, Sarn and Hakon had to move away quickly into the shadows to prevent being caught listening by the king. They waited out of sight, shuffling quickly backwards as Tam opened the door and light spilled out into the darkness, until the king left the building and passed out of sight. Lars accompanied Sarn and Hakon to the Inner City gates in silence. There he bade them a goodnight and returned to the keep. He wished to return to the library and open the locked drawers and cupboard, eager to discover what secrets may be contained within. He knew though that it would be best to wait until the next morning otherwise his actions may be viewed as suspicious.

Entering his room in the keep Lars was surprised to find Lady Talia waiting within for him, sitting in a chair by the cold fireplace. The fire wasn't lit and she had a heavy blanket wrapped around her shoulders. He bowed upon seeing her and said, "Good evening, Lady. To what do I owe the pleasure of this visit?" He tried to sound polite though in truth he was suddenly apprehensive as to why she was there, suspicious of her intentions.

"I am here to make sure you are the right man for my daughter," she said, standing, letting the blanket fall away to reveal she was completely naked beneath. "I know of only one way to do that."

Lars looked Talia up and down, feeling his body reacting as he did so. She had an amazing figure, with large, nicely shaped breasts and an enticing curve to her hips. Lars felt nature overriding common sense. He walked slowly towards Talia, all too aware of the bulge in his trousers and knowing that she had noticed it too.

Stopping very close to Talia he stretched his arms around her, feeling her breasts press against his chest. Lars trembled at the feeling of that soft flesh so close.

"Are you nervous?" asked Talia, "Or just excited?"

Lars remained silent, doubting he could speak without his voice betraying him. Slowly he reached down and picked up the blanket before he lost control of himself, draping it over her shoulders as he brought his arms back up and taking a step back before he spoke.

"As beautiful as you are I love and respect your daughter too much to betray her. And this would be the greatest betrayal of all. I could never do that to Amelia; *would* never do that."

Talia breathed a sigh of what Lars assumed to be relief and pulled the blanket tightly around her shoulders. "Thank you, Lars. I hoped you would prove to be as good a man as you seem. I'm sorry to have tested you in such a vulgar way but I had to know. My daughter's future happiness means everything to me and I would not have her live in a marriage of lies as did I.

"I loved my husband although I had good reason not to. He was unfaithful to me on many occasions, and even though it is common for a lord of Ragal to have many lovers it still made me feel as though I could never be enough for him. And he promised to share his bed with no other when we married. He betrayed the sacred words we shared that day. It wasn't until several years after our marriage that I discovered one of his many shameful adulterous acts had been commited with my own mother. A daughter's relationship with her mother is a very special thing and that hurt more than you can know. I would not have my daughter suffer the same fate and rather she discover now if you would be unfaithful than to live for years in a relationship where she would not be truly happy."

Talia lowered her head and was silent for a long time, then said, "Would you please turn your back while I dress."

Lars waited in quiet contemplation while Talia dressed. Something had come to mind as he stood there and was nagging at him constantly. He wasn't sure if he wanted to know the answer but had to ask the question anyway. "Does Amelia know that you are here and what you intended to do?"

"No," Talia replied. "I would not have my daughter suffer anymore grief and anguish than absolutely necessary." Then in a sudden rush of words she asked, "Would you please help me with the laces on my dress?" and turned her back to him.

Lars had done the same for Amelia several times now and knew what he was doing but he still wasn't quick as he figited with the thin cords. The door burst open and Amelia entered, saying "I have something to tell you." The scene that greeted her quickly led her to an obvious conclusion. "I never thought you would . . ." she blurted out, then stopped suddenly.

Lars caught movement out of the corner of his eye and turned to see Talia fervently shaking her head at her daughter. He quickly drew his own conclusions and fury roared up inside him at this latest deception.

"You knew!" he hissed at Amelia, then looked back at Talia, who hung her head in what he was sure was feigned shame. He glared at Amelia, his eyes burning with rage. "You clearly expected me to throw your mother out or be in bed with her when you walked in. Is there any limit to the deceit from the both of you?"

Lars took Amelia by the arm, uncaring of the gasp of pain his tight grip caused. He placed his free hand on the door handle and looked at her. "Go home. Your mother will follow you shortly. I am too angry for rational judgement at the moment. I will decide tomorrow if I ever want to see you again."

Talia watched as her daughter was pushed out into the corridor. The door swung closed and she was alone in the room for a few seconds until the door opened again and Lars re-entered.

"Where were we, *My Lady*," said Lars, using the honorific with clear disdain. "Ah yes, I was fastening your laces. Please turn around."

Talia did so and waited nervously as Lars approached, expecting some harsh words before she, too, was thrown out. What she didn't expect was for Lars to start pulling her laces back out, before running his hands slowly down her back, then up again, gently pushing the dress over her shoulders and down off her arms so it dropped to the floor to pool around her feet.

Lars caressed the sides of her body as his hands came back up and around to cup Talia's heavy breasts. She gasped as his fingers traced circles around the erect nipples, then turned to face him, her hands quickly moving to unfasten his trousers and reach inside to find him ready for her.

Talia took control of the situation then, her greater experience and confidence taking over. Pushing Lars back towards the bed, Talia started to remove his shirt. Reaching the bed Talia whispered, "Lay down," and as Lars did so she positioned herself above him and eased herself slowly down.

If Talia hadn't been so aroused she might have noticed what Lars had seen before they had even moved to the bed. The door had opened, ever so slightly, only just enough for someone to see into the room. And now, as Talia's eyes closed in ecstasy, the door opened further and Amelia stepped into the room, remaining silent but sickened by what she saw.

Amelia stood there, as Lars had told her to, until her mother's body shook as the orgasm took her. It was then that she slammed the door. Lars, too, could hold back no longer and his seed flowed, repulsed at himself for actually taking some pleasure from the sordid situation.

Amelia stood with her back to the door, shaking with rage, waiting a few seconds for comprehension of the situation to dawn on her mother.

"How could you!" Amelia screamed. "When Lars told me to come back in after a few minutes and he would show me exactly what sort of woman you really are I expected you would bolt out of the door and I would be lacing up your dress as we went down the corridor. But you didn't even protest as he undressed you; not even a single utterance of unwillingness left your mouth. Then you took over so completely it is easy to see how much you actually wanted this to happen.

"Was that your hope, your single intention of what you had me conspire in? You wanted Lars to fail your test so you could feel what it was like to have a man inside you again." She pasued as tears flowed down her cheeks. "Why, mother? Why Lars? You could have almost any man you wanted and most of them would remain discreet. Did you just want to hurt me, to take from me the one thing good in my life?

"How could you?" Amelia screeched. She waited then, silently fuming with suppressed rage, watching her mother, hoping for some show of guilt or remorse. None of which was forthcoming. Talia hadn't even moved from atop of Lars, looking more angered at having her pleasure disturbed than contrite. "You are nothing but a scheming whore!" screamed Amelia, and stormed out of the room, slamming the door again.

Lars threw Talia aside onto the bed, quickly dressing before turning to her. "Get dressed and get out," he told her, then followed Amelia out of the room. He ran down the corridor and leapt down the stairs, taking them four or five at a time. When he reached the doors he was about to ask the guards which way she had went when one of them pointed straight ahead, towards the maze of gardens and the fencing yard. "Thank you," said Lars and raced out of the door.

Moving into the gardens he had to slow his pace to a trot, otherwise he might miss any signs of which way Amelia had went. He found her by the sound of her sobbing, following it to the grave yard where she knelt next to the mound of earth that marked her grandfather's resting place.

He walked slowly towards her, unsure what her reaction would be. Now his anger had settled down he was ashamed of what he had done, found it difficult to justify his actions even to himself. It was just that he had been so annoyed with their scheming and Talia's manipulation of her daughter that he needed to show Amelia the kind of woman her mother truly was. Talia, although she played the betrayed wife who wanted nothing but security for her family, had her own motives, and would willingly use her only daughter to get what she wanted.

Not wanting to startle Amelia, Lars spoke softly as he approached. "I am sorry that you ever had to see that. Believe me when I say that I hate myself for doing it and took no pleasure from it." Amelia had stopped crying but Lars didn't know if she was listening to him or just trying to ignore him. "If we are to have any future together, if you even want to see me again after having to witness that, I needed to break you away from your mother's control. Otherwise there could be no trust between us, ever, and our relationship would be nothing but a lie."

Lars stood there in silence for a few moments, wishing Amelia would speak, yet also grateful for the silence. "I will leave you alone now," said Lars. "I hope one day you can forgive me." Lars turned and walked away, taking slow steps away from Amelia, hoping she would call him back.

He walked away in silence, each step harder than the last, completely disgusted with himself and the whole sorry situation.

Back at the keep he walked slowly past the guards and up the stairs towards his room. When Lars opened the door he was relieved to find Talia had gone.

Amelia sat beside her grandfather's grave long after Lars had walked away, long after the tears had stopped flowing. She was angry with Lars for what he had done; angry because he hadn't taken her in his arms to comfort her instead of walking away. The longer she sat there the focus of her anger shifted and found a new home.

She had listened to what Lars had said and knew for a certainty he was correct. Her mother was nothing but a controlling, scheming, manipulative bitch. Lars had been more polite in his wording but it amounted to the same thing.

She sat at the graveside, stewing, until her anger reached an explosive level. Rising, she brushed the dirt from her dress, and walked with cold purpose towards her home. Amelia opened the door quietly and stepped inside, then slammed it shut with all her strength, listening in satisfaction as the echoes boomed down the hallway and slowly faded away.

Amelia stalked across the hallway, up the stairs and down the corridor, her feet pounding loudly on the marble, almost daring someone to come out and confront her. She was disappointed when no one did. Entering her room she slammed the door before realizing her mother was sitting on the bed, waiting for her to return. "What do you want?" hissed Amelia.

"I would like you to forgive me."

"You ask a lot," said Amelia, her voice close to a hysterical shriek. "More than I am willing to give."

"I know," said Talia, cringing under her daughter's withering stare and harsh tongue. "I do ask a lot. Still, it is important that we make amends. I love you more than anything in this world."

"Love!" cried Amelia. "I doubt you know the meaning of the word. Love to you is just a tool, something to be used, not an emotion. It is something you use to bend others to your will."

"I do love you," Talia began again. "More than you will probably ever realize. Everything I have done is with your best interests in mind."

"Including sleeping with my betrothed? I wonder, mother, how you consider that to be in my best interests."

"I admit that was a mistake," said Talia. "I was seduced by Lars and shouldn't have allowed myself to lose control of the situation."

"Seduced," said Amelia, nodding, then added, her voice heavily laden with sarcasm, "Oh, that explains everything," her anger sparking again as she continued, "Do you take me for a fool! I was out of the room for little more than a minute. Lars would have to be the greatest seducer in the world to have got you undressed and . . . *inside* you, had you not been willing."

"The fact remains that if Lars hadn't initiated it after you left the room our coupling would never have happened," said Talia, clearly believing this to be an adequate explanation that her daughter would believe.

It wasn't.

"*You* were on top of *him*, mother, or have you forgotten. It wasn't as if Lars had overpowered you and was restraining you, taking you against your will. You didn't cry out or even try to resist. You wanted him and you were all too pleased to have the opportunity.

"You have tested Lars sorely with your scheming," Amelia accused. "He was simply returning the favour. If you had just said no it would have ended then and there. Lars wanted to show me what sort of a woman he believed you truly to be, so that you could no longer manipulate me.

"Now that I know the truth about you, you will never control me again. Never! Don't worry though mother. In public I will still behave like nothing has happened. I will not tell anyone about what you have done and ruin your reputation. You should understand that I don't do this for you but for our House. You can rot in the depths of Kra's hell for all I care, but I will not allow House Corban to fall apart because you are a whore."

Amelia waited for a response from her mother but none was forthcoming. "Get out!" she screamed. "The very sight of you disgusts me."

Talia rose and left the room, leaving Amelia alone to deal with her rage. Outside the room Talia's mother was waiting, having heard the full conversation. "That went better than expected," said Senara.

"Yes, it went quite well under the circumstances," replied Talia, and together they walked to the Atrium to relax before retiring for the night.

Inside her bedroom Amelia heard the exchange and listened in silence as they walked away, stunned that her grandmother was also party to the scheming. She rubbed a hand across her stomach as a fluttering began. Her courses were late, at least by ten days. At first she hadn't realized with all the death and tragedy and at first put it down to exhaustion. But her body had already started to subtly change and she was now convinced she was pregnant. She wanted to talk to someone about it but could no longer trust her mother with such information lest she use it for her own gains. She had thought about talking with her grandmother but with what she had just heard that was no longer an option. Most of all she wanted to tell Lars but was too angry just now, and confused by raging emotions, to do so.

Lars slept fitfully that night and was awake and dressed before Bollo knocked on his door for their morning practice session. The lessons were all over now and each morning they tested each others abilities, enjoying the competition, with Bollo introducing new moves he had not yet shown his student to see how Lars would react. After he had finished that morning Lars felt drained.

When he went down to the library he felt like copying Felman and stacking some books on the desk and hiding behind them to snooze. When he saw the locked cupboard though he became enlivened somewhat, thinking on what secrets he may discover within.

Lars took the key from his pocket and placed it in the lock, turning it slowly as the mechanism clicked and turned. Inside was a thick stack of parchment. He removed the lot and placed it on the desk. Intending to skim through them all and place those he found interesting in a separate pile for further perusal, he was surprised when he found he couldn't put a single one of them aside without reading the whole document.

Even though they were fascinating one and all, Lars did manage to form two piles; one for those he wanted to read again later and those he wanted to read again straight away. Several of the latter contained magical incantations, written in the ancient language, which he had learnt something of the year before when looking for information about the *Draknor*, and had learned in greater detail over the winter as he had started his training to become the next *Fa'ku*. These new spells were magnificent and could be used as very effective weapons.

Lars decided as he read through the documents another several times, he would need to practice the spells, to see just how effective they could be. To do so in the confines of the city could be dangerous not only to the citizens, but also for Lars himself. And he suddenly worried that if it was discovered what he had learned the king may try to use him for the city's needs, to assist in the coming war with the Ammelin, holding him there against his will.

Since Lars had returned to Ragal he had sensed a side to the king that he didn't wholly trust. Zief would do anything to protect his city, which was only to be expected, but Lars suspected there was a darker edge to the king that would also use anything or anyone as he saw fit whether they were at war or not. He now wondered about Zief's intentions when he had invited him to return to Ragal and also wondered if he would ever be allowed to leave. And knowing the king was responsible for imprisoning the souls of Ragal's nobles only added to his unease.

Lars, having memorized several of the incantations, locked the documents back inside the desk cupboard. He left the library and walked out of the keep itself to the stables. He found Enric, the stable master, outside in the training ring, breaking in a new horse. Enric looked up and saw Lars walking towards him. Tying the horse to an iron ring he came over to the edge of training area.

"How can I help you, Highness?" asked Enric.

"I need a horse," replied Lars. "I feel the need to ride and enjoy the freedom of the open plains."

"Unfortunately, Highness, the Low Plain is no longer as free as it once was," said Enric. "Let me arrange a guard for your protection."

"That will not be necessary," Lars assured the stable master, wanting no one there to witness what he was about to attempt. "I am more than capable of defending myself." And with these new spells there was more truth to his words than ever before. He now knew spells that would repel attackers and others that would reduce them to ash drifting on the wind.

"As you wish, Highness; I will saddle a horse for you." Enric looked down to Lars' hip, then back up. "Should you not at least take your sword, highness?"

"Of course," replied Lars. "I shall go and arm myself while you prepare the horse."

Lars returned to the keep and raced up the stairs towards the armoury, relieved to find Bollo already there. "Hello again," said Lars. "I need to get my sword."

"Planning on a little more practice?" asked Bollo. "Or is it something a little more adventurous? A duel to the death maybe over the honour of some fair maid?" he finished with a flourish of one hand as though he was brandishing a sword and looked to Lars, a deep grin spreading across his usually sombre face.

Lars burst out laughing and Bollo instantly straightened with a mock affronted look.

"Nothing so grand I'm afraid," said Lars. "I am going riding outside the city and there is still the possibility of bandits attacking so I must go armed."

"Very prudent of you," said Bollo, retrieving Lars' sword and scabbard from the rack and handing it over to him. "Enjoy your ride."

"I will," said Lars, fastening the sword belt. "Thank you, Bollo."

Lars returned to the stables just as Enric was leading a horse out, saddled and ready for him. He was surprised to find it wasn't Teari, as he had hardly ever ridden a different horse during his lessons.

Seeing his frown Enric explained. "Teari's has an inflamed fetlock, but this old fellow is just as easy to ride and enjoys the exercise."

"Thank you," said Lars, climbing into the saddle while Enric held the reins, pleased with himself at just how confident he had become around the large animals. "I should be back in a few hours."

Lars took the reins and heeled the horse forward. He made his way out of the quiet Inner City and into the mayhem beyond. He was still a little surprised at how well he could handle the nervous animal after what felt only a short period of training and how well the horse responded to his movements.

Relieved to finally pass through the gates he waited until he was clear of the roadway before taking the horse to a canter. He realized then he had forgotten to ask the horse's name, and felt a little guilty for neglecting that fact. He liked to know the name of the beast he rode, found it would respond better to his touch or instructions if he used the name.

Lars rode for over an hour in a south westerly direction away from the keep. Having no idea how effective these spells would prove to be he wanted to be far enough away from the keep to ensure he would pose no risk to the citizens and also that no one would be able to see what he did.

Stopping on the southern side of a large copse, Lars tied the horse to a tree, making sure the reins were tight so it couldn't pull free if the magic scared it. Lars walked around the copse to the west, until he thought himself far enough out of the way to be no danger to the animal.

Lars spoke the words of the first spell he had memorized, *"Pendalir foncalis globul varkril,"* and a small ball of red light appeared above his hand. He spoke another word, *"Annule,"* and the ball of light winked out.

Lars spoke the incantation again and the ball reappeared. He could have made the orb double in size, but with having no idea just how potent a weapon it could prove to be he didn't want to risk it. He examined the ball, watching as what appeared to be hundreds of miniature internal volcanoes erupted, spewing little streamers of fire, the constant disturbances filling the orb with swirling flames.

After a few more seconds Lars pulled his arm back and with a throwing motion, as had been described as one of the uses for this weapon in the text, launched the flaming sphere. It streaked through the air like a comet, a tail of red sparks blazing behind it. It flew a lot further than Lars had expected, until it was almost out of sight. It struck the ground and exploded with a flash of light and a clap of thunder, throwing dirt high into the air. Knowing he would need better control he thought back on what he had read in the text regarding this spell.

Calling the orb of light into existence once again, Lars concentrated on a tree over one hundred paces away, keeping his gaze fixed on it as he threw the orb. The ball of light blazed straight towards his intended target and the tree disappeared in the spray of splinters, leaving the stump and much of the debris in flames, some floating as embers on the wind.

Pleased with the results of this first spell he moved onto the next. Lars prepared himself, raised his hand, and spoke the words of the next spell, *"Pendalir foncalis globul ferinze."* This time a ball of blue light appeared above his hand, the inside of which crashed about like an ocean wave breaking against a rocky shore, throwing swirling mist that billowed within the confines of the orb.

Concentrating again on the same point, where the tree still burned, he threw the sphere. This one flew through the air, leaving in its wake a stream of misty vapour.

The ball reached its destination and blew apart in a spray of water and mist, soaking the area and extinguishing the fire. Steam rose into air as all the heat was washed away by the cold water. Lars was stunned with the effects of these first two spells and couldn't wait to try the third and final one he had memorized. First though he produced another blue orb and used it to extinguish the smouldering remains of his first attempt.

Satisfied the fires he had created were no longer a danger to anyone he moved further away from his horse for the last spell, after seeing the potency of the first two. He walked to a small copse several hundred paces away and moved between the trees to its centre. Composing himself for this final spell he thought about how effective the repulsion spell would be.

Lars spoke the words, *"Sordi repeluci,"* and immediately crouched down, as the document had warned was necessary. The inrush of air above his head, pouring in to fill the vacuum created as the spell took effect, was battering and deafening. Even crouching there he could feel how effective the spell was going to be, blowing anyone close to him from their feet. He could imagine the trees around him swaying outwards, away from him as they were pounded by the wind as the magic was released.

What he saw when the spell dissipated and the wind abated left him shocked and awed. The trees closest to him were completely gone, swept away in a shredded mess. A little further away some stumps remained, the tops splintered and ruined. Ten paces from him the trees were toppled, the leaves flayed from the branches. Further out the trees remained standing but were also leafless.

The spell had decimated the copse; Lars could only imagine what it would do to anyone close enough to feel its full effect. This force could also be focused as a stream, aimed in a specific, direction, but Lars was reluctant to attempt that. The document had described it as complicated and dangerous, certain wards having to be in place lest the user be dragged along in the spell's wake.

Lars returned to his horse, relieved at finding it hadn't broken the reins and bolted with all the noise he had made, leaving him with a long walk back and some potentially difficult questions when he returned. He mounted and rode slowly back towards the keep, surprised that soldiers weren't pouring out of the gates to investigate the explosions.

When he entered the city and passed through the gates there was no undue commotion indicating that the results of his magical weavings hadn't been heard at the city. As he passed through the streets though it didn't really seem so strange; the cacophony raised in the streets by all the vendors and citizens could drown out anything, and as he passed through to the Inner City and the wall of noise behind him faded, the wind blowing in from the ocean carried with it the constant crashing of waves breaking on the rocks.

He returned the horse to the stables, thanking Enric for his assistance. Returning to the keep he first handed his sword in to the armoury, then went down to the library to review the documents. There were other smaller spells he could try at his leisure and may occasionally be needed. The few he had already tried would be the most useful to him, as far as he could tell.

Lars rolled the documents and slipped them inside the loose shirt he was wearing, before locking the now empty cupboard. He had decided as he rode back to the keep that these spells were too powerful and dangerous to let them fall into the wrong hands. Such magic needed to be strictly controlled lest it be abused by those who cared only for the power it would give them over others.

Returning to his room he put the documents into the pack he had brought with him from Lokas, hiding them at the bottom under his other possessions. He ate some of the meal that had been left for him, removed his shirt, and poured some cold water into the bowl to wash with when a knock at the door drew his attention.

Lars opened the door to find Hakon standing there.

"I have come to say goodbye," said the warrior without preamble. "I will be leaving the city early in the morning. Your father will be expecting you to return with me, but I think you will be remaining here?"

"For the time being," said Lars.

"I will inform your father about the wedding," said Hakon.

"If the wedding goes ahead," said Lars.

"Having problems?"

"Some," Lars confirmed.

"Well, if you decide not to go ahead, many villagers will be relieved to see you return to Lokas," said Hakon. "The succession of the *Fa'ku*, may Krogos hold that day far in the future, must be certain. I suppose though with your younger brother, Bane, there is now more than one option."

Lars nodded yet remained silent on that point. Since he had returned to Ragal his life and perspectives had changed in so many ways, leaving him unsure of how he felt about returning home and training to be *Fa'ku*.

Instead Lars said, "Good luck on your journey. Be careful, there are still bandits in the area."

"They shouldn't bother me," Hakon assured. "I am of no threat to them and have nothing they would want."

They shook in the forearm grasp of the warrior and Hakon departed, leaving Lars alone. Lars sat down on his bed and thought about home. Unsure of what the future would now hold for him in Ragal such thoughts made him more than a little homesick. And now that Hakon was returning to Lokas it only made him feel worse.

Lars decided he needed some pleasant company, from those who would expect nothing from him. Removing the stone from around his neck he hung it on the bedpost, finished undressing and lay down in bed. It was still fairly early in the evening but he fell asleep easily.

He awoke several hours later and was surprised that he hadn't visited the dome. Feeling restless he stood and paced around the room until he settled somewhat. Feeling he may be able to sleep again Lars returned to his bed and lay down. This time as he drifted off he found himself immediately in the dome. Several spirits moved around the dome lazily. Most hung languidly in small groups and he could now easily identify Melissa with the newest spirits. Looking around he located Seeli and was shocked to see just how dim and insubstantial her spirit had become, almost faded away completely to a faint wisp that could be dissipated by even the slightest breeze.

Lars approached Seeli, kneeling down next to her, with his back to the dome.

"Hello Seeli," he began, expecting no response and receiving just that. "I am sorry that your release is taking so long. I feel I am so close now and you should not despair. I cannot even imagine how harsh your entrapment is, but keep your hopes up. Your freedom is close at hand," he assured, hoping it wasn't a complete lie. "I just need events to occur in a necessary order and your release will be assured. And I am working constantly to ensure these events come to pass as and when I require them." This last was a lie but he had the first inkling of a plan that could achieve what he promised.

"*Thank you, Lars,*" said Seeli, her voice as weak and insubstantial as her spirit. "*I will try and remain hopeful. Even though I can sense the uncertainty in your voice I trust you and know you will do everything you can for all of us. For my part I will try to stay positive enough to prevent my spirit from fading away completely.*"

"Please do so," said Lars. "It would mean so much to me. When I free the souls here I would find it hard to bear should you not be amongst them."

Unnoticed by Lars, Melissa had drifted towards them. "*Hello Lars,*" she said as she stopped before them.

"Hello Melissa," said Lars, then, indicating with one hand towards the group of souls Melissa had just come from, asked, "How are Parlen and Felman. I hope they are coping well?"

"*They are as well as can be expected.*"

"And Paolen?" asked Lars. "The difference in his behaviour since the arrival of these new spirits is incredible."

"*Yes, they have caused a remarkable change in Paolen, dragging him back from the incessant madness that has gnawed at him for so long.*" Melissa was silent in thought for a few seconds before saying. "*I only hope he can* remain that way," adding with undisguised desire in her voice, "Or that we will all soon be free."

"As I was just saying to Seeli, I am hopeful that day will be soon," Lars explained. "I need some events to occur in a certain order to make it possible, but recent information I have discovered could make that day much sooner than I had previously thought possible," he finished, meaning the arrival of an invading army from Ammelin, seeing no point in explaining it further to Melissa, at least not until he had it firm in his own mind.

"I can only pray that will happen soon."

"I also hope that it will be soon," Lars agreed. "I should leave now. It must be near dawn. I will return when I can."

Lars left the dome then and woke back in his room. The keep was still quiet so he retrieved the stone from the bedpost, hung it around his neck and went back to sleep, hoping to get a few hours before Bollo came for him.

Hakon left Ragal with the first light of dawn. He said his farewells to Sarn and his wife, telling them they should visit Lokas someday, to which Sarn had replied he was too old for new adventures. Hakon had laughed even though he was slightly saddened that he would likely never see them again. He had enjoyed his time in Ragal but was looking forward to going back home. He had tried to concentrate on learning new skills and not think about his wife and child too much. Each day made it just that little bit harder. In recent days he had been unable to get them out of his mind, and couldn't wait to get back to them. Now as he passed through the city gates he was experiencing a feeling that was very rare indeed for a warrior from Lokas; excitement.

His journey for the first few hours of the morning was a mix of walking and running through the rolling farmlands of the Low Plains before the land became dotted with clumps of trees. Rounding one such copse he came face to face with an armed man who had his sword drawn and had clearly been waiting for him. Hakon heard movement from behind just too late to stop the dagger been pressed to his throat and the second bandit's arm wrapping around his chest.

"What are they doing?" asked Theodin as an Ammelin soldier, named Traek, came up beside him. "One man is not a legitimate target. And he is clearly not a messenger or he would be riding out. He doesn't even dress like those from Ragal."

"Leave them to it," said Traek. "Every one we kill is one less we will have to fight later." Traek walked away, leaving Theodin alone.

Looking at the man they had captured Theodin thought the soldiers might be in for a surprise. The man had the look of a hardened warrior and may put up a good fight, unlike the farmers and traders they had attacked recently.

It was for reasons like this that Theodin was now beginning to suspect the Ammelin had lied, or at the very least exaggerated, about the brutality of the people of Ragal; and they were now proving themselves to be no better. Other than the soldiers who had attacked them that one night, the people of these lands seemed like good, normal folk, trying to make a living. Attacking a lone man, especially one who by his dress was not from Ragal, only risked drawing attention to their position and for little gain.

Hakon knew that no matter what these men wanted they were not going to let him live. He needed a distraction though, and it arrived in the form of a patrol heading straight towards them. The man holding Hakon moved his knife away from his captive's throat to point towards the column.

Hakon chose this moment to strike and with a quick movement slammed his head back into the bandit's face, hearing a satisfying crunch and feeling a warm spray of blood on the back of his neck as the man's nose shattered. The man still held on and Hakon had to drive his elbows several times in quick succession into the ribs of his assailant before that grip was finally released. The second man was already raising his sword to kill Hakon. The warrior rolled to the side and drew his own sword, facing the two bandits. The one with the broken nose had recovered somewhat and snarled threats as blood ran down his face, now prepared to defend himself.

In the trees Theodin saw the soldiers coming and ran to warn the rest of the Ammelin soldiers, shouting as he burst into the clearing they were using for a camp, "We have to leave, now! Soldiers are coming."

"Where are Franno and Derkiss?" asked the captain.

"It is too late for them," replied Theodin.

There was a moment's hesitation then the captain hissed, "You heard the man. Move out!"

The clearing became a mass of movement and was quickly empty and silent as the sad remnants of the increasingly smaller advance party dispersed into the forest, away from the soldiers.

Hakon could hear the thunder of hooves coming up quickly behind him and grinned at the men. "I thought you to be bandits at first. But no, you are Ammeliners, aren't you?"

The faces looking back at him showed surprise, shock and dismay in equal amounts.

"Yes, we know who you are," Hakon continued. "And we know why you are here. But ultimately you *will* fail."

Hakon stepped forward then, while his words still had them off guard, his sword moving with deadly speed, whipping out to take the as yet uninjured soldier across the throat. Blood spurted from the severed arteries and the man sank to his knees, gurgling, drowning in his own blood. After a few seconds he collapsed to the ground, dead. The second soldier turned and ran into the trees. The patrol was close enough now and quickly ran him down, intending to take him prisoner. The man had no intention of being taken alive and drove his dagger into his own heart before the soldiers could stop him.

The captain of this patrol, an elder son of House Tremar named Mornas, moved his horse close to Hakon. "Were these the only two that attacked you?"

"They are the only two I saw," replied Hakon. "There could be more."

"You are one of the warriors from the mountains who came here last summer, are you not?"

"Yes," replied Hakon. "I returned this year to train as a blacksmith with Sarn Plat."

"Where are you heading?" asked Mornas.

"Home, to Lokas," replied Hakon.

"We will escort you to the Clendan Hills. You should be safe from these bandits once you are clear of the Low Plains."

Hakon wanted to tell them they were not bandits but he doubted King Zief would want them to know the truth. Instead he said, "Thank you. That would be greatly appreciated," knowing the king would receive a full report of the incident and draw his own conclusions.

Hakon shared a horse with one of the soldiers and reached the hills before nightfall, a journey he had expected would take him more than two days on foot.

"Thank you again, Captain," he said to Mornas. "No doubt Lars will hear of this. Could you let him know I am safe?"

"I report directly to the king," said Mornas. "It will be up to him if Prince Lars is to know of this incident or not."

"Very well," said Hakon. "I wish you a safe ride back to Ragal."

"And may the Twelve Faceted God watch over you on your journey." Mornas turned his horse and without a backward glance led the column back to Ragal.

Hakon set off into the hills while a little light still remained, now even more excited at reaching home that much sooner.

It was late that night when Captain Mornas returned to present his report at the keep. Normally any reports would wait until morning but the king required reports of any incidents immediately.

Zief was seated in the antechamber at the rear of the throne room when Tam brought the captain to him. Zief looked at Mornas as he entered the room. The captain was tall, with long dark hair that flowed freely down his back. Other than several brief conversations at feasts Zief had hardly ever spoken to the young man who now stood before him.

"Report," said the king, with a frown that made the captain uncomfortable.

As Mornas relayed the incident, in precise detail, that frown only continued to deepen. Mornas finished his report with, "Do you want me to inform Prince Lars, Majesty?"

"No, that will not be necessary," said Zief. "That his friend is safe is good enough. There is no need to unduly worry him. Thank you, Captain. You and your men have made our lands a safer place this day; dismissed."

Mornas bowed and left the room, Tam closing the door behind him.

"I need more prisoners, more answers," said Zief.

"That may be difficult, Majesty," Tam ventured, "If suicide is a new tactic they are employing to prevent capture." Tam paused for a second before adding, "Still, such tactics may be only the choice of that one man. Maybe the fear of capture and what that might hold for him was greater than the fear of death."

"I can only hope that is so," said the king. "I need more information on these Ammeliners and their intentions."

"Hopefully next time our patrols will have more luck."

King Zief lapsed into thoughtful silence and Tam moved towards the door, waiting outside in case he was needed again. The king didn't require him again that night, nor did he go to bed, sitting through the long night wondering about the army heading their way. When would they arrive? How great were their numbers? Could they pose sufficient threat to conquer his city?

There were simply too many unanswered questions.

The day had passed much the same as many others for Lars. He kept himself busy but still occasionally found his mind drifting to Hakon returning home to Lokas and wishing he was going too. Each time he found his mind wandering in that direction he thought instead about all he could learn in Ragal, information that would help his people when he did return.

Returning to his room that evening he felt exhausted and cold. He built up the fire and lay down on the bed, and was asleep moments later. He awoke several hours later to a tapping sound that had featured in the dream he had been having and it took a long time to drag his mind away and back to the waking world.

That knock was familiar to him. Several times now he had heard it and it had been followed by an apology or another betrayal. This time he expected to be the one apologizing and was prepared to do so, if necessary, in the simple hope that things could return to the same as they had once been, before all the games and deceit.

Opening the door he found Amelia standing there, as expected. Lars stood back from the door to allow her to enter, letting Amelia walk into the room and sit before the dying fire. He closed the door before he spoke.

"I'm sorry," he began, standing with his back against the door. "I know what I did the other night was unforgivable. I just wanted you to see how badly your mother was manipulating you and even if that meant losing you at least you would be free to make your own decisions in the future." He wanted to say more but words failed him and an awkward silence developed.

"I am sorry too," said Amelia, growing uncomfortable. "The way I allowed my mother to bend me to her will is what started this sorry mess. I came here tonight because I needed to tell you something; well, two things actually. First, and this is no game of my mother's; she doesn't even know I am here or what I am about to tell you."

Amelia paused, taking a deep breath. "I am pregnant," she blurted, relieved at having said it at last, then held up a hand to stall Lars' question. "Second, what kind of mother would I make if I couldn't forgive the father of my child?

"You are right," she continued, "In so many ways. What you did with my mother was both disgusting and appalling. Yet it is no worse than the manner in which we both used you to get what we wanted. And you were also correct in assuming that if you hadn't done anything so traumatic I would never have broken away from my mother's control.

"Now I am free of her, and for that I thank you. I actually feel free, in control of my own fate once more. I will act normally when my mother and I are in public together, but she knows I want nothing more to do with her.

"I came here tonight to also ask one more thing that is of great importance to me. I want to know if you still wish to marry me." Amelia paused then, anxiously awaiting a response from Lars, nervously rubbing her hands together.

Walking slowly from the door to kneel before Amelia, Lars remained silent. He took her hands in his to stop her constant fidgeting. Lars looked deep into her beautiful green eyes, searching for any signs of deception. Finding none he said, "With all my heart there is nothing in this world I would like more than to marry you."

Amelia threw her arms around his neck, sobbing as emotionally charged relief washed through her. Even after all that had happened she still loved him and if Lars had rejected her she would have been devastated; and ruined. A single pregnant lady in Ragal would not be able to marry among the Five Houses and would likely be cast out of the city.

Lars moved to sit opposite Amelia, studying her. "Will we proceed with the wedding as planned, or would you rather move it forward under the circumstances?"

"We should leave things as they are otherwise it will arouse suspicion. Already there has been too much talk with us not been together lately. We should do something tomorrow to quash any rumours, maybe a horse ride and a picnic. We would need to have several guards accompany us and I could bring servants from my House. That should be sufficient for word to spread through the Inner City and silence the gossip mongers."

"Sounds wonderful to me," said Lars. "It will be good to simply spend some time together. We can keep the guards and servants far enough away that we can talk without half of Ragal knowing what we say to each other. How you can live under the constant scrutiny of everyone around you astounds me. Everyone knows what you do, where you go, and most of what you say. It would drive me insane if I lived like this for too long."

"It is hard at times," said Amelia. "I have learnt to mostly ignore the servants and the gossips. Sometimes though it does become too much."

They shared Lars' bed that night, holding each other close. Lars spent most of the night awake, thinking about becoming a father. Amelia slept deeply, feeling safe in his embrace and content that their relationship was back on course.

The Ammelin fleet moved towards Gravick under the cover of night, landing several ships at a time on a stretch of beach they believed to be overlooked by nothing other than rocks and trees. After studying the new maps they had procured, Admiral Vellan and his captains had selected this cove as the best place to disembark. Halfway between Ragal and Grandor it offered the best chances of their landing remaining undetected.

With the moon full and low in the sky the first ships dropped anchor and all the soldiers and supplies were unloaded, each man carrying all he would need for the assault. It took many hours to unload all the ships, others coming in to take the places of those that returned to sea, sailing away from sight of the coast. There were only a handful of minutes from dawn when the army formed up and set off towards Ragal.

The last of the fleet returned to sea then, the final few ships spreading out so as not to arouse suspicion. The fleet had its own mission to accomplish, needing to reform and be in position as the army began their attack on the city.

The army would have to move from cover to cover, in the hope no one would see them early enough to alert Ragal. Little did they know but they had already been seen, by a lone soldier returning to Ragal from leave in Grandor, after attending the funeral of his father. He had arrived too late to say goodbye to his father and the fact had haunted him since. The soldier, a man named Graf Wade, waited to see which way the army was heading, then rode hard to warn his king.

As Graf had Ragal in sight, just after the sun cleared the trees, he rounded a small copse and came face to face with several men brandishing spears. The horse reared, throwing Graf to the ground. The force of the impact left the soldier dazed and winded, unable to defend himself. Spears were quickly driven into his body and as life faded, with blood bubbling on his lips, a shining figure passed between Graf and his attackers, holding out its hand. Graf's spirit left his bloody body without a backward glance, his father at his side, feeling at peace and free from pain, his important message undelivered.

If the Ammelin soldiers had thought to question Graf they would have discovered the arrival of the fleet they had waited so long for and could have moved to join up with them. Instead they returned to the Low Plains to carry on with their mission.

RELEASE

The next morning dawned over Ragal with the sun rising to full brilliance into a cloudless sky. Bollo arrived at Lars' door shortly after. Even though he had slept little Lars was alert and ready in an instant. Their practice session went well, each man pushing the other to the limits of skill and endurance, testing each other constantly throughout. They both thoroughly enjoyed the practice, followed by a cool down run around the Inner City.

Arriving back at his room Lars found Amelia still sleeping. He removed his jerkin and used it to wipe the sweat from his face and body. Sitting down in a chair he watched her; the way her hair trailed over her bare shoulder as she lay on her side, breathing slowly and softly, blissfully unaware. Lars was still awed by her beauty, and even after all their troubles considered himself lucky to be marrying her.

After a short while Amelia stirred and opened her eyes. "What are you doing?" she asked.

"Watching you," replied Lars.

"Why?" asked Amelia, sitting up, smiling radiantly.

"Because you are truly beautiful," said Lars, then added what had so preoccupied his thoughts the night before. "As I am sure our child will be. I can now only wonder just how good a parent I will make. I never expected to be a father so young, or married for that matter."

"I know that feeling," agreed Amelia, "All too well." The smile slipped from her face as she added, "But I'm determined to be a lot better parent than my mother. I will never be like her. This child will be loved," she said, rubbing a hand across her stomach, adding with obvious distaste, clearly thinking of her mother. "Though I doubt I will be perfect I will always have its best interests in mind and not use this child to get what I want."

"I know," said Lars reassuringly, understanding how hard it was for Amelia. He stood and walked across to the bed, sitting beside Amelia and holding her close, letting her relax into him for several minutes before speaking again. "Let's get dressed for our ride. I will go and tell Enric we will need horses and to arrange a guard."

News of the ride reached Tam only moments after Enric was informed. Tam had told the stable master to inform him of any such requests. Minutes later Tam was at the door to the king's private quarters, explaining the situation. "Should I stop them from riding out, Majesty? After yesterday's incident it may not be safe."

"No," said Zief. "Allow it. Seeing two young nobles riding together may prove too much of an irresistible target to those spineless scum, and draw out enough of them to capture some this time. Send a patrol with them and increase it from the usual numbers. Not so much to arouse suspicion but enough to ensure their safety."

"As you wish, Majesty," said Tam, wondering himself if it was wise to do so.

Lars was only away from the room for around twenty minutes and when he returned Amelia was still in bed, laying with her back to the door, only partially covered, yet clearly naked, showing an alluring amount of flesh that had Lars' body responding before he even reached the bed.

Sitting down next to her on the bed, Lars ran one hand up Amelia's side, reaching around her body and cupping a breast in his hand. Amelia shifted onto her back to face him and Lars ran his hand down over her stomach and down to caress her inner thigh and slowly worked his way up.

Amelia asked, stopping his progress, "Should we be doing this, with my being pregnant?"

Lars felt his eagerness slipping away. "I don't know. I thought you would know."

"I'm not sure," said Amelia "I can't ask my mother, not now. She would only find some way to twist my pregnancy to her advantage." Amelia paused for a short time in thought before deciding, "When we return from our ride I will find someone to ask. I would rather wait until we know for sure."

"Very well," said Lars, rising from the bed and crossing to the washstand, feeling a little disappointed, even though he understood, and shared Amelia's concern for their baby.

Amelia rose and came up behind Lars, hugging him from behind, pressing her breasts against his back, wrapping her arms around his waist. "We still could, if you want to?"

Temptation warred with good sense in Lars' head. Turning to face her he said, "No, you are right," while fighting back desire. "I, like you, don't know if it would be safe."

They dressed and walked together to the stables, Lars collecting his sword from the armoury as he passed. Enric had worked fast while Lars was away. A guard of twenty men was already armed and mounted, awaiting their arrival. Two horses also stood saddled and waiting for them.

"Thank you, Enric, for your swiftness," said Lars. "I hadn't expected all to be in readiness when I returned. Or so many guards," he finished, casting a glance over the mounted soldiers.

"In truth, Highness," said Enric, using the excuse Tam had given him were he to be questioned, "The guards were already assembled to go out on a scheduled patrol. They will accompany you now instead. It is important our soldiers maintain a visible deterrent in these dangerous times."

"Well, thank you anyway," said Lars, taking the reins of the horse selected for him, the same he had ridden only a few days earlier. "What is his name?"

"He is Brint," replied Enric before informing them, "The kitchen staff are preparing the lunch you requested. One of the maids should be here shortly with it." As he finished saying it a maid appeared from the keep, carrying a basket, and handed it to one of the three servants that were already mounted, ready to accompany them.

"Your organization is commendable," said Amelia, placing a foot into a stirrup and swinging herself up into the saddle.

"I am simply performing my duties, My Lady," said Enric. "But it is good to know my efforts are appreciated."

"Always, Enric," Amelia assured.

"Always," agreed Lars, pulling himself up into the saddle, adding as he looked towards Amelia, "Shall we."

"Certainly," said Amelia, heeling her horse to a walk and turning it onto the path towards the gates.

Lars nodded to Enric and nudged his horse to follow Amelia, the guard falling in behind. Lars moved his horse up alongside Amelia's and looked up at the sky. "Hopefully the weather will hold fair," he said, looking at the dark clouds building on the horizon, marring what was otherwise a clear blue vista.

"We should be back before they close in," said Amelia hopefully.

Lars looked back at those clouds, way to the west, and knew it would likely be raining in the mountains of his home. It made him think again of Hakon and feel a little sad he was not at home enjoying the pleasant coolness of the summer rain.

As they passed through the gates and out onto the Low Plains, thunder rumbled in the distance. The storm was moving in faster than they had expected it to, the wind picking up as the clouds swept across the sky.

Lars looked to Amelia. "I don't think we are going to need that lunch."

"No," agreed Amelia. Twisting in her saddle she dismissed the servants, sending them back to House Corban, before turning back to Lars. "We are going to have to ride fast to have any enjoyment from this day at all." She looked to the clouds and at the land before her. "If we ride to that copse," she said pointing far into the distance, "and circle round it, we should be back before the rain hits." With a mischievous grin she added, "Race you," and kicked her horse to a run.

Lars dug his heels in and his horse lurched to chase Amelia. The guards called out a warning to wait for them, but seeing it went unheeded cursed and followed.

Amelia's horse was a little faster than Lars' and quickly increased the lead she already had. Amelia was gripping the reins tightly and was leaning low over the horse's neck, getting as much speed as possible from her mount, enjoying the feel of the wind on her face, the simple freedom of the open plain.

The copse was a long way off and after several minutes Amelia slowed the horse to an easy canter. The easier pace was sustained from then on, allowing Lars to catch her and the guards to close in again, though they still remained at a discreet distance.

Still several hundred paces from the copse, and now a few miles from Ragal, the land dipped and passed between towering pillars of stone, the area beyond peppered with huge boulders. The path narrowed here, with only enough room for one to pass at a time.

Amelia took the lead again. She knew this area well and with a wild laugh heeled her horse to a gallop, leaving Lars surprised and slow to react. Having a considerable lead as she passed between the stones Amelia was unprepared as armed men moved from behind the ample cover the rocks provided, brandishing spears, jabbing them towards her horse.

The horse, startled, slid to a halt, hooves skidding as it tried to find purchase in the loose mix of sand and stone, rearing again as another spear was thrust towards it, the sudden unpredictable movement throwing Amelia from its back. The horse, now rider-less, moved away from those threatening spears, snorting through flared nostrils, eyes wide with fear.

Lars, seeing Amelia was in danger, dug in his heels and forced his mount to greater speed. Closing the distance quickly he drew his sword and charged amongst the bandits, batting spears aside and cutting the right arm from one, taking it above the elbow as the man tried to bring his spear around. The next he took in the throat, slicing so deep Lars almost decapitated the man, the head tilting to one side, exposing the windpipe and gushing blood as the lifeless body toppled to the ground.

The others backed away then, and after a few paces turned to flee. It took a brief moment for the thunder of hooves to permeate his senses, for Lars to realize it was the guards charging in that had the bandits fleeing. Lars sheathed his sword and turned his horse around, seeing Amelia for the first time, his heart thundering in his chest.

Leaping from his horse Lars ran to Amelia's side, their escort running down the bandits as he did so. Most were summarily hacked to death, with only seven being rounded up as prisoners.

Before Lars reached Amelia he knew she was already dead; her skull had struck a rock that was now blood spattered; her head was misshapen and her right eye bulged grotesquely, threatening to pop from its socket. Blood also ran from her nose and ears, but there was no force to it, suggesting the heart within her body no longer beat in its natural rhythm.

Lars threw himself to his knees beside her, searching for any sign of life, even though he knew it to be pointless. No life remained within her body that he could detect.

He was about to pull her into a tight embrace when the stone that still rested against her forehead caught his eye, glowing strangely from within. He would not allow her spirit to be trapped, never allow her to suffer the torment of Melissa and the others imprisoned in that accursed dome.

Pulling at the chain, Lars eased the stone away so it rested in his palm. He looked at it for a few seconds, glancing furtively at the escorting soldiers to make sure they weren't watching. With a sudden flare of anger he slammed it against the rocks, smashing it into countless shards. He was sure he saw a wisp of pink smoke rise from it, moving in the same fashion as the spirits in the dome, before it was lost in the sunlight.

Relieved at least to have saved Amelia's spirit, he slipped the chain into a pocket and then pulled her lifeless body towards him, holding her close. Raging within at the injustices of life, Lars felt like cursing the gods, but he knew it was no god who had done this and he would personally wreak his revenge on those responsible.

Laying Amelia back to the ground he gently wiped the blood from her face. Kissing her on the lips he whispered, "Goodbye my love. May Krogos take you into his mountain hold and keep you safe until we can be together again."

Lars stood then and slowly drew his sword, closing his eyes and listening as the metal hissed softly, announcing its presence to the world, letting that sound fill him and calm him from rage to cold purpose. When his eyes opened again they were void of all emotion. Turning, he looked to where the guards were tying up their prisoners ready to escort them back to the keep. Lars walked slowly towards them, in between the guards, and raised his sword, bringing the point up to rest under one prisoner's chin. He was a bald man, a little taller than Lars, with a livid red scar running down his left cheek where he had been injured in another recent engagement.

"What is your name?" asked Lars. "Where are you from?" He already knew the answer to the second question but wanted to hear it for himself.

The man replied by spitting at Lars, hitting his face below his left eye. Calmly, Lars wiped the spittle from his cheek with his left hand, holding the sword steady with his right. Lars looked back at the man, his face displaying no emotion. The prisoner grinned and said something in language Lars didn't understand. Suddenly the grin dropped from his face, as did all other expression, as Lars drove his sword up into the man's skull.

Theodin, shaking with fear of what was to become of them, had watched as the young man, clearly the highest ranking of this group, had laid the woman's body reverently to the ground, said something clearly heartfelt but indiscernible from this distance. He had looked on with foreboding as the man drew his sword and walked over to place it under the chin of Captain Fellir, as if he knew who their leader was. The feeling of foreboding turned to dread after a short exchange and the sword was driven up into the captain's brain. As the sword was pulled free, Fellir's body sank to the ground in a heap of dead meat, with no order to the limbs.

Suddenly, that sword was turned on Theodin. Knowing he was about to die he thought of his family half a world away, and of the brother who he believed was still sailing towards him. As the man approached and positioned his sword the same as with Captain Fellir, Theodin closed his eyes and prepared to die with as much dignity as he could muster.

Lars waited for the prisoner to open his eyes again and asked the questions again. "Who are you? Where are you from?"

Unlike the captain, Theodin didn't immediately understand what was said to him. He had become quite fluent at the language used by the Ammeliners, but the difference in accents, the guttural tone used in the mountains, made it difficult for him to understand.

"My name is Theodin Hornshank," he replied in heavily accented Gravician. "I am from Sarl."

"Where is Sarl?" asked Lars.

"The other side of the world," replied Theodin. "Many moons away, even on the fastest ship."

"Why would men from Sarl travel so far to attack these lands?" asked Lars rhetorically, looking at no one in particular.

Theodin answered regardless. "I am the only Sarlen here. The others are from this land, or were once."

"What do you mean by that?" asked Lars, already knowing the answer but wanting to hear it from the lips of one of those responsible for the death of Amelia.

A few of the other captives began to shout, to stop Theodin's explanation. They were quickly, and in some cases harshly, silenced by the guards.

Theodin thought to resist but the sword that had dropped ever so slightly was brought quickly back as Lars said, "Answer."

Theodin swallowed hard. "These other men are from a village called Ammelin."

Lars held up a hand to stall any further words from the prisoner. He needed no explanation from the man, only confirmation of what Zief had told him.

And he had no need to even ask why they were there; except for the man before him.

"I understand why they are here," said Lars quietly, so the guards wouldn't hear. "But why are *you* here?"

"I am a guide; a navigator for the ships that brought us here."

"Then why didn't you remain with the ships?" asked Lars. "Why fight alongside them, against people you have never met, who have never lifted a hand against you and yours?"

Theodin was slow in answering. Breathing out slowly he said, "I don't really know anymore. I have heard so much about how evil the people were who used magic to banish their enemies rather than fight with honour and meet them on the battlefield. I thought then that such people must be fought, to stop their evil spreading throughout the world, lest it one day move to infect Sarl."

"And now?" asked Lars. "Now you have been in these lands and know something of the people here? Do you still feel the same?"

"No," replied Theodin honestly. "I have seen nothing of the great evil spoken of. The people we have been terrorizing are just normal, hard working folk; farmers and such. People just like me. Even the few clashes that we have had with the soldiers have only been regular fighting. I have witnessed nothing of the foul magic I was told to expect."

"Well, Theodin," said Lars calmly, surprised to find his rage was well under control, "I have no choice but to take you all back to Ragal, where your future will be decided by the king."

Theodin hung his head, suspecting he already knew what that decision would be.

Walking the prisoners back to the keep was a slow process and night was already approaching when they passed through the gates. The expected storm had completely covered the sky hours earlier, pelting them with cold rain for the rest of the afternoon. It had now slowed to a steady drizzle as the storm moved away over the ocean.

Lars had sent a rider ahead to inform the king of Amelia's death and the capture of the prisoners. Amelia's body was wrapped in cloaks and placed over her horse, the animal faring better than the rider from the attack. More soldiers had been sent out to escort them and nobles had been included to take command so Lars could ride back ahead of them.

Lars had refused, saying they were his prisoners and he would see them back to Ragal, for the king to do with as he pleased. As the column passed through the gates they were greeted by a howling mob of Ragal's citizens, all armed with rotten fruit, vegetables and in some cases rocks. They pelted the prisoners and howled abuse, stalling their progress. If not for all the guards they would have been torn apart by the angry crowd.

More guards joined them, creating a path, and the column was escorted through to the Inner City and marched straight towards the keep. Word had also spread through the Five Houses and the noble families lined the path, many of the faces displaying open hatred for the men who had killed family and friends. Parlen's mother and father were among them.

Parlen's father, Lord Hartin, placed a hand on his sword and drew it a couple of inches from the scabbard. Seeing this Lars moved his horse forward, to meet his gaze, and gave a slight shake of his head. After a tense moment Hartin nodded and released his grip on the sword, letting it slide back into the scabbard.

Outside the keep King Zief waited with Commander Tate Benellan and Tam at his side. Zief had been on edge since he had received the news of Amelia's death and the capture of the prisoners.

Lars was surprised to find Lady Talia was not with the king ready to claw the skin from the faces of her daughter's murderers, making him wonder if she even knew of Amelia's death.

Far to the left stood a beast of a man, who Lars did not recognize, waiting with undisguised excitement as the prisoners approached.

Lars moved ahead of the column, halted before the king, dismounted and bowed. "Your Majesty, I can see you received my message. I did not see Lady Talia as we we approached." He cast a glance back then to where Amelia's body lay over her horse.

"I am sorry for your loss," Zief lied smoothly, still believing it worth the cost to finally have the lives of these Ammeliners in his hands. "Lady Talia was consumed by grief and collapsed when she was told the sad news. Her mother is caring for her." Zief cast a glance over the slumped corpse and let his gaze move to the prisoners and held it there. "You can rest assured that those responsible will suffer greatly for what they have done."

The king started walking slowly towards the horse and Amelia's body. "Ragal can ill afford to lose our precious daughters." Zief reached out a hand to Amelia's dangling hair, searching under the cloak that shrouded her face and feeling for the stone that should be resting there. Finding it missing he turned on Lars, barely containing his anger. "Where is the chain and jewel?" he asked tightly.

"It broke when she fell," Lars lied with only a slight catch in his voice that could easily be mistaken for grief. Pulling the chain from his pocket he passed it to Zief.

The king took the chain and started walking back towards Commander Benellan. Running the chain through his hands he said, "Lady Talia will be disappointed. She would have wanted this as a keepsake."

Lars knew that Zief was lying but couldn't detect any hint of it in his voice and wondered how often someone had to lie to become so practiced at it.

King Zief motioned to the bald man to Lars' left, introducing him as they approached. "This is Tauros. He is the Dungeon-master here in Ragal, though he seldom has anyone in the cells."

"I didn't realize Ragal even had a dungeon," said Lars. He had only first heard of a dungeon several days earlier while perusing a book in the library otherwise the word would have meant nothing to him.

"It is deep beneath the keep," Zief explained, "Out of sight and out of mind."

Lars wondered just how true that statement was also, and just how many poor souls had been left 'out of mind' in the cells until they had died. "I would like to see this dungeon."

"There will be plenty of time for that later," said Zief. "Tauros will be too busy this evening processing these prisoners to have any interruptions. And I will have more than that to show you tomorrow," carrying on to explain at Lars' curious glance, "The new weapons are ready and will be moved to the bastions and assembled this very night whilst the city sleeps, ready for testing in the morning."

"That will be something to see."

"Yes, it certainly will," agreed Zief. "Now, you should go and rest while I deal with the prisoners."

"Very well, Your Majesty," said Lars, wondering what this *processing* would involve. "I leave them in your hands." Lars bowed again and walked away.

Intending to take Amelia's body to House Corban and return their horses to the stables he turned and found Enric already there and taking the task in hand. Several nobles had come forward, reverently eased Amelia's body from the horse and were carrying her to her home. Lars nodded to Enric, grateful for the Stable-master's aid, and headed for his room where he intended to order a hot bath and a bottle of wine brought to his room. His mind was too numb to think of anything more.

As he walked away Lars heard the king order, "Tauros. Take them down!"

Entering the keep Lars trudged up the stairs, weary beyond belief. At the top he found Bollo waiting for him. The Sword-master had no words of sympathy for Lars, knowing nothing he said would make him feel better. Instead he offered, "I'll clean and oil your blade."

Lars unbuckled his sword belt and handed it over to Bollo. With a tight nod of appreciation he continued on to his room. Finding it cold and empty he sat before the unlit fire and let tears flow down his face.

As Lars had walked away Zief had ordered the nobles to disperse and sent Tam to find out how Lady Talia was faring. Commander Benellan accompanied the king to the dungeons to see their new prisoners. Down the stairs, what passed for the Dungeon-master's office was crowded with guards and their prisoners. Tauros was taking them one at a time and placing them in separate cells, before dismissing the guard who accompanied each.

Seeing the king arrive Tauros ordered the guards to move aside and took the next prisoner to a cell. Soon all six prisoners were secured and all the guards dismissed, leaving Zief, Tate and Tauros alone with their new victims.

Little over an hour later, while he sat looking at nothing, a knock at his door brought Lars away from his daze. He still hadn't ordered a bath poured and his wet clothes were starting smell. It took several more knocks before he actually got up, wiped a dirty hand over his tear streaked face, and opened the door. Tam stood there, an unreadable expression on his face.

"The king bids you meet him in the dungeons," said Tam. "He believes you will be interested in what he plans for the prisoners." Tam looked as though he didn't share Zief's belief.

Having never been in the dungeons Lars found himself actually curious as to what they were like, pleased to have any distraction that would lead his thoughts away from Amelia's death.

Lars followed Tam through the keep and out to the dungeon entrance. Taking a lantern from the wall there Tam led Lars down the dark steps. Tauros stood at the bottom of the stairs, clearly waiting for Tam to return with undisguised impatience. He had his keys in his hand, one key already separated from the rest. As Lars stepped off the last stair Tauros thrust the key into the lock and turned, the well oiled tumblers within turning silently, the hinges similarly quiet as the door was pushed open.

Tauros let Lars and Tam precede him through the door, locking it again once they were inside, before leading them down the corridor to the room at the end.

As Lars walked into the room he was instantly disgusted to see the instruments of torture, found their very existence nauseating. This feeling only increased when his eyes drifted to the two men stretched out on the racks. He was relieved to see neither of them was Theodin, even though the Sarlen was as responsible as the other prisoners. All he could think of was Hakon, and the horrific injuries he had suffered at the hands of men who would use such tools to wring the answers from those unfortunate enough to fall into their hands.

His eyes met those of the king and he could see the malicious eagerness there.

"I have no interest in seeing these men in pain," said Lars. "And I would rather they remain unharmed."

"Well," Zief began, his voice filled with scorn, "while I respect your delicate sensibilities, I need answers. If these prisoners won't talk willingly then I will force them to do so, and have no qualms whatsoever about the methods I need to employ to get the answers I need. Of course, you may go. I don't wish to stress you unduly. I just thought you would wish to witness justice meted out on those who took what was precious to you."

"There is no justice in torture, only pain," said Lars, before turning and leaving the room, heading down the corridor and waiting for Tauros to come and open the door. It took several minutes, while Lars stood, looking at the jail and feeling the despair of the prisoners.

He was glad to leave when the door was opened but didn't feel the growing claustrophobia ease until he was back in the open air. Tam followed him up the steps and asked, "Is there anything I can get for you, Highness."

"A hot bath and some strong drink would be nice, Tam. I will be back at my room within the hour," said Lars as he walked away into the night. He had to walk twice around the Inner City before he felt relaxed enough to return to the keep.

In the dungeons, unperturbed by Lars' reluctance or his wishes, Zief tortured the two prisoners, receiving few of the answers he so desperately wanted. He stopped short of anything that would kill them, wanting to keep the prisoners alive so a sense of despair could settle in overnight while in their cells. He would question them again the next day, when they would be more susceptible to his methods.

If not, they would die.

It was well into the night, not long after he had finally laid down to sleep, when Tam was disturbed from his rest, to meet with a ramshackle group of farmers, who had arrived at the Inner City gates in the early hours of the morning, demanding to see the king. When Tam heard what they had to say he ordered a soldier to take them into the keep.

Tam instantly went to notify the king, who had also retired for what remained of the night. "The Ammelin army has landed, Majesty. Some farmers are here with news for you." The king quickly made himself ready to receive his citizens and Tam led him to the Throne Room, where petitioners would normally meet with the king to receive judgement.

As the king entered the farmers all knelt nervously, many never having being this close to their ruler before. The king walked forward and sat on the throne. He was anxious to hear what these people had to say, wondering if he could glean any important scraps of information. Sitting on the throne he commanded, "Rise and speak."

They all started jabbering at once, each one starting at different places. "Stop!" shouted Zief to cease the unintelligible racket. He singled out one man, who seemed a little more composed than the others. Pointing at the man Zief asked, "What is your name?"

The man fidgeted nervously before replying. "Samil Grewd, Your Majesty."

"Do you know all the details of this?" asked Zief.

"I think so, Your Majesty."

"Then would you alone please recount it for me. All you others listen carefully and if you know any other information, no matter how trivial, I will hear it at the end." Looking at Samil the King said, "Begin."

"Shortly after dawn a soldier arrived at my farm and said a fleet of ships had landed in Brant Cove. An army had disembarked and is heading towards Ragal."

Samil paused as the king looked towards Tam, clearly wondering about any news of this mystery soldier. Tam shrugged in return, knowing nothing of this. "Continue," said Zief.

"He ordered us," Samil began again, "to pack up and leave and head for the safety of these walls. On the way here we met with others, who the soldier had passed and warned. Then, when we were close to Ragal we came upon a mess of blood on the ground. A few of us followed the blood trail to where a body had been dragged into the bushes and left face down in the dirt. We turned the body over and found it to be that of the soldier who had warned us.

"We didn't know if he had been seen and intercepted, or fallen prey to bandits, but we didn't see anyone from the army he spoke of. We made haste for Ragal then to warn you, Your Majesty."

"Did this soldier give his name?" asked Zief.

"Not to me, Your Majesty."

"Did he give his name to anyone?" asked Zief of the others.

Most just shook their heads but one man finally stepped forward. He was short and hunched, dressed in little better than rags with hair looking like dirty straw and his face a mass of pockmarks from some childhood disease. When he spoke he displayed very few teeth. "He didn't give his name but my wife recognized him as her second cousin's brother in laws son, Graf Wade."

Looking over the assembled mass Zief said, "Thank you for delivering this information to me so swiftly, you all have my gratitude." Turning to Tam he ordered, "Escort these people to the Inner City gates and find Commander Benellan. Tell him of this army's imminent arrival and of the soldier's death. Then come to my chambers. I must don my armour. There will be no rest for any of us this night. And tomorrow could be a very day long indeed. With such a large army they will plan to lay a siege. It may be quite some time before any of us see a good nights sleep again."

With the first light of dawn Admiral Vellan led the fleet towards the keep, which even now could be seen with the naked eye. On the deck the cannons were being prepared, cleaned and loaded, ready to unleash a deadly hail of fire driven iron at the admiral's command.

Next to him stood Rubis Hornshank, looking at the mass of solid stone that grew larger every minute as they closed the distance. "Can such a thing be destroyed?" he wondered aloud, the question little more than a whisper.

"If it is built by men then men can destroy it," said Vellan. "Have no doubts, Rubis, this will be our finest hour. We were assured by the Farren Islanders that Ragal has no protection on the ocean side of the keep other than its thick stone wall. All they could do is use fire arrows and we will be far out of range for them to be a threat.

"They have nothing that can counter our attack. Today we will defeat our enemy and finally have the revenge my people have so long wished for. Today we will defeat evil. Today we shall reclaim the land that is rightfully ours."

If all that the admiral spoke of came to pass it would be a busy day indeed and one to rejoice; for Rubis it would mean he could finally go home. But the navigator still had his doubts. An awful sense of foreboding was threatening to overwhelm him which grew with each passing moment as did the keep and the high solid stone outer wall. Rubis felt that whatever happened today there would be little glory involved, for any of them.

Looking across at Admiral Vellan, Rubis could see he was brimming with excitement as he inspected one of the cannons, and wondered if the man had ever seen the destruction and merciless slaughter those guns could cause.

Amazed that Vellan believed they would meet no resistance from the keep on this side, Rubis decided it might be for the best if this fleet was destroyed to teach the man some measure of humility; if he survived.

If any of them did?

15

WAR

Lars rose the next morning unsure if he had slept at all. The whole night had been filled with visions of Amelia falling from her horse until at one point he remembered that she had been pregnant, and he had not only lost his future wife, but also their child. He imagined it would have been a boy who he could teach to hunt and use weapons or a girl Amelia could have taught to be a proper lady and would greet him each day with a smile and hug.

With a heavy heart he rose and opened the shutters, surprised to find the sky already light and probably only moments away from sunrise. Recently this had been the time when Bollo would come for him to start their morning practice sessions. Dressing quickly Lars picked up the wooden practice sword that stood in the corner behind the door.

Leaving the room he realized he had no idea where Bollo slept. A guard was always present at the stairs up to the Royal Apartments and Lars had to ask him where Bollo's room was. The guard point behind Lars, to the corridor on the other side of the grand balcony, "Across the balcony, Higness. It is the third door on the left. Lars walked quietly to the room door, surprised Bollo stayed in the less lavish side of the keep. But the plain corridor somehow suited the austere Sword-master. At the room Lars lifted the latch and slowly eased open the door, surprised to find it unlocked.

In the darkness he could barely make out the form of Bollo in the bed, breathing deeply. Lars raised the wooden sword and let it fall to the floor, where it clattered loudly. A stir from the bed and the blankets were cast aside. Bollo stood, fully dressed with his sword at his side and Lars' in his hand.

"I hoped you would come," he said, holding out Lars' sword. "But I thought it best to leave the choice to you this morning."

Lars' took the sword and belted it around his waist, his only response to Bollo's words a tight nod.

They walked out of the keep together and ran through their usual warm up, setting aside their practice swords as they entered the yard. Facing each other in the fencing yard they drew steel for the first time and bowed to each other as masters, with the sword blade straight in front of the face.

They paced around for a little while, making experimental thrusts with no real commitment, before Lars made his move, Bollo instantly bringing his own sword up to block. As their blades met there was no clanging of steel to be heard. Instead a thunderous explosion ripped through the air and the ground shock below their feet. This was closely followed by several more repetitions, deafening roars as the cannonballs struck, several of the iron projectiles whistling over their heads to land in the Outer City.

When the first volley ceased Lars and Bollo could see dust and smoke rising from the far side of the keep.

Both men sheathed their blades, rushed to the keep and up onto the roof. A large group of nobles had already gathered there, including the king, Commander Benellan and Tam. More followed behind, to see what calamity was befalling their city. Clouds of smoke erupted from ships several hundred yards out to sea and the next wave of the bombardment struck the keep, showering those on the roof with shards of rock.

One small piece of stone struck a minor noble, a guest in the keep, in the eye, piercing through to his brain, killing him instantly. Everyone else backed up several steps as servants rushed to help the victim, shaking theirs heads after checking for signs of life.

"Cannons," said Lars, unsure if anyone had heard him his ears were ringing so badly. Grabbing Bollo's arm he shouted, "I have to speak to the king!"

As Lars approached King Zief a numb feeling spread through his left arm and he looked down to find a shard of rock embedded there, just above the elbow. He pulled the shard out and worked his arm. It felt strange but he still had a full range of movement. He continued on and forced his way through the assembled mass to the king, who was loudly issuing orders to those nearest to him. Men rushed off, allowing Lars a clear path for the final few strides.

Lars stopped before Zief and shouted, "Cannons! They are using cannons!"

"So I suspected," replied Zief, and Lars was surprised to see the king was also bleeding from a cut above his right eye. "Do you have any ideas how we can counter this attack? By the time we moved our cannons up to here the keep will be a pile of rubble."

Just then, at a break in the bombardment, great horns sounded and all turned to the landward side to see an army moving onto the open plain and heading towards the keep. The horns sounded again but were drowned out prematurely, as the cannons roared once more.

"To the bastions!" roared Zief to the nobles. "Prepare to defend the walls!" Then he turned to Tate Benellan. "Get the prisoners! You know what to do!"

Suddenly the roof was clear of all but Zief, Tam, Lars and Bollo.

"Any suggestions?" asked Zief, in a voice mingled with rage and despair.

Lars thought about the orbs he could create with his magic and knew he had an answer to those guns. Just as he was about to voice it though a new idea blossomed in his mind.

"I know a way," he said, looking at the king, his face alight with hope. "You have souls here, just like we had in the caverns in Lokas."

"I don't know what you mean," Zief lied fluidly.

"Now is not the time to deny what I already know to be true."

"How do you know?" asked Zief, clearly angered that someone knew his secret.

"Now is not the time for explanations either," said Lars as another cannonball struck and they all had to crouch to escape being torn to shreds by flying debris. "Now is the time to act. I could use those souls like I did in the mountains, this time destroying those ships."

The cannons roared again, forcing his hand, and Zief shouted, "What do you need me to do?"

"Is there a way I can access the chamber where the souls are kept from up here on the roof, so I can direct the souls, to use them and still keep those ships in sight?"

"There is a keystone on this roof," said Zief. "The chain attached to the bottom of the keystone connects directly to a mechanism at the top of the chamber below."

"Where?" asked Lars.

Zief hesitated, clearly not pleased about any of this, yet believing he had no other option. "I will show you," he said and led Lars across the roof to an area that looked, at first glance, no different to any other. Behind him was the stout tower where the flag poles were mounted, and in front of him was a short section of roof before the outer wall met the ocean. He could see nothing that might be this keystone.

"Where is it?" Lars shouted as another cannonball struck the keep and the roof heaved beneath their feet. "We can't delay any longer."

Zief turned and pointed to the flags. "It is up there, in front of the centre pole."

Lars didn't waste any time and ran up the stairs to the centre pole. The keystone was easy to identify; it was hexagonal with a metal loop on top. Lars pulled the stone up, having to work it side to side so it would come free. After a short length of chain was revealed he felt the resistance of the mechanism Zief had spoken of. He pulled hard until it would come no further. Hoping that was enough to open the chamber below he cast the stone aside and stood above the hole, ready to receive and guide the souls.

Momentarily he thought about the year before when he had to take over as Channeler after his grandfather had collapsed. Then three of them had been involved in guiding the souls. Now it was all down to him and he felt a moment of doubt which he quickly pushed aside.

The first soul came as a jolt and he released an involuntary gasp, quickly closing his eyes, remembering that the souls would use his eyes to be guided. A voice entered his head, anguish clear in the panicked tones. *"Where am I? I thought I was heading to freedom?"*

Lars recognized the voice instantly. "All is well, Melissa. It is I, Lars. I have you and will release you soon. I just need to gather all the souls and release you at once. How many souls are there now?"

"One thousand and five souls, including myself," said Melissa.

"This shouldn't take long," said Lars, feeling a multitude of souls joining Melissa, who quickly soothed them.

It took no more than a few moments for all the souls to come to him and it was a struggle to hold them all at once. He was about to speak the ritual words when another doubt entered his mind. He needed to ask Melissa what she thought before he continued.

"The king needs me to use you as a weapon to destroy ships that are attacking the keep." Another wave of cannonballs struck as if to emphasize the importance of what he was about to do. "It is how I secured your release. But I still don't know for certain if your souls would be hurt at all with you being released in so violent a way."

"We will be unharmed," said Melissa. "But thank you for your concern."

"Very well," said Lars, and prepared to release them. He felt a moment of panic, realizing he couldn't remember the words of power to send them on their way. He calmed himself and thought back to the year before, when he had needed to take over from his grandfather. In an instant he had the words, opened his eyes, raised his arms to guide the souls towards the ships, and spoke the words of power, "Profundi sartarlan previ."

The souls erupted from him in a stream of white fire that shot out over the roof of the keep and across the ocean, where the stream broke up and dissipated harmlessly. Lars was worried for an instant, wondering if the souls had been hurt but he could see their wispy lights moving around, enjoying their freedom.

As the last soul left him, he heard the voice of the mad spirit, Paolen, say, "I always knew you could do it boy. I knew that you would be the one to release us." The spirit then joined the stream only to harmlessly break away from it like all the others. The stream sputtered and died, leaving Lars confused.

"What happened!" screamed Zief, racing up the steps to where Lars stood, grabbing him by the shirt and shaking him.

"I don't know!" shouted Lars, forcing himself away from the king's grip. "Maybe these enemies can repel the attack in some way? Or perhaps it just doesn't work over water?"

"You have failed me!" shouted Zief. "Now the keep is doomed thanks to your incompetence."

Lars was about to defend himself when another barrage of cannonballs struck the keep, throwing them both from their feet, the tower on which they stood was hit directly and substancially weakened. Lars recovered first and ran down the stairs to the edge of the roof, one hand raised and speaking the words, *"Pendalir foncalis globul varkril."*

A ball of red light appeared above his hand, and wasting no time he hurled it towards one of the ships with all the force he could muster, speaking the words again, forming another ball before the first one struck. And strike it did, in the centre of the deck, blasting apart wood and flesh, toppling the main mast. The ship was badly damaged but remained afloat

The next he aimed at the water line of the same ship, the following explosion ripping open a huge hole in the side that quickly filled with water, making the vessel list badly. He moved to the next ship in line, again aiming for the water line, then the next and the next, until twelve of them were sinking.

Lars stopped for a rest, suddenly feeling drained, his legs barely able to support him after drawing and releasing so much power. Zief came up beside him then. "What was that?"

"Just an ancient spell," said Lars, looking towards the sinking ships as he added, "A very effective one, so it seems."

"Then you didn't need to release the souls at all?" Zief accused.

"It seems not," Lars agreed, and left it at that, locking his gaze with that of the king, not looking away until the king did.

Looking at the remaining ships that were even now moving into position Zief asked, "Are you up the finishing this?"

Lars took a deep breath and nodded, raising his hands as he spoke the words to form another ball of fire. Zief moved quickly back, away from the dangerous magic, which brought a small tired smile to Lars face. He launched the orb, then another, continuing until he systematically disabled all the ships that had come to attack the keep. Five ships turned to flee near the end, but their retreat gained them no mercy. Lars didn't want to risk them returning and all five had the red orbs aimed and flying towards them, striking the sterns.

Admiral Rolan Vellan lay next to the stern rail of *Avenger*, dying, blood gushing from the ragged stumps where his legs had been. He would have screamed in rage and frustration had his throat not been burned raw from the fire and smoke that had engulfed the deck as the first of the fireballs had reduced the mainmast to a deadly rain of splintered wood. He didn't know if it had been a lucky guess that the flag ship had been struck first or if whoever worked that magic had known which ship commanded the fleet.

Rubis Hornshank crawled across the deck to kneel beside the admiral. "The ship is going down by the bow. I need to get you off now."

"Rubis, save yourself," said Vellan, blood flecking his lips. "Save yourself while you still can. I have failed in my mission; I have failed you, my people and my ancestors. I have failed you all. I am dying and I shall go down with my ship."

For a moment Rubis thought this to be more of the sentimental nonsense that was so often displayed by the admiral, but one glance at the spreading pool of blood assured him the words were true. Rubis nodded, a grim expression on his face. "It has being an honour to serve at your side," Rubis lied, having never developed a fondness for the man, or even a grudging form of respect or admiration.

"The honour is all mine, Rubis," said Vellan with all sincerity, the last words he ever spoke, leaving Rubis feeling a little guilty for his own low opinions. But Rubis had no time to lose. Water was quickly devouring the ship. The navigator cast his coat and boots aside and jumped into the ocean. After taking a brief moment to orientate himself the navigator began swimming towards the distant shore, having to work his way through wreckage and the dead.

So many dead, whose pale faces he knew would haunt him, if he lived long enough for them to do so.

Lars stood watching the smoke drift across the water, hiding much of what he had wrought. He rested against the crenelated outer wall, feeling suddenly sick, wondering just how many lives he had just ended with so little effort or thought.

Most of this part of the battle had been one sided, with very few cannonballs been fired in answer to the fury he had unleashed. Now all the ships that still remained afloat, only eight in total, looked as though they would not do so for much longer. Crews were abandoning them, the highest ranking among them launching skiffs and rowing for the shore, with the common sailors left to swim, and most likely drown or be bashed to death against the rocks.

Thoroughly exhausted, Lars sank to his knees, watching as the smoke cleared to reveal the full destruction he had unleashed. He thought of the prisoner, Theodin of Sarl, and wondered how many of those he had just killed were just like him, innocent men deceived into aiding these Ammeliners with their revenge.

For the first time he truly wished he had never returned to Ragal. Then he wouldn't have to feel the heartache of losing Amelia. He wouldn't have to feel the anguish that was now creeping up on him for slaughtering so many. And he knew it was far from over.

The horns blared again, pulling him from his morose thoughts. Dragging himself to his feet with the aid of a shattered merlon, Lars turned to appraise the next threat. He could see Zief and Tam standing at the landward side of the keep roof, no longer interested in the ships now they posed no further threat.

Lars moved up to stand beside the king, looking out on the approaching army. The city was a seething mass of activity. Looking to the bastions he could see the crews there preparing and loading the new weapons. A first volley was fired, all the new weapons working perfectly as far as Lars could see. The great javelins of the ballistae fell short. The cannonballs and rocks from the trebuchet, although short, were only just so and struck the ground, peppering holes in the front lines of the approaching army as sharp rock and metal fragments tore through armour and flesh.

Movement below caught his attention. The six prisoners were being marched out from the dungeons, trekking a slow route through the Inner City, and even slower through the Outer City where they were heckled continually. The group split up in the city, out of sight from those on the keep's roof.

The next volley was fired with no ballistae this time, the cannon fire and rocks landing right amongst the front ranks. Another volley was fired as soon as the weapons could be reloaded, then a halt was called and Lars wondered what was happening, why they would cease their bombardment and risk losing the clear advantage handed to them by these new weapons.

The prisoners were marched up to the bastions, three to each side, facing their fellow country men. Ropes were secured to metal rings on top of the bastions, the prisoners forced to stand on the wall with other ends of the ropes wrapped around their necks. As one the prisoners were pushed from the battlements, their necks snapping as the ropes pulled taught, one head completely detaching, the rope whipping back up, throwing the head in a high arc towards the enemy as the body slammed to the ground below.

The soldiers on the bastions cheered loudly, roaring insults to the Ammelin army. The weapons fired again, this time including the ballistae, the huge javelins striking solidly among the enemy, impaling several on each one.

"Why do they keep coming?" asked Lars of no one in particular, feeling despair creeping up on him with so much unnecessary death. "They are being slaughtered. Without support from the ships their cause is hopeless."

"They probably don't know yet," Zief replied. "They will be thinking our forces and efforts are split, trying to repel an attack on two simultaneous fronts."

Many fell to the deadly barrages as they continued to watch, quickly reducing the enemy's number by at least a quarter. Soon the enemy army was within range of the archers and, although shields were raised and armour protected them, some arrows found their way through to fell a soldier or two with each volley. Now, though, as each rain of arrows ended, the enemy returned fire with their own archers, finally spilling the blood of those at whom their hatred and will for revenge was directed.

The new weapons fell silent as the attackers moved in too close for even the ballistae. The Ammeliners marched on relentless, steadfastly sticking to their plan. Zief had expected them to try and lay a siege, cut off their supplies. It seemed now they were intent on ending this war quickly, throwing away lives if necessary to accomplish their goals.

Even with the numbers that had already fallen to Zief's new weapons, the attacking army was huge. They could afford to take heavy losses to finish it quickly. As they drew near Lars started to doubt whether the soldiers of Ragal could defend their city against such large numbers.

The archers continued to fire and crossbows joined them, picking off a few with each volley, taking their toll until the army reached the walls.

Swords were drawn as ladders were raised, the soldiers of Ragal interspersing themselves between their own archers. Others, armed but with weapons not held ready, threw rocks and poured hot oil, quickly followed by burning brands, onto the men crowded below. The screams were horrific and the stench almost unbearable as many of the Ammelin soldiers were burnt to death in the inferno that erupted along the base of Ragal's walls; and still more came.

More ladders were raised and cast down, only to be raised again. The arrows and crossbow bolts fired from below were starting take their toll on the Ragalan soildiers, creating gaps in the defensive line, allowing the first of the Ammeliners to make some progress up the ladders.

Enemy soldiers fought their way up, one rung at a time, repelling projectiles, spears and swords, gradually cresting both bastions and the length of the wall between them. The whole defensive line was a scene of unbridled carnage, where blood flowed freely, coating the battlements in its sticky redness as soldiers fought, some losing weapons and grasping whatever came to hand, some using just their hands to strangle or gouge out eyes, grabbing at open wounds to tear the skin further, speeding up the blood loss. Any advantage, no matter how small, was used in the most brutal ways imaginable.

Many of the enemy soldiers died before they got up the ladders, hacked at feverishly by the defenders, blood spraying into the air, creating a red mist. Where the blood finally settled the ground was turned to a gooey mud that sucked at the Ammeliners boots, hampering their efforts.

It was slaughter, plain and simple. Still the enemy pressed on, gaining ground, each pace and every rung on the ladders, paid for with blood.

More Ragalan soldiers raced onto the bastions and along the wall, fighting the Ammeliners back, suffering heavy losses themselves to do so. Lars watched, knowing Bollo would be down there somewhere, no doubt in the thick of it, and suddenly felt the urge to join him.

Without warning Lars drew his sword, Zief immediately stepping back and placing a hand on the hilt of his own weapon. Lars held up a hand and moved away, running through a series of warm up moves, seeing if he had the strength to join the battle. He still felt tired after wielding so much magic, but he had trained for this and knew from his many lessons with Bollo that he had pushed himself way beyond the point that he was now at.

He saluted Zief with his sword, sheathed it, and ran to the steps and down into the keep, emerging moments later from the grand doors at the front of the keep, running through the Inner City and towards the battle.

The noise in the Outer City was an indiscernible roar. Cry's for reinforcements mingled with those of panic, dismay, and disbelief. To Lars the number of reinforcements, drawn from other posts, were woefully inadequate to repel the monster that was the attacking army.

Common folk were massing, heading in the direction of the Inner City, hoping to find safety within those walls, impeding the reinforcements attempt to bolster their defences.

For the first time Lars realized that the city could actually fall to the Ammelin army, something he had thought impossible only hours before. Approaching the mass had not seemed so massive, but as they had reached the wall and spread out it almost seemed their numbers tripled. And they fought with a passion for vengeance, giving them a wild fury that made them hard to counter.

Reaching the northern bastion, and racing up the stairs with sword already drawn, Lars arrived at the top just as the first of the enemy soldier's was about to descend. Ducking under a wide swing, hearing metal hiss by above him, Lars drove his own sword forward and up, punching through the soft skin of the abdomen and up into the ribcage, cutting through heart and lungs.

The Ammelin soldier feebly tried to raise his sword but lacked the strength or the breath. The weapon fell from slack fingers as the body slumped forward then tumbled down the stairs as Lars pulled his sword clear and stepped aside so he wasn't pushed from his feet by the dead weight.

Stepping up onto the bastion Lars quickly appraised the situation and decided that within the chaos the enemy had the upper hand. He could see Bollo and Tate Benellan standing back to back, fifty paces away, surrounded and fighting for their lives.

Carving his way towards them, Lars did so in a fashion that brought him into contact with as many enemy soldiers as possible. Each Ammelin soldier that faced his blade fell to it. Remembering the hard lessons Bollo had taught him, Lars made sure each and every one of them was dead before he moved on, leaving a bloody trail in his wake.

As he attacked the outermost enemy soldiers who were completely surrounding Bollo and Commander Benellan, Lars had to laugh of the irony of being the only one fighting his way into the circle to join the target of that ferocious onslaught. He wondered why such a concerted attack was being directed at only two men.

It was unlikely they knew who Bollo was, and although it was probable they had seen Tate Benellan issuing orders, Lars thought the level of attack aimed at the pair was excessive, and decided it was probably because they had been identified as the best swordsmen and therefore the greatest threat, making one on one combat against them nothing short of suicide, meaning they should be despatched with haste, using the full force they could muster.

And still they fell, unable to get close enough, even though they pressed the attack from all sides. In no time Lars sliced a gap in the line and joined Bollo and Tate, the latter of the two swinging his sword several times before realizing it was in fact Lars. The three of them made quick work of dispatching the press around them and started to move together, constantly rotating as they worked their way across the bastion, taking down many of the enemy, their show of superior swordsmanship boosting the Ragalan soldiers to greater effort.

Soon there were not enough enemy soldiers for the three of them to continue fighting in this fashion and they were forced to split up and pursue individual targets. The reinforcements had arrived whilst they were fighting, and without enough enemy for every man to engage the remainder moved to the walls and started throwing back the attackers there, toppling ladders and cutting down any who made it to the top of the wall before those ladders, too, could be cast aside.

With the enemy driven back the action on the north bastion returned to one of defence. The southern bastion though was a different matter altogether. Beyond that a fire burned and Lars knew they were also attacking the main gate, intent on ending this war on the first day and not letting it drag on into a second, or even worse a siege, resulting in a long series of battles that would allow the surrounding towns and villages to come to the aid of Ragal.

Bollo and Tate had also seen this and with silent communication, which consisted of little more than nods, all three of them set out across the defenders platform on the wall between the bastions, constantly crouching as arrows and crossbow bolts whistled above their heads.

Twelve other soldiers, having no crucial task, followed them, watching as the leaders of the group summarily cut down any who they met along the way, all of whom were enemy soldiers, Ragal's defenders there already dead or dying and the whole stretch left undefended. Tate Benellan ordered the soldiers to hold the platform and continued on.

Arriving at the southern bastion Bollo called to Tate and Lars to resume their previous formation. The enemy though moved in too quickly, forcing them apart before they could group. Very few Ragalan soldiers, less than twenty, remained alive and fighting on this bastion.

Lars found himself driven away from Bollo and Tate as he fought for his life. He sorely needed every ounce of skill he possessed simply to remain alive. All too soon he found himself in a desperate situation and had to think fast as he was pressed from all around.

Speaking the words, "Sordi repeluci," Lars crouched down as men were thrown from their feet, bones shattered, internal organs punctured and split apart, killing them in an instant. He remained crouching until the roar of wind above him subsided.

When he stood again all fighting on the bastion had ceased, those left standing looking in awe towards the source of that devastating wind.

Lars took a moment to assess the situation and quickly decided to take advantage of the silence. He had seen enough violence for one day, was in fact sickened by his own part in this barbarism.

It was time to put an end to the fighting. "Stop this. Stop it now or I will destroy you all." He strode across the bastion, the combatants parting to let him pass, none willing to challenge him now. Even those perched on ladders, ready to leap onto the bastion, were silent and still.

Walking across to where he could see Ragal's main gate he conjured a blue orb into existence, speaking the words, "Pendalir foncalis globul ferinze." He had to concentrate on no fixed target, twenty or so feet above the gate. It was difficult to do but he feared the wood may have been weakened sufficiently by the fire that aiming straight at the gate may destroy it, leaving it open for the enemy to take advantage.

The ball of swirling blue light exploded in a spray of water that, even though it was a little too far, carried back towards the gate on the breeze. The spray sizzled in the fire but only marginally reduced the flames. Three more times Lars had to repeat the spell before the fire was extinguished. The smoke was replaced by clouds of rising steam.

Still those on the bastion were silent, the quiet permeated with cries from below, questioning the delay. Lars walked across to the land facing wall of the bastion and jumped up onto the wall, standing in plain view of the enemy. A single arrow was loosed at him and Lars, by the luck of its trajectory and the wind slowing its flight, caught it from the air, looked at it and snapped it in two, before casually casting the pieces aside.

Waiting for a few seconds, Lars let the impression that must have given sink in, knowing they would also see this as magic. "Enough!" he roared, his voice hoarse from the smoke and the wearying effects of prolonged fighting. "Enough! Cease your attack or you will all die this day, every last one of you! You may think you can win this battle but you are mistaken. Your fleet, which you no doubt still believe offers you support from the ocean, is nothing but a shattered mass of wood floating on the water or sinking away into the blackness. If any survive they are few in numbers and they are sorely in need of your help.

"Pull back now," he commanded, knowing he had their full attention. "Set up camp. Help your people from the water and tend their wounds." Lars thought about what King Zief would have to say regarding what he was telling the enemy. He cast the thought aside, carried on regardless. "We will give you this night to rest and discuss your options, few though they are. You can try and resume your attack but I will watch you all night long and if you continue hostilities on any level every last one of you will die without a single soldier of Ragal having to raise a hand in defence. If anyone else dies here I can assure you the losses will be all yours.

"In the morning, if you wish, a contingent of your leaders can approach the gates and will be granted access and an audience with the king. That is all. Retreat now or die."

There was some hesitation among the attackers and Lars suspected they doubted the truth of his words. Calling forth a red ball of fire he held it aloft for several seconds before casting it to land beyond their lines, yet still close enough to shower many in dirt.

He conjured a second and held it up again. "I can aim these with pinpoint accuracy and destroy your whole army within minutes. Retreat now or face annihilation." They didn't need a second display and within several minutes the bastions were cleared and the ladders moved away from the wall as the army pulled back, knowing they could do nothing to counter this magic, many muttering under their breath about the evilness of these lands.

Lars spoke a single word, "*Annule,*" and the red ball disappeared. Lars was relieved. He was exhausted and most of what he had said was a bluff; but it was a bluff that had worked and saved hundreds of lives.

16

WRATH

"What do you think you are doing," roared the king, racing up on to the bastion and pacing in a fury towards Lars. "You have no authority here. How dare you presume to offer these people peace? I want them all dead, now. You have denied my soldiers their victory; I demand you now destroy the enemy. Use your magic, kill them all."

"No," said Lars, quietly but with a firmness that would brook no argument. "I know you wish to put an end to these people once and for all. That is not possible. Look at them; they are all men of fighting age. The young, old and the women must still be in Sarl, where these people have all come from. If you kill them, you, or your son, will face the next generation in twenty years or so. This fight could rumble on for generations to come. Or it can be ended now, peacefully, without any need for further loss of life and removing the need to be constantly on your guard."

"Don't presume to lecture me on how I should rule my city or my people," said Zief, through clenched teeth. Bollo and Commander Benellan moved to stand at his sides. "I rule these lands, not you. And while you live under my roof you will live by my rules and follow my commands."

"I do now, and will continue to live by your rules," said Lars. "But if you mean by following your commands that I should slaughter those men out there, then you know nothing of my principles. I could never do such a thing unless threatened."

"If you won't do it then I will," said Zief, turning to Tate Benellan. "I want every soldier who can ride on a horse and formed up in fifteen minutes, ready to ride out and decimate the enemy while they are still vulnerable. And start those new weapons firing again before they are out of range."

"Don't do this, Zief," Bollo whispered, moving to stand in front of his brother.

"So you question my authority, too?" snarled Zief, nostrils flaring.

"No brother, I do not," said Bollo, fervently shaking his head. "You are the ruler between us, not me; never me. But if we continue with the battle after a truce has begun-"

"A truce I did not deliver or agree to," interrupted Zief.

"No, you didn't," said Bollo carefully. "Yet is has begun nonetheless. If you press an attack now, many more of our men will die. More of Ragal's women will lose their husbands and sons. The people of the Low Plains have suffered too much recently; first the *Draknor*, and now this long forgotten enemy, has taken a huge toll on citizens and farming, our whole way of life. To continue this battle could be the ruin of this land, your realm."

"To let those men live could also be the death of this realm," said Zief, calming now. "We have no way of knowing if any peace we agree to with them will be honoured. They may simply bide their time and infiltrate the city as traders, springing an attack from within our walls."

"That risk is always present with any traders coming to this city," countered Bollo.

After a long silence Zief said, "Very well. I will allow the truce to stand and meet with the Ammeliners. I can only hope I will not live to regret it," he finished, looking to Lars in a way that clearly warned if this meeting went awry, the blame would lie firmly with him.

Lars stood where he was as the king and his brother walked away, Commander Benellan moving off to issue orders to his soldiers, some remaining as guards while others began clearing away the dead.

Below, the enemy soldiers had detailed a detachment to do likewise, taking their fallen away one at a time to be piled on a hastily built pyre, some distance from the city. Lars watched as each man was identified and his name recorded, curses uttered on both sides as the bodies were carried away. Brush and wood was piled between and around the bodies.

After a long series of prayers were spoken, the pyre was lit, huge plumes of dark smoke rising into the evening sky.

A long time passed before Lars finally turned away. He had watched the enemy army while the Ragalan soldiers worked around him, taking away the dead, returning those that could be identified to their families. Water was hauled up to the battlements to wash away the worst of the blood but the stains would never be completely removed. The new weapons were checked and the supplies for them restocked.

Feeling guilty for not helping them, Lars simply stood witness, in truth too exhausted to do any more. He wanted nothing more than too sink to his knees and fall asleep on the stones. At first the pools of blood and lumps of flesh deterred him; later it was a sheer force of will that kept him on his feet.

The walk back to the keep was slow, one foot dragged in front of the other with painstaking slowness. The effort of it all was nearly too much. When he reached the stairs in the keep it took several moments of staring at them to muster enough energy to ascend.

Finally making it to the door to his room he pushed it open, staggered in, crossed to the bed and collapsed onto it. His sword dug into his side; unbuckling the belt he left it there and rolled away from it. Expecting to be asleep in an instant, Lars soon became frustrated as sleep evaded him.

It took a moment for him to pinpoint the source of his unrest before he realized it was a strange feeling, a constant belief he was being watched. He could sense a presence near him. Thinking back, Lars knew it had begun after releasing the souls. He had been too busy then to take much notice, the cacophony surrounding him drawing his attention away from anything other than the next task.

Now, laying in the silence of his room, the presence was a palpable force. He thought about which of the spirits from the dome would have stayed with him after they had been released and, although he wished otherwise, he knew it wouldn't be Melissa. Neither would Paolen stay with him. It took a few moments for him to sift through those he had met in the crystal dome before he arrived at a likely candidate.

"Seeli?" he asked softly as he sat up and shuffled to the edge of the bed. "Are you there?"

"I am," said the disembodied voice of the spirit. *"How did you know I was here?"*

"I can feel you near me," replied Lars.

"Do I make you feel uncomfortable?" asked Seeli.

"A little," admitted Lars. "But at the moment I am curious as to why you have stayed close to me at all?"

"Where else would I go?"

"Back to your family in the world of spirit," Lars ventured.

"I don't know how to get back there," said Seeli. *"Nor do I wish to; I owe you a debt for rescuing me and would not leave until that debt is paid. Honour demands I do no less."*

"But you are a spirit, who already knows what lies beyond the boundaries of death," said Lars. "You are no longer tied by the rules, morals, and beliefs you held to in life. And when I released you it was not so you could go from one confinement to another."

"I know that," said Seeli. *"Nevertheless, I will stay by your side until I feel I have repaid you."*

Lars felt Seeli wanted to say more and remained silent, giving her time.

"Life in spirit may be different in many ways," Seeli continued. *"But the sense of right and wrong remains as strong as ever, if not more so. Sometimes I feel as though it is all I have. You have helped me more than you could ever know. I could not leave you without helping you in what is to come."*

"Do you know what is to come?" asked Lars. "Can you see into the future?"

"Not really," replied Seeli. *"I do get feelings though, about people. I can sense a great deal of activity and torment in your future."* Suddenly Seeli burst out laughing; a wonderful thing to hear from someone who had suffered centuries of imprisonment.

"What is so funny?" asked Lars, seeing nothing amusing in her words.

"Sorry," said Seeli. *"I shouldn't have laughed. It's just that when I was young an old woman in the village where I lived claimed she could see into the future. When anyone asked her to read their future she would tell them they were going on a long journey. It became a bit of a standing joke in the village. I just sensed that you are indeed going on a long journey and it reminded me of*

that old woman." Seeli paused for a moment. *"That is the first time I have laughed in ever so long. It felt good."*

"I will be returning home before the winter. That is probably the journey you can sense."

"No," said Seeli with deliberate slowness. *"I can also sense that one, but the journey I speak of is much longer."*

"Do you know where?" asked Lars warily.

"No," said Seeli with a finality that ended the other questions forming in Lars' mind. *"I can't sense specifics. It's just a general feeling."*

Lars ran his hands over his face, the exhaustion making its presence felt again. "I need to sleep."

"I will move away from you a little," said Seeli. *"Hopefully then you will be able to sleep."*

Lars felt the spirit retreating across the room. He swung his legs back up onto the bed and lay down. Within a few moments he was asleep, more soundly than normal, content that Seeli would watch over him while he slept.

It seemed though that fate conspired to prevent his rest, and in truth the news that was delivered by a servant pounding on the door only moments later, could not have been more important to him.

"Lady Talia bids you attend the funeral of her daughter, your betrothed, Amelia Serillia Corban. It will be held at the Inner City graveyard in thirty minutes."

The servant waited and Lars' mind was too muddled from been dragged awake to wonder why.

"Do you have a reply for My Lady?" asked the servant eventually.

"I will be there," said Lars, closing the door.

Crossing to the wash stand Lars poured cold water into the basin and stuck his head as far in as possible, letting the coolness revive him.

He dressed quickly and headed to the graveyard, feeling Seeli trailing along behind.

The graveyard was already packed when Lars arrived. The king and his brother were there, standing with Lady Talia, who was comforted by her sister, the queen. Queen Seran held in her hands the Star Stone. It was the first time Lars had seen the stone in over a year. The stone glittered dazzlingly, seemingly capturing every scrap of starlight and transmitting it at three times the brightness.

Tam and Commander Benellan stood just behind the king and Bollo, several paces from the main group. Lars recognized many of the other nobles gathered there but, even though he knew he had been introduced to them, his tired mind failed to put names to the faces.

The coffin bearing Amelia's body rested above a hole in the ground, held up by two beams of wood. Without any direction Lars moved to stand at the end of the line. Seeing him, Bollo indicated for Lars to stand next to him and the commander.

The funeral began with the king moving to stand at the head of the coffin. "Thank you one and all for attending this funeral on a day that has already seen so much loss. But this is not a time for sadness. It is a time to celebrate Amelia's life. As painful as this may be, we have to remember that Amelia has gone to take her place with the gods, and shall live for eternity at their side, waiting to be reunited with those of us left behind."

Talia walked forward next, moving to stand at the head of the coffin as the king moved to the side. "Amelia was everything to me and the future of House Corban. She was my world. I would have done anything for her, to ensure her happiness."

Lars had to mask a bitter laugh with a cough.

Talia frowned but continued. "Amelia is now at peace, knowing those who killed her have had justice delivered on them this day," looking at Lars and adding with an accusing stare, "It is only a shame that any of them are still alive.

"However," she continued, her gaze returning to the crowd, "I thank the gods for the victory they saw fit to bestow this day on our great city." Talia looked down at the coffin. "Goodbye my beautiful daughter. I will miss you. All of Ragal will miss you." When Talia looked up again tears ran down her cheeks.

Next was Queen Seran who, stopping at the head of the coffin, placed the Star Stone upon the lid. "Ragal will indeed miss her daughter. Amelia was my lady in waiting and a good friend. She was loved by all who knew her and her death is a great loss to us all. May the Twelve Faceted God bless her soul and through the power of the Star Stone show her eternal peace."

As Seran spoke the final words it seemed the Star Stone shone a little brighter, as if possessing some form of sentience, reacting to her words.

The queen moved away and Bollo placed a hand on Lars' back, easing him forward. "It is your turn."

Lars walked forward to the ritual place, looking down on the coffin, totally unprepared for this. It took several minutes to rein in his emotions and gather some measure of composure.

"I may have only known Amelia for a short time, but I will treasure the days we shared for the rest of my life. She was the most important person in the world to me. I can only imagine what the future might have held for us. Now that can never be and all we are left with are the memories. I shall hold those memories dear until we can be reunited in the spirit world."

Lars moved aside then, listening as others came forward to share memories of Amelia. He watched as the coffin was lowered into the ground and covered with soil. As everyone else departed he knelt by the grave, remaining there until long after the whole city was quiet. He spent the time in prayer, and reflecting on what he had lost.

Finally Lars rose from the cold graveside, whispering, "May Krogos keep you safe at his side until I come for you," and trudged back to his room, falling onto the bed as dawn's light began to creep over the horizon.

Rubis Hornshank had found a large piece of wreckage drifting in the ocean. Heaving his upper body up onto the wood he used his legs to propel himself towards the shore. It was dark long before he reached within swimming distance of land, bone weary and way beyond the point of exhaustion. Only the will to survive had kept him going this far. He kept hold of the wood, fearing if he let go he would sink like a stone. He had already cast away most of his clothing, the dragging weight too much for him.

As darkness had fallen he had seen torches lit, the bearers moving up and down the rocky shore. He knew he could easily be heading into the arms of the enemy but had no option other than to continue towards them; it was either risk being killed by the Ragalan soldiers or face certain death at the hands of the ocean.

Closer to the shore and the waves began buffeting the wreckage, forcing him to abandon it and swim the last stretch. Calling out weakly as he drew close to the shore, he was relieved as the torches were turned towards him, the searchers holding out their arms to help him up onto the rocks.

He was relieved to find it was the Ammelin soldiers that pulled him from the ocean. He was questioned briefly and had the sad task of informing them that Admiral Vellan had perished in the battle, as had so many others. Rubis was escorted back to their camp, a long walk for his tired legs. He shook constantly, the cold ocean waters having taken their effect, sapping his strength.

When they reached the camp he was given a blanket and filled in on the details of the land battle, and the heavy losses they had suffered from the same foul magic that had so easily destroyed the fleet. The commanders of the land forces had many questions for Rubis, he being the highest ranking person they had recovered thus far.

Even with the dire news and an uncertain future, when Rubis was finally allowed to lay down he was asleep within a few seconds.

The next morning Lars was woken by someone pounding on the door. He felt as if he had only slept for a few minutes. Dragging himself from the bed Lars trudged across to the door. Opening it he found Bollo standing there.

"Is it morning already?" asked Lars. "I'll get my sword."

"Wait," said Bollo. "That time came and went hours ago. I was here then but decided to let you sleep."

"And now?" asked Lars as Bollo hesitated.

"The delegation from the enemy army is entering the Inner City," explained Bollo. "The king wants you to join him in the throne room to witness the discussions."

"Why?" asked Lars. "I thought he wouldn't want me anywhere near the enemy again after yesterday."

"My brother doesn't forget such things easily. Now, I think, although it took a long time for him to calm down, he can see that what you did was with the best intentions and not to thwart any plans he may have had."

"What plans would they be?" asked Lars, not really expecting an answer.

"The Ammelin are an old enemy and my brother would like to see them all dead," Bollo explained. "As, in all truth, would I. But what you said yesterday was true. The whole Ammelin people are out of our reach and we would only have to face them again in the future. I am not sure what my brother plans to do, and I am sorry to admit I don't entirely trust his intentions. I think your presence, as an outsider of the two armies, could offer some form of mediation, giving your own insights on any points of contention."

Lars was sceptical that Zief shared his brother's views and wondered what the king was planning. Not wanting to voice his concerns he asked, "Do I have time to wash and change."

"Of course," replied Bollo, adding with a wry smile, "We don't need you stinking up the Throne Room."

Lars washed and dressed quickly, brushing back his hair with his hands as he left the room. He had deliberately picked plain clothes, a mixture of browns, not wanting to stand out.

Entering the Throne Room he found the Ammeliners already there, standing in a group, talking amongst themselves, heatedly discussing what demands they would make. They clearly had many differing opinions on what was most important. It was obvious they hadn't prepared for this eventuality when making their plans to attack Ragal.

As one they turned when Bollo closed the door, all looking with undisguised contempt at the embodiment of their defeat. Without Lars' intervention the battle could quite easily have been lost, the Ammelin army now celebrating within the city walls instead of being escorted in to negotiate a lasting peace or face certain death.

Lars walked forward, unperturbed by their scrutiny. Sitting in the front row of seats on the right side he pointedly ignored the delegation. He didn't want to do or say anything until Zief was present lest he raise the king's ire once more. Lars had decided while descending the stairs that he would only talk if a question was directed at him. He wanted to stay out of what was about to happen as much as possible, constantly reminding himself that he would soon be leaving Ragal and any agreement forged today would not affect him in any way and that these people would be the ones who would have to live by it.

When the anteroom door opened and Tam stepped out Lars stood without waiting for the announcement, listening as Tam recited his litany of titles by which King Zief was known. Zief walked forward as the echoes died away, sitting on the throne.

Behind the king came Commander Benellan, standing at the rear of the throne. Bollo walked across to stand at his brother's right side and Tam took his position to the left. Lars, having been given no directions, stayed where he was.

"Who speaks for you?" asked Zief of the delegation.

There were a few mutters then one man stepped forward. "I do, Majesty. I am Captain Haig Daenneth. As things stand I am the highest ranking among the Ammelin army."

Zief sensed some uncertainty in the statement and asked, "Is that likely to change?"

"In truth, I am uncertain." Haig paused for a moment before explaining. "The overall Commander of this offensive was Admiral Rolan Vellan. He died yesterday when the ships were attacked by your mage," he said looking at Lars with disgust.

"I would like to know more of those who rank between yourself and this admiral," said Zief. "But first you should understand something. Prince Lars is not my mage or anyone else's. He is not even from Ragal but from the mountains and an honoured guest in my city. Your fleet and army suffered his wrath yesterday simply because your attacks endangered his life.

"I can see the contempt you hold for him and can tell you it is misplaced. He is a decent and admirable young man who lost his betrothed to your advance party's attack. He captured those responsible but instead of slaughtering each and every one of them he brought them back to the city as prisoners."

"And you killed them yesterday at the start of our attack," said Captain Haig Daenneth, enraged. "It was an appalling display of butchery, the likes of which we were informed you were readily capable of." The others of the delegation joined in with views of their own on this point.

Zief waited for the din to settle before speaking. "This is war; what did you expect. Remember, *you* attacked Ragal. You travelled all this way with the single intention of killing everyone in this city. Were you expecting us to welcome you with open arms?"

"The crime of your forefathers warranted such action," declared Haig.

"I am not my forefathers," said Zief hotly. "And I certainly am not responsible for their crimes; if indeed they were crimes. We both only have the truth as it was seen by those who passed it down to us. We have no way of knowing just how far those truths may have been distorted."

Lars was amazed at just how diplomatic the king was being. He was sure it was all a sham and deep down Zief was seething with barely controlled fury.

"I can only tell you what I know," Zief continued. "My grandfather, Hagan, did not sanction nor condone the attack on your village that sent you half way around the world. He executed those responsible and banned all forms of magic in our town."

Lars almost laughed at the hypocritical way the real truth was glossed over. Lars knew the story well and the true feelings of Hagan where the Ammeliners were concerned.

"How do we know what you say to be accurate?" asked Haig, deliberately not using the word 'true.'

"What have I to gain by lying to you?"

"Can any independent party verify this?" asked Haig.

Lars guessed this was the reason he had been brought here. "I can," he said without waiting to be asked.

"You can hardly be classed as independent in this matter," accused Haig. "And no doubt you only learned of this whole affair since you came to Ragal?"

"Not true," replied Lars. "I heard this grim tale from my grandfather before I ever came to Ragal. What the king says is true as I know it. Furthermore, my grandfather blamed the Zutaren traders for the chaos that troubled our lands and ended in the disappearance of your village."

"And what would bring him to such a conclusion, that he set the blame at the feet of the Zutarens?" asked Haig, clearly confused.

"They were responsible for selling the spells to those not trained in the use of magic or possessing any latent talent. The traders sold the very same spell that caused your relocation." Lars paused for a moment to let that sink in. "My grandfather believed that the Zutarens did this deliberately to destabilize Gravick and sow mistrust, making an invasion easier for them to accomplish."

"Did an invasion ever take place?" asked Haig.

"No."

"Then what your grandfather said was little more than idle speculation," accused Haig.

"Not so," said Lars, holding in check his own growing dislike for these obstinate people. "My grandfather was *Fa'ku*, the leader of our people, and could read the rune stones our people use to foretell the future. What he saw there confirmed his suspicions. Only several days after your village disappeared, the threat mysteriously ended. We can only guess why but the most likely reason is the death of the empress at the time. Maybe her successor had no wish to continue her efforts to retake these lands."

"But that still seems more like speculation than hard fact. Do you have anything more solid to back up your claims?"

Lars could only say what he knew. After a brief silence Lars was surprised when Zief verified what he had said. "Ambassadors from all across Gravick and Tibor have visited Ragal over the past few years. They have also met with their Zutaren counterparts. What they have told me of their recent history ties in with what Lars told you. The empress who ruled Zutar then did indeed die around that time."

Turning back to Lars Haig asked, "And has your grandfather seen any more threats from the Zutarens?"

"My grandfather died last year when these lands were attacked by the *Draknor*," said Lars, continuing quickly at the captain's obvious confusion, "It is a beast thought to be mythical until last spring. The creature did come out of the west but that does not necessarily mean the Zutarens were involved in any way. But it is strange that not long before the attacks the Zutaren traders had returned to these lands. Maybe they were here for more than just trade."

"And I have not heard news of a single Zutaren ambassador being injured or killed during those attacks," said Zief. "It may be that they all left the east before those attacks started."

"Excuse me for a moment," said Haig, and turned to the others of the Ammelin delegation and they began talking amongst themselves. After several moments he turned back, looking again towards the king, and asked, "Would it be possible to continue this tomorrow? We need to discuss this new information with our people."

"If that would better suit you I am happy to accommodate your wishes," replied Zief.

"Thank you, Majesty," said Haig, bowing and turning to leave. When the doors were opened Lars could see at least twenty guards standing outside, ready to escort the delegation back out of the city.

As the doors closed Zief turned to Lars. "Don't think that what I said today in any way means I have forgiven you. What you did yesterday was inexcusable and has forced me into a course of action which I would never have chosen. I must now unwillingly make peace with these people, although I would sooner walk barefoot through a snake pit.

"I would like to see you leave this city today, never to return; but as things stand it would not be safe for you to go outside these walls and I have no desire to anger your father and your people. You can remain as our guest until the situation is resolved."

Lars felt like saying, 'Your city would be nothing but rubble now, and your people all dead, if not for me,' but instead simply said, "As you wish," knowing this would infuriate the king all the more. He bowed and turned to leave, expecting to be called back and almost feeling Zief's stare boring into the back of his skull.

Leaving the throne room Lars waited for a while next to the door, waiting for the explosion within the Throne Room that he was sure would come. He was not disappointed.

"How dare he?" raged Zief, only a few seconds later. "The arrogance of the boy is astounding. We offer him training and hospitality and he dares show no regret for ruining my plans; or any concern for being told he will have to leave."

Lars could hear others talking but not loud enough to distinguish who was saying what. Lars moved away then, nodding to the guard and heading up the stairs to his room. He started packing his belongings, and the scrolls from Felman's desk. He couldn't let them fall into the hands of someone like Zief, who would use them only for his own gains, to control, conquer or destroy as he saw fit.

He felt like walking out of the keep right then but thought better of it. He needed to bear witness to the negotiations to ensure Zief acted honourably; or as close to it as his twisted ambitions would allow.

Instead Lars went up to the roof of the keep, picking his way through the mess of shattered masonry. The destruction would take months to repair, maybe even years, and the keep would need to be weather tight before the winter storms arrived, pounding the keep with spray and pouring down into the rooms below.

Looking out over the city Lars continued to observe the damage, evaluating the city's defensibility. The city could be made sound soon enough, leaving the cosmetic side of the repairs to be completed later. The main problem he could see was their forces had been greatly reduced, to a point where they couldn't effectively defend the full length of the wall. Further fortifications would need to be added in several spots to prevent any gaps. There would also need to recruit and train a high number of Ragal's young men to replace the dead, leaving other sectors short of labour.

Walking a circuit around the roof Lars surveyed the Inner City and the damage there. The four lesser of the Five Houses had escaped any major damage and could be repaired quickly. He spent a long time looking towards House Corban before carrying on. Stopping on the far side of the roof he looked down on the ocean far below. The wreckage, all that remained of the once mighty fleet, crashed against the rocks, being broken into ever smaller pieces. He wondered just how many bodies had been torn apart against those rocks before sinking away to be eaten by the fish.

All those deaths lay firmly at his feet.

17

A FRAGILE TRUCE

Lars had retired to his room when the sun set. He sat before the fire and deliberated on his next course of action. He again thought about simply walking out of the city and heading home but quickly reminded himself he needed to see how the discussions with the delegation turned out. It could affect life in the mountains if the talks went badly, and have detrimental effects for his people.

Lars also knew Zief didn't have the manpower to finish the enemy and wouldn't be able to attack them outside of Ragal's walls for fear of leaving the city defences woefully undermanned. If he ordered an attack and that force was beaten Ragal would undoubtedly fall. Lars couldn't allow that to happen, knowing such an outcome would also affect the stability of Gravick.

When he lay down to sleep that night he could still feel Seeli nearby but was a little saddened, knowing he would never again visit the dome or speak with Melissa.

At dawn, a knock on his door heralded Bollo coming to invite Lars to join him for a 'sound thrashing' in the fencing yard. Lars was only too happy to accept. As they began their sparring session Bollo said, "I half expected you to be gone when I came to your room today."

"It did cross my mind," Lars admitted, parrying a thrust. "But I decided it best to stay and witness the proceedings. What happens today could change the future for the whole of Gravick. It would be remiss of me to simply walk away from these discussions."

"True," said Bollo. "I, personally, am pleased that you will remain here a little longer. I enjoy the challenges you present each time we practice here and will miss them greatly when you leave. There are many other fine swordsmen in Ragal, a lot of them trained by me, but you are the best I have ever trained."

It was a rare display of emotion and sincerity from the king's brother, which Lars could only answer with a slight dip of his sword, an invitation for Bollo to strike. Instead Bollo stepped back and one pace to the right. Their practice from then on was a real test of trying to read the other's mind and predict their moves.

When they were done and heading back to the keep Lars said, "Thank you for your kind words. It means a lot to me that you rate me so highly."

"I only give praise when it is warranted," said Bollo. "You really are that good."

"Well thank you anyway," said Lars, and they walked back to the keep in silence.

Lars washed and dressed before eating the breakfast that had been left in his room. The portions were a lot smaller now than when he had first arrived, the kitchen staff getting used to how much he would leave each day and adjusting the amount accordingly.

He sat then in one of the chairs before the unlit fire. Resting his head back he closed his eyes and extended his senses. He could feel Seeli's presence, staying as far back as the room's confines allowed.

"How long will you stay with me?" he asked suddenly.

Seeli drifted closer. "*As I have already stated; until I deem my debt repaid.*"

"I thought you may have reconsidered what I said and would wish to return to your family."

"*I have considered it,*" said Seeli. "*But I shall stand by my decision. Time in spirit is seemingly endless. After the years I spent trapped in that dome a single human lifetime of relative freedom will be easy to endure.*"

"Will you be near me my whole life?" asked Lars.

"*Only until I feel I have repaid you for freeing me. It may be one month or ten years; maybe more. Future events will determine the length of time I am with you. And you don't have to worry about privacy; I will leave you alone as and when required—providing it doesn't compromise your safety.*"

Lars could think of nothing else to say on the subject. He didn't particularly want a spirit hovering around him for the foreseeable future and wished Seeli would return to the world of spirit. An awkward silence threatened to develop until a knock at the door rescued him.

"Come in!" said Lars.

The door opened and Bollo walked in. "The Ammelin delegation are on their way. My brother asks that you attend the proceedings in the Throne Room again."

"I wouldn't miss it for the world," said Lars. "I want to learn more about these people, and the lands where they were transported to. Trade will be vital to their survival on the Midd Plains. Maybe, when the talks are finished, I could barter a deal that would benefit Lokas. My people need to start integrating more with the rest of Gravick and bring ourselves up to date with current developments."

"Very wise of you," said Bollo. "As much as I despise the thought of the Ammeliners returning to our lands I can't help but agree with you and I only hope Zief can see the opportunities their arrival presents."

"Let us go and see where this day will lead us then," said Lars, standing and gesturing towards the door, following Bollo out and down to the Throne Room.

Lars sat in the same place as the previous day, watching as the delegation was ushered in, noting that the party had increased by two. One of these had a patch over his right eye and his right arm bound tightly to his chest. The other man looked largely uninjured except for a few cuts and bruises but had about him a haggard look that made him appear older than his years.

Something about this second man was familiar and it took but a moment to recognize what it was. Lars rose and walked across to the man, bowing as the stranger turned to face him.

"I am Lars Velaren," he introduced himself. "Forgive me if I am mistaken, but are you the brother of Theodin Hornshank?"

"I am indeed," said the stranger, returning the bow. "I am Rubis Hornshank, navigator of the main fleet."

"That this man destroyed single handed," interjected an Ammeliner, standing next to Rubis, the man's name unknown to Lars.

"So, you are the mage I have heard so much about?" queried Rubis. "I would like to talk to you more about that. But first, if you have news of my brother, I would like to hear."

"We spoke together when he was captured," explained Lars. "I am sorry to inform you that he died the day your army attacked." Lars didn't see the need to go into the details. The loss of Amelia was still too painful for him and Rubis didn't really need to know exactly how his brother's life had ended, only that he was dead. But he did add, "He will have been placed on the funeral pyre with the other fallen from that battle."

Rubis looked distraught at the news but the Ammeliner butted in once again asking, "If he was captured how was he a part of the battle?"

Lars was about to answer Rubis' questioning look but was saved by Tam announcing the arrival of King Zief. Moving back to his place at the bench Lars remained standing as the king entered the room and slowly positioned himself in the throne, taking an exaggerated amount of time doing so, picking up the sceptre and looking at it closely before placing it across his lap. It was the first time Lars had seen the sceptre since returning to Ragal. The king also wore a golden crown that Lars had never seen before, as if to emphasize his regal position.

"Welcome," said Zief eventually. "Have you discussed among your leaders what we talked about yesterday?"

"We have," replied Captain Haig Daenneth, clearly still the highest ranking amongst them. "We have accepted what you told us; that the blame in fact lies with the Zutarens."

Lars noted the captain's choice of words in not saying that they believed their account. Clearly they still mistrusted the Ragalan's. Yet, without any further proof, they could not reasonably continue to wholly blame Zief's ancestors for their suffering.

"So," continued Zief. "The question has to be what will you do now?"

Haig was silent for a moment before answering. "We would like to return to the Midd Plains, rebuild the home our people once knew. A small contingent would return across the vast oceans to Sarl, to bring the rest of our people home."

"A noble sentiment," said Zief, clearly taking pleasure in pointing out, "but without a fleet, or even a single ship, how do you intend to accomplish this?"

"We would have to rely on the good graces of our new neighbours," replied Haig.

"Indeed," said Zief, leaning forward. "I think you will find good grace in short supply in these lands. Only last year Gravick, Algor and

Tibor were ravaged by the *Draknor*. We had not yet recovered when your people began your attacks. These troubles combined leave us unable to offer any aid."

"I understand," said Haig. "I am sure the future will not be easy for my people but we are determined and resourceful. We will do this alone if we must."

"I don't think you will need to do that," said Zief, looking at Lars as a smile spread across his face. "I am sure Prince Lars will help you in any way he can, and accompany any you send back to Sarl to ensure their safe passage."

Judging by the satisfied look on Zief's face, Lars could tell this was the king's idea of revenge.

Although it was a blow, Lars was determined not to let it show and instead turn it to his advantage. He turned away from Zief and faced the delegation, bowing before speaking, using every extra second to order his thoughts.

"I would be honoured," he began, "to help your people return to the place your ancestors once called home. Winter will soon be upon us so the start of our journey north across the ocean must wait until spring. I will be returning to the mountains for the winter, leaving here at dawn tomorrow. Several of you are welcome to come with me and open trade negotiations. My people have suffered the greatest from the ravages of the *Draknor*, and we are not wealthy, but we will help you in any way we can, to ease your reintegration into Gravick.

"I can also introduce you to King Tomar of Thoran. His is the only city on the Midd Plains and they may also be able to help." Lars glanced to Zief who was fuming that Lars was offering help from his people and others, knowing it would make Ragal and the Low Plains look bad if they offered nothing. "Also," continued Lars, looking back at the delegates, "they would be able to introduce you to leaders of the other villages on the Midd Plains."

Captain Haig Deanneth spoke with obvious distaste. "I must say I don't relish the idea of spending time with the man who is responsible for killing more of my people than the whole of Ragal's forces. However, I can only hope you were acting in self defence and not with any malicious intent or hatred for us. And in truth any genuine offer of help can not be refused if we are to survive the coming months.

"Thank you for your offer of assistance, Prince Lars. May I invite you to spend the evening at our camp? You can meet my people before we leave in the morning." Turning to Zief, who was whispering something to Tam, Haig said, "If we are to leave at dawn there is much I need to attend to. First I must ask; will there be peace between Ragal and Ammelin?"

"Of course," replied Zief, as Tam turned and left the Throne room, adding in a rare display of complete honesty. "I need to look to securing my own lands and people and have neither the men nor the inclination to wage war outside of these borders. Rebuilding this city and the confidence of my people will be my task for the immediate future."

"Then our meeting is at an end," said Haig, bowing. "I bid you good day, King Zief."

Zief simply tilted his head and the delegation turned and filed out. Lars tried to do likewise but the king's voice stopped him. "Prince Lars, stay for a moment."

Lars turned and walked across to stand before the king. "Yes Majesty?"

"I know relations between us have been strained of late," said Zief, looking at Bollo as though he was to blame for Zief having to be civil. "I would not have you leave with the situation unresolved. In fact I would prefer you remain here a little longer. I would not trust these Ammeliners so easily."

"Nevertheless, I need to return to my people," said Lars. "And I must do so before the onset of winter. Also, I have given my word to the delegation and would not willingly go back on that."

"If your mind is set I will not try to dissuade you further," said Zief. "But I hope this will not be the last time we meet. I wish you well on your journey," adding with a sneering smile, "and on your journey to Sarl."

Lars didn't react to that, instead he simply bowed and said, "Thank you, King Zief." He held Zief's gaze for a moment then turned and left, expecting Zief to call him back again. Lars was pleased when he reached the door without any further comments and even happier when he closed the door behind him.

Walking slowly up the stairs he entered to the room that had been his home for the last time. He would pack quickly and leave quietly.

Opening the door to the room he realized he would miss the space he had enjoyed while living in Ragal. That single room was bigger than the hut his whole family shared in Lokas.

He changed his clothes for those more suitable for travel, grabbed his pack and placed the good clothes in the bottom before carefully adding the scrolls of magic and a couple of choice books he had selected from the library that contained engineering methods which would greatly aid his people. The pack was topped off with the remainder of his clothes and was placed by the door, his sword resting against it.

With one final sweep around the room he confirmed none of his belongings remained and was about to leave when a knock at the door stopped him. "Enter," called Lars, expecting he knew who it would be.

The door opened and instead of Bollo, Lady Talia entered the room, closing the door behind her and leaning back against it. "Leaving us so soon?"

"It is time for me to return to my home, my people. Ragal holds no future for me; my life here died with your daughter."

"That is not entirely true," said Talia, rubbing a hand across her stomach. "I may be with child."

"Really?" asked Lars impassively. "You truly expect me to believe that."

"No. But it is possible, you must agree." Talia smiled. "If I knew for certain either way I would tell you. I would never lie to you about such a thing."

"Then it would be a first for you," said Lars. "I doubt there is anything about which you wouldn't lie if it would further your goals."

"You mistrust me," said Talia. "I can't say I blame you with my history. But this time you are the one who is mistaken. We made love, and my courses are late. I believe I may indeed be pregnant."

"Amelia *was* pregnant, and that was a fact. Our child died with her," said Lars sharply, pausing at the quickly indrawn breath from Talia. "You didn't know, did you? Your own daughter never told you she was pregnant. Now you come here claiming the very same. Amelia's claim of being with child I trusted. Yours, *Lady*, I do not."

"You need not trust me," said Talia, regaining some of her previous demeanour. "Nevertheless, the truth is the truth." Talia paused, choosing her next words carefully. "I know you didn't want this. In truth neither did I. But we must face the future and if I am pregnant then you should be a part of your child's life. You could still be Lord Corban; if that is what you want."

Lars couldn't help feeling he was being drawn into another trap yet found himself believing Talia, even if it was highly unlikely. "I don't know what I want anymore. My life has been torn apart lately. Still, let me say that, although I know you are untrustworthy in the extreme, I am willing to accept what you say may at least be possible.

"How gracious of you," said Talia, sarcasm thick in her voice.

"I will be returning this way in the spring. I will come and see you and I shall discover the truth then."

"And what then, if I am indeed with child?"

Lars shrugged. "Only time will tell where the gods may lead me. I will be leaving these lands in the spring and travelling north to Sarl. If I return from such a long and perilous journey, then will be the time to decide."

"Very well," said Talia. "I can ask for no more than that. Indeed I expected a lot less." She walked to Lars and leaned forward, gently placing a kiss on his cheek. "Take care of yourself. I will see you in the spring." Talia left him alone then.

Lars sat down for a few minutes, struggling to take in what Talia had said and trying to detect any hint of a lie in her words or actions, and was distressed to discover he could find none. A short while later he stood, belted his sword around his waist and hefted his pack onto his shoulders.

Leaving the room Lars was surprised to find Bollo leaning against the wall opposite his door. "How long have you been here?"

"Not long at all."

"Did you overhear any of that?"

"Not enough to make any sense of it."

"Good," said Lars, filled with relief.

"Do you want to talk about it?" asked Bollo.

"Not really." He didn't want to explain even a little of the whole sordid situation.

"As you wish," said Bollo.

They walked through the keep and out of the Inner City in silence.

Bollo looked at the damage as they walked through the Outer City. Suddenly he broke the silence, saying, "Thank you."

"What for?" asked Lars.

"For saving Ragal," explained Bollo. "The damage could have been a whole lot worse. As it would have surely been had you not acted. Zief, too, is pleased that you stopped our city being destroyed, even if he will never admit it."

They continued on to the scorched main gates, where repair crews were already busy cutting out the weakened wood and replacing it as necessary. Bollo walked outside the gates with Lars before saying his farewells.

"I, like my brother, have reservations about you travelling with the Ammeliners. The only advice I can give you is to sleep lightly with one hand on your sword. Trust no one and be sure you always prepare your own food and drink. And I can only hope that if you return in spring we will have another chance to test each other in the fencing yard. Take care of yourself."

"You too," said Lars. "I'm sure you will be busy for the foreseeable future," he added, looking around at the damage.

"I just hope the gods see fit to grant us peace and allow us the time to rebuild," said Bollo. "The past two years have been hard, as you well know."

"I feel confident Gravick will remain trouble free for years to come," said Lars, saying the words but not wholly believing them.

"I'm not so sure," said Bollo, echoing Lars' doubts. "Others will see our misfortune as weakening us to a point where they may be able to take advantage of the situation and invade, conquering these lands easily."

Lars nodded but kept his thoughts to himself. "I should go," said Lars finally, offering his hand. "In case we never meet again, I would like to say it has been an honour to know you."

"Likewise," said Bollo, taking Lars' hand.

Neither of them was prone to long goodbyes so as they released hands Lars turned and headed towards the Ammelin camp. After several hundred paces he turned to wave, finding, even though he was not surprised, that Bollo had already gone.

HOME

Lars approached the Ammelin camp with a large amount of apprehension. Night was already approaching, the sun just setting. He wondered who he would need to ask for when the guards stopped him, expecting to be turned away. As it turned out he didn't need to worry: Rubis Hornshank was already waiting for him on the outskirts of the camp, along with another man Lars recognized from the delegation.

Lars wondered if the navigator knew the truth about his brother's death and was about to confront him. Or if he wanted to ask more questions until Lars revealed the truth.

"Welcome to our camp," said Rubis. "I have prepared a place for you to sleep." Turning slightly to the man next to him Rubis introduced his companion. "This is Eavitt Dargol. He, too, is from Sarl, and will accompany us next year. A small crew has already been selected to sail a vessel to Sarl."

"You have a ship?" asked Lars, thinking he had destroyed them all.

"Three actually," said Rubis. "Though only one that will be seaworthy in the near future. It is one of the ships from the advance party. The damage is largely superficial and, after minor repairs, will be used to tow the other two to dock in Grandor. A small group will remain with the ships to keep them safe and begin repairs. Eavitt will be in command of refitting the ships."

"I will make sure you have a fine and fast vessel to carry you on your voyage, Prince Lars," said Eavitt.

"Please, just Lars. Among my own people I am no one important. My father's position grants me nothing. I am not even a warrior, just another young man, yet to decide his course in life."

"I have a feeling fate is deciding your course for you," said Eavitt. "I doubt when you came to Ragal that you expected to be thrust into the middle of a war and gain a great victory for King Zief."

"No, definitely not," replied Lars uncomfortably.

"Or that you would be steered into such a journey as you will undertake come spring?"

"That's quite enough of that," said Rubis, seeing Lars' discomfort. "Lars didn't come here to answer questions; he is a guest."

"Of course," conceded Eavitt. "I am merely curious."

"I didn't expect a lot of things that have come to pass," said Lars, feeling the need to explain to Rubis about his brother and doubting he would get a better chance than this to broach the delicate subject. "I became betrothed since I arrived in Ragal, to a beautiful young lady from a high ranking family. Your brother was among the group who attacked us while we were out riding. Amelia was thrown from her horse and struck her head in the fall. She died instantly."

Rubis was about to speak but Lars forestalled him with a raised hand. He needed to get this out and didn't want to stop in the middle of it. Any sympathy from the Sarlen would only make him falter and threaten his resolve.

"I, along with the guard who accompanied us, captured your brother and all that remained of your advance party. I killed their commander and came close to doing the same to your brother, Theodin. I restrained my anger and your brother, along with his companions, was marched to Ragal as a prisoner. He told me about Sarl, about his family, and how he came to be in Gravick.

"Theodin seemed disillusioned about the reasons that had led him to participate in his mission. When your army came into sight all the prisoners were taken up to the bastions and executed by hanging in plain sight of your army. His body, if it still hung from the walls after the battle, will have been cut down and taken away and burnt along with the fallen."

"Thank you for sharing that with me," said Rubis after a long silence. "It can't have been easy, and I am sorry for your loss also."

"I am sure it is no easier for you to learn of your brother's death," said Lars, "Or of the unnecessarily brutal way in which it came about."

"No," agreed Rubis. "But Theodin always was a hothead. I pleaded with him not to go with the advance party. The chances of his survival were slim from the start."

"Enough of this moroseness," said Eavitt gruffly. "Dwelling on the past does no good for anyone. What's done is done, and while we should always remember those who have died before us they are now in the past. The future is for the living and that's where we should be looking towards."

"True, true," said Rubis, nodding. "And for the near future we'll all have more than we can handle keeping us busy. For the present let me take you to where you can sleep tonight."

Lars received a lot of different looks as he made his way through the camp. Some were wary, others indifferent. Most though simply stared with undisguised hatred. He was happy to find the area where he would sleep was on the outskirts of the camp and surrounded by the Sarlens among the army.

He lay down immediately, feigning tiredness, keeping his eyes closed until Rubis and Eavitt moved away. He hardly slept the whole night, expecting a knife through his heart. The night passed with infinitesimal slowness. When dawn came the army was up and moving in only a few moments, heading west, with a smaller group, made up of all the Sarlen's except Rubis, separating and going to deal with the damaged ships.

Lars remained with the Sarlen navigator at first, trailing along at the rear, feeling more comfortable there. Soon though Captain Daenneth sought him out for guidance on what direction they should take. From then on Lars had no option but to remain with the Ammeliners. He spoke seldom, and only when directly asked a question. The following days passed slowly, and three long days later they moved out onto the Midd Plain.

Finding food for such a large number was difficult and consumed a lot of time, dragging the journey out longer than Lars would have liked. The nights were getting cool now but the heat was still blistering during the day out on the Midd Plain. Lars heard more than a few comments about the starkness of the open plain, the miles of seemingly never ending grass, several wondering if they had travelled all the way from

Sarl, a lush green land, for burned grass a long way from the oceans they had all grown up next to.

Another concern that was often voiced over the following days was the lack of trees on the plain. They would have to travel a long way just for the wood they would need to rebuild their village. Lars felt a sense of despair building amongst the Ammeliners, which only grew as they crested a slight rise and looked down on what could only be classed as a minor indentation on the vast plain.

"This is the site of the original village of Ammelin," said Lars, indicating with a sweep of one arm, "The home of you forefathers." He could see the disappointment written clearly on their faces and could think of nothing to say that would make it better for them. Instead he stuck to the practicalities of the situation. "Can I give you some advice?"

"Any help would be useful," replied Haig.

"First and foremost you need to dig a well. There is water all over the plain during the summer but come winter the surface water will freeze. Then you need to start foraging for wood and food. The winter will be soon upon you so your efforts would be best directed to one large building that could house you all; a great hall if you will, or at least the beginnings of one.

"With that completed at least the combined body heat of so many will reduce the amount of wood you will have to burn to get you through the worst of the winter. Other than that you will have to decide as you go what will be best for your people."

"When will you return to the mountains?" asked Haig.

"There are still a few hours of daylight left," replied Lars. "I intend to get as far as possible before nightfall. If you have already decided on who will travel to Thoran I will be happy to guide them there."

"Four Ammelin men will accompany you. Two will stay in Thoran and the other two will continue on to your village. Also, Rubis has requested to go with you and stay at your village for the winter; if that is acceptable to you?"

"That's fine with me," replied Lars. "Are these men ready to continue?"

"I think they would like to spend this first night in our ancestral land before setting out again."

"Very well," said Lars, disappointed at the thought of more lost time. "We will leave at dawn."

Sitting on the gentle slope, Lars watched as the Ammelin men set to work with the few tools they had. They selected several spots and started digging holes, hoping to find water in at least one. Others scouted and made maps of the immediate area. Several men collected stones, to line the walls of the well if they were lucky enough to find water on the first attempts.

Soon darkness stopped work and everyone settled down for the night. The scouts had found a small stream only half an hour from what would be their home. And even better it was lined with trees and shrubs for a league or so, more than enough to build a hall, or so they believed. Many of the shrubs also bore fruit. It was decided though, among their leaders, following advice from Lars, they would need to find another source of wood as it would be reckless of them to cut down what could be a life line for their people. Lars had explained that they had a similar small wood close to Lokas, and no trees were ever cut down, but it was regularly harvested for fruit and deadfall for the fires.

They had also decided to speed up the process and save on wood by making bricks from mud and straw, both of which were in abundance with all they were digging up. And the wells were looking promising. Three of the four digs soon found soft mud and after another hour of digging those working in two of them were up to their ankles in water.

If there had been any way of providing light they would have worked on through the night to dig the well as deep as possible and start lining the walls. Instead it would have to wait until first light.

Lars lay down and soon the soft rustling of the grass lulled him into the best sleep he'd had in days. Dawn came on too quickly and he was woken by the sound of digging as work started up again. Walking down to see the progress they had made, it was clear water would be no problem for them. Two of the wells were already knee deep and were proving hard to clear the sucking mud. It would be a tiring day just to gain a few extra feet and line the walls to at least above the water level. But the wet mud was already being put to good use: moulds were made from some of the crates they had recovered from the ships and the first batch of bricks could bake in the heat of the day.

Wheat and barley grew on the plain at sporadic intervals, as carried by the wind and birds, and most of the day for those not digging would be spent collecting seed, both for the immediate future and so they could till the land and plant a proper crop the following spring.

"Good morning, Lars," said Haig, walking over from the other side of the well. "That is a good sight, is it not?"

"Certainly," replied Lars. "I am sure the future seems a lot less bleak than it did yesterday."

"It does," agreed Haig. "Yesterday this seemed like a lifeless and uninhabitable place. Today I can see why our ancestors chose it as a site for a village. And we can start making it better quickly. With so much water we are going to transplant some of the small trees and shrubs our scouts found at the river, adding a little touch of green that will eventually shelter us from the wind."

"It will all take time but at least you know your people can survive here for the immediate future."

"Indeed we can," said Haig, nodding as he looked around, grand plans forming in his mind. "Come, I will introduce you to the men who will accompany you."

A small group waited to one side and Lars saw that Rubis was already with them, each man with a pack at his feet. Rubis stood to the rear, unobtrusive, as the introductions were made.

"This is Heramon Storg," said Haig, introducing a tall, thin man, with a neat beard and oiled black hair. Heramon had removed his armour but still looked every part the soldier. "Heramon will go to Thoran, with Tarlis Bant." Haig indicated the next man in line who was a little shorter than Heramon but powerfully built. His head was shaven clean and had two outstanding scars, one a thick white mass of knotted skin that stretched across Tarlis' left check to the bridge of his nose. The second scar was a livid red gouge, still in the process of healing, that ran right across his forehead.

Next in line was Bardim Goc, the youngest among them, but still older than Lars. He was the first of the two Ammeliners who would accompany him to Lokas. His dark hair was close cropped and he had piercing blue eyes, a wide nose that had been recently broken and a square jaw. Bardim was the same height as Lars, yet despite his mean appearance, the man withered slightly as Lars looked at him. Lars guessed he was scared of the magic he possessed and would have to work at putting the man at ease for the journey ahead.

Last in line was Chad Frome, a short and wiry fellow with a narrow face that resembled a rat with straggling fair hair and a lazy left eye. Lars shook hands with each man in turn but wasted no more time on formalities.

"We have several hard days of walking from sun up to sundown before we reach Thoran," said Lars. "There I will speak to the gate commander. He should be able to introduce you to King Tomar. From there I will immediately head for Lokas. After we leave Thoran it will be another three to four days before we reach my home. By the time we arrive winter will already be starting so unless you want to stay there the whole season you will have to be quick in returning to the Midd Plains.

"My people will help you in any way we can, though that may not be much. Lokas is not a wealthy village and we are self sufficient with no need for trade. That doesn't mean we have no use for what anyone else can offer us. We have been long at war with the neighbouring villages of Balt in Algor and Thoran, which was then called Drakor.

"Those wars," continued Lars, "if indeed it could be called a war— long term skirmish might be more accurate—ended when the *Draknor* attacked. After that everyone was too busy merely trying to survive to wonder what others were doing. Now, if you are all prepared, we should be on our way."

"I would like to hear more about this *Draknor*," said Bardim Goc.

"And I would be pleased to answer any questions you have, but we can do so as we travel, if you please," said Lars, indicating with one hand that they should get underway.

Haig handed Heramon a small leather pouch, saying, "You know what we need most."

"I'll get whatever I can," replied Heramon, taking the pouch and placing it inside his vest.

Each man hefted his pack and shook hands with Haig as he wished them well on their journey. Moments later they were on their way, heading south west.

As they travelled Lars was constantly questioned by all four Ammelin men, asking about trivial things such as common plants and animals at first, before moving on to more in depth concerns, many of which Lars couldn't answer, such as the likely reactions from what would be their closest new neighbours. Lars could only tell them what little he knew of the places he had been to.

Rubis remained quiet during the day, saving his questions for night time as they were making camp. Shortly after noon, on the fourth day of their journey, they came within sight of Thoran. Before nightfall they reached the city and Lars wasn't surprised to find Commander Turral at the gate, impeccably dressed as ever, waiting for the small party of strangers that had been spotted hours earlier.

"Welcome, Lars, to Thoran," said Turral. "Who are your friends?"

"These men are an Ammelin delegation." Lars could tell by Turral's change of expression that he knew what had happened to their ill-fated village. "They have returned to Gravick from across the oceans, intending to rebuild their village on the same site. These two men are Heramon Storg and Tarlis Bant," he said, indicating each in turn. "They are here to speak with King Tomar and to purchase supplies, though any aid you could give freely, no matter how small, would be greatly appreciated. The other men will continue on with me to Lokas." He didn't see any point in naming them as he didn't even wish to enter Thoran, preferring to continue on while daylight permitted.

Realizing this Turral said, "You can leave these gentlemen in my care. I will tell the king you were here. He will be disappointed you couldn't stay for a while."

"As am I," said Lars, adding, "And thank you, for your assistance," before turning to Heramon and Tarlis. "I will leave you in the capable hands of Commander Turral and wish you every success in your negotiations." He bowed to them and turned to his other companions, indicating the road west, towards the mountains. "Shall we?"

The two Ammelin men looked disappointed that they wouldn't be staying in Thoran for the night but didn't protest. Rubis seemed indifferent. Lars started walking, leaving the others to follow or be left behind.

Three days later they had Lokas in sight. The snow had started before they were clear of the forest and only grew worse from there. All were unprepared and had to don multiple layers to stop the biting wind cutting through to the skin.

The gates of Lokas were closed as they approached, barred against the wind and it took long moments before they were opened. In the time it took to do so, Lars' parents had been told of his arrival and Alric and Mira were waiting as the gates creaked open, just enough the let them all pass through.

Mira ran forward and hugged Lars tightly, forcing the air from his lungs. "I didn't know if we would see you again. Hakon told us you were to be married and I feared you would never return." Mira scanned Lars' companions as Alric walked up to join them and asked, "Is your wife not with you? I was so looking forward to meeting her. Where is she?"

"Dead," said Lars flatly.

Mira, clearly saddened by this news, and troubled by Lars' curt statement, quickly changed the subject. "Will you introduce us to your companions?"

Lars, grateful to put aside the inevitable questions, was only too happy to do so. "This is Bardim Goc. He and his friend, Chad Frome, are from Ammelin." Seeing his father's interest piqued Lars added, "I will explain more about that later. They are here to talk about possible future trade. I told them our people would help if we can. Lastly is Rubis Hornshank. He is from a land called Sarl, and again I will explain more about that later.

"Gentlemen," continued Lars, "these are my parents, Alric and Mira. My father is *Fa'ku*, the leader of Lokas Village." Alric and Mira greeted each in turn before Lars continued. "Tomorrow will be soon enough for talking. For now we are all cold and tired. So if arrangements could be made for our guests I think they would like to rest for the night."

"Of course," said Alric, saddened at the loss of Amelia, whom he knew from the previous year and had told Mira all about. "We had already built another hut for you and . . ." Alric paused, realizing what he was about to say. "For you," he continued. "Your guests can stay there and you can stay with us," Alric finished, placing an arm around his wife.

"Thank you," said Lars, knowing he wouldn't be lucky enough to escape explanations until the next day. He fully expected to be awake well into the night, and indeed he was.

Alric was mystified that Lars could be so calm around men from the same army that had caused the death of his betrothed. Mira was distraught about the loss of the grandchild she hadn't even known existed. Kora also sat in on the conversation, keeping silent but listening with rapt attention. Finally Lars was allowed to sleep but found it hard to do so.

The next day dawned bitterly cold. Mercifully the snow had stopped and the sky was clear, allowing the sunshine to take some of the bite from the wind. Alric took the Ammelin men to talk with a select group of Elders, held in a large hut made of a wooden frame with hides stretched across them. What little heat those thin walls could hold was provided by a central fire, but the structure protected them from the wind. Mercifully the weather prevented a full council being held in the Council Square otherwise the questions would have continued all day in an endlessly repetitive stream. As it was all were chilled to the bone before they were done. Three staloks were gifted to their guests and twenty hides. Flint tools were also included and any other supplies that could be spared, pitifully few though they were.

Bardim and Chad left the following morning, while the weather still held, heading back to Thoran to meet up with their friends. The three staloks trailed docilely behind, tied to each other and led by a single tether. The south gates were just closing when a call from the guards on the north gate had Alric and Lars heading through the village to see what the fuss was about.

Three figures, heavily wrapped in furs, clearly labouring through the deep snow, approached from the mountain pass. Alric found it amazing that anyone could have survived travelling through the passes during winter. It took several hours before the figures actually reached the gates.

"Who are you and what is your business here?" called Alric from the wall.

"I am Banin," said the central figure. "Formerly of the Brotherhood of Divine Guidance, who reside in the Imperial Palace in Zutarinis. I must speak with the *Fa'ku*."

"You are," said Alric, surprised that the man knew of his title and its correct pronunciation.

"What I have to say should be said in private," said Banin. "Afterwards, who you tell shall be your choice."

"Very well," agreed Alric. "Open the gates." Turning to Lars he said, "Go and stoke up the fire in your hut. We will meet with these strangers there."

Lars nodded and raced off, wanting to make sure the hut was tidy, having already started moving what little he owned into the hut his parents had built for him and Amelia, in the hope he would bring his wife to live in Lokas. He wouldn't be living there himself just yet, instead letting Rubis stay there for the winter. He added wood to the fire and set about sorting his possessions into some form of order. Rubis in turn tidied away the few items he had carried with him in his pack.

For the first time since he had returned home Lars could feel Seeli close by but had no time to ask her opinion of their latest guests. He just finished in time for his father opening the door to let the Zutarens enter.

Letting each in turn remove the excess furs Lars was surprised to find one was a woman. When all were seated around the fire Alric asked, "What is so important that you would come through the mountains in such weather to seek me out personally?"

"First let me introduce myself and my companions," said Banin.

"Of course," agreed Alric. "Forgive me for forgetting my manners. I am Alric and this is my son, Lars. His friend is called Rubis and not from these lands."

The Zutaren leader raised an eyebrow but didn't comment on the Sarlen. "I am Banin. My companions are Damion and Rella." He paused for a moment before continuing. "War is coming to your lands."

"We always seem to be fighting with one foe or another," said Alric. "We are always prepared to defend our home."

"I do not underestimate the fighting prowess of your warriors, or your will to protect your way of life. But you cannot stand against the force that will some day come to kill your people."

"Who is this enemy you speak of? And what do you mean by some day?" asked Lars.

"They are Zutaren, like us," explained Banin. "Empress Shatala has decided she wishes to reclaim the lands of Tibor, Gravick and Algor, lands Zutar once ruled. Shatala has long harboured plans of sending the full might of her military to ensure this is accomplished quickly and any resistance dealt with immediately. This will be no drawn out campaign but a swiftly executed mission that will see every soul in this village dead on the first day.

"Her plan is to annihilate your people so no word can spread. Then her army can use the High Plains as a staging post before conquering the rest of Gravick. Genocide is her intention, so no further resistance can disrupt her future plans. Lands will be granted to those in her favour at the time."

"I think your empress will find we will not die as easily as she expects," said Alric.

"Shatala knows exactly what to expect," said Banin. "You have already been the victims of her schemes, although that did not go exactly as she had hoped."

"What do you mean?" asked Alric sharply.

"The *Draknor* that attacked your lands," explained Banin, "was no wandering beast but sent by Empress Shatala." Banin thought it best not to mention his part in controlling the beast. "She hoped the beast would create a lot more devastation than it did."

"It did enough," said Alric, tightly reining back his growing anger. "It will take years to recover from those attacks."

"I doubt Shatala will give you even one year. You may have stalled her plans but I doubt they have been abandoned. She will strike while you are weakened. Your defeat of the *Draknor* greatly vexed her and she has filled her mind with thoughts of revenge. The empress does not take defeat lightly."

"So why are you telling us?" asked Lars.

"Suffice to say we are no longer in favour with the Empress."

"Things change," said Alric.

"Not for me they won't," said Banin. "Shatala would have ordered me executed did she not already believe me dead."

"Where will you go now?" asked Lars.

"I don't know," admitted Banin. "I had only one goal in mind when we set out and that is now complete."

"Would you be willing to help us fight your own countrymen," asked Alric, feeling the strength of the magic within the two men.

"That I could never do," said Banin. "I may not be pleased with the actions of our current empress but I do love my country and my people.

And although I may never be able to return, especially after betraying her plans to you, I could never kill one of my own people."

"Then why tell us?" asked Alric.

"Even though I no longer owe her my loyalty this was not an easy decision for me, but I can no longer condone genocide," explained Banin. "Once I would have had no qualms in aiding her in the annihilation of your people. Even now I could have supported her still if I believed subjugation was her intent. There is no reasoning to her plans; she thrives on mindless slaughter. I come to tell you this simply to give your people the chance to flee and survive. I would advise you to move your entire village to the lower plains and resettle there. Hopefully then the empress will not totally destroy your people. To fight her army would be futile."

"I will decide that," said Alric. "But thank you for bringing us this information. The least we can offer in return is a hot meal and a warm bed for the night."

"Thank you," said Banin. "That will be most welcome."

Lars had been thinking about the spells he had used to fight the Ammelin. He asked Banin, "Does the empress have many powerful mages at her command?"

"Several hundred," said Banin. "And Shatala has magical powers of her own. Several of which are unique to her family line, who guard their secrets closely."

"Would she send the mages with the army?" asked Lars.

"Several would certainly accompany any troops to facilitate communication and relay the empress's orders," explained Banin. "You could not hope to stand against her huge army or such well trained mages."

"Our people, too, have powerful magic at our disposal," said Lars, suspecting that his own limited knowledge would be nothing compared to what the Empress could throw at them, as Banin soon confirmed.

"I know of the magic your people use," said Banin. "I even saw, and admired, your use of the spells you employed to save the people of Ragal. I must say you wielded those powers well; but they are nothing compared to what my people know. Unless your knowledge extends far beyond what I have witnessed I would advise not using magic against my people. They already consider you a trivial threat that can be quickly eradicated.

"If you do not use magic against them, it is likely they will not think it necessary to bring their mages into the battle. At least then it will be a fight of simply steel against steel; even if the odds are overwhelmingly in their favour. To use magic would bring about an attack that would finish the battle in an instant without a single Zutaren soldier needing to draw his weapon."

Lars had wanted confirmation but wished it hadn't been delivered in such a hopeless fashion. "Thank you," he said. "Our people will take that into consideration when the Council of Elders meet to discuss this."

Banin bowed his head. "I would not wish to leave you in any doubt as to how futile any resistance may be. I would not like to see your unique culture extinguished."

"I will have one of my warriors show you to where you can sleep tonight," said Alric. "You may wish to refresh yourselves before we eat."

"Thank you," said Banin. "That will be most welcome."

As they were led away Alric asked Lars, "Do you think he is boasting about his abilities and those of his people, in the hope that we will abandon our home? Perhaps he has been sent to attempt to accomplish their primary objective without a fight?"

"He doesn't strike me as a man accustomed to boasting," said Lars. "I think what he said is nothing but the plain truth as he sees it."

Alric thought much the same but was hoping a second opinion might shed a ray of hope on the bleak future Banin had painted for them. "Me too," was all he said aloud.

EPILOGUE

In Zutarinis Shatala bathed peacefully, in preparation for her forthcoming wedding. In less than two hours she would be married. The man she had selected was tall and well proportioned. More than his looks though Shatala had selected him because he was easily controlled, with no ambitions other than to please his empress.

Shatala was also already pregnant, though only six weeks, nothing that would prevent her enjoying her wedding night. Of course no official announcement could be made until several weeks after the wedding, but at least she could keep the wretched mages of the Farren Isles from pressing their attentions on her.

The thought repulsed her still.

Stepping from the bath maids sprang forth and wrapped her in the softest towels, drying her skin with the gentlest touch. Shatala was pleased with the way things were progressing lately. Her greatest problem had been averted for the near future. Secondly her expansion plans for her empire would get under way in less than two seasons.

It was time for Zutar to reclaim the full extent of her empire. Shatala would be hailed as the empress who had led them to greatness once more. She smiled at the thought, greatly pleased with herself.

On the Farren Isles the Circle of Five had just left the cave after their morning meeting. The Nefferanian had watched them leave. If the creature could have smiled it would have. After witnessing events of recent months, the Nefferanian was pleased.

Soon the one it had watched for many months would come to the islands and help it die. Death was all that was left to the once space faring creature. Living on the surface of Klendor, crushed under rock and the force of gravity weighing heavy, life was painful, and the constant draw on its power only served to finalize its thoughts.

Too weak to break free and with no access to the nutrients it needed to recover its strength, the Nefferanian knew that death was the only form of escape it could hope for and welcomed the thought.

Across the oceans, sleeping peacefully in a small village on the western coast of Zant, a young man named Shadaan, barely out of childhood, was blissfully unaware of just how much his life was going to change, and how swiftly. He thought he had problems being steered into an apprenticeship he didn't really want. But he had no idea just how trivial his worries would seem only a few short hours later, or where his life would lead him.

ABOUT THE AUTHOR

K eith Jones was born in April 1969, in Stockton-on-Tees, England. At the age of 18 he joined the British Army and served for 8 years, spending most of that time posted in Germany. After leaving the army he returned to the UK until immigrating to Canada in 2005. Since his time in the army onwards he has worked as a Heavy Duty Mechanic.

Writing has always been a passion, including completing a Creative Writing course at Hartlepool College.

Keeper of the Damned is the third book to be completed and published through Authorhouse and is the second part of a trilogy. With the third book in the trilogy also finished and several others started Keith hopes to be publishing again in the near future.